Also by Cheryl Robinson

Sweet Georgia Brown
It's Like That
If It Ain't One Thing

In Love with a Younger Man

a Younger Man

cheryl robinson

NEW AMERICAN LIBRARY

New American Library
Published by New American Library, a division of
Penguin Group (USA) Inc., 375 Hudson Street,
New York, New York 10014, USA
Penguin Group (Canada), 90 Eglinton Avenue East, Suite 700, Toronto,
Ontario M4P 2Y3, Canada (a division of Pearson Penguin Canada Inc.)
Penguin Books Ltd., 80 Strand, London WC2R 0RL, England
Penguin Ireland, 25 St. Stephen's Green, Dublin 2,
Ireland (a division of Penguin Books Ltd.)
Penguin Group (Australia), 250 Camberwell Road, Camberwell, Victoria 3124,
Australia (a division of Pearson Australia Group Pty. Ltd.)
Penguin Books India Pvt. Ltd., 11 Community Centre, Panchsheel Park,
New Delhi - 110 017, India
Penguin Group (NZ), 67 Apollo Drive, Rosedale, North Shore 0632,
New Zealand (a division of Pearson New Zealand Ltd.)
Penguin Books (South Africa) (Pty.) Ltd., 24 Sturdee Avenue,
Rosebank, Johannesburg 2196, South Africa

Penguin Books Ltd., Registered Offices:
80 Strand, London WC2R 0RL, England

First published by New American Library,
a division of Penguin Group (USA) Inc.

First Printing, January 2009
10 9 8 7 6 5 4 3 2 1

 REGISTERED TRADEMARK — MARCA REGISTRADA

LIBRARY OF CONGRESS CATALOGING-IN-PUBLICATION DATA:
Robinson, Cheryl.
In love with a younger man/Cheryl Robinson.
p. cm.
ISBN 978-0-451-22582-5
1. African-American women—Fiction. 2. Middle-aged women—Fiction. 3. Young men—Fiction. I. Title.
PS3618.O323I5   2009
813'.6—dc22   2008030626

Set in Granjon
Designed by Alissa Amell

Printed in the United States of America

This book is dedicated to Brian C.

Acknowledgments

First, and foremost, I am thankful to God. Last year was a journey that I was anxious to take. I felt His presence every step of the way. I am thankful to Him for the lives He allowed me to touch and the people He put in my path. I met some wonderful new friends and reconnected with people I have known nearly my entire life. For always being there for me so I never feel alone. I can no longer say I am awaiting a new beginning because You are leading me down the path I need to travel. I love You.

Brian, as you already know, but I will continue to tell you, you have added an entirely new dimension to my life. I appreciate our friendship. You mean so much to me that I had to dedicate this entire novel to you, because it was our friendship and my love for you that inspired this story. Some friends can make you smile at times, laugh at others, perhaps even cry. They give advice when you ask for it or perhaps when they feel you really need some, a shoulder to lean on, supportive words when you feel like giving up; you have done all of those things for me and so much more. Thank you for assisting me with the Atlanta aspect of the novel and for chauffeuring me around the city and particularly Buckhead, where most of the novel centers.

Thanks for taking me to the Mansions on Peachtree, giving me a brief history of the city, and always replying to my Atlanta-related questions lighting-fast, mostly via text. Even though I come to Atlanta often, I could never have known most of what you told me. I could tell I was getting on your nerves at times, although I know you would say, "No, you weren't, baby," but that's where your patience pays off (smile) and your generous spirit. Because with gas being as high as it is, I wish I would drive someone around for four hours, three days in a row, and fill up twice in one day. LOL. You know I would do the same for you because that's what friends are for. Thank you for being there and for at least making an effort to call me more and text less. It didn't work, but you tried. I have finally accepted the fact that you're a texter. I love you so much.

As always to my family: my parents, Ben and Velma Robinson, for their love and support. My sister, Janice Robinson, for continuing to act as my Detroit PR person as well as a good friend and big sister who I love even when we fight. To my nephew Brandon Robinson. To my nephew Sterling, who has grown up so quickly before my eyes—one day I'm changing your diapers, and then the next you've graduated from college and moved off to California. I feel like Olena, waking up and wondering what happened to all the years that flew by. I am very proud of you for going after your dreams despite the fact that your family tried to talk you out of going so far away. And I'm proud of you for passing the LSAT. I think it's wonderful that you realized so early on that this is your life to live.

To my Angels in heaven: my brother, Benjamin Robinson, Jr. My uncle Sherman and aunt Billy.

To my editors at New American Library: Kara Cesare

and Lindsay Nouis. As always, thank you for doing what you do so well. You two ladies are always the first to read my manuscripts and provide constructive criticism, which I rely on and trust. I hope our relationship continues, because my writing certainly will and Penguin Group feels like home.

To Sandy Kovach and Detroit's home for "smooth jazz," V98.7, for selecting my novel *Sweet Georgia Brown* as their April book club of the month and for hosting the book club meeting at the Borders in Dearborn, Michigan.

To E.Lynn Harris, one of my favorite authors, who listed my novel *Sweet Georgia Brown* among his favorites on his Web site, and for mentioning my name on K104 as one of the authors he reads. Thank you for the honor.

To author Connie Briscoe, another one of my favorite authors, for interviewing me for her blog, Page One, which again was truly an honor.

To author Kimberla Lawson Roby, another one of my favorite authors, who I had the pleasure of meeting for the first time at the 2008 National Book Club Conference and having lunch with. You could have sat at the table with Terry McMillan and Iyanla Vanzant, but instead when they offered to move your seat, you told them that you were fine where you were, allowing me the opportunity to tell you how much you inspired me at the start of my literary journey and how you continue to inspire me. Thank you for all of the advice you gave me during lunch and for being so kind and down-to-earth. I hope we keep in touch. Oh, and this year when I go to Detroit for my signing, I'm going to need to make sure you aren't right across the street giving away free lunch like you were at the library downtown when I was at the Borders in the Compuware building☺. That just wasn't fair.

To author Cydney Rax and author Electa Rome Parks, whose friendship has meant a lot. It's so nice having friends who are also writers and who can relate to all that we as writers go through as we try to have our stories told. Thanks for the encouragement.

To Curtis Bunn of the National Book Club Conference for allowing me to participate in the 2008 conference and arranging a giveaway with my book *Sweet Georgia Brown* to new NBCC members. I had a ball and look forward to attending next year. Even if I'm in the audience and not a featured author, I have to go because it is the best time I have ever had at a literary event.

To Green (Ricky) Moss III for all you have done for me through the years. For being one of the first to believe in me and invest your time and money in my dreams. You are like a brother. I love you.

To all who hosted my virtual book tour, including but not limited to: Marlive Harris of the Grits Literary Service for doing my online publicity; Yasmin Coleman and APOOO; the Sweet Georgia Brown Readers and Review Club on Shelfari.com, where we kicked it off with an online book release party that was a blast; AA Kulture zone; Sankofa Litarary Society; Genre Go Round Reviews; Yvonne Perry; Patricia Woodside of Freshfiction.com; Sistahfriend Book Club; Swaggie Coleman; Lauretta Pierce and Literary World.org; Delta Reviewer; Rawsistaz; Writeblack.com; authors of myspace; Bergers Book Review; Book Club Central; Ebony Farashuu; Vee Jefferson; the Real Divas of Literature; Renee Williams of All the Buzz; Bria of Ruminatingbria.wordpress.com, UrbanReviews.com, Rachel Kramer Bussel; the Peopleslounge.ning.

To the Cass Tech Alumni, particularly those from the

class of 1984. After all of these years, the alumni still keep in touch either through the personal relationships that we fostered or through the casstechhigh.ning.com. I voted for my high school in 2007 so we could win the Steve Harvey Hoodie award, which we did. I know that I'm a long way from high school, but there was something very special about the former pickle factory, and there will always be a place in my heart for Cass no matter how old I am.

To Lawana Durisseau Johnson for sending out blast e-mails to all of your contacts months before my novel *Sweet Georgia Brown* was released and for recommending my book for the radio station's book of the month.

To Laverne Brown, aka Missy of Readers Paradise, and Toka Waters: I want to thank you both. As two avid readers who enjoyed my novel *Sweet Georgia Brown*, you effortlessly took on a publicity campaign all on your own, which assisted me tremendously. Thank you so much. Words can't express how appreciative I am. Missy, thank you for sharing *Sweet Georgia Brown* with your book club and for passing out bookmarks and postcards while you rode the subway in Chicago. I was blown away that you would go to those lengths to promote my novel. It meant so much, and hopefully one day I can meet both of you to thank you personally.

To Trese Kennard and Patricia Golightly for reaching out to me on behalf of the Rosalind Williams and the entire Williams family. When I first made the decision to include a scene with Darrent Williams and mention the tragic events of his untimely passing in my novel, I approached it from the standpoint of how many lives his life touched. At the time, I had no idea somehow my book would get into the hands of his family, and they would reach out to me with so much support and love. Thank you for contacting me. You are always in my prayers. I am thankful to Darrent for touching the lives of so many. His spirit lives on in so many positive ways.

To Shannon Scott and Leah Evans; my friends since Gesu Elementary School, and that alone needs acknowledgment. Leah, this year, I am sure I will be in the D.C. area to promote my books, so we will get to see each other soon. And, Shannon, of course, I'll see you in Detroit.

To my girls in Dallas: Dewhana Jones, Agatha Clark and Cynthia Taylor—I miss y'all so much. Dewhana, you truly are the little sister I never had. And to Regina Smith, Charmette Brown, Pia Wilson-Body and Anthony Body, Derek and Nina Burke, and Chris Elliot. Thanks for everything.

To the many wonderful book club members, bookstores, retailers, and libraries and media that have helped spread the word about my books and me. Thank you. To everyone who has and continues to purchase one or more of my novels and allows me to walk on step closer to my dream of writing full-time.

Thank you and God bless—Cheryl Robinson

It's not the years in your life that counts. It's the life in your years.

1984

The robust aroma of freshly brewed Folgers coffee filled the interior of the silver 1980 Oldsmobile Ninety-Eight Regency with the burgundy vinyl top causing Olena's ears to ring with the company's slogan; "The best part of waking up is Folgers in your cup."

Olena was wide-awake, stretched across the backseat with a book in her hand and hope in her heart. She listened as the chirping sparrows welcomed the morning while her father eased the car out of the driveway of their Westside Detroit home.

"Put that book down, baby, and wave good-bye to your brother and sisters," said Olena's mother as she peered at Olena through the vanity mirror while she powdered her pale nose. A smile of pride soon surfaced for the fact that her youngest child was going away to college. "They all got their butts out of bed to see you off, so please be considerate."

Olena slid farther down into the burgundy velour seats. Her eyes piercing the page of the poem "The Gamut" from Maya Angelou's book of poetry *Just Give Me a Cool Drink of Water 'fore I Diiie*. "Wave for what? They know I'm leaving."

"Put that book down and wave, girl. Nobody's playing with you. They're not going to see you until next summer, young lady. You're going to miss your family while you're gone, especially your sister."

"*I am?* Are you sure about that?" Olena let the back window halfway down, stuck her thin arm out, and waved furiously as she plastered on a fake smile. "I'm *not* going to miss any of you all," she shouted, "except for you, Alicia, my best friend." She blew a kiss to her five-year-old niece, whom Olena's older sister had dragged from the comforts of a warm bed, and smiled as she watched her niece repeat the gesture.

"What are you reading now?" Olena's mother asked, seeming almost irritated by her daughter's preoccupation. "Eugene, turn on the interior lights so the girl can see, because all she's doing is pretending."

Olena glanced up from the page and recited a line, " 'Quiet my heart, be deathly quiet, my true love is leaving,' " followed by a deep sigh. "Maya Angelou's words literally send chills through my body."

Olena's parents took a momentary look at each other. "Are you sure she's ready to go off on her own?" Olena's father questioned as he waited at the stop sign on Greenlawn and Six Mile; he was hesitant to flip on the left blinker and turn. "I can go back if you don't think she's ready."

"For God's sake," Olena shouted, "I *am* ready. Take me to my new life. Allow me to press on, move past all of this misery and dread and march to the beauty and surrender of what can only be described as hope." She sighed.

"Was that deep enough? I'm trying to get as deep as Maya Angelou."

"Well, may I suggest you try a little harder," her dad said.

"You're almost there, baby" her mother reassured her.

Olena's eyes rolled hard enough to fall off the page, and they landed on a box of her father's business cards, which was stuffed underneath the seat. Again, her father belittled her while her mother tried to repair what was already shattered—her daughter's self-esteem, but Olena was working hard to correct that herself, and she wasn't going to give up. Not before she could stare in the mirror and love the reflection glaring back. That was the goal, and Olena wasn't going to give up until she accomplished that along with so many more.

Instantly, Olena felt the pain again, tried hard to exercise restraint. She was stronger than that, she would chant. The past deserved to stay there, but Stan was her everything, or so her mind said. Even though they were young, he was still all that she wanted at that time. Now all that she wanted was to get away, and so she chose to attend a historically black university in the District of Columbia, because it was far enough for her to feel like she was escaping. In Detroit, she had to face the reality of a situation that was too hard for her to leave behind . . . the loss of her first love. She had seen only pictures of the administration building at the university and two other photos; she had selected that particular college mainly because they had accepted her. And Olena strived to be accepted not only by a school but by others.

"I can't wait to be grown," she mumbled.

"Being grown is so overrated," her mother replied. "Enjoy being young. Youth only comes once."

Young and stupid, she told herself, *young and dumb, young and vulnerable. Young and misled.* Being grown gave her choices that she herself could make. Being young meant she had to do what her parents told her to do, when all they ever said was what not to do.

Nearly three hours had passed and Olena's eyes had closed shortly after her father took exit 2B on to Interstate 75 from the John C. Lodge leaving Detroit and heading for Toledo and Flint. She was now awake, but allowed her eyes to remain closed, relying instead on what she could hear rather than see: the sounds of her parents and their discussions on finances and retirement.

"Just be proud that the child is going to college, Eugene."

"I am proud. But I also wanted to retire. What was wrong with her staying at home and going to Wayne State? Now we have to pay tuition, room and board, and allowance. She could have gotten student loans. It would have been better for us."

"But it wouldn't have been better for her," her mother said. She fought for her children, even the two boys who were hers by marriage not birth. "I don't want any child of mine bogged down with student loans for ten years after she graduates. That don't make no sense!" her mother exclaimed.

Olena opened her eyes. " 'Don't make no sense'?" Olena repeated, shaking her head. "And you're a teacher for the Detroit Public Schools . . . but then again, you do teach special ed."

"I know I didn't hear you say something smart, and I'm sitting up here defending you," her mother said as she rolled her eyes toward Olena's, before focusing back on the conversation at hand. "One child is all we have to worry about putting through school. Just be thankful that our youngest decided to go. And all we have to do when we get back from dropping her off is put a game plan together on what we're going to do with the rest of them."

Olena loved her parents.

She respected her father and adored her mother, although both often unnerved her. Her father was so busy running his small typewriter-repair shop that his family often came last. He had a knack for maintaining and rebuilding most typewriter models and later became a dealer for several popular ones, like Brother, Royal, and Canon. Olena herself had a Canon AP300 electronic typewriter in the trunk of the car. She was bringing it along not only to aid with completing her college papers, but also to peck on when she had enough free time to make further attempts at writing something deep: a book she hoped to publish one day, perhaps about her life, her love, and her loss—her Stanley.

Olena's mother had completed her undergraduate and graduate degrees both while married to Eugene. Nancy Day was just forty years old and had already celebrated her twentieth wedding anniversary to her husband, who was twenty years her senior and had begun displaying signs of aging. A beauty and a beast was how Olena sometimes referred to her parents. And yet when she stared at herself in the mirror as she often did, Olena found no resemblance to either, but she knew she wasn't adopted. Knew for a fact she was her parents' child, evidenced by the pictures at birth all the way up until now. People would ask about her gray eyes and where they had come from. Sometimes she wouldn't comment; other times she'd say she didn't know. She wondered how it felt to be her mother. To have children who didn't resemble her. Children whose honey complexion felt dark in comparison to their mother's light skin tone. Not that complexion mattered in the Day household. They liked to preach that love was the only thing that made sense.

Olena's back straightened as her father turned right onto Howard Place and then onto Sixth Street Northwest. The appearance of the school wasn't at all what she had imagined—the surroundings, much the way she saw herself, a lot less perfect—the neighborhood of row houses and brownstones something she wasn't used to—most were run-down. But the people were just what she had hoped they wouldn't be: rich and beautiful—her polar opposite. Still she remained positive, because confidence was the one thing Olena lacked, but did a good job at faking.

They parked on Fourth Street Northwest in front of a massive dormitory structure that housed hundreds of freshman females—the Harriet Tubman Quadrangle, also referred to as the Quad.

"Wait," Olena shouted as her father reached for the door handle. She observed a strikingly beautiful female student standing beside the car that was in front of theirs. The young lady resembled Olena's mother more than Olena did. They were the same complexion and both had long, wavy hair. The young lady stood in the back of the Rolls-Royce beside her father and older brother while they removed expensive Louis Vuitton luggage from the trunk; young men driving by slowed their cars and gawked in her direction.

"Let them go first," Olena pleaded.

"What do you mean, let them go first?" her father said. "We're not in line. We can all go at the same time." He stepped from the car, followed by her mother. Finally, Olena trudged from the backseat and stood on the sidewalk, observing the massive residence hall and the constant flow of traffic moving in. She closed her eyes and smiled. Imagined what her new life might turn in to—a life without her mother's suffocating form of love and her father's constant negativity . . . a chance to explore . . . to get away from her father's office machines and concentrate on books . . . to find herself and perhaps even find real friends . . . or better yet, her voice in literature.

TWO

Olena is a Bitch.

Her head was stuck inside Maya Angelou's *I Know Why the Caged Bird Sings* as she negotiated her thin frame through four small patches of girls lingering in the lobby of the Quad with their fashionable book bags in tow, while she eased her way toward the elevator.

Even though there hadn't been much in her life to feel good about, Olena still made a promise to herself that she was going to do her very best to keep smiling.

Smile when inside she felt like crying.

An entire month had passed since her parents had dropped her off, and instead of making friends, she made a mysterious set of enemies. The same problem she had in high school had followed her to college. She knew it was her and not them—an aura that she was somehow emitting. But she didn't know what to do to correct it, wasn't quite sure if she even wanted to. Although, at times, Olena was amazed that she could be living among six hundred forty freshman females while not one seemed to like her. But that, her high school counselor would have explained, was all part of her paranoia. First of all, she didn't nor could she possibly know all six hundred forty Quad residents. *True.* And college students, particularly freshmen, were more concerned with fitting into the culture of campus life, meeting new people, learning their way around, and of course, excelling in their classes than with her.

Umm, well, if true, then why has my daily ritual become erasing hate from the message board affixed to my dorm room door? she would wonder.

She had listened to her older sister, who had enough so-called friends to fill a classroom. Would hear her pitting one against another, and Olena didn't want any part of that falsehood. Friends would only complicate her life. Pretend to be one, find out her business only to spread it. That had been her past experience not only with her friends, but with her first cousin Candice.

All she could do now was smile... even without friends.

And so she smiled as she glanced up from the treasure she had been reading long enough to observe some of the other students, whose noses twitched as their eyes crawled over her. She refused to feel sorry for herself. Refused to sing the lyrics from that same sad song she'd written her sophomore year in high school about how no one loved her—the one she continuously played for her family like a needle stuck on a broken record—Olena could sometimes be annoying—wallowing in self-pity, yet determined to overcome, to move on—to let the past be just that. To Olena, it didn't matter that she seemed to be disliked by everyone. For at that moment she was lost in Maya's world.

Olena halted suddenly in the hallway as an epiphany fell over her. She knew exactly what she wanted out of life. She had known for years, but pushed the need further and further in until the desire to write was lost. A month had passed and not one page to her story had been typed, but many had been stored in her mind—an entire outline— the beginning, middle, and end.

The long-haired, light-eyed, small-waisted girl traveling behind her, the one possessing all of the Louis Vuitton— the purses and the complete luggage set—whose father, a surgeon, had driven her to school from Roanoke, Virginia, in a Rolls-Royce—the one who was parked in front of Olena's father's car whom the young men on campus craved—whose older brother drove a Porsche and was just as handsome as his sister was beautiful—the one whose boyfriend was an upperclassman and a Kappa—slammed into Olena's back. Olena immediately turned to face her so she could express regret, only to be flipped off and cursed at. Her eyes immediately fell back to the pages filled with words that flowed like a calm river with fresh water to quench her thirst—words expressed by her favorite author's own disappointments and obstacles that she fought to overcome, and so once again, Olena came to the realization that words would be her only cure, serve as therapy to her soul—bound pages that people would flip through and dissect, and then Olena herself could learn through her critics what was right and wrong about her life. Not through a high school counselor who only knew Olena from her school chart or by a child psychologist still working on her doctorate degree and who wasn't even equipped with a license let alone the know-how to help Olena move past her grief. Neither had ever helped Olena, nor had her family. She still felt like an outsider living outside of her.

The dorm room that she shared with her cousin Candice, who had also attended the same high school as she, was at the very end of the hallway on the fourth floor of Wheatley Hall—one of five halls comprising the quad. Their room sat beside a phone booth and just steps away from the door that led to the stairway—a convenient enough location; perhaps too convenient for the perpetrator(s) who wished to slander Olena's good name. As she strolled off the narrow elevator still engrossed in her book, she sauntered toward her room and stumbled over an eraser.

One day they're going to steal my damn eraser, she thought as she knelt down to retrieve it. And that would irritate her more than the nasty messages they scribbled, because Olena never wanted anything that belonged to her—she didn't care how small—to be taken away. She had a fear of abandonment that had sparked in high school after her boyfriend tragically left her.

Olena erased the words *is a bitch* from the message board, but left her name because she appreciated the skillful manner in which the person had written it. It was obvious that they had taken extra time and even demonstrated a little care when they designed the text, while also letting her know just what they thought of her. From day one, she had felt as if they had hated her. *They* were mostly all of the girls who lived on her floor, particularly those from the East Coast. But Olena had no idea why. It was not as if she had ever spoken badly about any of them. *Hell, I have never spoken to them at all. Oh, well, perhaps that is one of the reasons,* she thought. But at least she smiled, which was a lot more than some of them did.

Olena had retreated into her own little world ever since her sophomore year in high school. It wasn't every day that a person discovered their boyfriend lying in a pool of blood, dead at the age of fifteen; so if Olena was a bitch, then she might have had good reason to be.

Olena's first cousin Candice, who was Olena's aunt's child, assumed that the East Coast girls hated *them* because they were from Detroit and people from Detroit had a reputation for being tough. Candice thought they, being the East Coast girls, might have been intimidated by Olena and Candice, and as a result they might have decided to put the fear in Olena and Candice before the cousins had an opportunity to do the same. Olena felt that her cousin's analysis was very fitting because both she and it were ridiculous. Neither one of them looked tough. Candice was overweight with a pretty face, and most everyone loved her because of her infectious smile and outgoing personality, which was quite the opposite of Olena, who might have had a more sincere heart than her cousin and an even prettier smile, but she lacked the personality to garner any lasting friendships.

No, those East Coast girls were referring to Olena—she was certain—and not to her cousin, after all. They had put Olena's name in front of the B word and not Candice's.

"Candice," Olena said with her back leaning against the door and her hand still clutching the knob, "I know my true calling. I want to write. I'm going to change my major to English, and I'm going to try to write for *The Hilltop*. Did you know that Zora Neale Hurston cofounded that paper? There is just so much history here."

"Who is Zora Neale Hurston?"

"You don't know who Zora Neale Hurston is? She was an author during the Harlem Renaissance who wrote *Their Eyes Were Watching God.*"

"Whose eyes?"

"That's the name of one of her most popular books, and

she is one of my favorite authors aside from Maya Ange-lou. So I've decided I'm going to become a writer."

"What were you going to major in?"

"Sociology."

"Girl, what can be done with either one of those majors besides teach, and I thought you didn't want to teach?"

"I don't. I want to make some real money so I can af-ford Louis Vuitton too."

"Anyway, I heard there's a step show tomorrow in the valley. And you know there's going to be some fine guys there. Do you want to go?" One thing Olena could say about her cousin was even though she was overweight, she never let her size stop her from getting out and being seen.

"Why are you asking about tomorrow today? Ask me then." Olena left, upset that she had opened up any of her desires to her cousin, of all people. Only temporary amne-sia would have caused her to forget the fact that the peo-ple on all sides of her family tree were negative, even her mother at times.

THREE

The loud chatter coming from outside awakened her.

It was Saturday morning. She raised the window to peep out, and noticed a crowd heading down to the valley.

"Girl, you better get dressed," said Candice. "They're getting ready to step in the yard. Hurry up. I'll meet you down there. I'll be standing near Founders Library—that's if I can get a good view from there. Just look for me. Not like I'm hard to spot." Candice closed the door behind her.

Candice was the outgoing one with a natural gift of gab. The one who spoke to everyone she came in contact with. So it was no wonder to Olena that five girls trailed alongside Candice as she walked out of the quad while Olena observed from her bedroom window. But this, Olena found, came natural for someone like Candice, someone who was grossly overweight as many of the women on Olena's mother's side were, including Olena's mother, who lived in a constant state of both dieting and denial. But no matter how much she deprived herself of the greasy foods she loved consuming, her hips continued to spread. However, Candice was the largest of all the women in their family by far. Big enough to be labeled obese by her doctor and told if she didn't shed a hundred pounds soon she'd risk losing her life, not live to see twenty-five. Many of their relatives hated to see her coming, because she served as a reminder of what they could turn into if they let their love for food consume them the way Candice had.

"Why couldn't she wait for me?" Olena wondered as she sat up on her twin bed, trying to compose herself. She slid her feet inside of her rubber-soled sandals and stood. She dreaded the large, dark, boxy showers that were in the hallway only a few steps across from her dorm room. She often found herself dancing around a roach she was too scared to smash.

Olena couldn't find her cousin among so many students, but she did notice a young man from across the yard as he stood in the valley on the steps near Rankin Memorial Chapel. His arms folded, he observed the various fraternities and sororities stepping. He himself was a member of one, as evidenced by the T-shirt he was wearing. He was an upperclassman, she could tell by the regal manner in which he stood, brewing with self-confidence, a seriousness captured in his eyes.

She paced slowly, nearly creeping past him, afraid to establish eye contact. She felt his stare as she stood a few feet away. Her next-best asset, aside from her eyes, trailed her.

The pounds she packed on went straight to her behind. From her peripheral vision, she noticed he had begun walking down the steps toward her. It was then that she fled. He was perhaps the most attractive man, aside from Stan, that she had ever seen: tall enough, taller than her, but not so tall that he appeared awkward to her. To Olena, he was the right mix of everything: an average build; chestnut complexion—*perfect* was the only way Olena could describe him, perhaps too perfect for her.

That same night, she and her cousin attended social hour at the Blackburn Center. This time she noticed him as soon as she stepped through the double glass sliding doors, and he her for whatever reason. He broke away from the sizable crowd he was standing with and followed behind her and Candice as they headed down the stairs.

"Excuse me, Olena" he said, "but I believe you dropped this earlier in the yard." She was embarrassed to see him holding her student ID, particularly since she hated her picture. "You look so much better in person."

"Thank you," she said, snatching the card away from him. Olena's eyes told her cousin to leave, which she did.

"My name is Andrew. And you probably hear this a lot, but you have some beautiful eyes—the kind that stare at a man and make him immediately start confessing. I couldn't lie to you. And I'm not lying when I say I want to get to know you better."

She smiled. She liked him and his pickup lines.

"What's this really all about?" she asked. "Are you on line or something? Did one of your frat brothers put you up to this?"

"On line?" he laughed. "We haven't even started a new line, and I crossed mine two years ago."

"Are you a senior?"

He nodded. "I'm usually only on campus for classes, but from time to time I like to take in a few of the activities. And I'm so glad that I decided to do so today."

"So you don't live on campus?"

He shook his head. "I live in Silver Spring." He noticed her confusion. "It's in Maryland, which isn't that far. What about you? Do you live in the Quad?"

"Yes, unfortunately."

"Well, if you ever want to get away, give me a call. Do you have a pen and piece of paper?" She shook her head. "Well, let's see if you can remember this." He rattled off his ten digits, repeating them three times to allow them to stick.

She repeated the numbers silently as he stood in front of her. "Give it to me again without the area code. I can look that up, but seven digits are easier to remember."

"I will, but just this one last time. We don't forget what's important." He rattled the digits off again. "Now I hope you can remember that."

When he left, she scurried out of the center and hurried back to her dorm room, reciting his phone number the entire way. Her heart was beating rapidly from the excitement of meeting a man who was popular enough to belong to a fraternity—a man who took an interest in her when there were so many other girls on campus more attractive than she that he could have had and, in Olena's mind, should have directed his attention to. And so, for a brief moment, she didn't trust him. Questioned his motives and wondered if his intentions were serious. She always went so many steps ahead of where she should have, always put the cart before the horse, because she longed for the connection she and Stan had shared, or the one she thought they had; needed to replace the void in her heart by any *man* necessary.

The first call to Andrew was made Sunday evening after much contemplation. *Was it too soon?* she wondered. Just one day after meeting him. Would the phone even ring, or would a recording state that she had reached a number that was no longer in service? It was still hard for her mind to grasp the fact that she had met a man so handsome that even his smile made her insides melt.

She convinced herself to dial the number, and surprisingly he answered.

"What are you doing?" she asked.

"Waiting for you to call, wondering if you forgot the number."

She smiled. Wanted to confess to him that she had left directly after he had given her the number and headed for the Quad so she could write it down before it became lost in her mind, along with the many other thoughts that occupied her there, but she decided to play it as cool as she possibly could, which for her and the circumstance wasn't cool enough.

"What are you doing tonight?" he asked. She could hear the sounds of Coltrane in the background and realized how mature he actually was. He was more man than upperclassman.

"Nothing. Just sitting here. And you?"

"Sipping a glass of wine and listening to jazz. Just relaxing. Care to join me?"

"Yes," she said, without hesitation. She wanted wine—red or white . . . didn't matter much. She wanted Coltrane. But more important she wanted him.

"What time is your first class in the morning?"

"I'm not a morning person, so I only have one class, and it's not until one."

"I find it funny how people often tell you more than you need to know . . . more than you ask for."

"Huh?"

"Huh? You're too intelligent for that response. I didn't ask if you were a morning person. I simply asked about the time of your first class. I'm going to teach you how to keep your life simple. Not share any more than you need to, because the average person really doesn't care. Would you like that?"

She nodded before speaking and then said, "Yes, I need that."

"What else do you need, Miss Olena Day? Tell me in one word."

"In one word?" she questioned, afraid to admit the truth that what she needed, what she longed for came with time, and that was love.

"Do you want to get away from there? I'll come get you if you like. Teach you things that you can't learn in class unless the subject is sex."

"I don't know. Maybe not. I don't really know you, and I'm not ready for those kinds of lessons."

"I noticed the way you looked at me, Olena. I know that you are ready. The greatest thing about going off to college as a freshman is when you realize that you're now grown and that you can make your own decisions. Your parents probably live hundreds of miles away, and what you do in your spare time is nobody's business now but your own."

She liked the sound of everything he was saying, particularly the part about her being grown. It was true that she was hundreds of miles away from her parents. But she lived with her bigmouthed cousin Candice, who would surely tell her own mother, who in turn would tell Olena's.

And then she'd have to contend with the harassing calls from Nancy Day as she explained to Olena what good girls didn't do. Stan had already taught her how to be naughty. Now she was hoping Andrew would pick up the lesson so she could earn an advanced degree.

"So I'll ask you again, Olena Day. Would you like to come over? Do you want to get away?"

"Yes," she said, without even thinking. "Yes," she repeated. "I'd love to get away."

"I can be there in an hour. Just pack a small bag."

"Why me?" she asked, still confused by his sudden attraction and in need of clarification. Could this finally be love? He was like Stan, matching him in his attractiveness, but unlike Stan, Andrew had confidence.

"I'm not following your question."

"Never mind. I'll be downstairs waiting for you."

"Don't go down too soon—the stairs, that is. I won't be there for an hour. Around nine o'clock."

She left a note on Candice's bed—a form of blackmail that basically said she wasn't coming home that night, but if Candice told one soul, Olena would be forced to disclose to Candice's mother that Candice wasn't following her diet and that instead of losing weight, she had packed on ten additional pounds. That would be enough to cause Candice's mother to get on the first plane available and snatch her daughter out of school, take her back to Detroit, and immediately admit her to a hospital.

By ten till nine, Olena was standing in the entranceway of the Quad, looking out at the cars that whisked by, realizing that she didn't know what kind Andrew drove. By nine thirty, she was ready to turn around, head back to her small room, rethink her pain, mourn Stan more, and hate herself for trying to move on. But then a black Mazda

RX-7 with tinted windows pulled in front of the building. Her spirit told her it was Andrew. She stepped out of the building toward the car. Her senses leading her to the man she was trying to convince her heart would be her next happiness. She heard the door unlock, and so she opened it and climbed inside.

"Sorry I'm a little late. Got caught up on the phone with my parents. It's their thirtieth wedding anniversary."

"Oh, how special. Where do your parents live?"

"In Monroe."

"Monroe? Where's that?"

"Louisiana."

Her eyes widened. "I've never met anyone from there. Are you Creole?"

"No. Do you want me to be?"

She snickered. "I was just asking."

He drove on Georgia Avenue before turning onto Piney Branch Road for a couple of miles and then entered Maryland. He continued on SR-320 and veered left on Manchester—the road leading to his apartment building, which was another large structure, but smaller than where Olena resided. The drive was short, which was good because she didn't have enough time to analyze his silence. Instead, she fantasized about what the night might bring. If he asked to have her, she would oblige because sex was something she also craved. *Was she addicted?* No. Her cousin Candice was addicted ... to food—and only the worst kinds, those high in cholesterol and saturated fat. She would wake up in the middle of the night to eat, gnawing the way rats do. Olena was glad to have one night of freedom, as she was sure her cousin was. No more sneaking for either one of them. Food was what Candice desired—sex was what Olena longed for.

Stan had been Olena's first and last lover. But once they had become sexual, not a day went by that he wasn't inside of her. Whether that meant sneaking into a bathroom stall at the Renaissance Center after skipping school to go watch a movie, or going to his house after school because his mother was a nurse and worked the late shift, they found a way to express their love. Now she longed to be held again . . . to be touched. She imagined Andrew easing himself into her. Prayed this time love would be real, and that this time it would last.

"What are you thinking about?" he asked, after pulling into a reserved parking spot.

"Honestly?"

"Honestly."

"Two words this time: *making love*."

And that was the beginning. For everything she had thought Stan had allowed her to experience, Andrew had taken their encounters several steps further. She was earning her master's—not just her master's, because according to Andrew, she was working toward earning a PhD (a pretty hard dick). He became her total preoccupation. It was difficult for her to study. Impossible for her to do much of anything aside from cook for him, do his laundry, make sweet love to him at night and most mornings, play the wife, the lover—so many roles done privately behind the closed door of his apartment.

Their only separation during the entire school year was for one week in November when he went home to Monroe, and they didn't speak once. She had no way to. He didn't give her his parents' number. Instead he promised to call and never did. Not once. She knew what that meant. Knew she could either leave him or accept that her state of mind was merely a dream . . . and this was not love . . .

not Stan . . . not what she longed for. But then for the rest of the year, he remained in D.C. She didn't go home for Christmas, and neither did he. She stayed with him in his apartment for semester break also.

"Do you love me?" she asked him one night while they lay in bed, spooning each other.

"*Love* is such a strong word. That's what you're seeking, but not what I want, at least not now. I appreciate what we have."

She wanted to ask him what it was that they had exactly . . . besides great sex. And why it was they could never be seen together as a couple. Why she had to settle for an apartment instead of the movies or dinner? Was he ashamed? She wanted to know who he loved if he didn't love her, because surely there was someone. But she was afraid to ask the question, because she didn't want the truth. Instead, she said, "Do you have someone back home?"

"Why did you ask me that," he snapped, "when I'm here I'm with you? Not a day goes by that we aren't together. What does that tell you?"

It told her that even in his truth there was something missing. That, as much time as they spent together, she still felt a void. It told her that she was needy for him, and she wished she could focus on her studies instead. Earn something while away at college other than his PhD with which she couldn't do anything in the real world.

"Why me?" she asked.

"What do you mean, why you?"

She shrugged. "I mean, you could have any girl on campus just about and there are a lot of pretty ones. Why choose me?"

"I don't need a pretty girl to make me look better. I

look good enough standing alone. Besides, I think you are pretty. Your eyes are beautiful . . . so is your body."

"I'm skinny."

"It's a turnoff when a person points out what they perceive as their own flaws. One man's junk is another man's treasure."

"So I'm your treasure?"

"You sure aren't my junk."

Some nights they made love with their bodies, other nights with their souls; and that was one of the nights that their minds connected. She knew while lying on his chest and feeling his heart beat steadily that she had found her void—a man who didn't need her to be beautiful, only needed her to be who she was, and if she didn't yet know who that was, then she would allow him to show her.

"I think that you're perfect," she told him hours after the light on his nightstand went off.

"No one's perfect, baby," he said, kissing her forehead. "Sleep tight."

FOUR

"**A**re you okay in there?" Andrew asked, followed by persistent knocks.

Olena was on bended knee when he opened the bathroom door. Her arms hugging the toilet as she vomited. "Shit, don't tell me you're pregnant. That's the last thing I need right now. I thought you were on the pill."

"Maybe I'm just sick."

"Aren't you on the pill?"

"I missed one day, but I doubled up. I'm probably just sick."

"You're probably just pregnant. When you go to campus, go to the university clinic. Take a test and find out what's wrong with you. I pray you're not pregnant."

"If I am—"

"Don't even speak it, because if you are, we have a problem. Go to the clinic as soon as possible."

And so she did. She sat. Waiting patiently for her name to be called, wanting so many times to leave. If she were pregnant, she'd find out eventually, when her stomach grew with their love. If she was she would be happy, even if Andrew claimed not to be. His feelings would change. If he loved her, he would certainly love the child they produced together, but *if* was the big question.

"Olena Day," the nurse called.

Olena stood. Her nervousness caused her to repeatedly sweep her hands down the front of her jeans in an effort to straighten the nonexistent wrinkles.

"Olena Day," the nurse repeated when she observed that Olena seemed to be lingering in the waiting room not willing to step forward.

"Yes, I'm here."

"What did they say?" Andrew asked as soon as she sat inside his car. He kept the car in park, awaiting her response before pulling away from the Quad. "Well, what did they say? Are you?"

She nodded.

He sighed heavily before shaking his head. His eyes were transfixed with anger that he directed at her. "You did this shit on purpose. You were trying to get pregnant, weren't you?"

"No, I wasn't trying to get pregnant."

"Trying to trap me. Trying to mess up my life. I'm not ready for a baby, and I won't be for a very long time. An abortion is cheaper than child support, so I'm going to go ahead and pay for you to get one."

"For me?"

"Yes, for you."

"Andrew, I wasn't trying to trap you," she said, placing her hand on his thigh that he quickly removed. "I hope you don't think that I was. I love you."

"You know what? I'm really not in the mood. Go ahead and get out."

"I can't stay with you."

"No. Look at what all of this playing house got me—a baby on the way. I'm twenty-two years old. I'm going to graduate magna cum laude. I want so much more out of my life than a baby with you. Why would you think I'd be ready for that?"

"I'm eighteen. Why would you think I am? I'll get rid of it. I just don't want to lose you. I can't lose you."

"Get rid of it and you won't lose me. Next week I'll take you to the clinic."

"Okay, but please let me stay with you tonight. You were going to let me before you knew I was pregnant."

"I know, but the fact that you are just blew my mood." Her eyes closed when she heard the automatic doors unlock. "I'll feel better when it's taken care of."

She leaned over to kiss him, but stopped after he shook his head. She pried herself from the passenger seat and trudged back into her dormitory. She was in jeopardy of losing another life, and all of a sudden she hated the life that was growing inside of her. Couldn't wait to rid herself of the burden. Next week couldn't come quick enough.

Olena cried while she waited for her name to be called at the abortion clinic; cried because at that moment she wanted to keep her baby even if Andrew didn't want her to.

He had dropped her off. Said he'd come back in a few

hours, wouldn't even wait with her as if the baby was her problem alone instead of theirs. Not even two words were spoken as he drove her to the clinic. "Hey," was all he said as soon as she got in his car, and even that was thrown out drily.

While she was lying on the cot in the clinic, she thought about so many things. About the doctor at the university who slid his gloved finger inside her vagina and pulled it out when she wouldn't lie still enough for him to perform a pelvic exam.

His impatience and frustration caused him to say, "I'm sure you've had bigger things up you than this," but Olena was too numb to feel. "You're pregnant," was his conclusion as he snatched off his rubber gloves, balled them up, and tossed them in a nearby garbage can. He turned in her direction, shaking his head. "I feel sorry for your parents, who are paying for you to have a good education, and instead you're going to have a baby."

"Don't feel sorry for my parents," she said as she sat up, sliding her feet from the stirrups. "Feel sorry for me." The doctor left the room, letting the door slam behind him.

She thought about Stan, her high school sweetheart, as she lay waiting for her pregnancy to be terminated. For, at that moment, she felt no better than him because she too was taking a life . . . just not her own.

"Olena, the doctor needs to talk to you," the nurse said. "He will be in shortly."

"Is something wrong?"

"He just needs to discuss something with you. He will be in very soon. You may sit up if you like."

She raised herself. Held the sheet to her chin and waited for the doctor to enter. *Soon* for Olena meant he would enter when the nurse left. Instead it took him nearly twenty minutes, and when he came, she didn't like the news he came bearing.

"It appears that you have conceived twins. And when this happens, we need to make you aware, because in some cases, the mother changes her mind and doesn't want to go forth with terminating the pregnancy. Do you need time to decide if you still wish to proceed?"

"I would like to ask my boyfriend, but he dropped me off. I just need to call him at home."

"You can use one of the office phones."

Olena smiled as she dialed his number. Certain that this news would excite him, cause him to reconsider his position. He answered on the first ring. "Is it all over?"

"No."

"What's taking so long?"

"I'm carrying twins."

"It takes longer to get rid of two?"

"No, Andrew. The doctor thought we might change our minds since I'm pregnant with twins."

"If I don't want one, why would I want two? So I can be doubly miserable. Don't call me again until it's over."

FIVE

Now that the babies were removed, so was Andrew. They rarely saw each other. The times spent at his apartment had dwindled from every day to none at all. The excuse he served was that he had lost focus on his studies and needed to buckle down with just a couple weeks left before graduation, before that one, he had made up some other. Now, she was back at the Quad, back to the slander on her message board—back to being a bitch. But what others thought of Olena didn't matter much because she knew that even if no one loved her, Andrew always would, or at least she still hoped so.

Eight months of nearly every night in his arms, except for a one-week separation, and now Olena was back alone, and still couldn't wait to be grown. Couldn't wait to graduate from college and get a good job, marry Andrew, and have beautiful children. She didn't need a white picket fence, didn't need a fence at all—not even a house—just love to live inside of. He was mad at her now, but she was certain it was merely a phase that would eventually pass.

Yes, Olena had issues, which even she dare not deny. And college was to serve as her second chance. The step before true adulthood—the place people went in search of themselves and their future was where she went seeking love.

She sat in the phone booth directly outside her door to phone Andrew. Praying that he'd answer, but instead his machine did. She left another long message, pleading for forgiveness. Promising to do whatever he said. "I miss being held by you," were the last words she spoke before his machine cut off.

Olena knew that life could be hard, but she was determined to succeed even when life had labeled her a failure. Not life, per se, but love, first and foremost. She had tried her hand at loving a young man once in high school, and that relationship had failed miserably. Tried again in college, and she couldn't yet determine their status, but it didn't seem promising. Now Olena could finally relate the words she heard her mother speak so often about how anything worth having should take some work to get. She had been easy to Andrew, and now there was nothing she could do to turn back the clock but pray that she hadn't messed it up too badly.

While Andrew was heading for an honor of great distinction upon graduation, Olena was failing. Not because she wasn't smart—her grades had gotten her accepted into Howard—but mainly because she rarely attended class. The only course she excelled in was sociology, since it dealt with human social behavior, which was a topic she found fascinating, particularly when it came to asking why a person did certain things or behaved in certain ways, but why Andrew was suddenly ignoring her even after the abortion she couldn't make any sense of.

She was trying to remain hopeful. But that was before she entered her dorm room.

"Girl, did you hear?" Candice searched through the contents of a milk crate filled with what looked to be every current issue of the popular black magazines.

"Hear what?" Olena exclaimed.

"I just had my hands on that *Jet*. What did I do with it?" She continued digging through the pile. "Girl," Candice said, swirling the word as if she were gargling, "I picked up my mail on my way back from the grill and my *Jet* came. You will never guess whose wedding was being announced." Her head nodded, her lips purshed, and her eyes glowed as she delivered the bad news. "Your man Andrew, if I can ever find it."

"Stop playing. I don't believe that."

There had to be a mistake. Candice could never get any of her stories straight, even back during their days at Cass Technical High School. She had reported Vincent Doolittle, Olena's secret crush freshman year, dead from a terrible car accident. Well, it turned out that three of the most popular boys from their high school had died after rushing home from a house party, but none of them was Vincent. Olena fainted when she saw him strolling down the corridor. As a result, a rumor had spread that she was pregnant. And if she had been, she would have changed her name to Mary, because at that time she was still very much a virgin and, as she often reflected, wished she would have remained one.

Olena's sophomore year of high school was by far her most trying one. It was the year her boyfriend Stan had committed suicide. And yet Candice offered not one word of condolence. Instead, she became the main source of more rumors. That Olena had broken up with him days before he took his life. *Not true*. That Olena had slept with his best friend, and he had walked in on them. *Never*. That he was gay. *Please*. Olena confronted her cousin, who vehemently denied Olena's claims, but Olena's spirit told her otherwise. And, as she would learn through the years, she should always listen to her spirit.

"I know, girl, one of the finest, most eligible men on campus taken," said Candice. She took a short break from administering misery to finish eating her onion-laced corned-beef hash and stewed spiced apples. She soaked her buttermilk biscuits in white gravy. All of her food was compliments of the much beloved and world-famous Florida Avenue Grill. She was gobbling down her meal so quickly that one would assume it might be her last for the day. But Olena knew better; she knew that her cousin would hike back to have the pigs' feet for lunch and the spare ribs for dinner, and she had the nerve to wonder why she couldn't lose even one of her two-hundred-plus pounds. While Candice's mother wondered why the Weight Watchers' plan she was paying for wasn't paying off. Olena was the last person to call another woman fat, since she hated when people referred to her as anorexic. Besides, at times, she wished she were fat, because being thin had never won her a prize.

After Candice finished her breakfast, which included the fried pork chop that she had slid from the take-out container on the sly, she continued with her assessment. "I knew it was just a matter of time. The two of them are from the same hometown. They've been dating for over four years, and she's pregnant."

Pregnant? Olena thought. She had allowed Andrew to convince her that he wasn't ready to become a father, and he had driven her to a clinic in Baltimore to rid himself of the burden of caring for a child conceived by a woman he never loved.

"How pregnant?" Olena asked Candice as her hands strangled the edge of her flowered comforter.

"I'm not sure. Okay, here it is." She pulled the *Jet* magazine out of the crate, flipped to the wedding announcements, and handed the magazine to Olena.

Olena froze when she saw *her* Andrew in the upper-right-hand corner, grinning beside a light-skinned black woman with long blondish strands.

"So that's what she looks like," Olena mumbled. "I knew there was someone else."

Candice's hearing was as good as a canine's. "Yep, that's her. Light, bright, and damn near white. She doesn't look pregnant either. I think it's the way they cropped the photo, because my sources say that she's at least six months."

"Who are your damn sources?" asked Olena angrily. She was ready to burst. Eighteen was too young to feel the way she did—like she was having a heart attack. And at that moment she hated Candice more than Andrew and even more than Stan. In fact, she didn't even hate Andrew or Stan. She was just disappointed in both of them. At that age, she didn't realize young men lied in order to have sex. At that age, she didn't understand that she would be better off keeping her legs closed, that a man didn't fall in love as a result of a climax. She should have learned that with Stan. No, she wasn't upset at Andrew. He was just a young man in love with a beautiful woman—his high school sweetheart, and Stan, who had been hers, it was hard for her to even think about without becoming teary-eyed.

Olena had believed that Stan loved her and that she was his best friend and the woman he would one day marry. Six months later he took his life without warning. Nothing could affect her the way that had. Nothing could . . . nothing had . . . and nothing would. No more tears would be wasted on Andrew. She would have to tough it out. Move on and patiently wait to be grown.

"I couldn't wait for you to get here so I could tell you," Candice said.

Candice is too much like the evening news, Olena thought. She was supposed to be Olena's flesh and blood, but she could never report anything uplifting, only something tragic. Olena realized that Candice wasn't much of a friend either after she said, "As pretty as his fiancée is, I don't understand why he would ever cheat with you."

"What is that supposed to mean?"

"Girl, you're my cousin, and you know that I love you, but I have to be honest with you—you don't have anything on his fiancée. Look at how long and pretty her hair is. And I can tell from the photo that she's thick. Men like a woman with meat on her bones. Something they can hold on to."

"I have long hair."

"Yeah, but you use a maximum-strength relaxer to get your stuff straight, when all she has to do is wash and air-dry. And let's face it. Most men, especially most dark-skinned men, love light-skinned women. And you are far from light-skinned."

"Andrew doesn't have a complex with color. And he's not dark-skinned either."

"It's not a complex, Olena. It's a preference. I'm light-skinned and I know firsthand what most black men prefer because they've told me."

"Oh," Olena said, "so you've had a discussion with *most* black men? And they told you they preferred a light-skinned woman like you? Then why haven't you ever had a man?" Olena's heart was pounding so hard, it sounded like she was playing the drums. She knew the next time she opened her mouth, it would be to tell her cousin off.

"Girl, I can tell you're getting upset, so let's change the subject. Are you pledging next year?"

Pledging? Is that stupid girl asking me about a sorority, while I'm not only mad as hell but in mourning? I'm about to lose my man and then my mind. The last thing I want to contemplate is pink and green or red and white.

"Wasn't Auntie an AKA?" Candice asked.

Olena looked at her crossways and rolled her eyes. How many times did Olena have to remind her that neither one of her parents was a member of any Greek organization. Olena's mother was a teacher, and the only thing she had ever pledged was allegiance to the flag.

"I don't believe you," Olena said, this time pacing the small dorm room.

"Believe that I'm pledging? Girl, I have the application and everything. But it's hard as hell to get on line here, too damn political. It would be easier if I had lineage."

"I don't believe Andrew is getting married and his girlfriend is pregnant. I don't care how beautiful she is. He thought I was beautiful. He told me so. He loved my eyes."

"A man will tell a woman anything to get some."

"You know what? You're the bitch. Not me. So why my name has to be the one scribbled on that board is beyond me. You sit here always trying to put me down any chance you get like you're all that. And you're my cousin . . . my very own flesh and blood, and you claim to be my friend.

Hell, with friends like you, I need to start associating with my enemies, because maybe blood isn't thicker than water."

"What's wrong with you? I was just telling you because I thought you'd like to know."

"You thought I'd like to know what? You thought I'd like to know that the man I'm in love with is getting married to another woman and they're expecting a child? Did you really think I wanted to know that? Maybe that's something that I need to know but it sure in hell isn't something that I want to know. And did you really think I'd want to know that he never found me attractive because I'm not light-skinned? There's nothing wrong with the way I look. You may have a problem with how you look, but don't try to transfer your problems over here. I'm *fine* in more ways than one."

"You do have pretty eyes," Candice told her.

"And you have such a *pretty* face," Olena rebutted, knowing how much Candice hated hearing people say that.

"Mom," Olena said as she sat in the phone booth two floors below her dorm room, because she didn't want those East Coast girls or Candice to overhear her conversation and see the tears that were sure to flow. "I can't make it out here. I want to come home."

"Are you failing?"

"She's failing?" She heard her father yell. "I told you that she wasn't ready to go away to school."

"Your father could have gone into semiretirement last year, but he continued to work the extra hours at the shop so we would have enough money to put you through col-

lege and so you wouldn't have to worry about paying back
student loans. I know you're not failing. Are you failing?
You're too smart to fail."

"Well, tell Dad he can go ahead and fully retire this
year if he'd like. Yes, Mom, I'm failing."

"Are you failing?" her mother shouted. This time the
octave on her voice elevated, and Olena had to remove the
receiver from her ear for a second.

"Why can't I fail? Krystal failed. Why am I the one
always pushed to the limit?" Olena screamed. "I can't concentrate. I need to come home."

"Are you pregnant?"

"She's pregnant?" Olena's father shouted. "She better
do something about that."

"What do you suppose she does about it, Eugene?"

"Krystal had Alicia at fifteen, and you still watch her
while Krystal's at work," Olena said.

"I watch Alicia to help out Krystal and because that's
my grandchild."

"Well, you have more than one child, Mom. You have
three other children, and I'm your youngest. Maybe if you
showed me a little more love—"

"We love all of our children just the same, and you
know that."

"I told you she wasn't ready to go away. We just wasted
our money," Olena's father added.

As her parents continued with their usual drawn-out
back-and-forth exchange, Olena parked herself in the
phone booth, assessing her regretful past. She could have
turned to drugs after Stan's death. She had been tempted
to do so. But she had never been the type to experiment
with something that could alter her mind, with the exception of men, who always seemed to.

"I don't know, but I do know that she can't bring a baby into this house," her father continued.

"Well, I'm not going to turn my back on my child and grandchild," her mother said.

"I'm not pregnant," Olena said faintly.

"Why didn't you take the girl to get on birth control before she left for school? You know those kids have sex when they get off on their own," said her father.

"Will you tell Dad I'm not pregnant? I'm not good enough to be someone's mother or someone's wife either."

"She's not pregnant, Eugene," Olena's mother shouted.

"Well, then, what's wrong with you? Why can't you buckle down and study? Get a tutor if you need to. You don't have to fail."

"I'm sad."

"Sad? You want to come home because you're sad?" her mother asked.

"Sad?" her father shouted. "She can handle being sad. She better get glad."

"I can't handle being sad," Olena shouted back.

"Olena, what are you sad about?" her mother asked.

"Sad for myself. Sad for my life. Sad that I have no *real* friends and that the one boy who loved me didn't love me enough—"

"What that boy did wasn't because of you. It was something wrong with him. He had problems."

"So I guess something being wrong with all of my friends is the reason I can't keep any of them."

"You're better off without them. Real friends don't leave. Get over him and move on with your life. It's not always about some boy, Olena. Why can't you see that? Is that what's causing you to want to come home now—some boy?"

"No. He's not a boy. He's a young man. He has his own place, and he listens to Coltrane."

"And I bet you listen to all his jive too, don't you? You will learn," her mother said, screaming at the top of her lungs, "to leave those boys the hell alone and concentrate on Olena Day."

"I didn't think another young man could hurt me more than I've already been hurt."

"Do you know what's going to hurt you more than some young man, as you like to call them, more than some *boy*? Not getting an education. That's what will really hurt you. Now what you need to do is stay there and finish your degree and make something of yourself so that you'll not only have something to offer the world and the real man who will come along one day, but more important you will get an education to further yourself. You have to be stronger than that, Olena. Remember what your high school counselor said."

"That woman never helped me. No one has ever helped me. Not that psychologist either." And then the tears came—the tears that she had been resisting ever since Candice had showed her the truth. Her sight temporarily blinded from the pain and disappointment and regret of falling in love the first time with a boy who couldn't cope with life and the second time with a young man who couldn't cope with her. "Never again."

"Never again what, Olena? You have been doing so well. It's the only reason your father and I agreed to let you go off to school. And because we knew Candice would be there with you."

"Candice!" Olena shouted. "I hate that girl with all my passion."

"Candice is not only your blood but also your friend."

"Well, this isn't about Candice being a friend. This is about me being miserable. I want to come home."

"You can't come home, Olena. You have to stay there and make it. Take summer classes if you have to. This is your future we're planning. Do you know how prestigious it is to obtain a degree from Howard? I wish my parents could have afforded to send me there, or to any school, for that matter. Your father paid for my education. I was twenty and pregnant before I went to college. I refuse to let you ruin your life."

"She can come home if that's what she wants to do," her father shouted, "less money out of our pocket. But she's going to have to get here the best way she knows how. We're not driving there after her. I've wasted enough of my gas and mileage on her."

"The best way I know how?" Olena repeated.

"Your father's just a little upset right now, Olena, and rightfully so."

"Well, Mom, I can't help that I don't like it out here. I wish I was different, but I can't help the way I'm made. I let certain things get to me and this one thing has gotten to me bad."

"What one thing?"

Olena wondered if she should tell her mother. She knew if she did she'd have to brace herself for Nancy's wrath, and the more she thought about what would inevitably be her mother's response, she decided to leave what wasn't well, but was well enough, alone.

"If you aren't coming to get me, fine," Olena said. "But trust me, there will be hell to pay." She stood. "I would never force a child of mine to do anything. But that's okay. The tears I shed today, I won't shed again. And, Momma, despite what you say, I can't wait to be grown."

twenty-five years later

Twenty-five years' worth of regrets, Olena reflected as she eased her way through the security line at Orlando International Airport, heading for the Big Apple on business. If she could wipe her entire slate clean and start from scratch she would, including the previous seven years, even though the last seven accounted for not only a sizable six-figure income that she earned in her sales profession, but also a ballooning 401(k) portfolio with investments that paid off nicely. But along with the money also came an affair for her not only to remember, but always regret. The sex was great, but the sinning was so shameful. Now, nearly a year had passed since she put an end to their relationship, telling him to go back to his wife.

Olena was husbandless, childless, and in her mind homeless. On the weekends she lived in her parents' retirement home in the Villages, a community development district twenty miles south of Ocala, Florida, while her parents traveled the Western states in their RV. During the week her home sweet home became the Embassy Suites in Manhattan. Most of her friends her age from school were married; some had said, "I do," a second time, and a few even a third. Most had children who were either about to graduate from high school or college; a few were even grandparents. But Olena was the complete opposite. At forty-three she had never been married, and she didn't have nor did she want any kids. She didn't have the patience for children. Having kids meant sacrifice: attending PTA meetings, soccer practice, band, basketball, and whatever else they decided to participate in unless she forced hers to be introverted the way she had been as a child. No, it wasn't a need for her to consider motherhood. Besides, she'd waited too long. What Olena was ready for was to hop into a convertible and live worry-free, and by the beginning of the New Year, that was exactly what she had planned.

Is this my midlife crisis? she often wondered. She thought men were the only ones to have those, but now she wasn't so sure. The thought of growing old had never concerned her, because she was committed to staying young. And by that, she meant looking and feeling her very best. But the idea of missing out on life, which was what had occurred to Olena, was beginning to frighten her. She didn't want to reflect in twenty-five more years and then have fifty years' worth of regret.

The TSA agent glanced at Olena's driver's license and then up at her. "Is this right? What's your date of birth?"

"June 12th."

"Of what year?"

"Sixty-six. Too bad it's not eighty-six, right?" she said

with laughter as she stared across at the TSA agent's blank expression.

"Do you have a second form of ID, ma'am?"

"I wasn't a *ma'am* a minute ago. Now that you know my age, I'm all of a sudden a *ma'am*?" Olena removed her passport from her Louis Vuitton bag and handed it to the agent, who took a second to inspect it. "Okay, thank you," she said as she stroked her highlighter across a small section of Olena's boarding pass.

One hundred dollars is all it would have cost Olena, but she had run out of time, and now all of the upgrades to first class were sold out. So she was back to feeling regular—the way she had in college. Even the seat—20F—the *F* stood for *failure*—reminded her of her college days, or rather the day she left the District of Columbia after dropping out of college the second semester of her sophomore year and flew home. She'd had enough money from her last paycheck to purchase a plane ticket to Detroit and pay for cab fare to her parents' home. Once she arrived, her parents had barely spoken to her . . . and this carried on for nearly a year, other than occasional grunts from her father and lectures from her mother. She was lucky to have a home to return to, her mother would caution. "How could you?" she would ask Olena on the rare occasions she broke her silence. "How could you withdraw from your classes, get a refund, and spend the money we were investing in your future on all of these clothes?"

"I didn't spend the money on clothes. I worked and saved and bought my own clothes. Besides, I only got a partial refund anyway. Just a couple thousand dollars."

"Just?" her mother's head shook. "Well, it doesn't matter. You disappointed us, and that's what counts now. Two years and all you have to show for it is twelve hours."

Instead of attending classes the last semester of her sophomore year, Olena had worked full-time at the Bloomingdale's department store in Chevy Chase, Maryland. She had ridden the Metro every afternoon and evening for five, sometimes six, consecutive days to surround herself with fashion. At that time, her biggest claim to fame wasn't her sales, but rather the fact that she had alerted security to a ring of shoplifters just hours after eyeing a sketch that had been passed on to her by her manager. When Olena wasn't assisting customers in the men's department, she would float through the women's designer-apparel section. Trying on outfits she couldn't afford, but dreamed of one day owning. In high school, she had envisioned a career as a fashion designer, until she failed her first sketch class and resigned herself to the fact that she wasn't cut out to design anything more than a perfect life—one she had been sketching for too many years.

The one thing worthy of noting that Olena participated in on campus her sophomore year was the fall fashion show, which was a big deal at Howard. The audition process felt long and grueling to those who tried out. The names being posted outside the director's door was an exciting moment for all who appeared on the list. Freshman year Olena also auditioned but didn't make it. Finally after two tries, Olena's name appeared.

Somehow, she had managed to get past the fact that Andrew had lied about loving her and had left her to marry the woman who really did have his heart—a woman who Olena's research discovered, was a first-year medical student at Howard, but who obviously didn't attend Howard undergrad.

Olena would throw her thoughts on the fashion director and away from her past. He was an upperclassman, and at six foot four and with a muscular build, he appeared to be all man, but was actually someone else's man—some other man's man, that was. Olena's world crumbled at the after-party for the fashion show, which was thrown at a row house a few blocks from Cramton Auditorium, where the fashion show had been held. Olena saw him—the fashion show director—huddled in the corner tongue-kissing another man, who was as tall and big as he was.

She rushed into the bathroom to compose herself, only to discover three of the most beautiful girls on campus—who Olena considered to be role models—snorting cocaine. The three young ladies—one of whom had attended the same high school as Olena but graduated two years before her—not only modeled in the fashion show, but were all professional models. She never expected to find them bent over and holding a small cut-off straw, sucking their life away through their nostrils.

In a matter of seconds, Olena tumbled. First, she had assumed Andrew loved her. Not only was that not true, but it was last year's lie, and she had been trying to move on. But also what followed was a new set of misconceptions. She never assumed the fashion director would have an interest in men. If there was such a thing as a man looking gay, he didn't, so why did he have to be? she had asked God while she cried into her pillow late that night. More tears shed over a man, even after she swore Andrew would be the last one she would cry over.

For the latter part of her sophomore year, Olena had shacked up with a young man she had met on campus. He had never attended college, but he carried a briefcase with him every morning when he left his apartment for his so-called job. He wore jeans instead of a suit and always had wads of cash. In retrospect, she realized, she had been living with a drug dealer.

One hundred dollars to upgrade her seat meant all the difference in the world. One hundred dollars was her peace of mind—one less passenger to sit beside—a complimentary meal and glass of wine—plush seats. And distance between her disappointing past and her anticipated future. She wrote better in that section—composed her thoughts a lot clearer—felt more like somebody. If she had been in first class, she would have been focusing more on the words flowing from her Montblanc on to her Moleskine pocket-sized notebook rather than the shape of the clouds outside her window. The woman sitting beside her with diarrhea of the mouth wouldn't have been heard in first class. She would have been hidden behind the curtain, distanced nearly twenty rows back. The child who was continuously kicking Olena's seat wouldn't have been behind her, and life would have been better as life always seemed to be for those who could afford the best, and Olena could and she certainly could have afforded to upgrade. It was against her company's policy for employees to book a first-class flight in advance, but they would reimburse upgrades that were made available at the airport.

Olena had had every intention of arriving at the gate well before it was time to board. And as soon as the attendants arrived and the flight schedule was updated to the one she was on, she would approach their post and inquire about an upgrade as she always did. But today she had been detained. So once she realized she was going to miss her flight and be placed on standby, she went to the Borders inside of the airport in search of Walter Mosley's book on writing, but spent too much time there and then even more time on an incoming call from her ex's wife. Hugh had a wife before he became Olena's ex, but back then it hadn't matter to Olena as much. She had gone through a period where her morals and values had been placed on hold for what could only amount to as momentary pleasure. And this time she had wasted seven years instead of eighteen, but all total had thrown away twenty-five . . . and now she was forty-three and wondering how so much of her life had escaped her.

She thought back over the six years she had shared with Hugh. Times that she had convinced her mind were special, even though, the real special times were never shared with her. Holidays were reserved for his family; his wife and small child. She was merely a fling, and as the years passed, she understood how low her position was in his heart and she refused to settle. Now she realized just how sneaky the pair had been. She had even been to his home, met his beautiful, unsuspecting wife. Smiled in the woman's face, eaten her food . . . even held their child. Sat across from her at the dining room table and pretended she was there to get hooked up with Hugh's friend Hendrix so Hugh could prove to his wife that Olena was simply one of his employees and nothing more. So she would stop paying attention to the way Hugh gazed at Olena as if his eyes were playing back the many times they had shared together. Their entire relationship wasn't fair. Hadn't been fair to his wife or to Hendrix, who was still one of Olena's good friends, although he never understood why he and Olena didn't move out of the friendship zone or why she refused to become intimate with him, when the truth was she was serving it up to his friend, and to that day Hendrix still had no idea. But it particularly wasn't fair to Olena, who had convinced herself that she was being loved by a man who had already made a commitment to another woman—a man who was nothing more than a cheat. She deserved so much more, and finally one day nearly a year earlier, she decided it was time to end six years of suffering. Six years of sneaking around. Six years of betrayal; of sharing a man who even if some day in the future would belong to her she probably wouldn't trust enough to want.

One more kick from behind and Olena had had enough.

Her head spun around so quickly that she nearly got whiplash. "I'm not going to go this entire flight with your son kicking the back of my seat. I'm trying not to be rude, but if you don't mind, can you control that little foot of his? He's old enough to know better." She turned back to face the clouds.

"Do you have kids?" the woman behind her asked.

Olena's eyes closed momentarily from anger. *Did she have kids?*

"No, I don't have kids. But what does that have to do with your kid kicking the back of my seat and disturbing my flight? If I had kids, I would make sure they were mindful of others."

"Bobby, don't kick the mean lady's seat again, okay?"

The mean lady's seat? Olena mouthed.

"If she's mean, why can't I kick her?" Bobby said, giving one last swift jolt.

Olena shook her head as a flight attendant approached.

"Is everything okay over here?" the flight attendant asked Olena. "Are you having a bad day?"

"Yes, I sure am," Olena said. "But I only have an hour and forty-five more minutes before we land, and I should be doing a whole lot better then."

Olena was in fact having a bad day, which, while rare,

happened on occasion, and she was finding those times to come even more frequently. One minute she would be overelated at nothing in particular—a euphoric feeling would suddenly fall over her—and then in a matter of seconds sometimes, she would crash and panic, worry without being certain what it was that had caused her so much concern. Her friend Shelly, who was also in her forties, had suggested to Olena that she might be going through the change—a notion Olena quickly rejected. In Olena's mind, she was still young. Never mind the fact that she spent a fortune at Sephora on antiaging products. She couldn't explain how more than half of her life had somehow escaped her. It was as if one day she had fallen asleep at eighteen, and the next morning she awoke and was forty-three. But the truth for Olena was that her emotions *were* getting the best of her. Her clock *was* ticking, but in a different way. It wasn't about the desire to have a child. No matter how many celebrities made the news for having babies—even the ones in their forties, Halle Berry included—Olena had already pushed that desire aside years ago. It was about a desire to have . . . period. Not a desire to have money, because after years of obsessing on just that, she was finally in the position where she earned a lucrative six-figure income. But what of her life made it seem of any substance? The airplane flights, taxicab rides, hotel stays, and dining out for three meals a day mostly alone or entertaining clients who only knew her by her facade had all seemed so passé. She could have never imagined that the saying *Money can't make you happy* would be the least bit true, but it was turning out to be so.

It was one thing to look different, which she had definitely achieved, but another thing to be different, which was something she still needed to work on. After years of obsessing over long hair and a shapelier frame, she finally decided to cut her boring shoulder-length mane into an angled bob that rivaled Victoria Beckham's. She'd even carried a picture of the pop star that she tore out of *People* magazine into Lavar Hair Designs on West Seventy-second Street on Manhattan's Upper West Side to make sure her stylist achieved the same look, and while the results weren't exact, they were even more to Olena's liking. As for her body, she was a slender woman, and no matter how much she stuffed down her throat, very few pounds would stick, so finally she decided to stop caring so much. If being thin meant black men wouldn't like her, because black men supposedly preferred a woman with meat on her bones, then there was nothing she could do. At forty-three, Olena knew it was more about her accepting who she was than worrying about whether others would. Besides, she had achieved her best shape yet through regular exercise. At five foot nine and a size eight, she was twenty pounds and two sizes larger than her college days. But as slender as she still was, she had her trouble spots, like her stomach, which no amount of crunches could flatten, so instead she relied on Spanx body shapers to suck in what stuck out. She spent money on getting her teeth professionally whitened every year, and treated herself to a facial once a month and a manicure and pedicure twice a month at Bliss 57. And to accent her gray eyes, she discovered the Anastasia Brow Studio at Sephora on Fifth Avenue. She spared little expense on looking her best, because she had learned early on that people judged others more from what they saw on the outside, and if that wasn't appealing, very few would stick around long enough to discover what, if anything else, was.

She doodled in her Moleskine as the plane climbed to

cruising altitude, and thought about so many things as she increased the volume to the music coming from her iPhone in order to drown out the annoying sounds coming from coach. Wondered how many wrong men it would take her to love before she stumbled upon a real one. Glanced at the calendar on her phone and focused on the end of the month, when life at Lutel would end for a year and she would embark on a journey of self-discovery during her paid sabbatical. She couldn't wait for the next four weeks to buzz by. There were just three more work-related meetings she needed to attend. One was the mentoring session she was on her way to New York for. She was sitting in on one of the newer key account managers sales calls to assist with the close. The next was the annual sales conference in which she was the keynote speaker. Her topic, How much are you willing to sacrifice for success? And last, but certainly not least, finalizing the multimillion-dollar sale of Lutel's most expensive state-of-the art telephone and teleconferencing system to Olena's largest client, the Loyal Hospitality Group. It had been installed nearly three weeks prior, but the Loyal Hospitality Group was having problems with the system and had contacted Olena about canceling the agreement.

When all three of those meetings were over, her schedule for the remainder of the month would be light. And come the New Year her life would suddenly become her own for a change.

SEVEN

For the first time in seven years, she was conscious in the taxi as the driver went from JFK International Airport and took the Belt Parkway west to the Brooklyn Battery Tunnel. Aware enough to observe him veering left after exiting the tunnel and then following the signs for West Street, where he made a right and drove five blocks and then turned left onto Murray Street and went one block and made a left. The hotel sat on the corner of Murray and North End.

The taxi cab driver pulled around to the main entrance on North End Avenue and let Olena out at the Embassy Suites—her home away from home.

Didn't take Olena long to snooze the disappointments of the day away. At approximately 7:34 p.m. EST, she lay slumped over the sofa bed in the living room of the Embassy Suites, fully clothed and snoring. She had unintentionally fallen asleep clutching her corporate BlackBerry after reading her friend's e-mail. Her laptop was still powered on while her VPN token, which provided her with access to the company's network, lay beside it. The television was tuned to the Movies-on-Demand home screen. Her Louis Vuitton luggage blocked the entrance to the bedroom. The room service trays rested on the dining room table—the food barely touched.

The foul fish smell from the leftover Maryland crab cakes and seafood gumbo had caused her nose to continuously twitch and awakened her, at which time she pushed the cart out into the hotel's hallway and returned to the sofa and the e-mail that she had fallen asleep while reading.

The subject line read: New Beginnings.

It was sent by Shelly Ford, a dear but distant friend.

As you all know I'm moving on to the sunny state of Arizona. Wow! Today will be my last day with the company, so please discontinue using this e-mail address after today. Please send e-mails to my personal address at shelly44@xol.com.

Please K.I.T. Remember that from high school ... Keep in touch! ☺
xxoxo

Arizona? Olena had wondered. *Why Arizona? Is it another corporate relocation? No, she says it's her last day with the company. After sixteen years, Shelly is finally leaving the job she hates.*

Olena and Shelly had met nearly ten years earlier, while both were employed by the same financial services company. Shelly was in human resources while Olena was a retail credit analyst, servicing automobile dealers in the Greater Detroit area. Olena left the Motor City and headed south after she realized that the relationship she was in was more bogus than some of the automobile deals she used to decline. After she quit the finance company where she had been employed for twelve years, ever since she had graduated from the University of Detroit Mercy, she accepted an outside sales position with Lutel Industries, a leading telecommunications company in the U.S., and at that time she assumed she had found her new beginning.

Olena had relocated to five states with Lutel, the fifth stop bringing her to a regional sales office in Orlando, Florida, a city forty-five miles south of the Villages.

She and Shelly had stayed in relatively close contact over the years. Even though they had fallen off talking on the phone and e-mailing, they touched base on holidays with a free Hallmark e-card Shelly usually sent out. Now the e-mail Olena had just received was her reconnection to not only one of her good friends but to the truth—a new beginning—which was exactly what Olena needed.

She had never taken a vacation. The four weeks off that she earned each year she forfeited, opting instead to optimize her commission, which she could never do if she weren't there to smile in her clients' faces and convince them that they needed to upgrade the phone and teleconferencing systems they had just upgraded one or two years earlier. The company's top brass considered her an overachiever, which to Olena meant she had what most Americans during trying economic times could only dream of: job security. But her position wasn't that secure. Like many other industries, there were rumored buyouts, takeovers, layoffs that at times made the *Wall*

Street Journal and other notable publications, but she tried not to worry herself with things that were out of her control, and besides, she had saved quite well for her rainy day.

Eighteen work days remained before she had three hundred sixty-five days to discover who she was, giving her a small taste of what retiring at *fifty* would seem like.

But I'll be fifty! she thought.

Fifty.

Five-O. More than half of her life would already be over. She already felt like half of her life was over.

Will I still look good at fifty? she wondered.

The e-mail from Shelly forced Olena to quickly assess her own life or rather the lack of one. She lived as if she were certain she would see tomorrow. Lived for the future, rarely taking time to enjoy the present, and too often dwelling in the past. Her weekends were spent sleeping, recovering from a week on the road, and on Sundays she packed and prepared for the next week—a cycle that seemed unbreakable.

The hotel phone rang loudly, startling Olena out of her restful sleep.

"Good afternoon, this is Olena Day," she said in a professional tone, too sleepy to realize she wasn't at work and the call hadn't come from one of her clients but rather her niece Alicia.

"Afternoon?" chirped Alicia, an aspiring actress living in Los Angeles and chasing her dream, and on the verge of giving it up. "Check your watch. It's not even late morning on the West Coast. What are you doing?"

Olena yawned, wiped the sleep from her eyes, and sat up, trying to regain consciousness. "I was halfway asleep. I had a bad day, and I have a long one tomorrow. I can't even remember closing my eyes. Do you mind if I call you back tomorrow?"

"Yes, Auntie, I do mind. Wake up and talk to me. I feel like I'm in the middle of a nervous breakdown, and I need your help."

"I promise I'll help you tomorrow."

"Did you hear what I said?" Alicia snapped. "I'm on the verge of a nervous breakdown. What makes you think I have until tomorrow?"

"Don't talk like that." Olena struggled to compose herself. She had a crick in her neck, and her right shoulder was stiff. "What's bothering you?"

"What? It's not just one thing, Auntie. Life is bothering me . . . love . . . hell, almost every thing. I don't see how you do it."

"Do what?"

"Forty-three years old . . . never married . . . no kids. I'm thirty, and if I'm not walking down the aisle in a white dress, standing at the altar and saying *I do* to someone soon, I might just end my misery."

"What about your dream? Are you going to end that also?"

"What dream?"

"You forgot your own dream?"

"Oh, you mean my aspirations of becoming an Oscar-winning actress? That's not my dream. That's a damn fantasy. If I hadn't been running and chasing after that since I was eighteen, I'd probably be married by now."

"Honey, everyone who's married isn't happy . . . and everyone who's a parent doesn't want to be one. Define your life based on your own desire and not on what society says you should want. If you want to act, act. Continue doing what you're passionate about."

"That all sounds good, but I also want to be in love."

"Talk to me about your life. Love will always disappoint, so it's not even worth discussing."

"You don't miss being in love?"

"The only thing I miss right now is my rabbit pearl."

"The vibrator?"

"That's right. It was confiscated at the airport and I feel like I'm going though withdrawal. I might have to take a cab to an adult novelty store." Olena silently counted to five and waited for her niece's reaction.

"Auntie, your life sounds so sad and lonely. I don't want to end up like you."

"Gee, thanks. I didn't realize I had ended up any kind of way."

Alicia blew her nose. "Well, I mean, you miss a vibrator, Auntie, and not a man."

"Because the men I've had haven't been as reliable as my vibrator."

"Oh, God, Auntie, you are depressing me. It's a rubber dick. Stop talking about that thing like it's real."

"Okay, I will, if you'll stop crying to me like your problems are real. Crying just because you're not married?" Olena hadn't cried in more than twenty years. She had shed enough tears all through high school and her first two years in college that now she was all cried out. She didn't even cry at sad movies, not even *The Pursuit of Happyness,* when Chris Gardner was called to the boardroom and told that he was the one selected for the job. Even some of the men in the theater had been in tears.

"I'm not crying just because of that. Why is it that some people succeed without even trying? Jennifer Hudson won the damn Oscar for her first role."

"Are we still discussing something that happened over

two years ago?" Olena asked."It's time to move on. You should have been happy for her. I was ecstatic. That was the highlight of my evening."

"Happy for her? What about me? She pops out of *American Idol* and gets a role starring opposite those A-listers like Eddie Murphy and Jamie Foxx, when I've been in Hollywood for twelve years, and the best I can do is a damn play that's not even a Tyler Perry Production."

"You couldn't have played Effie anyway."

"You're missing my point, Auntie."

"No, I'm not missing your point. You're missing mine. Listen to me. I think you are doing fine with the plays. Doors will open up for you soon."

"When?"

"Probably when you least expect it."

"Please, Auntie, don't start one of your sermons. How about a door opening up when I need it most instead of when I least expect it?" Her cries echoed through the phone. "I try my damnedest with everything that I do. Even the men I love . . . even though not one of them is worth shit. Only with me because they like the way I look, which makes them shallow, and I have to ask myself if I want to be with a man who is mainly with me because I'm beautiful."

"Well, if there's one thing you don't lack, that's confidence."

"Auntie, of course I know I'm beautiful. How many times have I heard that since I was a child? But has my beauty allowed me to find love? No. And jumping from one man's bed to the next gets old quick."

"Try celibacy. It will help you gain clarity."

"The clarity I lack I make up for in the orgasms I achieve, even though my orgasms haven't been worth it. These men—black and white—all men haven't been worth it."

"Well, get a rabbit. Every woman needs one. And trust me, you'll have multiple orgasms."

"Stop, Auntie. I need a man and not some damn vibrator."

"You don't need a man. You would like to love a good man who also loves you, and there's nothing wrong with wanting companionship," Olena yawned. She wasn't going to let her niece's trials and tribulations carry her back to a place in time that she had no interest in revisiting, which was her past. She was determined to live as Eckhart Tolle described—in the now, which she knew even though she had only made attempts at reading both of his books, but had never made it past the first chapter of *A New Earth*. She had downloaded to her iPod the weekly Internet series that Oprah hosted and watched it on occasion.

"This too shall pass," Olena said firmly. "I'll call you tomorrow. This is your pain body I'm speaking with now."

"My what?"

"So you lied to me when you said you bought *A New Earth*. It's not too late to pick up a copy. *You* really need to read it."

"I thought you sold telephone systems. Now you're selling books."

"Now I'm selling phone systems. One day I will be selling books—my own, but I can't concentrate on that day. I can only focus on what is now, and I suggest you do the same. Leave your past behind. You're not hurting right now. Buy the book, and see what I'm talking about."

"What's the book about?"

"I haven't had the time to read it, but if Oprah recommended it, it must be good. I'll call you tomorrow."

EIGHT

Olena tried to drown out her yellow cab companion. It had been bad enough listening to her niece complain about her lack of love the night before, but now she had to hear it from a woman she was trying to train—one she barely knew. She didn't care about how long the woman had been married or how many kids she had or the schools they attended. And she really didn't care that the woman suspected her husband of having an affair.

"Did you hear what I just said?" the woman whined. "My husband gave me an STD."

Olena wanted to sound sympathetic when she responded, but it was hard for her to pretend with anyone other than a client. Still, she gathered up all the empathy she could muster and said, "I'm so sorry to hear that. Is everything okay now?"

"Okay? How could it be? He gave me an STD, Olena."

"If you want my advice, I'd say you need to focus on work—the one and only thing that I found will give you back as much if not more than you put into it."

"Give *you* back, Olena, because you've mastered this whole art of selling, but I'm really not cut out to do this. It's nothing like pharmaceutical sales. I miss my job. Too bad they downsized."

The cab pulled in front of a downtown skyscraper. Olena exited, but noticed her companion had stayed behind.

"Aren't you coming?" asked Olena as she stuck her head inside the cab.

The woman shook her head. "No, Olena. I don't want your life. I don't want to eat, sleep, and breathe Lutel. You can have it."

"But this is your account, not mine. I'm just here to help with the close not do the entire presentation."

"I'm sorry, but I have to do what's best for me and my happiness."

Olena closed the passenger door and stood on the curb in front of the office building, watching the cab as it pulled away. She started to call her manager, but decided to wait until after she had closed the deal.

Olena kept her presentations brief. She didn't use her Power Point slides as a crutch, preferring instead to focus on the actual product—the phones. Ten of which were lined up on the conference room table. Lutel's newest model was at the end, farthest from the decision maker—a female who appeared to be in her early thirties, with impeccable taste and a wonderful shoulder-length haircut that Olena marveled at.

"The best part of our new twenty-four system," said Olena as she circled the table, passing out the slim portable phones to the management personnel who were present, "is this state-of-the-art touch-screen mobile device that accompanies the landline and performs more like a miniature laptop with phone capabilities. When it is released in the beginning of the year, the mobile device will be available only to corporate subscribers of Twenty-four. The phone number to your landline converts to your mobile when you are away. It's as easy as pushing one button to automatically call-forward your line."

"All of this sounds quite nice, but it also seems too costly for our budget," the decision maker said.

Olena's eyebrows signaled confusion. "But your company's reputation is built on customer service. You are the best at what you do, and when you partner with the right telecommunications company, you will continue to be. For five consecutive years, you have won the JD Power Customer Satisfaction Award. Are you sure your company can't afford our most admired system? Because if you can't, what if the runner-up can?" She risked offending the decision maker with her sly comment, but Olena knew just how to phrase her question with the right tone. " It's something to consider, anyway."

"She quit," Olena said into her wireless earphone to her manager as the cab pulled in front of a prestigious skyscraper at 1211 Avenue of the Americas between Forty-seventh and Forty-eighth streets. Olena grabbed her black Epi leather Louis Vuitton briefcase from the seat beside her, stepped out of the cab, handed the cab driver a fifty-dollar bill, and told him to keep the change, but made sure he provided her a receipt for the full amount so she could expense it all. "But on a brighter note, I'm sure I closed the deal."

The attendant held the door open for Olena, who strutted through with her head held high as usual and her hips swaying to the rhythm of an imaginary melody. Olena lived for song. Her ears remained tuned to a station in her head that played continuous hits—some oldies but goodies like the Isley Brothers' "For the Love of You," Minnie Riperton's "Memory Lane," and Phyllis Hyman's "Prime of My Life."

"What do you mean she quit? Just like that she quit?" her manager asked.

"No, not just like that." Olena took the elevator to the twentieth floor.

"Well, what did she say?"

"She said her husband gave her an STD, and she said a bunch of other things that I barely paid attention to. And then she said she couldn't do it—something about being true to herself, all that same garbage. She never got out of the cab."

"Why can't all of our employees be like you?"

"Probably because they all have a life."

"So what's the rest of your week like?"

"Well, I'll visit a few of my key accounts before I fly back to Orlando. Then I'm heading out the middle of next week for the sales conference in Atlanta. I'm sure I'll see you there. I'm not sure why I was appointed the keynote speaker this year. I don't know how to tell people how to do what I do, and I'm not sure if I did know how to say it that I would. I love being number one. I don't want to give up my edge."

"Just do your best. I'm sure you will because you always do."

NINE

What good is having money if I'm not happy? Olena still wondered. As if finding the answer to that question would somehow cure her. And she wasn't truly happy. She returned from the laundry room with a small pile of lingerie, which she placed neatly inside the mesh compartment of her luggage, preparing to leave for Atlanta next week instead of New York this time.

She sat lifeless on the edge of the sofa with her blue Bliss at-home facial plastering her face as she stared at her laptop and VPN token, which rested on the coffee table in front of her. She picked up the phone to call Hendrix, but as soon as she began dialing, the house phone rang.

"Olena, what are you doing?" said her cousin Candice in a near whisper.

"What do I normally do on Sundays? Nothing." For Olena, the best part of Sunday was *Sixty Minutes*, but even that wasn't as much of a highlight now that Ed Bradley had passed. "What's wrong with your voice?"

"Oh, girl, you know how Delbert hates for me to talk on the phone."

"And you know how I hate to talk to you on the phone when I have to strain to hear you." Candice had changed. And while it was something she needed to do, Olena had hoped her cousin's transformation would be as a result of the passing of time instead of the pressuring of a man. She preferred her cousin the old way, before the bariatric surgery and the major weight loss. Back when *Jet* weddings and the latest gossip about the stars ruled her existence. She used to be irritating to Olena, and the two would often fall out, but at least she was something back then—something more than what she was now, which was some man's pet. But Olena didn't even consider Candice to be Delbert's pet, because even a dog is man's best friend. Candice wasn't anything to her man. "Do you know what I can't understand? How you can allow that man, that baby daddy to four baby mamas, to dictate where you go, what you wear, and even who you talk to on the phone?"

"I didn't call for that same old lecture. I have someone that I would like for you to meet."

"Someone you would like for me to meet?" Olena asked with laughter. "Maybe you should keep him for yourself, because you're the one in need of a new man."

"At least I have a man." At least she *finally* had a man was what Olena wanted to say to her cousin. He was the first man Candice had ever had. When she had been close to three hundred pounds, she hadn't had too many suitors, but at one hundred fifty pounds and shrinking, she now caused her fair share of heads to turn.

Olena said, "You may have a man, but he's a piece of one . . . and I don't want any part of the one you're trying to hook me up with. I'm trying to get myself in order. I've got some major issues of my own that require my full and undivided attention, which means that I don't need a man up in my mix." She was trying to convince herself more than her cousin.

"I think you would really like him. He's Delbert's cousin."

Olena burst out in even more laughter, and then she began coughing because she had gotten choked. She cleared her throat. "Do you honestly think that I want to meet anyone even distantly related to Delbert? I would never be with a man who monitored who I talked to on the phone, monitored my wardrobe. As much as I like to shop, do you think I'm going to let a man tell me what I can wear? No, baby, I'm not. Maybe it wouldn't be so bad if he had good taste, but Delbert doesn't, and if there's one thing that I absolutely can't stand, it's a man who wears cheap shoes."

"He's a good man. I don't care about his shoes. He makes me happy. You really are too picky."

"I'm willing to compromise in some areas, but my hot buttons need to be pressed." It was sad for Olena to consider how desperate her cousin had become and not because her man wore less expensive shoes than Olena preferred; but all for a man she barely knew; a man whom she had met online on a Christian dating Web site who seemed more like the devil. A man who had convinced Candice to move from D.C., where she had settled after she graduated from

Howard University, and leave behind a well-paying, highly sought GS-14 job with the federal government, where she had been employed for nearly fifteen years and start over in Jacksonville, Florida, at the city-government level, because as Candice was known to say, "You never know what you'll do for love?" Well, Olena knew what she wouldn't do, and that was to be a fool like her cousin. She had already been there and already done that. The definition of insanity was doing the same thing over and over, and Olena knew she was many things, but crazy wasn't one of them . . . at least not anymore.

"His cousin isn't anything like Delbert."

"So even you admit there's something wrong with Delbert."

"No, that's not what I'm saying. I'm just saying they are different. Just meet him. He lives in Florida also. He's an executive for Disney World. He just bought a brand-new Mercedes. And he recently built a home in Celebration. Delbert said he paid over eight hundred thousand dollars for it."

"You're telling me things that really don't matter. I don't need his money. I have plenty of my own. If he's all that, why is he alone? What's wrong with him?"

"You're alone. Is there something wrong with you?"

"As a matter of fact there is—a whole list of things too long to even mention."

Candice laughed. "Girl, you're too crazy. One date. That's all I'm asking. You never know. You could be blocking your blessing."

"The man who tried to holla at me at Florida Mall as I was walking to my car from Nordstrom said the same thing. And I said to God after he walked away, if that was my blessing, go ahead and block it."

"If you change your mind about meeting Delbert's cousin, call me."

"Don't worry. My mind is all made up. I don't want to meet him. Call up another one of your enemies and see if you can manipulate them into letting you ruin their lives."

TEN

Olena couldn't believe it, but it felt like love at first sight as she stood inside of the Magic Kingdom, outside of the Mainstreet Bakery, feasting her eyes on the most gorgeous man she had ever seen, who just happened to be her same age, and looked just as young as she did. She ate her ice-cream sundae and studied him: flawless olive skin; salt-and-pepper hair that lay flat against his head in a natural wave pattern; and perfect teeth. She ran his statistics down in her head—the ones that Candice had given her. He was single, had never been married, had no kids, a great job, and a nice home. And now she could add handsome and well-dressed to the list as well . . . with nice shoes.

Her last-minute decision to meet Flint, Delbert's cousin, was turning out to be more than she bargained for—a lot more. Initially, the call she placed to her cousin was one she made because she had suddenly become stir-crazy from staying inside.

Flint was cordial, though he rarely maintained eye contact with her. Olena tried to think of things to talk about, and when all else failed, she resorted to what she knew best: Lutel. She talked about her job as they walked through Magic Kingdom. Talked about how successful she was and how much money she earned. Discussed the Loyal Hospitality Group and how she had closed the largest deal in Lutel's history, but they were having second thoughts and her negotiation skills were going to truly be put to the test. For nearly three hours straight, she bragged about her career, while all he said in return was "Mmm-hmm" or "Really."

Finally, at six o'clock, Flint said, "Well, Olena, I know you have to fly to New York in the morning."

She shook her head. "I don't fly out until the middle of the week."

"I see. Well, still, I promised your cousin the evening wouldn't go long. I really appreciate you coming out, and it was a pleasure meeting you." And then he shook her hand.

After she arrived back at her parents' home, she called Flint, but his voice mail picked up.

"Hi, Flint. I was just calling to say I thoroughly enjoyed myself, and hopefully we can see each other again since we live so close." Then Olena did something she swore she wouldn't do—she called her cousin.

"Has Delbert talked to his cousin yet?"

"Yes."

"Okay, and . . . what did he say? Does he like me? My heart hasn't throbbed like that at first sight of a man in years." She noticed that she had been talking for nearly ten minutes straight to Candice's continued silence. "He didn't like me, did he?"

"It's not that he didn't like you."

"It's just that he didn't like me."

"Well, he thought you were cute, but just not his type. I just found out tonight that he likes Hispanic women. His last four girlfriends were either Cuban or Puerto Rican."

"Did he think I was going to be Hispanic? You're not Hispanic, and I'm your cousin."

"I'm not Hispanic, but I guess because I'm so fair and the way my hair is some people think I'm Hispanic."

"You mean the way your weave is?"

"Most of it is mine. I only have one track of weave."

"Well, it must be a very long and a very thick track," said Olena, letting her cousin know that she wasn't all that she wanted to make herself out to be. Giving Candice a little of her own medicine.

"He thought if you weren't Hispanic, you would at least be fair-skinned. He has a preference for fair-skinned women, and he likes fuller-figured women—women who are around my size. And I didn't realize he's into younger women, much younger, like under thirty. But he thought your eyes and smile were beautiful, and he said you had great teeth."

"You don't fuck a woman because she has great teeth." Olena shook her head. She was so disappointed that she almost . . . almost—never would she shed a tear. She wasn't that hurt.

"But, honestly, he was more turned off with your obsession with your job. He said he wanted to throw up. He is looking for a woman who doesn't even want to work."

"So basically I'm too independent, too skinny, too old, and too black, but I have great teeth and pretty eyes. Just

what a man's looking for. Well, thank you again for ruining my life and taking me back to my college days," Olena
said as she slammed the house phone down and collapsed
onto her pillow.

"Fuck you, Flint, Michigan. You're not even that big of
a city, anyway," she said, and fell out in laughter. "I don't
care that you don't like me because I'm black. Yes, I am
black, and I'm proud. Why do I have to be Hispanic? Why
do I have to be light-skinned to be loved? Mixed if I want to
be considered beautiful if I'm not white? Afro-Caribbean,
Afro-Asian, half something to be loved. Why can't I just
be a black woman and be loved? Why are black women
labeled as angry? Is that too fuckin' much to ask? Fuck
you, Flint. Fuck you. Fuck you. Fuck you." She threw one
of the sofa pillows across the room. "I'm not obsessed with
my job. I've got two more weeks of that bullshit, and I'm
out."

ELEVEN

Olena took her aisle seat in first class, pulled out her iPhone, went to iTunes and hit the Leela James CD cover. While the rest of the passengers boarded, she listened to "Soul Food," one of her favorite tracks.

"Excuse me," a deep voice said. The man stood in the aisle, shoving his carry-on in the overhead bin directly above her. "I'm sitting next to you. If you want the window seat you can have it. I prefer the aisle since I'm kind of a big guy."

Kind of a big guy, she thought as she gave him the once-over. That was an understatement. He was six foot four and more than two hundred pounds, closer to three, but more muscle than fat. She slid into the window seat and stared out, ignoring the man.

"I'm Jason," he said, awkwardly extending his hand. "Jason Nix."

She heard him, but since her earphones were on, she could pretend not to. However, he was persistent and had the nerve to remove her earphone from her right ear and repeat, "I'm Jason, and you are?"

"Listening to music," Olena said, as she shoved her earphone back inside of her ear. It wasn't that men annoyed her. Just the other night she had prayed for God to send her one. It was just that the urge for one would come and go, and at that moment it had vanished. Not that she could be certain that he was even flirting, and she hoped that he wasn't because as she proceeded to inspect him through her peripheral vision, she discovered that she wasn't attracted to him in the least. He smelled way better than he looked. She recognized the scent as Clive Christian's No. 1 Pure Perfume for Men. She wiggled her nose and glanced over at the man. Wanted to ask if he was wearing a fragrance that retailed for two thousand three hundred fifty dollars but decided against it, because she knew her nose didn't lie. She had become familiar with the fragrance that Neiman Marcus sold in a one-ounce handmade crystal bottle decorated with a radiant brilliant-cut white diamond on front. Olena loved surrounding herself with the finer things. The lady behind the fragrance counter at Neiman's had allowed her to sniff a sample of the oriental-amber fragrance, a scent Olena would never forget.

She thought about the advice on meeting men her male friend Hendrix had given her days earlier, and decided to turn off her music and focus her attention on Jason. If nothing more, they could be friends. She reminded herself that she needed more of those. And a male friend would have male friends, and who knew where that could possibly lead, even though knowing Hendrix had never led to any introductions and she was certain that was only because he had been so persistent in the past in trying to ease himself out of her friend zone.

"I'm sorry. I didn't mean to be rude. My name is Olena."

"That's a pretty name for a beautiful woman. Do you live in Orlando or Atlanta?"

"The Villages. And you?"

"I've never heard of the Villages."

"It's near Ocala, where Wesley Snipes was on trial."

"Oh." Jason nodded to signal his familiarity. "I travel between Atlanta and New York—mainly New York during football season. I was just here for a couple days taking my sons to Disney World."

Sons, she thought. *Strike one.* "Oh, where are they now?" she asked, pretending to be interested.

"They're still in Florida with their mother. I'll be back next week to get them."

"Just them or their mother also?"

He smiled. "Just them."

Olena started noticing people acknowledging him as they walked past. People he appeared not to know, so she realized that she might be sitting next to someone who was known even though she didn't know him. And considering how much he paid for a bottle of cologne, she knew if nothing else he had money, but quite possibly he also had fame.

"I don't want to stereotype you just because you're a big, black, well-dressed man sitting in first class. I know that doesn't mean you're an athlete."

"I am."

"Are you famous?"

He smirked. "I used to play football for the Falcons, but I retired last year. Now I'm a commentator for FOX, and I also do some work with TBS. Does that make me famous?"

"It depends. Were you a starter when you played?"

"Yes."

"Did you play in the Pro Bowl, and did you have any major endorsement deals?"

"Yes, I played in the Pro Bowl every year since my rookie year, and does a McDonald's commercial count for a major endorsement? I'm negotiating with T-Mobile. I might do the Fav-five series with Charles Barkley and Dwayne Wade, and add a little twist since they're basketball players and I'm football."

"Are you serious? I love those commercials. The one they did on Super Bowl was hilarious when Barkley said either you play better or call in sick. Oh, that was so funny to me. So I guess you are pretty famous."

"Little bit. But as famous as I might be, I'm glad that you didn't know me."

"I'm sorry. I don't follow football, basketball, or baseball, either. I barely have enough time to follow life."

As the airplane taxied the runway and prepared for takeoff, Olena shut her eyes and said a prayer to God that if Jason was her blessing to make sure she didn't block it, at least not before she got to know him a little better. He had passed her initial warning indicator—he wasn't broke.

"What drink are you having?" he asked Olena, lightly nudging her shoulder as two of the flight attendants began pushing the beverage cart down the aisle.

She opened her eyes. "Cranberry juice will be fine."

"Two cranberry juices."

She sat, sipping on her cranberry juice and eating the full pasta dish that was set on her tray. After she finished, she handed Jason her empty containers to give to the flight attendant passing by with a plastic bag. "Well, I usually sleep during my flights. So I think that I'll attempt to do that now."

"Would you like to lie on my shoulder?"

"On your shoulder?" She perked up. Even if she wasn't all that attracted to him, the fact that he might be drawn to her was flattering, particularly after she had been rejected by Flint. And Jason was famous to boot, with a heavenly scent lingering in his space. "You don't mind?"

He shook his head. "Mind? I'd be honored." He raised the armrest that separated their two seats.

"I wish I had my digital camera with me. I'd have someone take a picture," she said as she snuggled comfortably in his arms, "and I'd sell it to the paparazzi."

"Why stop at a picture? I have a camcorder at home. You can come by, and we can make our own movie."

"All right, Ray J. I think I'll have to pass. Good night."

"Do I get a kiss?" he asked, puckering his lips.

Olena turned and noticed two of the flight attendants rolling their eyes in her direction. "What's wrong with them?"

"They want to be sitting where you are, instead of standing pushing carts."

"Be nice."

"I offered you my shoulder for the entire flight. Isn't that being nice?" Her large eyes glanced up at him, and she smiled. "You're eyes are stunning, but I'm sure you hear that a lot."

"This is the first time that I've heard it from you."

"Have a good nap."

Olena slept better than she had ever before. Part of it was his scent. But then also it was his large frame. He was like a teddy bear, and she didn't normally like that type, but she thought nothing was wrong with trying something a little different. But then she had to remind herself to slow down. The man had just offered his shoulder, not his entire life.

"Sweetie, it's time to wake up," Jason said, as he tugged at her finger. "We've landed." She could have sworn she felt his lips brush against her forehead. Her eyes opened slowly. She had been lying in a small puddle. Her hand was resting in his crotch. She snatched it away and gasped. "I slobbered on your good shirt. I know it cost a mint, didn't it?" She wiped the corner of her mouth before covering her entire mouth. "I'm so embarrassed. Please forgive me. It was your cologne. It just knocked me out. I'll pay for your dry cleaning."

"I probably won't ever clean it," he said with a smile.

Olena didn't understand. She had gone all of this time with one lame excuse of a man after another, and now suddenly while on a flight to Atlanta she met a famous man who decided to treat her like a star, even though she was dressed like a college student.

Most of the other passengers were lined up in the aisles, pulling down their bags. She had checked all of her bags, with the exception of her purse, which was underneath the seat in front of hers and a Louis Vuitton duffel that Jason grabbed from the overhead bin and handed to her. She grabbed it quickly and stood.

"It was nice meeting you," she said as she stood in front of him, waiting to exit the plane. She didn't want to be disappointed if he didn't ask for her number or make the next move, but if he didn't she certainly wouldn't. So instead, she was getting ready to flee, better to do it that way than to stay and wait for something that might never happen as she had seen in her life many times before.

"Olena, hold up for a minute." Jason limped toward her. "My knees are bad, and I can't walk as fast as a young woman with long, shapely legs like yours."

"You're just full of compliments today, aren't you? Even though you can't even see my legs."

"I love it when a woman leaves something for the imagination. You are so beautiful to me."

"What's so beautiful about me?"

He looked at his watch. "I don't have enough time to tell you, but if you give me your number and allow me to take you out to lunch, or hopefully even dinner or perhaps both, I won't spare words."

"Do you have a pen?" she asked as the two engaged in an intense stare down.

"I have better than that. I have a pen and something to write your number on. How about that?" He handed her a ballpoint pen, along with two of his business cards. "One is for you to keep." He flashed a smile, and she noticed his pearly whites and deep dimples. His looks were improving by the second.

She handed him back his pen and one of his business cards without writing down her telephone number. She tucked his business card inside the zipper compartment of her Louis Vuitton purse. "I'll call you." She wiggled a few of her fingers and pranced away.

There was something up with him, Olena thought. She took one last glance. *Call me, please,* he mouthed, with his hands clasp together in prayer.

TWELVE

"**M**y name is Olena Day."

She strutted from behind the curtain of the makeshift stage and stood briefly at the podium. The Evergreen Ballroom inside of the Marriott conference center sat four hundred in a classroom-style room that was filled to capacity. She made full use of her wireless microphone as she floated through the rows of tables. She might have had a difficult time crying, but fake smiles came easily. She had to always appear to be happy. And why shouldn't she be since she was paid so well? she'd often remind herself. She had spent most of the morning at a spa for the full-service treatment so that she could be digital camera and camcorder ready by one in the afternoon when she was scheduled to speak. She wanted her bob more pronounced, so she had had the stylist stack and shorten the back so that her sides appeared even longer, and then she had asked for a black rinse to hide the few gray strands that had popped up overnight, the same way her age had.

"I have been employed by Lutel Technologies for seven years. I am the number-one senior key accounts manager not in the district . . . not in the region . . . but in the country. I am where each one of you should want to be. I have far exceeded not only the company's expectations for an employee but also those I initially set for myself. Commitment to excellence, which for me translates into customer satisfaction, starts and stops with you. The product that we are selling is not a phone system—it is simply ourselves."

She didn't care what her peers thought of her; most of them she didn't know, nor would she ever. It didn't bother her one bit if in their silence they were cursing her out as she floated through the aisle. There was nothing better than being the best, which was exactly the position she was in with her company. *But how long can I remain on top?* she often wondered. If she decided to return from her paid sabbatical, she would come back at the very bottom, and everything that she had worked so hard to achieve over the years would be gone just like that. For five of the almost seven years that she had been employed with the company, she had been number one. She couldn't imagine starting over.

When her hour-long speech ended, she took questions from the audience.

One woman stood and said, "How do you balance your professional life with your personal life?"

"I gave up my personal life for my professional one—next question."

She had a reputation for being direct and to the point. Olena's belief was the more a person said, the less they truly knew.

"What was the one thing that you did to propel your career to the next level and become the number-one salesperson?"

"I can't answer that question, because I'm not a salesperson. Now, if you would like to rephrase the question . . ."

"What was the one thing that you did to propel your career to the next level and become the number-one senior key accounts manager?"

"So you don't think that I'm a salesperson. As much as my ego wants to say that I'm more than a salesperson, no matter how many fancy titles companies come up with, the fact is that I am one. Most of us in the world are always selling ourselves to someone."

The questions poured in, and her answers remained brief. And then she brought it all to a close. "I want to be the best at everything that I do, and right now the only thing that I do is work, and I'm the best. If I were a mother, I would be the best. If I were a wife, I would be the best. But what I am is an employee of Lutel, and I am, their very best." She received a standing ovation, because who didn't like a success story? And she was surely one. The president and chief executive officer came onto the stage and shook Olena's hand.

"Let's give Olena Day another hand. She is the best, and we're excited to have her on our team. Now it's up to each one of you to determine how you can get to where she is. Don't think that it's impossible. Hard work and dedication," she heard him saying as she was stepping behind the curtain. She hadn't even left yet for her sabbatical, and they were already trying to motivate her peers to take her spot. *To hell with the company,* she thought. She was ready to contact a BMW dealership and purchase a convertible. Buy another plane ticket to Atlanta before she chickened

out and ended up spending her year off at the Villages instead, blending in all too well with the fifty-five-and-older
crowd. She might have been forty-three, but she wasn't
dead, and despite what her niece thought, she wasn't that
sad and only a little lonely.

"**L**ook, Olena," said an enthusiastic Carrie, the front-desk receptionist at the Loyal Hospitality Group, as Olena walked through the double glass doors, followed by Taj and Anish, her two colleagues who joined Olena to provide their technical expertise. "He finally did it." Carrie stood and pranced over to Olena, with her left hand extended to expose the large rock on her ring finger. "And I didn't even have to give him an ultimatum."

"And you're still working here? Girl, I would have given my one-minute notice."

"Olena, girl, you're crazy. I love my job."

Olena really was crazy. Here it was the fourth and final day that she and her team were meeting with the top brass of the Loyal Hospitality Group, trying to keep their phone system intact, and she had just told their receptionist she should quit. Even though it was just a joke, she prayed no one overheard.

Olena moved her hand closer into view and beamed at the huge pear-shaped diamond.

"Very nice," Olena said, releasing Carrie's hand as she started to make her way through the building walking toward the glass offices that lined the back wall, and as she walked, she focused on the women in their cubicles, observing their left hands, for the presence of the wedding rings that many wore. Sometimes, she found herself staring at married women and wondering why them and not her. Was she too tall? Men seemed to gravitate toward petite women, and she was five-nine. Was it because she didn't have kids, since most of the women that she knew with kids all had men who weren't necessarily their children's father? Maybe she needed to expand beyond black men. Several of her black female colleagues had white husbands. But Olena loved black men: the good . . . the bad . . . just not the ugly . . . and especially not the ones wearing cheap shoes. Maybe it didn't matter. She was already married to her job. Between the plane rides, the yellow cabs, and the hotel stays, her life really had room only for frequent-flier miles, American Express Rewards, and Hilton Honors.

As she approached Milton Kirk's office, she noticed that his door was shut, and the lights were off. His administrative assistant, Jill Johnston, greeted her.

"Olena, Mr. Kirk had to fly to Pennsylvania for a family emergency. And the other managers are all out as well, but they did leave me with a directive. Unfortunately, they decided to rescind the agreement. The system is just not working out for us. I'm sorry," she said as she handed Olena a sealed envelope.

Just like that her six-figure commission check was gone—
not to mention the hassle Lutel would be put through to re-
install Loyal's old system or perhaps a different one, if they
were even given that opportunity. And, of course, Olena
wouldn't be the one to negotiate any new deals that might
be decided while she was on sabbatical. During a conference call, they had pointed out all the problems with Lutel's
phone system that their technical support team had been
looking into: an echoing sound that customers complained
of hearing, an occasional disruption of service, and landline-
to-cell-phone transfers that often disconnected. But Olena
really thought they'd be able to work through most of the
glitches, and if not, maybe she could upgrade them to the
Twenty-four system, but that was not being released until
January, and they said they couldn't wait that long, even
though it was only a few weeks away at the time.

"Thank you, Jill. I will have my sales manager contact
Mr. Kirk, because I'll be away for a while."

"That's right. You're going on your sabbatical. Con-
gratulations. That's a great benefit. I wish I could take a
year off with pay."

"Thanks, but I need it, especially after this."

"I know, Olena, but I'm sure they'll decide on another
system. They're very pleased with you. So have you decided where you're going?"

"I'm heading to Atlanta." Olena took out her sales
manager's business card.

"Oh, really, why there?"

Olena shrugged. Didn't want to tell Jill the truth about
her decision being based partially on a man whom she had
met on the plane, and even though she didn't feel the least
bit attracted to him, she loved the cat-and-mouse pursuit
that she had never been privy to. In fact, they had spoken

nearly every night for the past week, and she had agreed to spend New Year's Eve with him. "I've always wanted to live there, and whenever I retire, I'm thinking about making it my home. Please be sure Milton gets this." Olena handed her manager's business card to Jill.

"Well, enjoy."

"Oh, I will. Take care."

"I'm about to throw up," Olena said underneath her breath to her two colleagues as they quietly left the office suite and headed for the elevators. They waited until they were in the cab to vent.

"None of them were there? Bunch of cowards couldn't even tell us to our face," Anish said.

"I had a feeling after the conference call that they were going to rescind," said Taj.

Olena sat quietly in the cab. Looking out the window at the hundreds of people traveling by foot, she wondered what each of their lives was like. Did they have someone special at home, or was it all work, the way her life had been? All work and a damn six-figure commission check that she wasn't going to earn now.

"Let's go drinking," Anish said.

"The Embassy gives us free drinks after five," said Olena. "I don't feel like going out."

Anish looked down at his watch. "It's only two. I'm going to be wasted way before five, and you should be too. Do you know how much money you just lost?"

"Isn't that the truth?" she said, fighting back tears. "Take us to the nearest bar," she told the cab driver.

"There's an Applebee's at the Embassy," Taj yelled out. "Blue motherfuckers for everybody."

"I don't like the way that sounds," Olena said. "I'll stick to my usual pomegranate or chocolate martinis."

"No, this day calls for some blue motherfuckers."

The cabdriver pulled in front of the Embassy Suites on North End, and even though they were sober, they still all stumbled out.

Taj, Anish, and Olena were sitting at the bar. Each had a drink in their hand and another round on the way.

"We flew all the way down here for nothing," Taj said. "Freezing our fuckin' assess off in this dirty-ass city when we could be back in sunny Florida with our families."

"I love New York, or at least I did. What a way to ring in the New Year. But since I'm here, I'm going to stay here and watch the ball drop in Times Square," Olena said, lifting her glass. "A toast." Olena knew all too well how to have a good time. She had perfected the art of pretending. In some ways, she could be the life of any party. And even though it was all a facade, she was the only one who knew.

"A toast?" Taj questioned. "To what?"

"I don't know. I guess to blue motherfuckers. I've never had one before now, and I see how they got the name, because I'm feeling blue and I'm fucked up like a motha'."

"I don't think that's why they call them that," Anish said.

"Well, that's why I call them that," Olena said. "And since I'm the one who just lost six figures today, and all you lost is time with your damn family, I'll go with my theory. How 'bout that? At least you have a damn family."

*   *   *

Three hours later, Olena returned to her room. Taj and Anish were still at the bar drinking when she left. She felt a little more than a slight buzz as she stumbled down the hallway.

When she entered her room, the first thing she did was open the curtains in the bedroom so she could take in the spectacular views of the Hudson River. Usually her rooms had views of the city, but she was glad this time she could look out at water because that put her at peace. *Then maybe I should go jump in the river,* she thought cynically.

She sat at the small desk wedged into the corner separating the two large windows that held the gorgeous view, and flipped open the black portfolio to peruse the room-service menu. Tonight, she decided to try the salmon and have a three layer brownie à la mode for desert. *Did I eat while I was drinking?* she wondered. She honestly couldn't remember. Well, even if she had eaten, as thin as she was, she could stand to eat again.

Olena had so many problems, and she hid them all in her work. And now work was ending for a year, and she'd have to face them head on. For one thing, why didn't she have many friends aside from her niece Alicia? Not any real friends. She understood why she didn't have any friends at work, because she was never in the office. But even before she had taken the Lutel job, she had lived thirty-six years, so what had happened to the people she should have met and developed lasting relationships with along the way? Why was she still the bitch that those girls wrote about on her dorm-room door? The reason Olena didn't have friends was the exact same reason she had never had a man to truly love her for her.

There was something about *her*.

What was it? she wondered.

She picked up the phone and called her niece Alicia to ask, "What is it about me?"

"Huh?" Alicia said. "What is it about you?"

"Why are you my only friend?"

"I'm not your only friend. I'm your niece. What about Renee?"

"I lost contact with her years ago. Last time I saw her, she was married and had just had a little girl. I think I'm her daughter's Godmother."

"You mean you don't even know."

"I'm pretty sure that I am. Try having my life and see how much you can keep up with. Back to my question. Why are you my friend? What do you like about me?"

"You're my aunt. Do I have a choice?"

"Well, thanks a lot. Of course, you have a choice. You don't have to like me."

"Okay. Then I don't."

"What? You don't have a choice. You're right."

"Auntie, did you ever have any friends who weren't family aside from Renee?"

"When I was six, my best friend was Carla Morrison. We started the Barbie doll club together. She was the president and I was the vice-president. We recruited about five other girls to join, and then they all voted me out."

Alicia began laughing hysterically. "You got voted out of the Barbie doll club, Auntie?"

"That's right. I got voted out of the damn Barbie doll club that I helped found," said Olena angrily.

"Are you drunk?"

"No, I'm not drunk, are you?"

"You're drunk. What's wrong, Auntie? You were fine when I talked to you last night. What brought all of this on?"

"I lost the account."

Alicia gasped. "You lost the account and all of that money too?"

"Do you know money doesn't mean a thing if you're not happy? Not one blue mothafuckin' thing. It doesn't mean shit if you don't have anyone to share it with. And I am not happy. Not . . . at . . . all. That's all I want—all I've ever wanted: just to be happy, Olena."

"I'm Alicia. You're Olena."

"I know that," Olena snapped. "So what if the Loyal Hospitality Group doesn't want our funky little state-of-the-art fiber optic bullshit system, and I'm not going on my sabbatical with a six-figure commission check in the mail. I'm still getting my six-series BMW, regardless. I have enough money in my checking account. I don't even have to touch my four-oh-one-K for that." She opened her laptop and logged on to BMW's Web site. "I'm looking at it online right now."

"What are you looking at online?"

"The BMW experience . . . oh, my God. Now that's living," Olena said as she watched the video presentation. "What kind of house is that? What country were they in when they filmed this? I can't believe how some people live."

"Can I call you back?" Alicia asked.

"No, you can't call me back," Olena shouted, "not until you answer my question. And now that I really think about it, there was also Mary. She was my best friend when I was in the fifth grade, until she got mad at me because I was her secret Santa and I got her a book of Life Savers because your grandmother was too cheap to take me to the mall so I could buy Mary a real present. My mother forced me to give Mary—a girl who wore braces—candy for Christmas."

"Did you try telling Grandma that the girl wore braces?"

"You know your grandmother just as well as I know my mother. Do you think she cared that the girl wore glasses?"

"I thought she wore braces. Not glasses."

"You know what I mean. Her exact words were, and I'll never forget them either." Olena paused because she had forgotten her mother's words. "What was it that she said?"

Alicia began laughing. "What have you been drinking?"

"Blue motherfuckers."

"Oh, you're torn up."

"I remember now. She said, 'You better give that girl that candy. If she can't eat it, she might know somebody who can.' Mary was so hurt that she was crying the entire day at school. I felt like shit once I was revealed to be her secret Santa. Everyone else had nice gifts, and I gave that girl a book of Life Savers that *might* have cost five dollars, and I do stress *might*. She was my first, my only, and my last best friend."

"I'm your best friend."

"You're family. But why am I crying over friends? Michael Vick had friends, and what good did they do him?"

"Get some rest. You'll feel better in the morning, if you don't have a hangover."

"I wonder if Jason was one of Michael's friends. They played for the same team."

"Go to sleep, Auntie. Get some rest."

"Can we get back to my question please?" Olena shouted. "Miss Get Some Rest. I don't want to rest. I want to think. Think about what my problem is. So what is it?"

"Read *A New Earth*. You'll learn how it's not good to do so much thinking. You don't want to end up lost in thought, Auntie."

"What is it about me? Please answer the damn question."

"What is it about you? Let me think on that and get back to you tomorrow when you're back in your right mind and won't care."

"I might not make it through tonight. I'm staring out at the Hudson River, and I'm tempted to go jump in."

"Yeah, right," Alicia said, doubting her aunt's sincerity.

"Do you think I won't kill myself? Stan killed himself. The coward. I wish he was alive today so I could kill him myself."

"Auntie, get some rest."

"No, I want my answer right now."

"Okay, that's what it is about you. You're not the only one in the world, Aunt Olena, who can be busy. When I call you and want to talk or want your advice, what do I get from you? 'Oh, call me back. I'm on a conference call' or 'I'm getting ready to board this plane or rent a car or catch a cab, check into the Embassy.' But when you want to talk, everybody had better drop every damn thing immediately and attend to your every need. And if they don't, what do you do? Threaten to kill yourself. That's just not right."

"You're usually not busy, Alicia."

"Well, I am tonight. I'm on a date."

Olena's heart sank. She wanted to be happy for her niece and resist being so sad for her lonely self, but she couldn't help it. She was so ready for love . . . not marriage . . . just love. "You met someone? Tell me about him."

"I can't tell you about him now because he's right here."

"Just tell me where you met him."

"Blockbuster."

Olena's nose curled. "Is he that big of a flirt that he was trying to pick you up while you were browsing through new releases, because you don't flirt?"

"No, he was helping me find a movie. He works there."

"Wait a minute?" Olena said, waving her index finger. "You mean that you met someone who works at Blockbuster?"

"Yes, what's wrong with that?"

"The last time I went inside a Blockbuster, from what I can remember, all the people who worked there were in their twenties *if* they were even that old. How old is he?"

"He's in his twenties. Well into his twenties."

"How well into his twenties?"

"Well into his twenties. Almost thirty."

"How old, Alicia?"

"Twenty-six."

"You're thirty-one. I guess that's okay."

"Thank you for your approval. I'll talk to you this weekend."

"This weekend? What happened to tomorrow?"

"I'm going to be busy tomorrow."

"Too busy for your auntie?"

"Yes, Auntie, too busy for you, just like sometimes you're too busy for me. So I will talk to you this weekend."

"My body might wash up on shore by then. There's a small pad here. I'll be sure to leave behind a note."

"Okay. That will be good, so at least you will have written something before you leave this earth, because it doesn't seem as if you'll ever start your book."

"I started on my book at the airport. The first chapter is finished. But it's so sad no one will want to read it."

"Talk to you this weekend," Alicia said as she ended the call.

After Olena got off the phone, she dropped to her knees. "Oh, God, You're not going to forgive me, are You?" She had finally figured out why her life was so miserable. It was those six years of sinning. Sleeping with another woman's husband, and now Olena was expecting God to bless her with a man. Forget everything she had done to destroy someone else's marriage and bless her instead. She knew God didn't work that way. He couldn't possibly. What she realized was that she had to fix herself first. Fix herself from giving love before she even felt love and then trying to convince her mind that that was what it was so she could trick her heart in the process. She was so messed up . . . or maybe it was just all those blue motherfuckers

It was not only the last day of the month, but also New Year's Eve, and the dealership was staying open until five for the holiday. The inside was packed. In the center of the madness sat the top salesperson, a young white male sporting spiked blond hair, wire-rimmed designer glasses, a semi-expensive suit, and very loud cologne. His customer—a gray-haired, middle-aged black male with a good job and questionable credit—was wearing a postal uniform. Sitting beside him was his wife, a well-built, nicely dressed female who appeared to be much younger than her husband.

Tension was thick at the preowned superstore. The salesperson placed a sheet of paper—referred to as the four square—in front of the customer and proceeded to go over the price of the car, the customer's payoff amount along with the amount the dealership was giving him on his trade. There wasn't a down payment so the only other issue to discuss was the man's monthly payments.

"Sir, I just need for you to sign right here," he said as he pointed the tip of his pen at the signature line, set the pen down, and didn't say another word. The golden rule in the car business was the first person to speak loses. There was brief silence as the customer along with his wife glanced at the retail installment contract along with the four square.

The salesperson stared at the board hanging to the side of the sales tower in full view of the customers. He was the first name under Team A because he was the top salesperson on his team. Numbers one to thirty were written at the top of the board along with nineteen Xs that were placed beside his name. Box twenty was shaded green. The salesperson's thoughts were consumed with the fact that one more X was all that he needed. Just one car shy of hitting his twenty-car objective, and he would be awarded a two-thousand-dollar bonus.

He watched his customer's hand ease toward the pen. But then the man's wife snatched the pen away and said, "We're not paying six hundred dollars a month for a damn used car." She stood and grabbed her purse, which was hanging on the back of the chair. "Let's go."

Three of the managers eyed the situation from the sales tower.

"He needs that deal," the general sales manager told the used-car manager as he picked up his phone and dialed Matthew, but the call went straight to voice mail. "I guess he's in with a customer."

"It's actually five hundred eighty-five dollars, ma'am," the salesperson said. He was trying not to break a sweat, but he knew he couldn't let this customer get away because it was anyone's guess if he'd get another customer who would buy a car that day.

"Five hundred eighty-five dollars," the woman said with laughter. "We can't even buy gas for that guzzler with fifteen dollars—so, like I said, six hundred dollars."

The salesperson looked at the woman's husband, who threw up his hands. "It's all on what she wants. I don't want to get beat when I go home."

The salesperson laughed but neither the customer nor his wife did.

"You damn right, it's all on what I want, and I don't want an Expedition, no way. You need to come down on that price and give us more for our trade. Seven thousand dollars for a Magnum RT makes no sense. I can get more than that from CarMax. In fact, maybe that's where we should have gone. It's not too late. We haven't signed any paperwork."

"Ma'am, you came to the right place," the salesperson said, looking over at the sales tower. Imagining how much hell and grief he would face if he ended the month one car away from his goal. "You've spent nearly two hours in here already. Why not leave today with a new car for the New Year?"

"The New Year won't be used, so why should my car be?" the woman said.

"A preowned car," the salesperson corrected.

"Well, the only way we're leaving today with a preowned car is if we get at least fifteen thousand dollars for our trade and our payments are no more than five hundred dollars. Can you do that? If you can, you've got a deal."

"Let me see what I can do. Just give me a few minutes."

He marched over to the sales tower.

"Those bougs want a five-hundred-dollar payment. I've got the third-base coach in there, and she's talking about how much we're paying for the trade. He's doing whatever the fuck she says. I need this damn deal."

"Go to the box and get *him*."

The salesperson marched from the preowned super-center, through the Nissan store and Infiniti store, and into the BMW dealership, where the primary finance director's office was housed. He stood pacing with a file tucked under his arm.

Matthew glanced over at him, wrinkling his thick brows as he pushed his square-rimmed glasses farther up the bridge of his nose—a gesture that let the salesperson know he had ticked Matthew off.

Help me, the salesperson mouthed through the glass door.

"Does he need you?" one of Matthew's customers asked as all three of them watched the salesperson pace nervously.

"That's one of my salespeople. He'll be fine. I may need to step out for just a moment."

His customers nodded. "We understand," one of the men said.

"Now there are many options that are available to you. We base this menu on the options we think would best suit your needs."

The salesperson knocked on the glass door—a very bold move.

"Excuse me, if you can. I need to step out for a moment." Matthew stood tall and lean, leaving his Brooks Brother suit jacket resting on the back of his leather chair. The French cuffs to his crisp white shirt were rolled up, his suspenders were loosened, but his Burberry check woven tie was knotted tightly and still on straight. "Are you out of your damn mind?" he said to the salesperson as soon as he exited his office, closing the door behind him. He rolled down the sleeves to his shirt and buttoned them. "Don't ever interrupt me when I'm in the middle of closing. What's the problem?" Matthew asked the salesperson, who had now broken out in a sweat.

"I'm one away from meeting my goal, and I can't close my fuckin' customer. Mitch said to come get you." The salesperson handed the customers' file to Matthew. "I was that close to getting the paperwork signed, and then the third-base coach had to open her damn mouth."

"Is she signing with him?" Matthew asked as he looked over the credit file. "Because she might need to. He's had multiple BK's and just got out of one a couple months ago. My new buyer isn't like Shayla. She's going to want to see a year's worth of reestablishment."

"Her credit is worse than his," the salesperson said. "And she's talking about she wants fifteen thousand for the trade and a five-hundred-dollar payment."

"She obviously doesn't read the news? People are in the market for fuel-efficient automobiles, not a 2005 Magnum RT with close to eighty thousand miles on it. They're going to be upside down. They owe fifteen thousand on that car, and no one is going to give them that—*no one*." Matthew pulled a second credit report from the file. "Is this her credit report right here?"

"Yeah, that's it."

"Whoa."

"Yeah, they're both a couple of bougs trying to fake like their credit is bullets."

"Her credit isn't that bad," Matthew said, as he studied her credit report. "I've seen worse. She just has too much credit, but at least she pays it. I have a few angles I can use on them. I'll be right over there."

"Man, I need you now. They're ready to walk. How much longer are you going to be in there?"

Matthew handed the customers' file back to the salesperson. "I'm closing my customers on the back end. It won't take me long to knock their heads off. Just give me a few more minutes."

"Please, man, I need this deal. I need it bad."

"Don't worry about it. It's yours. Trust me. Just go back over there and tell them that you talked to your finance director, and they need to call him Santa because they're going to have Christmas again before the end of the year. Make sure you tell them that. Their Christmas is coming again."

"Their Christmas is coming again before the end of the year. Okay, I sure will."

Matthew took a deep breath before turning back around and entering his office. "I am so sorry for that interruption," he said as he sat behind his desk. "Now where were we?"

"That's Santa? Mmm, he's cute," the woman said as she observed Matthew approach the desk. "But he looks a little young to be Saint Nick." She snapped her fingers. "He reminds me of that singer, the young one with the nice body who can dance. What's his name?" she asked her husband.

"Chris Brown."

"Yeah," she said skeptically, as her nose twisted. "Oh, so you think he's got a nice body too?"

"Don't start, please. You've always said you thought he was cute, so I knew who you were talking about."

"Well, this is Atlanta, and I did find that Bulldog business card in the house with a man's name and number written on the back." Matthew's face tightened at the mention of the popular gay club that had been situated on Peachtree in the heart of midtown for more than thirty years.

"I told you that wasn't mine."

"So where did it come from? The only other person who lives in the house is our five-year-old son. I don't think he knows anything about clubs."

"Hello, ma'am," Matthew said as he extended his hand toward her. "Lovely blouse, and it fits you so perfectly. I love the vibrant colors."

She smiled. "Thank you."

"That is an International Concepts design, isn't it?"

Her eyes enlarged. "Yes. How did you know that?"

"My wife loves Inc." She looked down at his left hand and noticed the platinum wedding band. "And their pattern is unique to any other design."

"That's so true."

The woman's husband said with an attitude, "So your man over here tells us you're Santa, and Christmas is coming again for us this year. So what you got besides compliments?"

"That's right. I am Santa. And I've checked your credit. In fact I've gone over it twice." He pulled a chair from the desk beside them. "Do you mind?" he asked the wife as he slid the chair in between the couple.

"Not, at all. Is that Issey Miyake you're wearing?"

"Yes, it is."

"I love Issey Miyake."

"You love Issey Miyake?" her husband asked. "Well, why haven't you ever told me that?"

"Because you're stuck on that damn Cool Water, Edwin."

"But if I knew you loved Issey, I would have bought a bottle."

"Well, why do you have to know what I like? Why can't you just automatically wear it. Just be quiet and let Santa speak."

"I understand you're looking for more money for your trade, and that you would like for your payments on this car to be around five hundred dollars. I definitely agree with you," Matthew said, maintaining eye contact with the wife and ignoring the husband. "I did go to bat for you on the trade. I even had it reappraised. What I'm coming up against is the mileage and the accident. You were involved in an accident in March—is that correct?"

"How did you know that?" the wife asked.

"The appraiser ran a Carfax, which is standard when we're trying to justify giving someone more than the car is actually worth. We need to make sure of the condition. Things we have to consider as we prepare for resell. The other issue is the mileage. You're already at eighty thousand miles. Not to mention Chrysler Motors is discontinuing the Magnum, so we're dealing with an obsolete unit, and since it's not destined to be a classic, seven thousand is actually a generous amount. However, I do have another vehicle I am sure will be much more to your liking and can hold the negative equity better. Let me just have a porter pull it around for you."

Matthew walked over to the key machine and punched in the code. The salesperson was on his heels. "Man, it's too late in the game to switch units. You could be costing me a sale."

"They're not going to close on that Expedition. The

wife doesn't like it. That's the whole issue. I took a look at her credit file, and like I said, she's overextended. Plenty of store cards—Saks, Nordstrom, Dillard's, Victoria's Secret . . . you name it, she's got it. She's all about image. They'll close, just not on that car."

"What are you going to put them in?"

"My demo—the QX56."

The salesperson let out a hardy laugh. "I want to see this. I couldn't get them to close on an Expedition at a nearly six-hundred-dollar payment, but you're going to close them on a damn Infiniti at probably an eight-hundred-dollar payment?"

"Absolutely. And not only that, I'm going to convince my buyer to give me a seven-percent interest rate and we're going to mark it up two points and load them up on back ends, so actually they'll be out the door at around a nine-hundred-fifty dollar payment." Matthew winked. "Because I'm good like that."

The salesperson shook his head. "I can't believe this. You really will be a legend if you do all that. I'll even buy you dinner."

"All right. Take me to Chops."

"Fair enough. Just close it. I have to see this."

The porter parked the black Infiniti QX56 in front of the dealership.

"There's your new car," Matthew told the wife.

"Now that's what I'm talking about. Why didn't you show us that?" she asked the salesperson.

"In all fairness, I was driving it," Matthew said. "That used to be my demo. It only has twenty-five hundred miles on it."

"I want that car," she told her husband.

"But, baby," her husband said, "if you think the payment on the Expedition was going to be high, what do you think the payments on an Infiniti are going to be?"

"I don't care. I want it. You get what you pay for, and I'm willing to pay more for what I want," she said as she looked Matthew up and down from the top of his freshly cut head to the bottom of his expensive shoes. "Much more."

Matthew stood outside beside the QX56. The man's wife was sitting behind the wheel.

"Now, Mrs. Smith, remember to come back within thirty days on that WEOWE so we can get it all detailed for you."

"Okay, and tell your wife I said hello." She honked the horn as they pulled off.

"Wife?" the salesperson asked and shook his head as Matthew walked toward him. "Tell her I said hello too."

"I will in about ten years when I get one."

"I don't know why you think that fake ring helps."

"It puts husbands more at ease, and the wife feels that I'm stable and can be trusted. It's funny how women seem to flirt with me more when I put the ring on then when I don't. My, how times have changed."

"You haven't been around long enough to see the times change. How old are you?"

"Old enough to handle all my business."

FIFTEEN

"Matthew, there's a client by the name of Olena Day holding on line three for you. She submitted an application on our Web site."

Matthew glanced over at his desk clock. It was quarter after four. Forty-five minutes before closing early for the holiday, and he had barely eaten. His Wendy's bag had been tossed to the side of his desk, with eight chicken nuggets, an order of fries, and chili that was now cold still inside. His stomach was growling and his head pounded slightly. He was trying not to think about the onset of a possible migraine. And even though that day would be a short one from their usual eight o'clock closing time, it felt like he had been there for two days already.

"Okay, give me a few minutes to retrieve her application, and I'll pick up the call. Thanks."

Matthew swiveled his leather chair around to face his

thirty-two-inch flat-screen monitor, pulled the keyboard tray out, and entered his mainframe password.

"Okay, Olena Day. Let's see what you're made of. Are you bullets or a boug?" He studied her application. "Where is her credit? She's a ghost." He snatched his receiver up. "Thank you for holding. This is Matthew Harper. Am I speaking with Miss Day?"

"Yes. I was just calling to check on my application."

"Well, from what I'm looking at, there isn't a credit score."

"All of my credit is on TRW, but I don't have that much credit. I haven't had a need for credit. Most of my expenses are company related."

Matthew shook his head. He already heard his buyer's no. He surely couldn't get two favors in the same day, and he needed the Smith deal that he had signed on the bank's contract before receiving approval.

"You mean Experian? TRW is now referred to as Experian. Okay, hold on and let me pull that bureau for you. Miss Day," he said after taking her off hold. "Now, I want to make sure I have all the correct information. You are interested in the six-fifty-i convertible, correct?"

"Yes. That's the car I want."

"And it says here you're going to only be financing five thousand dollars."

"I'm actually paying cash for the entire thing."

"You want to pay for the car with cash? The MSRP is eighty-seven thousand dollars."

"I do realize that, and I can write a check for the entire amount."

"We accept cash, and in fact, we have several cash customers. But, Miss Day, in your case, since your credit is somewhat limited, may I suggest you put half down on the car, and finance the other half for a couple years just to build up your credit?"

"I don't need to build up my credit. And I'm not interested in leasing either. Anything I want I can afford to pay for."

"There's nothing more powerful than good credit."

"But I'll be paying interest."

"But your interest rate will be very low. What number can I reach you on in the morning? My banker already went home for the evening."

"I can give you my cell. But I'll be on a plane tomorrow and very busy for the next several days as I prepare to move to Atlanta. I want that car, and I don't want to wait forever to get it."

"Okay. What color would you like it in?"

"Black sapphire with château pearl leather interior and maplewood trim. I'd also like the premium sound package and the cold-weather package, and anything else you can think of that will make my driving experience superb."

"We don't have the exact one you're looking for in stock. I will either have to locate one or place an order."

"That's fine."

"Will it be possible for you to drop off a good faith deposit?"

"That won't be a problem. Do you need certified funds or will a personal check be fine?"

"A personal check will be perfect. I'll have you approved well before you arrive, and I'll also leave a message on your voice mail."

"I can definitely be there first thing in the morning on the ninth."

"That's perfect. Have a Happy New Year."

"Same to you."

SIXTEEN

Olena and Jason arrived at the retro-styled Chop Suey restaurant on the second floor of the Renaissance New York Hotel on Seventh Avenue three hours before the New Year.

The lights were dim and the music was loud—the perfect atmosphere for New Year's Eve.

They sat at the front of the restaurant at a sexy table with reddish orange leather chairs. The floor-to-ceiling wall of windows on three sides boasted outstanding views of Times Square, which were perfect for the ball drop.

"Did you request this table, or did we luck out?"

"I reserved it."

Olena imagined it was costly, but then again, Jason was a star, so maybe there was no up charge, but there were a lot of stars in New York, so maybe that really didn't matter.

Olena selected the ginger chicken while Jason ordered

the Wagyu ribeye. He added lettuce-wrap oysters, rock shrimp, and scallion pancakes for both of them to enjoy while they waited for their entrées.

Olena's eyes leaped as two waiters arrived with all of their appetizer dishes and arranged them around their square table.

"This is quite a feast."

"Save room for dessert, beautiful." The two maintained eye contact, a gaze he refused to break. She saw for the first time a *sexy man*, worthy to be named so, as he was by *People* in 2006.

She shook her head. "Maybe a dessert wine."

They ate and drank mojitos into the New Year. As the alcohol began kicking in, she stood and pulled Jason up by his muscular arm. Then the two danced near the table along with many others who were in the festive mood.

And then the countdown began.

10 . . . 9 . . . 8 . . . 7 . . . 6 . . . 5 . . . 4 . . . 3 . . . 2—Happy New Year.

He leaned and whispered into her ear. "Happy New Year, Mrs. Nix."

Her eyes widened as the party horns blew. The confetti dropped, and he placed a top hat on each of their heads and leaned into her lips to give her a kiss, but she drew back. "Not even a little one?"

"I suppose a little one is okay," she said as she grazed her lips over his.

"I love a woman who's hard to get. I have another surprise for you, beautiful."

"Do you really? Which is?"

"If I tell you—"

"I hate surprises, so please tell me."

"I rented a suite in the hotel for us."

"Like I said before, I'm celibate. And like you just said, you like a woman who's hard to get."

"I can be a gentleman. It's a two-bedroom suite. You have your room, and I have mine. We can wake up and have breakfast. Spend New Year's Day together. I thought you would like that."

She shook her head. "I would if I didn't have to fly out at six in the morning. I really need to be heading back to my own hotel so I can get a few hours of sleep before I head to the airport. As of one minute ago, I'm officially on my sabbatical."

"I understand. I guess I'll have to get a rain check in Atlanta since you're moving there to be with me."

"I am?"

He nodded. "Of course that's why you chose Atlanta. You just haven't realized it yet."

SEVENTEEN

An entire year. The possibilities were limitless, Olena thought as she carried a basket of laundry onto the lanai of her parents' home and sat on the leather sectional so she could fold clothes and pack. She had flown home to gather up some things before heading to Atlanta. Whatever she left behind, she was donating to Goodwill—including the contents of the ten-by-twenty-foot shed she was renting from Neighborhood Storage Center that housed the furniture from the three-bedroom home she once owned in Southlake, Texas.

She removed the BMW brochure lying on the coffee table and began flipping through. One line on page five caused her to imagine how wonderful her life could be: *Before you decide what to drive, first discover what drives you.*

What does drive me? she wondered. Money had, but that was truly past tense—not that she was going to give any away, as she had arranged for her personal effects that she was leaving behind. She was pround of the fact that she was a millionaire, even though she never referenced herself as one; ecstatic that in a mere seven years she could grow not only her personal income, but also her investment portfolio. But if a person's life could be traded on the stock market, how would hers fare? Olena was certain hers would cause it to crash.

People were getting laid off from their jobs. Factories were shutting down left and right. Even Olena's favorite coffee shop, Starbucks, had announced plans to close six hundred stores. And in the midst of so much economic turmoil, Olena had the opportunity to enjoy one year off with pay, *but* without her commissions, which averaged five times her base salary.

Maybe they're really trying to tell me something and giving me a year to think about it.

She walked into the spare bedroom that her parents had converted into an office, and studied the bookshelves filled with novels, none of which were written by her, and wondered how she could let twenty-five years escape her without setting aside at least one to write. Over the years, she had purchased and read hundreds of novels from authors of various genres. And of course, she owned every book Maya Angelou had ever penned. At one time, she had even belonged to the book club Phenomenal Woman, which was named after one of Maya Angelou's poems, but that was well before Olena switched to a career in sales and could find little time to read.

But now she had one year to herself. One year not only to return to her first love, reading, but also to write her great American novel . . . and maybe find love again.

She wondered if Andrew was still married or if he

had finally woken up and realized how wrong he had done Olena. After all, he had cheated on his fiancée with Olena, which to Olena meant there was obviously something missing in his relationship. His wife was a doctor, and she couldn't possibly have time for him or his intensely charged sexual appetite. Olena, on the other hand, knew how to cater to a man. Unfortunately, for her, it had always been the wrong ones. She caught her breath at the mere thought. Hated herself for stooping so low as to be willing to wait on a man who didn't choose her first to possibly settle for her on his next go round.

She thought about Andrew often, much more than Stanley. She would say that was because she knew where Stanley was at all times. She could go to Elmwood cemetery in Detroit and visit his grave if she wanted. Sit in front of his headstone, press her hand on the ground and come to terms with the fact that he was six feet under. But Andrew . . . he was like a dead man walking—a man who had dropped out of her life, but was still very much alive.

She missed some parts of their relationship. The fact that the best sex she had ever experienced was that which she shared with Andrew at the ripe age of eighteen. She could still recall how rapidly her heart would beat whenever he would thrust himself inside of her. She had never—of course not before him, and not even after—been brought to such climaxes during an orgasm, not even with her rabbit. She longed to be loved in that way again—for the sex to be so wonderful that the reality of the situation could become skewed—mind-altering, pulsating love that made her scream out obscenities.

Olena put her desire for love aside as she continued to flip through the BMW brochure. Soon enough she would be driving around expensive metal while other women had their men to ride.

Maybe . . . just maybe . . . her mother was right, and being grown was overrated. In some ways, Olena missed her youth. Missed how rebellious she could be. How she would let her mother's ideas of how Olena should behave go in one ear and out the other, along with her father's negative tirades. Right or wrong, she had attempted to make her own decisions back then. She regretted dropping out of college to avoid getting kicked out. She would have preferred to have a degree from Howard University hanging on her wall as opposed to one from University of Detroit that she had boxed up and stored.

She was certain that Mr. Magna Cum Laude Andrew and his doctor wife were living the good life, while she was simply living. She needed to remind herself that she wasn't the last single woman standing. There was of course Shelly, who was happily single and also without children. Three years older than Olena even. But now for some reason, she had decided to move to Arizona. If not for a job, it was most likely for a man. The last time Olena had spoken to Shelly was nearly two years earlier. Shelly had met a nice man through a mutual friend—a man who was her same age and had also never married, didn't have children and didn't want any. They had traveled to Rome by cruise ship.

Italy. Now that was a place made for a storybook. Perhaps I should have taken a little more time in deciding where I was going to spend my year, Olena thought. *Maybe I should have considered another country instead of another state. Hasn't it been said that foreign men make the best lovers?*

No more regrets, Olena had decided. Atlanta it was, and Atlanta it would be. She shook away all of the negative thoughts that Candice tried to plant in her about Atlanta and the men who lived there. Her primary goal was to re-connect with herself and discover her truest desires—to feel complete and perhaps if she were fortunate she just might meet a nice man. And then she remembered that she had already—a man, for some reason, she wasn't really attracted to. She wasn't sure if she could trust a man that well known with so much money. She could only imagine how many women she already had. *No, thank you.*

An entire year and this was what she was promising herself she would do.

First and foremost, she was going to write that novel that had been stuck in her head for years. The one about Clara, who reminded her in some ways of herself, only Clara was married and miserable. Put aside any ideas of a memoir and concentrate on bringing her fictional charac-ter to life. Then she wanted to do a bit of traveling. This would be well after she settled into Atlanta. After she had driven her car around town long enough to be bored with it; after she had purchased a condo and furnished it off nicely—perhaps even hired an interior decorator. Well, after she spent half her savings in one year. And what sense did that make? None. But Olena wasn't trying to make sense. Now she was just trying to live.

She snuggled her body against the leather sectional. Closed her eyes in an attempt to dream about the perfect life she had one year to find.

Olena had checked into the Embassy Suites at Centennial Olympic Park in downtown Atlanta, and was pleasantly surprised that she was automatically upgraded to the gov-ernor's suite on the eighth floor due to her diamond status as a Hilton Honors member. But that wasn't her only shock of the day.

There was a knock on Olena's hotel door within minutes of her arrival. She glanced through the peephole and saw a deliveryman holding two dozen beautiful lavender roses.

Her eyes lit up as she scribbled her name on the delivery slip and then read the card.

For a woman with undeniable taste. I can't wait to meet you in person. I'm sure you are just as lovely as you sound. Sincerely, your new friend,

Matthew Harper

She smiled and picked up the phone to call him, but then thought, *My new friend, huh? We'll see.* She tossed the card in the small garbage can in the foyer. It was a nice gesture on his part, as well as a great sales technique. So instead of calling him, she called room service and later phoned her niece.

"Are you in the ATL, Auntie?"

"Yes, I am."

"Hallelujah, my aunt can finally have a life. Remember what Walter Mosley said, 'This year you are writing your novel.' "

"I know. I have his book with me, and I'm getting ready to read some of it."

"So how was your plane ride into Atlanta?"

"I knew I forgot to tell you something. When is the last time we've spoken?"

"The last time was when you were tripping after drinking some blue motherfuckas."

"And then what about the time before that?"

"I can't remember, Auntie. I've been busy with auditions and my day job, why?"

"Did I ever mention to you that I sat next to a famous man on the plane who said he used to play for the Falcons and retired last year? Jason somebody. But until I can get on the Internet and Google his name I can't confirm or deny his statement. I mean, I believe that he was a professional athlete, but I don't know if he's as major as he says he was. He might be one of those guys who warmed the bench."

"Jason Nix?" Alicia asked, excitedly. "If it's Jason Nix, I can confirm his statement. He didn't warm the bench. Far from it. Is that his name? Tall, muscular, chocolate brown skin, and very handsome," Alicia asked.

"That's his name, Jason Nix."

"Jason Nix is so damn beautiful. Finer than Reggie Bush in my opinion."

"Who is Reggie Bush?"

"You don't know who fine-ass Reggie Bush is? He plays for the New Orleans Saints."

"Is that a football team?"

"I can't believe you don't follow football . . . and you don't even know who Reggie Bush is. He dates Kim Kardashian?"

"Who is she?"

"Auntie? The next man you come across ask him who she is—he'll know."

"I'm sorry I haven't been able to follow much of anything besides all of those sales presentations that I had to give. And if I was going to follow any sport for the men, it would be basketball. You, on the other hand, have always liked those bodybuilding-protein-shake-drinking types. I prefer tall, slim, well-groomed men, with good skin and nice white teeth."

"Jason Nix is tall, well groomed with good skin and beautiful teeth. He's just not slim. Four out of five sure isn't bad, especially when it's Jason Nix."

"Well, we just sat next to each other on the plane, and I slobbered on him."

"You what?"

"I slobbered on him. I was laying my head on his shoulder, and when I woke up, his whole left shoulder was wet. I was so embarrassed."

"You slept on Jason Nix's shoulder. So then what happened? Did y'all exchange numbers?"

"Girl, you are twenty phone calls and a date behind."

"You went out with him? You went out with Jason Nix? Auntie, your life is starting to finally sound exciting. Maybe there is hope for you after all."

"Meeting a man means there's hope?"

"When that man is Jason Nix, it does. Doesn't he have a girlfriend who's a popular singer. Isn't he dating Kelly from Destiny's Child?"

"Kelly from Destiny's Child? How old is she? Oh, my God. I can't compete with Kelly from Destiny's Child. She's all of twenty-five. Well, it's a good thing I'm not into him."

"I'm really not sure if they're dating, Auntie, and you know how those celebrities go in and out of relationships anyway. I don't want to give you the wrong name . . . so Google it. I think he may have even dated Serena at one time too."

"Oh, Lord, these are babies you're naming off."

"Does he know you're forty-three?"

"He didn't ask, and I didn't tell him."

"Let him fall in love with you first, and then spring it on him. So, Auntie, now that you're in Atlanta what are you plans?"

"My plans?" Olena asked, reflecting on the day before when she had packed her life into two suitcases. "I'm getting a new car. I don't want to live in a hotel the entire year, so I'll check out some condos to rent, maybe buy if I like this area enough to live in once I retire. And of course I'm going to write." Of course, she was going to write? She had pulled out her Moleskine notebook on the plane, but didn't scribe one line. She couldn't claim to be lost in translation, more so in thought. She had to add diet and exercise to her list of to-dos. "I think I might even try being a vegetarian."

"Auntie, every day you are reminding me more and more of these fakes out in Hollywood."

"Why? Just because I no longer want to eat meat. I already eat salmon three days a week. I don't eat beef and try my damnedest to avoid pork, so why not just call it what it is?"

"What next? Dreads."

"I wouldn't mind it, but I don't think that would go over so well at Lutel."

"Well, I hope you stay on course with your writing. Who knows? Your book could turn into a movie and then I could star in it."

"I'm sorry. I love you and all, but I don't believe in nepotism. You would have to earn the role."

Alicia's laugher escaped loudly. "Earn the role? So you would jerk me around worse than Hollywood, huh?"

"Sweetie, I'm just playing. Let me first write my book and then get it published. If it turns into a movie, you can play the lead. Even if your acting was as bad as Fantasia's when she was playing herself in her life story, I will still give it you."

"That's more like it."

After her conversation with Alicia ended, Olena moved from the dining room table, where she had just finished eating the room service she'd ordered, to the sofa, where she was reading Walter Mosley's book *This Year You Write Your Novel.* She had just turned over to page three, and asked herself the question how could she tap into her unconscious mind, when the telephone rang.

"Good news," Matthew Harper said. "You're approved. We'll have to order the car, and I will need you to sign the contract and provide me with a check for good faith."

"I can drop by tomorrow with the check."

"I really appreciate it, Ms. Day. It was a pleasure speaking with you, and I look forward to meeting you in person."

EIGHTEEN

It was the ninth, and Olena was coming into the dealership to complete her paperwork and drop off a deposit so that her car could be ordered. Her appointment was set for nine in the morning, and it was a quarter after eight, and Matthew was trapped in an all too common traffic jam on I-20. The highway was bumper to bumper like on most mornings in metro Atlanta; it was filled with people who lived in the suburbs and commuted into the city like Matthew, who resided in Tributary. He counted his blessings. Things could have been much worse. If he had been placed at the Acura store, he would have had to travel the complicated Tom Moreland Interchange, which often became gridlocked.

Thoughts of his job weren't too far from Matthew's mind—those of Sam, the new secondary finance manager and Rock, the new GM, both transplants from a Toyota dealership who arrived on January first. The two stuck together like peanut butter and jelly. He didn't trust either one of them, especially not Sam, who loved to brag about how much experience he had in the car business, but always messed up the paperwork, and caused major delays in getting their deals funded by the banks.

Matthew had merely suggested in a somewhat assertive manner that Sam return the postdated check he had accepted from a customer because it went against company policy. It was at that point that Sam told Matthew to "Get the fuck out my face." This, only a few days after Sam had started working there.

"Do I sense a bit of hostility?" Matthew joked with the sales manager standing beside him before turning back toward Sam. "Don't let the Brooks Brothers suit fool you. *I* run this place. And *you* . . . you need help walking—old man."

"Look, *little* boy, when you grow up to be the man that I am, then maybe I will listen to you, but for now, I don't want to hear any shit you have to say."

Matthew snickered. "When I grow up to be the man that you are? What kind of man are you? Do you know? Are you even a man or somebody's bitch?"

Matthew continued to ride to work in silence. He had placed a can of Coke in the cup holder beside him to nurse his throbbing head. He had hung out the night before at Jermaine Dupri's club, Studio 72, with a few of his frat brothers and then ventured on to Magic City, but he was starting to have his fill of the night life. It wasn't about the money, because he made enough to pay all of his bills and splurge without worrying about his lights being shut off. But Matthew was frugal, and the more money he kept in the bank, the better. Besides, long nights of partying like those left him dragging the next day with a migraine he'd spend hours tending to.

A Chrysler Sebring was parked outside of the preowned store in a space reserved for preferred clients. "We've got a duck in the pond," the sales manager told Ryan, a salesperson who was first up for a customer.

The dealership had yet to open its doors for the morning, and there was already a customer waiting.

Ryan observed the woman dressed in sweats and a baseball cap as she exited the base-model sedan. He grabbed a brochure of the new one series. "I'll hand her this through the door or direct her to our preowned store. I'm not going to let her interrupt my morning coffee."

"Don't judge a book by the cover," Matthew said. "You never know."

"That's easy for you to say. You're not in sales. Hey, Bill, how much can you give our client for that fine luxury automobile she drove up in?" Ryan asked the used-car manager.

"She's going to have to pay us just to take it. This isn't Enterprise."

"She wouldn't qualify for one of our pens, and we give those away free," Ryan taunted.

Olena stood in front of the locked glass door with a friendly smile plastered across her makeup-free face while the entire sales and management staff stared in her direction.

"Tell her to come back with a qualified cobuyer."

"Who knows? She might be one of Lil Bow Wow's personal assistants. Didn't one of them come in the other day?"

"No, it was someone from Jermaine Dupri's camp."

"You guys are so damn rude," Matthew said. "You're just going to leave the young lady standing out there. If she can't afford a car, there's nothing wrong with dreaming?"

"Except when it's on my time," Ryan said. "I only get paid when they close, not when they dream."

"One day, she might have the money." Matthew walked to the door and unlocked it.

"And that should be the day she comes in."

"Good morning," Matthew said, greeting Olena with a smile. "You're here bright and early."

"I told you I would be."

"You told *me* that you would be? We've spoken before?"

"Yes. I'm Olena Day."

"*You're* Olena Day?" He asked as he looked at her baggy sweat suit and Lutel baseball cap.

"Please excuse my appearance. I worked out this morning, but I don't smell. I did the pretty workout and didn't even sweat. I would have put on my tailored Brooks Brothers suit also," she said with a wink as she stroked the lapel to his jacket. "I started to change, but I figured this was just going to take a second. I'm just here to drop off the check so you can order my new drop top."

"You're Olena Day?"

"Yes. Why do keep asking me that?"

"You sound a lot older over the phone."

"I don't know why. Maybe it's my professional voice," she said as she pulled the check out of her purse. "Here's my check for ten thousand dollars. Is that enough good faith?"

He took the check from her. "I'll be right back."

"Okay. I'll be right here."

Matthew strolled casually into the sales manager's glass office as he glanced back at Olena a few times in total disbelief. She was standing in the showroom, eyeing the six series that was on display.

"What's up with her?" the general sales manager asked.

"That's my client . . . Olena Day, the one who was approved for the six series."

"What? Can't be. Get her ID. This might be identity theft. Didn't Olena Day have a fraud alert placed on her bureau?"

"Yes, but it was cleared by the bank."

"Which means nothing if you're a relative of the victim who knows the real Olena Day's personal information. She's probably Olena's daughter. Look at her. You know that woman's not forty-three years old. She's closer to your age than mine. Ask for her driver's license? She's not driving away with one of our cars."

"We don't have the color she wants here anyway. We have to order. Here's her good-faith check."

"Does she honestly think she's going to go from the car she drove up here in to a six series? I don't think so. She can keep her check. Tell her we need certified funds."

"How am I going to explain to her that she now needs certified funds when I already told her a personal check was fine?"

He shrugged. "Policy change. There's a lot of fraud in this business, and you need to know the warning signs."

"Is it because of the way she's dressed that you're skeptical?" Matthew asked the general sales manager as they both eyed Olena, who was looking at the luxury cars in the showroom as if she had never been around any in that class.

"No, I just don't have a good feeling about that one."

"Miss Day," Matthew said as he returned to the show-room floor, "are you trading in the Sebring?"

"No. That's a rental."

"Then I just need to make a copy of your driver's license? We need it to finalize the paperwork."

"Oh, yes, of course. No problem." She searched through her bag and gasped. "Oh, I must have left it at the hotel. I changed purses yesterday. I can run to the hotel and come right back. The hotel is just right downtown. It won't take me long to get back."

"Of course, take your time. Oh, and the personal check. Is it possible for you to stop at the bank and get certified funds?"

"Certified funds?" Olena asked with confusion. "Why? You told me over the phone that a personal check would be fine?"

"Well, there's been a policy change."

"Did the policy change when I walked through the door?" Olena asked as she scoured the white faces in the showroom. "I thought I was in ATL, not back in Florida. Didn't Obama win this state? Okay, *my brother*, or half brother . . . you're a little too light to be one of my brothers. I'll bring you certified funds." Her stale joke only seemed to amuse her.

"Was that funny?" He shook his head.

Olena rolled her eyes. "You're not the only BMW dealership in town." Olena glanced down at his feet. "Nice shoes though and very expensive. You may not have tact, but at least you have taste."

"I'm not the one coming in here pretending to be someone I'm not," he said under his breath. "Why do *we* have to scam? That's what they expect from us. Why do we always have to prove them right?"

"What are you talking about when you say *we*?"

"You know exactly what I'm talking about." He grabbed Olena's arm and pulled her off to the side. "Why are you trying to get a car in your momma's name?" he said through gritted teeth.

"Are you serious, or am I on *Candid Camera*?" she asked as she combed the showroom. "What do you mean, why am I trying to get a car in my mother's name?"

"You're not forty-three."

"I appreciate that you don't think I am, and I take that as a huge compliment. But trust me, I am every bit forty-three. Do I really need to dress up just to do business in here? If I were white—"

"Please, don't pull the race—"

"Well? Am I lying?"

"This has nothing to do with race."

"Well, young man, whatever it has to do with, I could teach you a thing or two about satisfying a client. I feel offended, and a client should never leave feeling that way. Take it from the number-one account executive for Lutel."

Matthew clapped his hands slowly three times. "I'm so proud of you."

"I'm proud of me also," Olena said. "Now I'm going back to the hotel to get my driver's license. But I'm not stopping at a bank to get a certified check. When you tell a client you can do something, you're supposed to deliver. I asked you if you needed certified funds or if a personal check would be acceptable. You told me a personal check would be fine. If you can't work with that, I guess I will have to go to another dealer." Olena marched through the showroom. "I'll be back in less than an hour."

Matthew stormed into the sales office after Olena left the dealership.

"She said she's coming back. She left her driver's license at the hotel, got mad at me because she's trying to pull a fast one." Stopped short of talking about his own people, but pulled back, couldn't go there, not in an office filled with whites, because then he'd be a sellout, but he couldn't help that sometimes his people frustrated him. He knew that the sale was too good to be true. The woman claimed forty thousand dollars in income a month. Not that it wasn't possible, but he had his reservations, because in his business he had seen so much.

"Oh, yeah, sure she's coming back," the general sales manager said. "And I'm selling a hundred cars today."

"She said she would, and I think she might. But she wasn't getting a certified check, because I told her we could accept a personal one, which I did."

"I'm not even worried about it. She won't be coming back. She doesn't have a valid driver's license in the name Olena Day. That's why she did everything online."

"I hope she comes back."

"What's that?"

"Nothing," Matthew said as he watched the Sebring drive away.

NINETEEN

"How are you enjoying my city?" Jason asked. He called Olena as she was heading back to the hotel from the dealership.

"I'm not. I was just treated like doodoo at a dealership."

"Doodoo—that's so cute. Just tell it like it is. You were treated like shit."

"Okay, I was treated like shit just because I didn't put on one of my thousand-dollar outfits. Sometimes, I just don't feel like dressing to impress. That's something I have to do at Lutel. I just don't feel like always having everything in place."

"They don't treat women that great at dealerships, anyway. It's always best to take a man along. Next time you go, take me."

"I'm going to be heading back there shortly. I have to

go back to the hotel to get my driver's license, so I guess I'll change."

"Then I'll come to the hotel and pick you up . . . chauffeur you down there. I'll guarantee they'll treat you better with me by your side."

"Oh, I know they will then."

"Hey, and there's no need to change. You don't have to dress up for those fools. Just for me later tonight when I take you out. Deal?"

She smiled. "Deal, but I look like doodoo too."

"I'm sure you don't look like shit. Don't let those fools play tricks with your mind."

"I almost feel like going to another dealership, but they do have my check."

"They'll treat you right . . . trust me. This happens to the best people from time to time. Dealerships are not the most pleasant places to go, but usually high-line stores are a lot better."

"Well, they think that I'm trying to pull a fast one, so I guess that's why they're being rude. They don't believe I'm my age—" she let slip out, but Jason didn't question her. "Are you on your way?"

"Yep. I'm already downtown, so it won't take me too long to get to you."

"Well, look who's back," the general sales manager said. He was sitting at one of the salesperson's desk that faced the guest parking, when he noticed Olena step out of the passenger seat of a Bentley Azure. He picked up his phone to call Matthew, but there was no answer on his line. "Find Matthew," he said to a porter. "Let him know that his customer is back. Who's that man she's with? He looks familiar."

"That's Jason Nix," Ryan said. "I guess Matthew was right. You can't judge a book by the cover. Can you believe we dissed Jason Nix's woman?"

"*You* dissed Jason Nix's woman," the general sales manager told Ryan. "I merely asked for certified funds, but a personal check will be fine."

"I guess so."

The porter grabbed a global electric motor car and hurried through the expansive lot. He spotted Matthew pulling his new demo into a parking spot.

"Your customer is back," the porter told him.

"Who?"

"Miss Day."

Matthew smiled as he checked his watch. It had been more than an hour, nearly two. "Oh, really? Let her know I'll be right there."

A few minutes later, Matthew entered the showroom. His wandering eyes were in search of Olena.

"Where's Olena?" he asked the general sales manager.

"Behind Jason Nix. And she ditched the Sebring for a Bentley. Who knew?" He shrugged. Matthew noticed Jason Nix, but couldn't find Olena, who was standing behind Jason, because his large size swallowed up her slender frame.

"Told you not to judge a book." Matthew walked over to Olena and Jason. "Miss Day, or I guess I should say Mrs. Nix, I'm sorry."

"Miss Day is correct. This is my friend. Here's my license."

Matthew glanced down at it, paying close attention to her date of birth. He shook his head.

"What's wrong?" Olena asked.

"Nothing's wrong. I just can't believe you're forty-three. You don't look that old."

She cringed. So much for not letting Jason know her age. "That old? What is that supposed to mean?"

"Nothing. I just need to finalize the paperwork if you don't mind coming into my office."

"Paperwork? I told you that I wouldn't be signing a contract at this stage."

"I understand," Matthew said as he led her to his corner office, noticing Jason was following. "Alone."

"Do you want me to be in there with you?" Jason asked.

"Miss Day, some of the information is personal, so if you don't mind . . . ?"

"I'll be fine."

"I'll wait in the car. It shouldn't take too long, should it?"

"No, she'll be out in less than fifteen minutes," Matthew said. Olena followed him into his office. "Please take a seat." He closed the glass door. "I have your contract ready to sign." He removed a manila folder from one of the file drawers in his credenza and slid it in front of her. "By signing now, you are guaranteed a special interest rate that may not be available whenever the car is delivered. And, as I went over with you on the phone, your new BMW comes with a four year, fifty-thousand-mile warranty."

"Excuse me, but I forgot my lips." Olena removed a small compact and a M•A•C tube of lipstick along with a separate tube of lip gloss and started to apply color to her full lips. "I'm so oily. I need to go to the day spa." Matthew's eyes followed his client closely as she removed a monogrammed handkerchief from her purse and began patting her neck and center of her chest. "Excuse me. I'm so hot, and it's not even warm in here."

Matthew grinned. "I seem to have that effect on women."

"It's called menopause, young man. It has absolutely nothing to do with you."

"You're a little too young for that, aren't you?"

"Just a minute ago forty-three was old. Now I'm too young. Make up your mind, and let's hurry this along. My man is waiting."

"Is he your man or your friend? Just a minute ago you said he was your friend. Now it's time for you to make up your mind."

"He's my friend, but who knows what the future might bring?"

"That's so true," Matthew said, his eyes piercing hers. "Who knows?"

"Young man, if there's a cost involved with this ultimate service, I'm not interested. I'm sure you're a wonderful salesperson, but you're going up against the best." She extended her wrist toward him. "Do you see this watch?"

"Yes, it's very nice."

"It is . . . isn't it? And it's also Louis Vuitton, who is one of my favorite designers. Not that I'm attached to things, but I'm using it to prove my point. Do you have any idea how much it cost?"

"I'm sure it was expensive."

"Twenty-three thousand nine hundred dollars. Do you know how much I paid for it?"

"Twenty-three thousand nine hundred dollars."

"No. Nothing."

"A gift from Jason?"

"No, a gift from my employer, for being the best. Never try to sell a master salesperson. *No* means *no*. I'm sure my eighty-thousand-dollar vehicle will live up to its reputation, and I won't have to worry about all the back-end products you're trying to add on. I know you have a quota to meet. Unfortunately, you won't meet it with me." She stood and tore up the thirty-six-month retail installment agreement for the vehicle. "I need my vehicle here in four weeks, because that's when I'll be back. And I won't be financing it. I'll be paying cash."

"But, Miss Day, I really want to explain to you the benefits of financing, as well as taking out an extended warranty, even with an eighty-thousand-dollar automobile, and this is not taking away from BMW's standards but rather enhancing the overall experience—"

"Slow down, baby—"

Matthew knew he felt an attraction toward her, but it was at that moment—the moment when she was telling him how to do something or rather the words that she chose, words that evoked a sexual reference—that he became even more intrigued.

"Remember what I said? When I say *no*, that's exactly what I mean. When I first came in this dealership you and yours treated me like a second-class citizen. Now, after I've resurfaced with Jason Nix, I'm not only good enough for your car, but your warranty too. Well, no, thank you. Have a good day, sir."

"Would you like to have dinner with me later?"

"Young man, are you asking me out on a date?" Olena said with a wide smile. "I'm flattered, even though I'm probably old enough to be your mother," she said, hoping he would take her hint and volunteer his age.

"Both of my parents are in their fifties, and, no, you're

not old enough to be my mother. I'd like to take you to dinner. Just think of it as my way of apologizing for the treatment you received earlier."

She smirked and stroked the back of her hand across his smooth skin. She hadn't been into light skin men since Stan, but he wasn't Stan. He was Matthew Harper, and to her just as handsome as one of her favorite Hollywood hunks, Hill Harper, so she said, "I'd love to."

"Well, are you available tonight?"

"Not tonight," she replied, thinking of her date with Jason. "Tomorrow night will be fine or Sunday or any day next week."

"And you're sure Jason is just your friend."

"Yes, just a friend."

"With benefits."

"No. I've downsized, just like so many of these major corporations. I too can no longer afford to offer benefits."

He grinned. "I'm sure things will turn around, and you'll start to offer benefits, especially if you find a good friend that really deserves them."

"Young man, just make sure you get my car here ASAP. I'm waiting for my BMW experience."

"Well, in the meantime, there's always the Matthew Harper experience."

"The Matthew Harper experience? I'd like to know more."

"It's just one of those things that's hard to describe and better to experience. Would you like to take me for a test drive?"

She smiled. "Let me get back to you on that."

She left his office with a smile that wouldn't vanish and

one that followed her into Jason's car, where he sat talking through his Bluetooth.

"You ready?" he asked as he ended his call.

She nodded. "Yep, I sure am." She watched as Matthew strolled out of the dealership looking intent, his hands tucked inside his Brooks Brothers pants.

"**W**hat time should I pick you up?" Jason asked Olena as he pulled into the circular drive of the Embassy Suites to drop her off.

"Maybe eight."

"Six or seven would be better. I'd like to start the evening off early, so I can have all night with you."

"You're so suave."

"Suave? Haven't heard that in a while. Must be your age."

"Don't start with my age."

"I love older women, and that's no line. So where would you like for me to take you for dinner? Do you like Italian?"

"I love Italian," she said.

"I'm Italian."

She laughed. "You're not Italian."

"You made me want to be the way you said *I love Italian*."

"Well, I love soul food also."

"Good. Now I don't have to deny my heritage in order for you to love me. So let's see, soul food, huh? I'm going to take you to the Harlem Bar, but the place gets packed quickly, so let's shoot for six."

Even though he was Jason Nix, and she was sure that women wanted him more for what he had than for who he was, she didn't need his money. But still, she was using him that evening—not for a free meal, because she could pay for her own—not for sex, though she could use a toy, but just because she was tired of being alone.

Olena played it cool as she sat beside Jason. This time he was driving an Aston Martin Db9. He headed southeast on Marietta Street toward Foundry and made a slight left on Edgewood, less than a five-minute drive from the hotel, and then parked along Edgewood Avenue, close to the eclectic bar.

It was hard for him to keep his eyes off of her.

"How many cars do you own?" she asked. "I hope I don't sound materialistic, because even though I am, I can afford to be. I'm also nosy."

"Five," he said nonchalantly. "The food is great here. You're going to love it. Ken Borders, the executive chef, used to do some personal-chef services for me a while back," he said as they opened their car doors simultaneously. "I would prefer to open the door for you, if you don't mind." She slammed the door closed and waited for him to walk around to the passenger side and open it. She glanced up at the hours on a sign posted on the bar and restaurant:

NOW OPEN DINNER NIGHTLY
6:00 P.M.-2:30 A.M.

He grinned. "Even though I know you can probably afford to open your own door too."

"I won't even respond to that. So this place is small, huh?" she said as she stepped out, wearing a Juicy Couture design. Jason was sporting a fresh haircut and a pair of shoes that were even more impressive to Olena than the ones Matthew had worn. She had to admit that he was a well-groomed man. He kept his nails short and well manicured and his face cleanly shaven at all times, with the exception of a neatly trimmed mustache. And every time he smiled and his cheeks sank into dimples, she melted.

"If I haven't told you already, you look lovely as always."

"You told me once when you picked me up and a few times in the car."

"Well, I'll probably mention it a few more times this evening, if you don't mind."

She smiled as she walked beside him, especially when he took her hand. But she was also aware of the stares shooting in their direction. He was stopped a few times for autographs. She couldn't imagine what it was like being him and then thought about how Denzel Washington felt, and wondered if he and others like him could ever leave their house alone, or if they always had to have security and an entourage. At least, Jason wasn't that famous. He was a star, but he could still lead a seminormal life.

Olena and Jason sat at a table near the window with a good view of the performer Leaf. Before she started singing, she sat with a guitar in her lap talking about a song on soul mates meeting at the right time.

Olena glanced over at a wall near the bar and noticed the film *Cleopatra Jones* being projected on it, taking Olena back to a time when she was truly young and innocent. When the most she ever worried about was making it home from Gesu Elementary School in time to watch *Gilligan's Island* to see if the crew would finally be rescued. Accompanying her would be a goody bag from the party store filled with a couple of packages of Indian Head salted pumpkin seeds, a Marathon bar, a Faygo grape pop, and a bag of Better Made barbecue potato chips.

"Do you remember the Marathon bar?" Olena asked.

"No."

Olena's attention drifted to *Cleopatra Jones*. She could still remember the movie's tagline: *She's "Ten Miles of Bad Road" for Every Hood in Town!* Remembered also how much she wanted to be Cleopatra Jones until *Don't Mess Around with Foxy Brown,* and Pam Grier became the next bad girl on the big screen in 1974. So many years had passed, so many memories to treasure and many others to leave behind.

The bar took Olena way back.

She gazed at Jason, who stared back at her, but remained silent. His confidence was appealing to her. However, love at first sight it wasn't. Nor at second sight either. In a suit he didn't appear to be as huge as he had on the airplane or even earlier that day when they had gone to the car dealership, but judging by the way he had to squeeze his big thighs underneath the table in the restaurant, his clothes were obviously deceiving.

"Sunday and Monday are usually for football. I fly out of town on Thursdays and fly back on Tuesday. Wednesdays I'm usually free," Jason said as he took a break from perusing the menu.

"Today is Friday, so shouldn't you be out of town."

"This week is different. I took some time to be with my sons. My boys are my life."

His boys were his life. She wanted to be someone's life, and it was obvious that she would never be his, so for all that mattered, Monday, Tuesday, Wednesday, Thursday, Friday, Saturday, *and* Sunday could have all been for football, because she didn't need any one of those days to be for her. Not when she would come in no higher than third place in his heart, so there was no reason to start feeling any attachment.

"Do you date Kelly from Destiny's Child?"

"Nope and never have. I don't know where that rumor came from."

"Serena Williams."

"No, but I'm definitely a fan."

"I bet you are."

"Of her game."

"I'm a fan of yours also," said Olena right before she shielded her face with the menu. "I know what I want," she said as she set the menu down.

"Me too," he said as he stared across the table at her, studying her full lips.

"I'll have the maple-glazed peppercorn-crusted salmon, because salmon is very good for you."

"And I'll have the smothered pork chops, because they may not be good for you, but they're damn good. Your mind seems to be somewhere else," he said as he watched her eyes continue to wander. "Is something wrong?"

"Nothing," she snapped. Did he really want the truth, the whole truth, and nothing but the truth, so help her God? He might have had nice, perfectly straight snow-white teeth topped off with flawless dark chocolate skin that was the same color as her favorite piece of See's Candies with the butter-cream center. *But*, and this was a *big* one, he reminded her too much of Hugh. She used to love big men. That was all she had ever wanted: a two-hundred fifty to three-hundred pounder. But that was before one broke her heart and nearly broke her back. Here he could barely catch his breath, and Olena had thought it was because he was so big. But no, it was because he was chasing too many women, and he was tired. So whenever, and if ever, her celibacy came to an end, she didn't want to spend her nights climbing on top of Jason to get some, and he certainly was too heavy to get on top of her. She had made that mistake in the past. It was the reason she now had to get a Swedish massage once a week for the rest of her life. *So there it is in a nutshell. He's too damn big for me!*

"You're sure nothing's wrong."

"No. Well, just so you know," she said, sipping on her drink, "I'm practicing celibacy."

"How do you practice not having sex?"

"You know what I mean."

"No, seriously, what do you do? Lie in the bed and say to yourself, 'No. Stop. It's too soon. Let's get to know each other first. Not before marriage.' "

She laughed because she thought his remark was funny, and then he laughed because she was laughing, and from that moment on, she liked him because he had a sense of humor, and a man who could make her laugh would always score big points.

He took a sip of his superfly while she tasted the dreamtini she had ordered strictly for the name.

"So you retired last year. How old were you when you started in the league."

"Twenty."

"Wow, you played a long time, huh?"

"Ten years."

"Ten years? And you retired last year, so you mean to tell me that you're just thirty-one?"

"That's right."

"Where are the people my age? Have they all dropped off the face of the earth?"

"You act like you're so old. I once dated a woman who was fifty-five and fine. And let me tell you that woman had some good stuff."

Olena's eyes rolled. "Excuse me, but I'd rather not hear about another woman's stuff, if you don't mind."

"I'm sorry. I forgot who I was with for a minute. That's man talk."

"But it is slightly encouraging to know that my stuff can still be considered good by a thirty-one-year-old when I'm fifty-five."

"Age is just a number."

She laughed at the classic line.

After their meal came, they focused a little more on the food and less on each other. Finally, to break the silence, she asked about his children, when she really wanted to ask about his ex-wife and what had caused the divorce. "Do you have any pictures of your kids?"

He removed a heart-shaped diamond-encrusted locket from his key ring and slid it over to her.

She opened the trinket and studied the two small boys and their chocolate complexions. "How old are they?"

"Jason Junior is six and Jamal is three."

"Cute," she said, sliding the locket back to him. She yawned. "Are you ready?" she asked as she stood up from the table. "It is getting somewhat cramped and loud in here."

"No." He remained planted firmly in his seat. "I'm sorry. I was just practicing celibacy."

"Ha . . . ha . . . ha," she said as she tossed her American Express green card on the table.

He tossed his black American Express card on top of hers.

"Well, I have my portion. Why should you have to pay for both of us?"

He picked up her card and handed it back to her. "I asked you out, remember? I'm a gentleman, and I can afford to pay for us both."

"Everyone in here already knows you're rich. No need to pull out the black card."

"I'm not concerned about what anybody in here knows. I'm just interested in getting to know you better. Are you going to let me? Go ahead and say no. Practice that celibacy, baby."

"Shut up. Yes, I am going to let you."

"I prefer hearing yeses to nos. Would you like to spend the night with me?"

"Hell, no, . . . How's that for a no?"

"You're bad."

TWENTY-ONE

Hello, beautiful. I'm running late. I should be leaving in another thirty minutes or so. I will text you when I'm pulling up to the hotel.

"**I**s he serious?"

"What?" Alicia asked. They had been talking on the phone for nearly an hour. Olena had told her niece nearly everything about her date the night before with Jason, but she had failed to mention the fact that she was going out to dinner with a younger man—just how much younger was what she didn't yet know and could only speculate.

"Matthew sent me a text to tell me that he was running late, and then he said that he'd text me when he got here. What's wrong with picking up the phone?"

"Another date, Auntie? I see why you picked Atlanta

as the place you wanted to spend your year in, so much for the male shortage."

"It wasn't because of the men."

"No, I guess not, considering so many of the men there are gay."

"Okay, Candice."

"What? Am I being negative?"

"You're being Candice. That's worse than being negative. But can you believe he texted me? Jason didn't text me to tell me he was on his way. He called me."

"How old is this guy? That's what young guys do?"

"I didn't ask. I'm assuming he's around Jason's age, around thirty or thirty-one."

"How old does he look?"

"Well, if I was going by the way he looks, I'd assume he was fifteen. I'm going by the way he acts. And in all of my dealings with him, which haven't been many, he's conducted himself in a very professional manner. He's at least thirty."

"But thirty . . . that's thirteen years younger than you. Thirty—that's my age."

"Well, baby, if you can date men my age, I should be able to date men yours. It's only fair. Besides, we're just having dinner. Not getting married. I'm simply keeping my options open. I wouldn't mind dating a younger man but that's it, because a younger man can't do *beep* for me."

"Auntie, don't tell me that you're looking for a jump off?"

"A what?"

"A casual-sex partner—a jump off—a freak, Auntie."

"Oh, you mean what all of my past relationships have been? No, I'm definitely not looking for that. See, your mind went one place and mine was somewhere else. I'm just having fun meeting new people and dating for a change. I need to do more writing though."

"Writing or dating—you decide. You haven't done either in quite some time."

Olena was staring at Matthew while she sipped on her second glass of merlot after taking a bite of salmon. She had absolutely nothing to lose, so she decided to flirt while they sat in the dining room of Ruth's Chris steakhouse, which was located in the hotel's lobby.

"So, Matt . . . do people call you *Matt*?"

"No, they don't. They call me Matthew."

"Sorry, Matthew. Well, tell me something about yourself?"

"What do you want to know?"

Olena shrugged. "Whatever you want to tell me. Oh, but I do want to know one thing. Do you have something against the phone?"

He laughed. "As a matter of fact, yes, I do."

"Which is?"

"I hate the phone. I would much rather text."

"Detached, are you?"

"No, but sometimes the sound of a person's voice can irritate me, and I end up with a migraine. I've suffered from those ever since I was seven."

"Really? Poor baby," Olena said, poking out her bottom lip. She glared over at him. His prescription glasses turned her on; they made him look like a cool nerd. He had both intelligence and an innocent sex appeal about him. "What happened when you were seven?"

"I thought I was Superman, and I jumped off the top

bunk, and my nose started bleeding. My mom took me to the hospital, and they did a CAT scan, and that was when they discovered I had migraines."

"I've never had a migraine."

"You never want to have one either."

"So you prefer to text?"

"I'd much rather see you in person and talk to you that way." He really couldn't blame it on his migraines, although he often did, but the truth was, even if he didn't suffer from those if it couldn't be said in a text message—which he averaged six thousand of monthly—then it most likely wouldn't be said.

"So what I'm hearing you say is that you have a hard time expressing yourself."

He nodded. "It is easier for me to say what I feel in a text message."

"I'm surprised to hear you say that because isn't that a real young thing to do? My nephew's twenty-three, and that's what he does. I thought by the time a person reached thirty that he would have grown out of that."

"I haven't reached thirty yet. I'm only twenty-five."

She choked on his words. Spit her wine out after some of it went down the wrong pipe, because the minute she learned his age, her next reaction was to shout, "What?" But a mouthful of wine made it nearly impossible to do so. "I'm sorry," she said as she used the napkin to wipe the wine from the corners of her mouth and her ivory sweater. She cleared her throat several times because she was still choking.

"Are you okay?"

"I'm not sure if I am," she said, clearing her throat once more. "Twenty-five?" She stared at his youthful face—the one she had grown so attached to from nearly the minute she had laid eyes on him, even after he insulted her at the dealership, even though she never let on. And yes, she saw every bit of twenty-five. "So you must have just graduated from college."

"I graduated from Morehouse three years ago."

"Wow." Now any thought that she may have had of flirting while she was feeling slightly buzzed had been removed. Knowing his true age had sobered her up quickly.

"Look at the time. It certainly flies when you're young— I mean, having fun. Thank you for dinner."

"But you barely touched it."

Olena signaled for the waiter. "At my age, you really have to avoid eating this late, but you're nowhere close to my age, so you don't have to worry about that for quite some time."

"What's with all the references to my age all of a sudden? We were having a good time, and as soon as I mentioned my age, you lost your appetite."

"No, silly, I didn't lose my appetite because of your age. I just lost it. Like I said, it's too late for me to eat such a heavy meal."

"Salmon is heavy?"

The waiter came over to their table and removed their plates. Matthew had eaten all of his entrée, and since Olena hated leftovers she didn't ask for her food to be wrapped up—just for the check.

"I have an early day tomorrow. I have a presentation. I need to go back to my room and prepare."

"A presentation? I thought you were off work for a year."

"Technically I am, but it's a long story to get into."

"Especially when it's a lie, right?"

She removed her American Express card from her wallet and threw it on the table. He slid her card back over to her and took the check from the waiter. "Didn't I tell you I was taking you out? So that means I pay," he said as he removed his platinum American Express card from his wallet. That was the second time Olena had heard that statement, and she was glad to know that chivalry wasn't dead, even when the man was in his twenties.

"You have a platinum card at twenty-five?"

"I also have a house and a job that allows me to have both."

"I'm so proud of you. My nephew is around your age, and he's phoning home every other week for a loan, but in all fairness, he's in law school. I can't believe I met someone who is just two years older than him."

Matthew shrugged. "And he's still in school, but I've been out in the real world for three years."

"Three whole years." She smirked. "How cute? Well, thank you for dinner and for the beautiful purple roses. This did make up for my poor treatment at the dealership."

"So you did get them? I was wondering."

"I got them and they were beautiful. I was surprised they were purple. Is that your favorite color?"

"No, black is my favorite color. Can I at least walk you to your hotel room?"

"I think I'll be safe riding the elevator up eight flights."

"It's not about safety. It's about me being a gentleman."

As they waited for the elevator, his phone started to vibrate loudly.

"You better get that. A text is coming through." The elevator door opened and they both stepped inside.

He glanced at the display. "Oh, this is my best friend from South Carolina," he said as he typed back a quick response.

She rolled her eyes and thought, *How young and rude of him,* but then she wondered why she even had the slightest tinge of jealousy with a man she barely knew who was basically the same age as her nephew.

As they walked out of the elevator and toward her room, he was still texting and finally she had had enough.

"Can't you wait?" she asked as she turned to face him. He was lagging far behind because he had to slow his pace to type.

"Wait for what?"

"To return all of those text messages. I mean when I'm with someone, whether it's a client or my man, I give them all of my attention. It's just the natural order of things. I came first. When you leave me and go to your car, then you can return your messages, which will be in all of ten minutes."

"Are you serious?"

"Yes, I'm very serious."

"The first text was from my best friend, and then a couple of my frat brothers started texting me too."

"I don't care who's texting you. Just be respectful."

"Yes, Mother."

Olena placed her hand against her chest and gasped. "Did I sound like your mother?"

"I'm just playing, but I had to get you back for all of those comments you made earlier about my age. I'm still a man . . . just a young one."

They lingered in front of Olena's hotel door to say their good-byes.

"So even when it becomes final with your car, that

doesn't mean it has to be final with us, does it?" he asked as he looked down at the floor.

"I don't understand what you're asking." She lifted his chin so that his eyes would face her instead of the ground. "Try that again."

"Can we do lunch tomorrow?"

"How are we going to do lunch when you're at work?"

"Tomorrow's Sunday, and it's my off day." He backed Olena into the doorway and started to kiss her. And she didn't resist. He pulled away from her slowly and winked. "I'll call you later, beautiful. I'm going to take a nap when I get home. It's been a long day. Maybe we can do dinner instead. I'd rather do dinner. Wouldn't you?"

She gazed at him as he strolled off.

"What a fine specimen," she said as she stood by the door and watched him until the glass elevator delivered him to the lobby. She couldn't wait to call her niece.

"Well," Alicia said.

"Well, what?"

"Age?"

"We kissed."

"How old is he?"

"Quite a bit younger."

"Younger than thirty."

"Minus five."

"Minus five from thirty. Oh, hell, no. You mean to tell me that he's twenty-five. Is that what you are saying?"

"Yes, that's what I said—and a very mature twenty-five, I might add."

"That's an oxymoron."

"Whatever. You can be mature and be twenty-five."

"Auntie, what happened to your philosophy on younger men?"

"What philosophy?"

"Oh, hell, you mean one kiss and you've forgotten your own philosophy?"

"I know that I may be robbing the cradle. So have me arrested," Olena shouted. "But you can't because he's legal. Lord, forgive me for the sins I'm about to commit. You're used to it with me. And guess what."

"What?" Alicia said.

"As much as I'm starting to become attracted to Jason Nix, I'm even more attracted to Matthew Harper."

"Have you lost your damn mind? You are forty-three, and he is twenty-five. Get a calculator and subtract the difference because it's too large for you to do in your head."

"And he asked me out again, so I get to see his fine behind tomorrow too. I want to hurry up and go to sleep, because I can't wait to wake up."

"I can't wait for you to wake up, Auntie. Wake up and realize he's way too young.

"Just be glad I'm attracted to the man."

"You're right. I'm glad. Eventually you'll come back around to your senses, I hope."

"Keep hope alive. Keep hope alive," Olena chanted.

"You'll come back to your senses after I call your nephew and tell him you're dating a boy young enough to be one of his classmates."

"Do not call your brother and tell him anything. . . . hello. . . . Hello." Alicia had hung up. Not ten minutes had passed before Olena's cell phone rang.

"Auntie."

"Well, hi, Maximillion. How's it going?" she sang. "What a pleasant surprise. How is UCLA law school treating you? I was meaning to call you. I know you're a struggling first-year law student, so I wanted to send you some money via Western Union. Is a thousand okay?"

"Auntie, I'm not calling for money, but a thousand's fine."

"Can I use Anywhere, California, for the code city?"

"Auntie, we can come back to that. I'm calling you about a very serious subject. "Are you dating a man my age?"

"No, absolutely not."

"Are you sure?"

"I'm positive. Who told you that lie, your sister?"

"How old is he, Auntie?"

"How old is who? I went out with Jason Nix. You know him, don't you? He's thirty-one."

"Not him. And yes, I heard. But the other one—the one Alicia said was my age. How old is he? Is he younger than me?"

"Younger than you? Be serious."

"Is he older than me?"

"If he's not younger than you and he's not your age, then that means he's older than you. You're in law school—you should know that."

"How much older?"

"Huh?"

"Auntie, how much older?"

"He's twenty-five."

"Twenty-five. Okay," he said calmly. "I guess it's okay if I bring home a woman who is forty-five then."

"Huh? Forty-five. Why didn't you say thirty-nine? At least she would be younger than me instead of older than me."

"Okay, a thirty-nine-year-old then. You'd be fine with that, right?"

"Huh? Well, it all depends. You are out there in Hollywood. Is she rich and famous? I can make concessions for someone like that."

"If you can date a man my age, I can date a woman your age, don't you think?"

"No," Olena said firmly. "You're going to want to have kids one day, and when I say one day, I don't mean tomorrow, and if you date a woman my age, that's how quickly they'll want to drop one on you. I am not dating that young man. We simply went out to dinner. I consider him to be my new friend, and that's it."

"So after dinner, did you kiss your new friend?"

"No, I did not kiss him. He kissed me."

"Auntie, how could you kiss someone my age? Think about how sick that is. I'm getting sick."

"I see that I really have to watch what I tell your sister. Please don't tell your grandmother. She's getting up in age, and she really doesn't need her blood pressure raised. And don't tell your mom, because your mom will definitely tell your grandmother, because she loves to ruin my life as much as she can. So expect your hush money by the morning."

"If it's hush money, I need two grand."

"You really are your mother's child, aren't you? Nice to finally hear from you. At least now I know what to do to get you to call me."

"What's that? Next you're going to start dating my friends."

"Good-bye, Maximillion."

*   *   *

She woke once she heard the elevator door chime, and smiled at the advent of a new day, realizing she had two male frinds she wanted to get to know better. Both single—however, one was divorced with two boys, which was more responsibility than Olena cared to handle. Perhaps that was the real problem. Maybe it had absolutely nothing to do with his large frame and not even his fame. Maybe it was as simple as the children. Her patience had worn thin after thirty-five, and his boys were practically babies; three and six years of age. She'd have to make sacrifices in order to be with him, like trips she'd have to forgo during a time in her life when she needed more, or would she? He was wealthy, she reminded herself. Money provided options.

So what was the real reason she didn't like dating men with children? Maybe it was just the children. She had given up two of her own years ago because a man told her to do so, and she would be damned if she'd turn around and help raise someone else's after she had killed her own. Her thinking was harsh, but in her mind very real. That was the side of Olena that even she didn't like displayed—the part that was still angry with a past filled with bad choices; the part she found impossible to let go.

Later that morning, she sat at the large dining table to enjoy a breakfast of fresh fruits and muffins that room service had delivered. With the dishes pushed to her side and her laptop powered on, she began outlining her untitled manuscript. As she reached for a strawberry, she typed:

> Who is Clara? Clara is a young woman who has it all; beauty . . . brains . . . and money as a result of her marriage to a much older man, a world-renowned surgeon. But who

is Clara really? She is a woman with a dark secret . . . a lust for power . . . a hunger for the finer things . . . and a strong desire for sex—a longing so intense that she would live a double life—one as the wife to Dr. James Elliott and the other as an escort.

Olena deleted the paragraph. She had to remind herself that she was writing a love story and not erotica. So who was Clara? She still had time to figure her out.

TWENTY-TWO

Do you still want to go out to dinner? if so i know of a great place.

Olena took a moment to contemplate her answer to Matthew's. She considered her nephew's feelings for less than a second and texted back:

Sure i'd love to.

At Two Urban Licks, a renovated warehouse turned restaurant, there were a few things she found worth noting. For one, Matthew didn't open her car door or the restaurant door, which she found to be rude, and without question Jason would have done both. And he walked ahead of her instead of beside her almost as if the two of them weren't together. Her hand was left holding on to her purse strap instead of his. And what was with the lack of eye contact? When she was with Jason, he couldn't keep his eyes off of her. And of course, there were Matthew's phone calls and his constant texting.

"You're rude," Olena said as she licked the sauce from her fingers after enjoying a baby back rib. She felt comfortable enough with herself that she didn't mind if Matthew noticed, especially after he'd demonstrated that he wasn't a true contender. And even though finger licking wasn't proper etiquette, she couldn't care less. If only she could feel the physical attraction toward Jason as she did for Matthew. If only Matthew had Jason's manners. She'd have the perfect man. And what age would she want them to be? Honestly, closer to her own.

Aside from the ribs, their table was filled with salmon chips, a cheese plate, and crab beignets.

"I'm rude. You're the one licking your fingers."

"True. But you didn't even open the car door or the door to the restaurant for me. You seem so distant and all of this texting— I don't know if it's your age or what?"

"I'm sorry," he said, turning off his cell phone and handing the device to her. "Keep it."

"That's the only way you can go without sending a text? If I hold your phone hostage?" She shook her head, refusing to take the phone away from him. "You can keep it." By this time she could hear her own phone vibrating in her clutch purse as it rested on her lap. She was tempted to check to see who was calling, but then she'd be placed in the same category as the one she'd put Matthew in—*rude with no manners.*

The waiter approached their table for the second time after dropping off the appetizers.

"Hennessy and Coke, please," Matthew said.

"May I please see your ID, sir?"

"My ID? Are you serious?" Matthew said as he reached for his wallet.

"Very."

Olena covered her mouth for a second and then went back to sipping her pomegranate martini. "He didn't ask to see mine," she taunted.

"And you're bragging about that?" Matthew teased.

"Simply pointing out that obviously you look like a baby," she said, pinching his cheek.

"If I look like a baby, and you like the way I look, then what does that say about you? Hmm? Something to think about."

"Thank you," the waiter said as he handed Matthew back his ID.

"He just made it, didn't he?" Olena said to the waiter, who grinned.

"I'm sure you're not too far behind."

"I'll be sure to leave you a big tip."

"I don't like it when you tease me about my age," Matthew said.

"I'm just playing with you, baby."

"Well, I don't like it, because it makes me feel like I don't have a chance with you."

"Do you want to have a chance with me?"

"Very much so," he said as he took her hand and kissed it. Now he was beginning to redeem himself. He massaged her hand and forearm, and his sensual touch sent sparks throughout her body.

"Okay, enough."

He grinned. "Are you getting hot?"

"A little."

"If you like I can give you a full-body massage later tonight."

"Leela James needs to perform here," Olena said, changing the subject. She tapped her table to the sounds of the Almost Blue band, which was performing that evening.

"Leela who?" Matthew asked.

"Leela James. She's a great artist who hasn't yet received her just due." Olena took more sips of her pomegranate martini. "Your favorite artist is probably—don't tell me. Let me guess. Soulja Boy."

"Actually, Earth, Wind and Fire is my all-time favorite."

"Earth, Wind and Fire," Olena said with laughter. "Are you kidding me? Earth, Wind and Fire." She shook her head before asking the waiter for a second drink. "What do you know about Earth, Wind and Fire?"

"You don't like Earth, Wind and Fire?"

"Oh, no. *I* love Earth, Wind and Fire, but then again, I grew up when they were at the height of their popularity, so I know all about them. Commodores too. Kool and the Gang also. That's not only real music but also road music. My parents drove me all the way to Howard listening to their music. What do you know about them?"

"Howard?" he asked. "My dad went there. What year did you graduate?"

"I didn't. Not from there, anyway. I only attended for two years." *Two years,* she thought. Her biggest regret smacked her in the face. Two years at Howard, and she left without a degree or her man, Andrew. She had loved hard back then. Loved the way any man would want a woman he loved to—loved blindly . . . innocently and regardless of consequence. She could have forgiven him for just about anything if he hadn't forgotten about her. If he hadn't left her for another woman and started the family he claimed he was too young for. She cleared her throat in an attempt to also clear her mind.

"Okay . . . okay, Kool and the Gang." Matthew started snapping his fingers and singing "Get Down on it." " 'Get down on it if you really want it,' " he sang. " 'What you gonna do! Do you want to get down? Do you?' "

"No," she said, shaking her head. "Okay, so you might know a little of Kool and the Gang. But who doesn't know that song?"

"Who else did you mention, the Commodores? Okay, let's see." He looked over at Olena and smiled. " 'Oh, she's a brick . . . house. . . . She's mighty . . . mighty . . . just lettin' it all hang out.' " He sang nearly half the song through Olena's laughter. "Who else, my personal favorite, Earth, Wind and Fire." He started singing "Reasons." " 'Now, I'm craving your body. Is this real? Temperatures rising—' "

"No, stop, please. Stop," she said forcefully.

"What's wrong, baby? You don't like that song?"

"You just took me someplace that I didn't want to go." She let out a deep sigh and then raised her finger for the waiter. "Another one please." She stared at the fourteen-foot wood-fire rotisserie and watched the blue flames flicker.

"So where did the song take you, baby?"

"Somewhere," she said as she thought of her first love and the tragic way in which she had found him dead. She had finally forgiven him, but she would never forget. He had taken his own life, which was horrible in and of itself, but to call her over so that she would be the first person to discover him dead—the first person to see his head blown off and brains splattered against his bedroom wall as if she had done something to him, and then to have a continuous tape playing with "Reasons" as if there was some sort of symbolism for that song—*their* song—to be played as if perhaps all of the reasons were a lie, as the lyrics said.

"You tell me I have a problem expressing myself. Why can't you?"

"Some cans don't need to be opened," she said and sighed. "Besides, the place it took me was well before your time."

"There you go again," he said as he downed his drink. "You love throwing my age in my face, don't you? Okay, here's the deal," he said as he snuggled up closer to her in the booth. "Tell me something I don't know about you— something you've never told anyone—and I'll tell you whatever you want to know about me."

"You have to go first" Olena said.

"What do you want to know?"

"You're a young man."

"I am."

"Surely, you're dating."

He shook his head. "I don't believe in dating. You have friends and then you have a relationship and the relationship is based on a solid friendship."

"So don't you go out with your friends?"

"Of course, but those aren't dates. If we go to dinner or a show, it's just a friend going out with another friend to dinner or to a show."

She sighed. "Okay, I'm trying to understand this new way of thinking."

"Is it a new way?" Matthew asked.

"I think so. In my day, aside from the fact that we didn't text, we picked up the phone and talked to each other. We also dated. We weren't afraid of commitment."

"I'm not afraid of commitment. I've had a commitment. I had a commitment in college, but she went lesbian."

Olena shook her head with laughter. "What do you do to these women?"

"Now you sound like my parents. They asked me the same thing. Oh, and she also tried to kill herself, but she said it was just a case of getting ahold of some bad weed."

"Really," Olena said in a near whisper. "That's terrible."

"Everyone else said bad weed wasn't why she tried to kill herself."

Olena quickly changed the subject. She didn't want her mind focusing on suicide any more that evening. "Well, back to you, baby."

"I love it when you call me baby."

"It's not hard to do in your case, since you really are one."

"Trying out your material for Def Comedy Jam? Well, keep trying."

"Who are your friends?"

"You don't know any of them."

"I might."

"You don't."

"Oh, you think you're the youngest person I know?"

"Yes, or at least the youngest person that you know who lives here. Naturally, my frat brothers are my friends. Cameron, my old college roommate, used to be a good friend of mine. Actually, I've known him since my senior year in high school. I used to hang out with him and another buddy of mine named Terrell."

"So why did you fall out with him?"

"He fell out with me. I don't have a problem with him. I believe in keeping my friends. He needed a place to stay, and I didn't want a roommate at the time. Still don't. If it was a matter of him staying with me for a week or two, even a couple of months, I had that, but indefinitely was something I didn't have. I like my own space, and he wasn't giving me a time frame on how long he was going to be there."

"Why did he need to stay with you in the first place?"

"Because at the time he had lost his job, but honestly it didn't seem like he could keep one. Ironically, now he has two. Back then, he told me that he was going to lose his house, but he still has it. Sometimes you just need to give your friends tough love. I mean I've reached out to him in the past after a friend of mine was killed in a drive-by shooting, but I guess the friendship is over, because he didn't try to reach back out to me."

"Well, how did you reach out to him?"

"I sent him a text letting him know that I had lost a dear friend in a drive-by shooting, and as a result it made me realize how short life truly was, and how holding on to grudges makes no sense, so I apologized for anything I may have said to offend him and told him that we'd known each other for many years and that I valued our friendship and hoped that the two of us could remain friends."

"And?"

"He texted me back saying *Sorry for your loss.* That was back in August, and I haven't heard from him since, except when he had Terrell call me on Labor Day to invite me to a cookout. They said it was a last-minute thing and for me to bring some girls."

"Oh, so you're the one they call when they need some girls—ladies' man."

"Not really. I just have a lot of friends."

"And . . . are there any special women in your life? Friends with benefits."

"No. I'm scaling back on my benefits also."

"So you're not sleeping with anybody."

"Just me, myself, and I."

Olena didn't believe him, but at that stage in their friendship, whatever he was willing to share with her was good enough.

Neither she nor Matthew wanted the night to end, which was evidenced by how long they lingered in the restaurant as if the two were old friends reminiscing. The waiter continuosly checked on them and told them there wasn't a rush, but his actions displayed otherwise, particularly after their drink orders stopped but their conversation continued.

"So tell me, when are you going to get out of that hotel and settle into the city? Have you been looking for a place?"

"I contacted a Realtor for an appointment next week."

"You don't need a Realtor. I already know where you need to live."

"Really? And where is that?"

"Mansions on Peachtree—it's a high-rise condo."

Her face beamed. "That's what I was looking for."

"I'll take you by there since your car will be in next week."

"Will it be in next week? That was a fast order."

"We located one for you."

"Ooh, I'm so excited."

"I'd love to get you excited about something other than a car."

"Do young men only think about sex?"

"I don't know. Do we?"

"Did I mention I was celibate?"

"Celibate?" He grinned. "Is that a religion? Never heard of it."

"You probably haven't, young man. You probably really haven't."

How did this happen? she wondered. How were her legs wrapped around Matthew's neck while his tongue vigorously massaged her clitoris? She could only remember him saying, "Trust me," after she let him in her suite to continue the interesting conversation they had started in the car. They were talking about relationships and the differences between men and women, and in their case they could take it a step further and talk about the differences between young women and older women and how that related when it came to relationships. But they began kissing quickly, nearly as soon as he walked through her door. He unzipped her dress. He didn't seem fazed by the fact that she was wearing a body shaper as he eased that off next. She was impressed that he didn't mention her modern-day girdle, but maybe he had seen them before. She tried to suck in her stomach, but he had already seen her small pouch. He pushed her thighs back and stuck his head between them. With her eyes closed, she enjoyed his long tongue while it lightly stroked her clit. His licks felt just as good as her rabbit ears. In fact, they felt so good that she searched the mattress for the remote thinking it was her rabbit.

"Lick it faster, baby."

"I love that you're cleanly shaved. Are you always, or did you do it special for me?" He used his tongue to slowly separate her vaginal lips. "You want it faster. I can do that. You want it in a circular motion or a pumping one?"

"What are you doing to me down there?" she asked. "This is—"

"What is it, baby? This is what?" Her head was twirling while her hands lightly massaged his head. "This is what, baby? Talk to me."

"Oh, Lord Jesus. Oh, God, forgive me for my sins that feel so good. Oh, Jesus . . . Oh, thank you, Father." She couldn't say it was crazy or that it was good or bad. "I'm celibate, Matthew."

"So am I. This is what celibate people do to take the edge off."

She came back to her senses. "Then stop. Okay, stop. Thank you. That was good." She looked down at his head still bobbing between her legs. He was skilled with his tongue, to say the least. And she knew a young man or any man who knew how to please a woman to that degree had had plenty of practice, and for a second it bothered her, but it never turned her off, because he was too busy turning her on. "I'm not going to have sex with you, Matthew. I know you're assuming because I'm an older woman that I'm easy. Isn't that right?"

"I don't want you to have sex with me. I want you to enjoy what I'm doing. Stop talking and relax and just enjoy."

"Why don't you want to have sex with me?"

"Because you're not ready for me. You're not ready to just enjoy sex without a commitment, are you? Would that be so wrong?"

"I have my rabbit for that."

"Like I said, you're not ready."

"I'm not," she said as pushed her lower half away from him. "You're so right. I'm not. I need to use the bathroom?"

"Be my guest."

"Is that how you treat your guests?"

"Just the real special ones."

"That was a turnoff," she said, and then shut the door right after he winked at her.

"It was a joke!" he yelled at her. "Lighten up."

She snatched the door open. "So now I'm too dark for you too. Young or old—you men are all alike."

"*Lighten up* is simply an expression."

"I made a mistake letting you go there."

"But it was a mistake that felt real good, didn't it? And it tasted good also."

"I am trying to practice celibacy. Don't come at me like that anymore. Do you hear me, young man?"

"Yes, Mother."

"Whatever." She stood in front of the mirror enjoying the sensation that was still vibrating between her legs. If he had been her rabbit, she would have kept going well into the night . . . for hours. Now she had gotten older and more practical or practically prudish. The relationship wasn't going to go anywhere, so why not enjoy what he could offer her? She opened the bathroom door and walked back into the bedroom of her suite. "I want some more."

"How many licks does it take to get to the center of your Tootsie Pop?"

She shrugged. "That's for you to find out."

TWENTY-THREE

"Good morning, Miss Day," Matthew said into his phone. "How did you sleep last night?"

"Like a baby. You know. . . . You were there."

He was parked at the entrance to the Embassy Suites, sitting behind the wheel of Olena's new car listening to the Strawberry Letter on the Steve Harvey Morning Show about a woman having an affair with her husband's brother. He was dressed in a casual outfit: slacks, a sweater, a leather jacket, and a pair of shades, because even though it was a chilly January day, it was still very sunny. He'd left early for work because he knew Olena's car was arriving, and he was going to get it detailed before the showroom opened and more cars came in and the detailers got busy.

"Your baby is here. I'm outside the hotel, sitting in it."

"My baby's driving my baby."

He grinned. Appreciated how direct she was with him.

He knew that he didn't have to worry about her being a challenge, because at her age, he figured she didn't think she still needed to be. In Matthew's mind, mature women were go-getters instead of game players. They knew exactly what they wanted and weren't intimidated by the process, which was why he had been surprised the night before. Actually, his surprise came when she stopped shy of letting him penetrate her, but if there was one thing he had plenty of, it was patience.

He smiled as he watched her glide through the revolving doors. She was beautiful in a pair of relaxed-fit jeans, a cashmere jacket, and fashionable boots.

"I don't get to drive my baby?"

He shook his head. "I need to chauffeur you through the city so you can sightsee."

"So where are you taking me first?"

"I want to show you that place I was telling you about."

"The Mansions?"

"Very good . . . and by the way, you look very nice . . . and when I left this morning and headed for work, I couldn't stop thinking about you. . I wish you wouldn't have made me stop."

"Another time."

He drove out of downtown to the affluent Atlanta neighborhood of Buckhead. Made a left turn on Stratford Road from Peachtree and pulled up to the building's entrance. "This is it. Where I think you should live. I'm not sure how much the rent is or how much you are willing to spend, but this is the spot."

"You make it sound like a club. Should we go in?" she asked as she noticed the valet coming toward them. "Or do I need to go back to the hotel and change? I don't want the same treatment I had at the dealership."

"You look wonderful. There's absolutely no need for you to change. Do you want to go in? Are you ready to buy?"

"I'm ready to look, but I'm also ready to eat. I'm starving. But it won't hurt to peek inside while we're here," she said as the valet held her door open. She walked toward the entrance with her head tilted upward as she eyed the tallest building in Buckhead. "I wonder if we need an appointment."

"Someone will be free," he said, and then heard her stomach growl. "Don't worry, baby. Our next stop is IHOP."

"Once I saw the English garden, I was sold," Olena said as she sat across from Matthew in the tiny booth at IHOP. "I can imagine myself sitting out there writing for hours." She surveyed their surroundings. "This is the smallest IHOP I have ever been in."

"It's Buckhead, baby. Told you it was small. The one out by my house is a normal size."

She flipped through the pages of the book for the Mansions that the Realtor had given her. "Where do you live, honey?"

"In Douglasville."

"A young, single man who has it going on."

"I looked at an apartment in the Atlantic Station area, but I couldn't live like that."

"You couldn't picture living carefree like I'm about to."

"I couldn't picture paying someone to live in something that I don't and won't ever own—that I have no tax benefits for. It's different for you, because you will own that, and when you go back to work—"

"If I go back to work."

"Right . . . well, you'll only be home on the weekends, so a condo would be better for you than a house."

"Does it make sense to pay that much money for something that after this year I will most likely only occupy on the weekends, though?"

Matthew had lost track of their conversation. He was too busy eavesdropping on the two women sitting in the booth directly beside them.

"What is wealth, true wealth?" the woman with a book and notepad by her side asked the woman sitting across from her. "Most Americans don't have a clue, let alone most black Americans. It's not living beyond your means, like we see so often in Atlanta. I own three homes. One was appraised at two hundred thousand. The other a little over a hundred thousand, and then my condo is worth one hundred eighteen thousand."

Now Olena was also listening, watching the woman's friend, who sat directly beside Olena, nod her head in silence as she sipped her coffee. "This book talks about how to retire with wealth, because Social Security isn't guaranteed, and the sad truth is that so many senior citizens aren't in any position to retire. They have to work until the day they die, but that will not be me."

"Some older people," her friend chimed in, "like my parents, help their children and grandchildren, which takes away from the money they've invested—"

"Stop right there. If your parents are still helping their grown kids, then that's their own problem. You can't take what you don't have. At a certain point you have to say no. Older people have to plan better and they have to teach their children or should have tried to teach them how to save and invest rather than overspend so when they became adults they wouldn't have to borrow from them."

Olena could sense that the woman's friend was becoming frustrated. The conversation was exhausting for even Olena to listen to.

"Now, that's an afro," Matthew said softly as he watched two women walk past them and sit in the booth directly behind Olena. "Turn to the side."

"No, Matthew."

He put his sunglasses back on. "Look in my glasses. Can you see now?"

She laughed. "Not really."

"Look in my glasses, baby. You should be able to see that 'fro."

She leaned forward and studied the image reflecting through the light brown tint of his shades. "I see it. Yes, that is quite a 'fro."

"They're together."

"Who is?"

"The two women behind you. The one with the afro is the man."

"How do you know they're together, Matthew?"

"This is Atlanta, baby. I see it all the time. There are just as many lesbians in the city as there are gay men. Besides, you can just tell. They are complete opposites, and usually friends are similar—dress the same, even in some ways look the same. One is feminine while the other is very eclectic and slightly masculine."

"Well, if they are, that's okay."

"I just like to observe people."

"And I like to observe you. You look so perfect. I haven't noticed one scar or even a small mark on you. How can that be? Didn't you go outside and play when you were a child? You never scraped your knee?"

"I did. I guess my mother took good care of her baby. Made sure the bruises healed properly. I don't know. No one has ever pointed that out to me, so I don't know how to respond. Although, all you've really seen are my hands and my face. It was too dark to see my body last night, but you felt my tongue, didn't you?" He caressed her leg from underneath the table. "To really see if your statement is true, you'd need to see all of me, wouldn't you?"

"It was dark last night, Matthew, but you're so light that you glow in the dark. I saw all of you."

"Not the way you can see me in broad daylight. Besides, I need a massage badly. Would you like to give me one?"

She blushed. "I would, but they're going to wonder why it took you six hours to deliver a car."

"I told them I wouldn't be coming back. They know you're an important client. And I told them I promised to take you around and show you some sights. There's one sight in particular that you should find rather interesting."

The natural light shone through the sheer drapes in the bedroom.

She didn't have massage oil, so Olena improvised with a body butter by Carol's Daughter, which she smoothed over Matthew's back.

He lay completely still as she started lightly massaging his head, paying attention to the area behind his ears. She worked her way down to his neck and spent most of her time on his back.

She stopped for a minute.

"You promised me an hour."

"I know." She didn't want to seem too forward as she placed her hands on his large behind and rubbed. "You have a better butt than mine."

"I doubt that. Let me see yours."

"You saw mine last night."

"No, I didn't, baby. You don't glow in the dark."

"You're right," she said as her hands squeezed harder on his butt. "I don't."

"Your hands feel so good, baby. One hour . . . you promised."

She worked her way down one leg at a time before arriving at his feet.

"Why are your feet so ice-cold? And look how white they are. Do you ever get out in the sun?"

"All the time."

"With sandals on?"

"Yes, with sandals on."

"You have pretty feet. No rough skin, no corns, no bunions."

"And I hope you don't have any of that going on, do you?"

"No," Olena said, putting her foot in his face. "My feet are beautiful, and they don't stink."

"Okay," he said, drawing his face back. "They may not stink, but it's still rude to put your feet in someone's face."

"Sorry. I just wanted to show you that you're not the only one with pretty feet."

"Are you ready to do my other side?" he asked as he attempted to turn over. She tried to use her strength, but he overpowered her in a playful manner.

"I'm not ready to see it," she said, covering her eyes.

"You're acting younger than some of the young chicks

I had to put down due to their immaturity. I thought I had met a grown woman."

"You did." Olena peeled her hands away from her eyes. "I just don't want to see it yet." She said, making sure her eyes didn't fall below his waist.

He sat up on the bed. Olena used the sheet to cover his lower half so she would feel more comfortable while speaking with him. "What was last night, baby?"

"My rabbit substitute."

"I've had enough of hearing about that damn rabbit. Last night I was all inside you."

"Your tongue was—that's different. Like you said, it helped get the edge off."

"Has it been a while for you?"

"Over a year."

"That's a while."

"I've gone longer."

"There's nothing wrong with having sex. I'll use protection."

"Do you have some with you?"

"No, but I can go out and get some. They may even sell them in the store in the lobby."

"By that time the mood will be blown."

"Then I'll just be careful."

"I'm very attracted to you, Matthew. But it's just not time."

"How about getting some more of my tongue?"

"No more tongue either. I enjoyed spending the day with you but maybe it's time for our day to come to a close. You think?"

Are you going to drive me to the dealership? That's where my car is. I drove yours here, remember?"

"You can stay over if you like, but that would mean you'd have to wear the same clothes to work tomorrow."

"Only the detailers saw me today. And besides, I'm not a woman, so that doesn't really concern me. But I will need a toothbrush because bad breath would concern me."

"We're in a hotel, so an extra toothbrush won't be a problem."

They relaxed most of the evening. They ordered room service and watched a movie on demand from the still-in-theaters section. They didn't talk much. She got the feeling he wasn't in the mood to hear another person's voice. She could tell from the few times she attempted to speak how each time he would rub his forehead. She definitely didn't want to be the cause of one of his migraines. While her eyes were on the TV screen, her mind was on her story and her characters.

"Do you mind if I leave?" Olena asked.

"Where are you going?"

"I'm going to go downstairs to get you a toothbrush."

"Dang, are you trying to tell me something?"

"No, silly. Actually, I'm going downstairs to sit in the atrium and write for about an hour, and while I'm down there, I'm going to get you a toothbrush. Do you need anything else?"

He shook his head. "You don't like my company."

"I love your company. But I'm really not interested in this movie, and I am in a creative mood. I have to seize this moment. I hope you don't take offense."

"Not at all baby."

"If you need me, text me. I'll have my phone."

Olena sat in a love seat in the hotel's lobby with her Moleskine notebook resting in her lap; her mind was completely transfixed to her story and not the young man who way lying in her bed only partially clothed in a wifebeater and boxers. She opened her notebook and took the pen that was stuck between pages out so she could start writing. "It doesn't have to be perfect," she said to herself. "It just has to be something."

And so that was what she started to write, something. And she wrote something for nearly two hours until a text came through.

Just checking on U. U said an hour. It's been over 2. I don't want to disturb U if U R busy.

I am still writing but I will be finished for this evening in another fifteen minutes. Did U need me to bring U anything?

Just U, baby.

She smiled at the thought of her new friend and then continued writing.

TWENTY-FOUR

What R U doing?

Writing or trying to . . . I'm getting used to texting, or maybe i'm just getting used to texting U. I miss U, and I can't wait to see U tomorrow, or are U up for some company tonight?

I miss U too, baby . . .

Seconds after Matthew had sent the message, a call came in from his friend Terrell. "You wanna go to Pin-Ups tonight?" Now Matthew was texting Olena while he talked to Terrell on his cell phone.

"Tonight? Nah, man."

"Why not? You're off tomorrow. You haven't been to the strip club in a minute."

"And you haven't called me in a minute either. We used to be boys but because Cameron decided for whatever reason that he wanted to give up the friendship that meant we still couldn't hang?"

"Man, it's not that. I've just been busy. Besides, I called you last."

"Okay, now you're sounding like a woman—and a young one, at that."

"Nah, I'm just saying you're always so busy with your job. I'm always the one dropping you a line. You can call too."

"Well, man, I don't feel like dropping that kind of money. I'd rather keep my cash in my own pocket. Let some other man make it rain."

"What kind of money, man? Who said we were going there to try to make it rain? It's Wednesday—five dollars for drinks and dances. We can stay an hour and spend twenty dollars."

"Yeah, right," Matthew said to Terrell. "It cost twenty dollars to park."

"You can park in the back for seven."

"Oh, and you also want me to drive? Hell, no. Where's your boy Cameron? He's always down for the strip club."

"He's spending time with his girl tonight. I don't mind driving, but you're the one pushing that black seven-series Beemer."

"How do you know what I'm pushing? I've probably changed my demo out five times since the last time you saw me in one."

"Come on, man, and go with me. It'll be like old times.

We don't have to stay long—an hour, long enough to get a few dances and a couple drinks."

"Every time we go to the strip club claiming we're going to only stay an hour, we end up in there for three or four. We're not in college anymore. This is the real world, and I can put my money to better use."

"In college, we didn't have bills or money, and we still managed to go to a strip club a whole lot more than we're going now."

"You went a lot then and you go a lot now. I'm not in the mood."

"You're not in the mood to have naked women with big asses and tiny waists catering to your every need?"

"Nope, because I know the game now, and I don't fall in love with the strippers anymore. Just like my salespeople sell cars, those girls are selling a fantasy."

"You always had fun when you went so come on. Hang with your boy."

What R U doing tonight? U never answered me . . .do U want company? It always takes U so long to respond.

I'm not doing anything. Just relaxing as usual. It was a long day at work.

U R so young, and it seems like U never go out. Is that how it truly is?

Yep. I work so hard that by the time I get home, I just want to chill. And a lot of times I'm just not in the mood to go anywhere. Tonight I have a bad migraine, and I'm going to bed after I take a shower.

They arrived at eleven to a packed crowd and a briskly moving line. He sent Olena a sleep-tight text, but then tossed his phone in the car before receiving her response because camera phones weren't allowed inside the club. Terrell and he walked through the metal detector, passed the ATM machine, and stood in line to pay for admittance before going through another doorway, where they were patted down.

The main stage was in the center of a large room. One dancer had just walked on and wiped the pole down. Terrell scoured the club, pointing out dancers he thought had the sexiest bodies, and in a club that boasted of having more than one hundred dancers nightly, he had plenty to choose from.

"Do you want to see my pussy?" a dancer said to Matthew as he sat on a bar stool at a high table and proceeded to knock back his first drink.

"Do you want to show me your pussy?" Matthew asked.

She was wearing a schoolgirl uniform. Her long hair was pulled into two ponytails, and as much as Matthew had pretended that strippers no longer fazed him, that one was starting to. There was something about her make-believe innocence and the way she was licking her lollipop that was turning him on. So much so, he paid for a second song. But soon he noticed her attention start to wane. She was focusing on the other side of the room, where the stage that was used mostly for private parties was.

"Jason Nix is in the house, and I'm one of his favorite girls. So, sweetie, I'll have to get with you on another night, because that brother over there knows how to make it rain," she said as she climbed off of Matthew.

"I can make it drizzle."

She grinned and stroked the side of Matthew's cheek. "You are very cute, though."

Matthew observed ten of the best-looking girls gravitate to the area where Jason and his small entourage were sitting.

"Like I said," he told Terrell, "it's all a business. I'm ready to go."

"Ready? Two lap dances and you're ready to go just like that?"

"I didn't want to come here to begin with."

"I'll buy you a lap dance . . . two . . . and a drink . . . and some chicken wings."

"That's twenty dollars. You'd better save your money, besides Jason Nix has the best dancers."

"There are at least ninety more women in here. You couldn't have possibly seen them all."

"I've seen enough."

By twelve thirty, Matthew was heading to his car with three drinks and four lap dances still in his system. He wasn't ready to go home after he dropped off Terrell. All that grinding had put his mind on something other than sleep. He could have called up Spellman; she was always down for a late-night rendezvous, but he had Olena on his mind. He wanted to finish what they'd started and since he was already excited, what better time to do so.

First he texted Olena, and then he called her.

"What are you doing? I want to see you."

"Is this a phone call?" she asked. "I thought you were in bed, honey."

"I was, but I can't sleep. I have you on my mind."

"Really?"

"Yes . . . really. Ever since that night you let me taste you, that's all I can think about . . . and now I need more than just a taste. Trust me. I won't ever leave you."

Those were the words Olena longed to hear. "How do you know you won't ever leave me?"

"Because I won't. Trust me. Look at the text I sent you."

"One four three?"

"You know what that means, don't you?"

"No . . . what?"

"Think about it."

"Why don't you just tell me?"

"Just think about it."

"One four three." She thought about it. Knew it was familiar. Figured it was probably a song, and then she started humming the melody. "Musiq Soulchild's 'One four three.' It means *I love you*. Do you love me, baby?"

"Yes, very much so."

"Come over."

TWENTY-FIVE

She stood in the open doorway in a short robe belted at the waist that exposed most of her full cleavage. Her large nipples protruded through the black satin and stood just as erect as his penis.

Making it to the bedroom wasn't a part of their plan, nor to the sofa. The dining room chair was as far as they got before their sex exploded. She straddled him, her hands gripping the back of the chair, the lower half of her body grinding him.

She didn't feel ashamed for taking what she wanted . . . for pleasuring herself. She was able to press PAUSE on the tapes that ran through her head. Didn't hear her mother reminding her of how a good girl was supposed to behave. She was far from a girl. She was a grown woman who knew what she wanted, and she wanted what she was sitting on top of. She wanted that man—that younger man—and so she took what it was she had been denying herself for the past year. The licking was nice, but the lovemaking was better.

"Baby, I'm about to come," he said after forty-five minutes and several positions. He pulled out of her just in time to avoid any mistakes.

Hugh, the last man she had been with, could never spend the night, but Matthew could. They lay in each other's arms, and she felt as if God had forgiven her. That was the only way she could explain meeting someone as wonderful as Matthew. Someone who promised so early not to leave her and she believed him. Even if it sounded like game, it was one game she was willing to play.

Olena awoke in the middle of the night, her eyes focused intently on Matthew. She wanted to touch him, but was too afraid he might awaken if she did. He was sleeping so peacefully. She wished he never had to leave, except for work, and then he would return to her afterward. She knew she loved him, and she wanted to do all she could for him. She wondered what fueled him, what made him happy. Was age truly just a number in his mind? Or was that a line he had given her? Would he leave her also— not the way Stanley had, but the way Andrew had? For another woman, maybe his high school or even college sweetheart—a woman closer to his own age, a relationship that would be more acceptable to society; a woman he could have kids with and the two could grow old together. Who was she fooling? Their relationship would never work just as her relationship with Andrew had never worked. Andrew had promised Olena the same exact thing—never to leave—and where was he now? He'd left years earlier so Olena had no idea.

She snuggled against him as they lay spooning each other. His hand began fondling one of her breasts; his erection stirred underneath the sheet. *What happens to a woman who has sacrificed sex for success and along the way ended up alone?* she wondered. She wasn't alone now and never wanted to be again.

"What did you do last night?" Olena asked Jason. Not that she cared, maybe slightly, but not the way she would have if he were Matthew.

He called her in midafternoon just to shoot the breeze. Asked why they hadn't talked in several days and accepted her excuses that she was busy writing but she hadn't picked up her Moleskine in days.

"I went to the strip club."

"You went to the script club?" Her words came out twisted, the same as the thoughts running through her head.

"No, I went to the strip club not the script club."

"You know what I meant."

"But those girls were throwing out plenty of lines, so it might as well have been the script club."

"And I'm sure you were throwing out plenty of cash too."

"I made it rain a couple of times."

"You're gloating. I can hear it in your voice. You're so proud of the fact that you patronize strip clubs."

"Baby, it's Atlanta. We're known for strip clubs—Magic City is world-famous."

"Is it really world-famous?"

"Most men go to them from time to time, and it's been months since I went to one."

"Well, I don't believe most men go to them. In fact, I know of one that I doubt does."

"And who is that?"

"Don't worry about who it is, but every man does not go to strip clubs."

"Well, if I could have been with you, I wouldn't have gone to the strip club. But you've been ignoring my calls. I can't believe I've only seen you once since you've been here."

"You're too busy with your commentating. You don't have time for me."

"Football season is almost over. I can make time for you when I'm in town. But I'm starting to wonder if you can make time for me. After all I did give you my shoulder to rest your head on, but instead you slobbered on it. Maybe that was a sign."

"The whole purpose of my sabbatical is for me to re-connect with my inner self. I'm getting ready to move. And like I said, I've been trying to write."

"I'd like to connect with your inner self."

"Good-bye, Jason."

Olena sat on the edge of the bed after she ended the call with him, and smiled as she scrolled through pages upon pages of text messages that Matthew had sent to her just from that morning alone when he left and headed home. Today was his day off, but he wanted to get some rest because they'd kept each other up well into morning.

Have U ever gone to a strip club, baby?

It took Matthew nearly thirty minutes before he sent back a response.

Y U ask? It was a long time ago. Not something I have done recently. Y? Yes, Y?

Just wanted to know if all men go to them, and I guess they do.

Not all men, baby. I don't enjoy them that much, not like I used to. it's all a game. A stripper is just a fantasy. I'd much rather spend my time and money on U.

U are really something, Mr. Harper. Something to behold.

I want more of U.

Is sex the only thing U want from me?

Her text went unanswered for several hours and then he sent:

I'm on my way to get more. R U ready for me, baby?

She understood how a friend of his college girlfriend's could have shown up at his dorm room and asked that he perform oral sex on her, saying that she had heard from his girlfriend how good he was. Supposedly, he refused, but Olena wondered how true that part was. Not that it mattered, because at that moment the only thing Olena was concerned with was how wonderful her clitoris was feeling.

He dangled his tongue between her vaginal lips. Dipped and scooped. And then came the moment Matthew waited for.

"Oh, Jesus," Olena sang. "Thank you, Father, for this tongue that I'm about to receive. Amen."

He laughed but kept licking. Knew he had her. Knew it wouldn't be long before her head was buried between his legs, and she was doing anything she could to please him. He told her that he wasn't into getting head so she would want to give him some. Pretended it didn't faze him so she could show him that he never had a woman do it the way she could. He anticipated the moment her lips tickled the head of his penis, her hands cupped his balls and then moved vigorously up and down his shaft.

He rolled on his back, placed his hands behind his head, and allowed her to fully examine her prey.

"Get on top of me, baby," he said.

He took her hand and placed it on his shaft, moving it up and down. "Get some lubricant and watch me come. Jack me off, baby."

"I can't."

"Why can't you?"

She peered down at him, examined his penis, licked her lips, and wanted badly to taste him. "Because I want it for myself."

Her lust for him drove him wild. He pinned her on the bed on her back. "I'll just have to keep eating your pussy until you can't take any more."

She spread her legs wide in the air, did splits while lying on her back, and surrendered herself to feeling like more of a woman than she had ever felt before. She understood why people liked their opposites—understood interracial dating better now; understood older men desiring younger women—and of course, she related to cougars, even though she didn't understand the need for a woman to be labeled.

Didn't really understand why an older woman being into younger men seemed shameful. There was something about having what you were so far from being that could heighten a sexual experience, at least in her case it was. If she had been the type to cry, now would have been one of those times she would have chosen to. Not because she was sad, but because she had never felt so good.

Olena stood in the middle of apartment number one, staring through the famous leaded glass window Margaret Mitchell had looked out of while writing *Gone With the Wind*.

Earlier that morning after Matthew left, Olena had decided it was time to get out and see more of the city, starting with some of the nearby sights. She was searching for some additional inspiration that would get her pen flowing. And so it just happened while she was flipping through the visitor's magazine in her suite that she stumbled upon information on the Margaret Mitchell House and Museum. And now she was standing in the very apartment where Margaret and her husband, John Marsh, had lived from 1925 until 1932.

The docent-led tour lasted nearly an hour and a half, but was extended to over two once Olena entered the gift shop to browse. She was both inspired and saddened by Margaret Mitchell's story—from the way she lived to her untimely death. It was obvious to Olena that Margaret Mitchell was an extremely talented woman and a woman with a secret life that involved a commitment to the black community during a time of segregation. Not only had she regularly contributed to a scholarship fund that helped several black medical students, but she also was instrumental in efforts for the desegregation of the city's police department. Olena could relate to Margaret on so many levels—not only because she was a writer who for many years kept her unfinished manuscript tucked away, but also because she was a woman who had captured the heart of two men: one an ex-football player and bootlegger who Margaret married first only to divorce somewhat quickly and go on to marry John Marsh, a newspaperman. They moved into apartment number one, which Margaret referred to as *the dump*, and she wrote her masterpiece. Sadly, ten years after the movie premiered she was struck by an off-duty cabdriver while she crossed the street at Peachtree and Thirteenth, just three blocks from *the dump*, only to die five days later at Grady Memorial Hospital at the age of forty-eight. Olena of course had never married, hadn't written anything worthy of a Pulitzer. She had yet to engage in any philanthropy, and couldn't imagine doing all of those things by the time she was forty-eight, nor could she imagine dying at that age either.

She sat in her car in the parking lot outside of the museum with the replica of the Margaret Mitchell House resting on the passenger seat. Before pulling off, she tried to digest what had transpired so far that day.

Olena was in Atlanta—the city she had chosen that had not chosen her—and this time things were going to be right. She was going to find love; she already could feel it. She was going to finish her novel. She was going to smile and mean it for a change She was wide-awake and loving it.

"I'm forgiven," she whispered, and then repeated it to herself loudly. Olena was forgiving herself for not being the smartest or the prettiest, perhaps not even the most ambitious. But, she realized after leaving Margaret Mitchell's home, each person had been granted life without an expiration date, and it was time for her to start living as if her life was still good, hadn't been spoiled yet, was good till God said otherwise.

TWENTY-SIX

What are U doing for Valentine's Day?

Olena had already been in Atlanta for a little over a month, and most of that time was spent with Matthew. When they weren't making love, they were texting each other to discuss how they couldn't wait to make love again. They'd go out for dinner and a movie occasionally, alternating on picking up the tab. But having sex was a constant. And then the gift-giving started with an iPod Touch, because she knew he wanted one but was too frugal to buy it for himself. He thanked her a million times and seemed to cherish it. And then she bought him a few other things—small things like Walter Mosley books since that was his favorite author and iTune gift cards to show him she was thinking about him so when Valentine's Day

approached she wondered if he would do the same—do
something to show her that she was thought of.

Valentine's Day?????

Yes. It's not next Saturday, but the Saturday after
that. What are U doing?

I don't believe in Valentine's day, so I'm doing absolutely nothing.

U don't believe in it?????

That's right? I don't believe in it. I don't need
to use an excuse of 1 day to show my love for
someone.

Interesting. I've always loved February 14. Sorry
to hear you don't.

The day before Valentine's Matthew sent Olena a beautiful bouquet of two dozen roses from Flowers.com with a
lovely note attached:

*I love you, and I thank God for the day we met. You are
better to me than I am to myself, and for that, you are
the best friend I have ever had and will ever have.*

She cut the stems, arranged the flowers in the accompanying vase, and set them on the dining room table;
then she smiled every time she floated past. Hugh used
to send her flowers on holidays as his way of apologizing

for his absence, but he had a family and a valid excuse for keeping Olena at home alone. What was Matthew's? she wondered.

"Don't make any plans for tomorrow," Jason said after calling her on the hotel phone. He was driving on Interstate 85 with his two small sons, who were sitting in the backseat of his Escalade watching a DVD.

Jason no longer had anything to complain about, because in the past two weeks alone, they'd seen each other nearly every day. Matthew's work hours were becoming longer and longer, and his admission about Valentine's Day had turned Olena slightly off. She was starting to wonder if he was selfish, if a lot of people in their twenties were concerned more with themselves than others. She tried to think back to her twenties, but that was a time period that she had actually blocked out of her consciousness. She and Jason went to the movies, and she learned quickly that they both shared a passion for the big screen. Of course, there were the usual dinner dates at posh restaurants throughout metro Atlanta. They'd also attended a comedy concert at the Fox Theater, and Jason hinted both in person and over the phone that he wanted the two of them to take a trip together, even if it was just for an extended weekend.

"Honey, why are you calling me the day before Valentine's and telling me not to make plans? Don't you think if I was going to make them, they would have already been made?"

"And if you had, you would just have to break them. No one should be more important than me."

"Really now?" She smiled, because slowly but surely he was starting to win her heart over. "So what plans do you have for us?"

"I'm taking you out to dinner with my mom and step-dad, and the rest is up to you and my mom."

"I'm going to meet your mother this soon? I barely know you. I feel privileged."

"You should. And for appearance's sake, act like you're in to me."

"Okay, I'll try."

"See, I knew you weren't into me."

"It was a joke. I'm still getting to know you. I like to take things slow."

"For an older woman, you sure act like you have nothing but time."

"What's that supposed to mean? Am I supposed to feel like my time is running out or something?"

"Maybe not running out, but running down. Like the hourglass. Eventually your sand will run out."

"I hate you for that."

"I love you too. It was love at first sight, and I can't wait to see you tomorrow, beautiful."

Olena had no idea when she strolled from the Embassy that a black stretch limousine would await her in the circular entranceway. She expected to see Jason in one of the many expensive cars he owned.

The valet held the door open for Olena as she climbed inside.

"Oh, Catch, she's so pretty," Jason's mother said.

"Thank you," Olena said with a big smile.

"Oh, you're welcome, baby. And she's so polite. At least I know you didn't meet this one at Magic City. She's just a down-home, regular-looking black woman with regular hair and regular features . . . just regular."

Olena's smile dropped suddenly after she realized the compliment had been altered. She was nervous as all eyes landed on her and her Tracy Reese dress.

"Momma, I've never brought a dancer home."

"Just to the hotel, huh?" she said.

"Momma, this is Olena. Olena, this is my heart . . . my mother. She's very outspoken, so don't let her shock you. She's bound to say or do anything. And she loves for everybody to call her *Momma*."

"Nah, not everybody, some of those women friends of yours I don't want calling me *Momma*. In fact, I don't want them calling me anything at all. You can call me *Momma*, though, baby. I'm a pretty good judge of character, and you don't strike me as a gold digger."

"Oh, no, I'm definitely not that," Olena said, smiling.

"No, Momma, Olena's not a gold digger. She loves to let a man know she doesn't need his money because she has plenty of her own and can take care of herself."

"There you go, baby. I don't blame you. Let 'em know they have to work for yours. I raised eight—count 'em—eight boys by myself, and I did that on not that much money at all. So I know firsthand that a woman can take care of herself. That's what my boys are used to seeing, and that's the type of women they like." Jason's mother winked at Olena. "Do you like my son?"

"Very much."

"I raised him to be real down to earth and very romantic. Every now and then he gets a big head, but I just smack him when he does, and he comes back down to earth real fast. Some women are gold diggers and other women wouldn't know what to do if they struck gold. Baby, you're holding a Lotto ticket right there, so you might as well scratch it off."

Olena smiled; she appreciated Jason more as a result of meeting his mother.

"Last Valentine's Day Catch and my husband took me out, and he didn't bring nobody, so I know you must be special. Come over here and sit next to me," his mother patted the seat beside her. "Let me get a real good look at you."

Olena moved from the seat beside Jason to the one beside his mother.

"Catch is my nickname in case you're wondering," Jason said.

"We've called him *Catch* ever since he was five, because he could always catch a football. So my son tells me that you're forty-three." She removed her glasses and studied Olena's face. "What you be drinking, olive oil?"

"No, ma'am."

"Ma'am? Don't be losing no points with that *ma'am* shit. How old do you think I am?"

"Maybe fifty."

Jason's mother patted Olena on the thigh. "We gonna get along just fine. I'm sixty-six, baby."

"You look so good."

"So do you, honey. How do you stay looking so young? Have you found the fountain of youth?"

"I wish," Olena said, looking over at Jason's mother.

"Oh, Lord, I thought she was regular. Her eyes aren't. What color are they?"

"Gray."

"Spooky. You scared me for a minute. Are those yours or are they Pearle Vision's?"

"Mine."

"Girl, where you get those eyes from?"

"Doesn't she have some pretty eyes, Momma? That's what I first noticed."

"My eyes?" Olena asked.

"After your lips."

"Awww, shookie, shookie now. Don't hurt my baby, because he ain't nothin' but a big teddy bear. His ex already hurt him. You know she was a fool to leave him. Only thing she did right was have my grandkids, but she's not fit enough to raise them. She's getting child support, but ninety-five percent of the time, Catch has the kids."

"Can we not talk about her? I want to have a nice evening," Jason said.

The limousine pulled up to a glass office building with a canopy that sat on Peachtree Road directly across from Phipps Plaza.

"What's this place, Catch?" Jason's mother asked. "This don't look like Bone's to me."

"It's Bluepointe, Momma. It's an Asian-type restaurant."

"The way my stomach is growling, you got the nerve to take me to some Asian restaurant."

"It has an Asian influence, Momma. It's not an Asian restaurant."

"Every time I eat Chinese food, I'm hungry fifteen minutes after I finish. I thought you were taking me back to Bone's."

"And every time I take you out, you want to either go to Bone's or the Palm. It's time for you to try something new."

"Have you ever been to Bone's, baby?" his mother asked Olena.

She shook her head. "Never."

"See, it would've been new to your date, so you still could have taken us there."

"I'll be taking Olena to every nice restaurant the city

has to offer in the near future, Momma. But if you want to go back to Bone's I'll take you there. It's Valentine's Day, so I will take you and Olena anywhere you want to go."

"Olena, baby, do you want to eat here or Bone's?"

"I've never been to either, so it doesn't really matter, Momma. I'll leave it up to you."

"Aww, she called me *Momma*. How sweet? I like this girl with her scary gray eyes. Well, we're here now. I'll try it since you went to all this trouble, and knowing you, you probably made reservations."

"Of course, I did. You think I'm going to have them keep my two favorite ladies waiting."

"You know you're special when you're with your man on Valentine's Day," Jason's stepfather said to Olena as they walked from the limousine. Olena thought about Jason's stepfather's statement and wondered who the special lady Matthew was with on the holiday he supposedly didn't believe in. The idea almost put her in a bad mood, but she had to try to live in the moment, and at that moment she was with a man who was trying his best to impress her the most.

"I'm trying to let her know that she's special," Jason said as he stood to the side and held the door open for his mother and Olena.

"And you're doing a good job," Olena said as she walked through the door.

"I guess I'll try their New York strip," Jason's mother said with her nose twisted as she perused the dinner menu. "But if I was at Bone's I would have ordered the sixteen-ounce, bone-in, dry-aged New York strip that I know for a fact is good."

"Momma, I'll take you there next weekend."

"I guess Olena thinks I'm ungrateful. And I'm really not, although I am waiting for some flowers or a gift or something . . . box of chocolates . . . something."

"If I gave you a box of chocolates, you would throw them back at me," Jason said as the waiter handed him a square Tiffany box with a white ribbon, and two other waiters set two bouquets of a dozen long-stem roses on the table—one in front of Jason's mother and the other in front of Olena. "Happy Valentine's Day, baby," Jason said to Olena as he set the box in front of her.

"For me?"

"Yeah, for her?" asked his mother. "You just met her a month or so ago. It's not time to break out the teal box just yet, Catch."

"Ooh, boy, you spoil your women. Make it hard on the next one," his stepdad said.

"Who says there's going to be a next one?"

"I don't even want to open it," Olena said.

"Please open it," his mother said. "I want to see what my son spent his money on."

Olena untied the white bow and slid off the box lid. Inside was a flat, square, velvet case, which she took out and placed in front of her.

"The box is too big to be an engagement ring."

"Like you said, we just met," Jason said. "Besides, I would never propose on a holiday. Only cheap men do that."

"Open it, girl," his mother said.

Olena opened the case and revealed a platinum bracelet with round brilliant and marquise diamonds. "Oh, my God, this is—"

"Expensive," Jason's stepfather said.

"If she got that, then I know my gift must be at home in my driveway with a big-ass red bow on it and a Mercedes emblem."

"Momma, every day is Valentine's for you."

"Every day and today."

"Your gift is at the house."

"I know it had better be, and I know what it had better be, because that bracelet right there cost about thirteen thousand dollars, so I know my gift cost at the least ten times that."

"You will be happy. It's something you said you wanted."

"I know what I said I wanted—an S–six hundred. But whatever you get me is fine." Jason's mother flashed a smile in her son's direction. "Catch, you know where we should go after we leave here?" his mother said.

"Where, Momma?"

"To the Sundial, so Olena can see the city."

"I'm not taking Olena to the played-out Sundial so we can stand in that long line to wait for an elevator and get packed in like cattle."

"What's the Sundial?" Olena asked Jason's mother.

"A very nice restaurant and bar on top of the Westin that revolves to show the city. You would like it. Sometimes my boy can be so selfish."

"Oh, really? I'm selfish," Jason said. "You're going to see how selfish I am when you get home, because a selfish person doesn't drop that kind of loot on a gift."

"Or this kind either?" Olena said. "Thank you."

"I'm sure he's waiting for his thank-you tonight."

"Momma, she's celibate."

"Celibate? Well go ahead and sell a bit. My son can afford it."

"Momma!"

Olena covered her mouth and blushed.

"That's something I heard a comedian say on TV. It was just a joke. I'm trying to see if she has a sense of humor, that's all," Jason's mother said.

"Hold out your wrist, beautiful, so I can put on your bracelet."

"No, Jason, I can't accept that," Olena said.

Jason's mother's eyes burst.

"Why not?" Jason asked.

"Because it cost way too much. The roses are lovely. Let's leave it with that . . . and the dinner. Thank you."

"Girl, you got some good game on you," his mother said as she slammed her elbow on the table and extended her wrist toward Jason. "Then I tell you what I'm going to do. I'm going to accept the bracelet on your behalf, and think about you every day that I wear it."

"But, Momma, I didn't buy the bracelet for you. Your gift is at the house."

Olena said, "Let your mother have the bracelet."

"Girl, you got some good game because I'm over here falling in love with you too," his mother said. "Let Henry slid it on me so he can feel like he did something for me for a change."

Jason handed the bracelet to his stepfather, who in turn slid it on his wife's wrist. "Happy Valentine's Day, beautiful," Henry said.

"Yeah, Happy Valentine's Day, beautiful," Jason said, leaning his face into Olena's.

"Give my son some sugar, girl. Go on and give him at least a little smack." Olena laughed as she turned her cheek toward Jason's lips. "As much game as you got, you need to be in the NFL. She's playing hard to get. Well, he's going to be hard when he gets it."

Olena burst out in laughter.

"Momma, you're really embarrassing me," Jason said. "I'm sorry for the way my mother has been acting."

"You don't have to apologize. I love your mother. She's hilarious."

"What do you think about me?" asked Jason.

"You?" Olena asked as she looked at him and his mother and stepfather. "I like you a lot. I think that you are a very considerate man."

"Is he getting some tonight? That's all he wants to know," Jason's mother said.

"No, that won't be happening. Sorry."

"Whoop, there it is," his mother said as she poured a glass of Krug champagne from the bottle resting on the table. "Now, aren't you glad I'm wearing this bracelet and she's not?"

"No, Mom. That's not why I bought it for her."

"Tell her anything. I know better. But Happy New Year's to the both of you any way . . . and of course Happy Valentine's Day."

After dinner, the limousine driver took them on a tour of Buckhead. The driver headed down Peachtree past Pharr Road. They rode by many of the sights Olena had already seen with Matthew. But she hadn't noticed the billboard that stood over the Geek Squad building.

Luxury is coming to the Streets of Buckhead.
Boutiques, restaurants, hotels,
residences, offices.
Arriving Fall 2009.

The billboard helped Olena come to a decision. "That's where I'm moving," Olena said, pointing to the mansions as the limo approached the skyscraper. She wanted to live in Buckhead; it embodied the type of atmosphere that she had grown accustomed to through her extensive travels to New York. Parts of Atlanta, such as Buckhead and Atlantic Station, were very cosmopolitan, and while she had toyed with the idea of renting, she wondered why should she rent when she could afford to buy.

"Pull next to the building immediately to your right," Jason asked the driver through the intercom.

"Ooh, chil', you gonna live way up there?" Jason's mother asked as she stuck her head out the window and gazed up. "More power to you. I couldn't do it. Anything past the third floor is out of the question for me. I'm scared of heights."

"Since when are you scared of heights? Since when does a person scared of heights ask to be taken to the Sundial?" Jason asked.

"I don't live at the Sundial, do I? All these nice homes in Atlanta—I wish the hell I would be caught living in something like that. But that's for you young jet setters, who can take care of your own selves and don't need a man for nothing . . . not even a diamond bracelet from Tiffany's." Jason's mother flashed the bracelet. "You sure you don't want it back?"

"I'm positive," Olena said.

"Good, because I wasn't going to give it to you no way." Jason's mother burst out in laughter.

"My mother is in rare form this evening, which means she really must like you."

"Oh, yeah, Jason, she's a keeper—a woman with her own money is good for one reason."

"What's that, Momma?"

"She can lend me some when I need it. It's always better to have two people to hit up when you need a loan."

TWENTY-SEVEN

Matthew was standing at the island in his European-style kitchen, fixing a late-night gourmet dinner for two. His mind was preoccupied with thoughts of Olena and their lovemaking while Tanisha sat at the dining room table. She removed a rose from the vase that held the two dozen Matthew had given her, and held it to her nose.

"What are you making, baby?" she asked.

"Salmon, asparagus, wild rice, and Caesar salad—a healthy meal for a change."

"I don't really like salmon."

"It's good for you."

"It is?"

"Yes, very."

She smiled. "Well, I'm sure I'll love anything you make for me. May I have a glass of wine to go with my meal?"

"When you turn twenty-one you may."

"I'm turning twenty-one next month."

"Then next month you can have a glass, but not before then."

Tanisha was a junior at Spellman. They had met the year before through mutual friends; her sorority sister was dating his line brother. Things got off to a somewhat quick start. She was cute, fun, young, and free-spirited. She held out on sex for the first few dates, but when they started, she didn't hold back anything at all. They swapped nude photos, watched pornos together, and made their own with their digital cameras. He started with Tanisha the same way he had started with Olena with oral sex—letting his tongue do all the talking. She was more controlled—didn't scream out the way Olena had, didn't take him to church— no amens while he licked her. She wasn't as much into receiving as giving.

"Should I date?"

"Should you date?" he asked as he set the plate of salad in front of her. "I don't know. Should you? Have you met someone you want to date?"

"Men holler at me all the time. What do you expect?"

"Men or boys waiting to become men? Do they own their own homes? Do they work and make the kind of money that I do?"

"Well, no, but they are willing to commit."

"Because they have nothing to give and therefore nothing to lose."

"So I guess I should date."

"Date," he said as he set both plates down and returned to the kitchen for the drinks. He poured sweet tea in her wineglass and pinot grigio in his.

"Just like that."

"I'm not one to stand in the way of anyone's happiness, baby."

"So you don't care?"

"I'm not saying I don't care, but I know what I can give, which right now isn't much."

"Why?"

"We've had this discussion too many times in the past. Let's eat before the food gets cold."

She sighed and looked down.

"Eat, baby. Waste not want not."

After dinner, Tanisha ran upstairs to prepare her surprise. "Do not come up here before I tell you to, baby. Promise me."

"I won't . . . I promise," he said, his voice dragging as he stared at his cell phone, wondering why Olena hadn't returned either of his text messages. He picked up the phone and dialed her hotel, asked for her room number—817—the governor's suite. The phone rang several times before switching to the automated phone-mail system. Then he called her cell phone, and it didn't ring at all before connecting to voice mail. He decided since today was Valentine's to leave a message, because she wouldn't expect it since he didn't believe in the holiday.

"Hello, baby. I'm just calling to wish you a Happy Valentine's Day. You're probably writing your soon-to-be masterpiece. I sent you a couple text messages earlier and never received a reply, which isn't like you. I hope all is well. I can't wait to see you again. Sleep tight, baby. I love you."

He turned and found Tanisha standing nearby with her arms folded and a look of sheer disgust.

"Who was that?"

"A friend."

"Who?"

"Why?"

"Because I think it's very rude to call some chick on Valentine's while you're with your valentine. I thought you told me Shayla got married and moved out of state."

"She did."

"Then who was that, because it wasn't Angel. So who else do you have? That woman with all the kids?"

"No."

"Who then? Who did you call up telling her to sleep tight and that you love her?"

"I'm not used to you questioning me like this, and quite frankly it's a turnoff."

"And I'm not used to you leaving messages on some chick's voice mail on Valentine's Day either."

"Enough with the Valentine's Day. It's just another day as far as I'm concerned. If you must know, she's a client. She purchased a six series BMW from me, which is a very expensive car."

"Just because I don't have my own car doesn't mean I don't know what a six series BMW is. I know it's expensive."

"She's rich and she has rich friends. Jason Nix is one of them."

"So if she's just a client, why did you tell her that you love her?"

"It's something rich people say to each other . . . like saying good-bye."

She tossed him a look of skepticism. "So you don't like her?"

"That woman is forty-three years old—almost as old as my mother."

"Well, all you hear about these days is older women with younger men. Nick Cannon married Mariah Carey."

"I'd marry Mariah Carey too, baby. Now I'm not saying the woman doesn't like me."

"Oh, so that old woman likes you? I'm telling your momma."

"Tell her. She'll just laugh. She knows her son, and she knows I wouldn't mess around with a woman who's damn near the same age as her."

"Matthew, you'd better not mess with an old woman like that. I can't stand when those old men try to holla at me. I want to marry a man close to my age—four or five years older at the most and definitely not younger. She needs to be ashamed of herself. She's got a serious problem. She must be desperate."

"In her defense, I am a handsome young man, and I wouldn't refer to a woman as being desperate because she likes me."

"You're twenty-five, and she's forty-three." Tanisha shook her head. "Anyway, are you ready for your surprise?" Tanisha took Matthew by the hand and led him up the stairs into the master bedroom, where several Valentine's Day foiled balloons were floating the largest one said *I Love You* and was tied to the headboard.

"Happy Valentine's Day," she said as she handed him a gift bag with a Hallmark Mahogany card stuffed inside the rose-colored tissue.

He read the card, which was filled with references to love, and then reached inside and pulled out the Cross Pen box. "Thank you, baby. I can always use a nice pen."

"I know it's not the Mountain Blank that you're always talking about."

"Montblanc, baby. It's not, but this is still very nice, and I will write with it every day."

"Don't let any of your customers use it."

"Clients, baby. And most of my clients have Montblancs."

"Well, I'm sorry that I couldn't afford a Montblanc. I'm a college student. Not a forty-three-year-old woman chasing a younger man."

"Enough." He walked into his walk-in closet and removed the Victoria Secret's bag that he'd hidden. He decided it was time to see her in something other than sweats or cotton thongs when she was trying to be sexy. He'd bought her the type of lingerie he liked seeing a woman in—the type Olena wore—since he knew that Tanisha couldn't afford to buy that either.

She pulled out the pink lace flyaway baby doll and the matching silk panties. "Aww, baby, it's beautiful. I'm going to put this on right after we get out of the Jacuzzi." She pulled off her dress, dropped her Hanes cotton bra and panties, and slipped into the tub, which was illuminated by a dozen tealight candles circling the granite edges.

The evening was nice, but still predictable. He knew what to expect. Could count on her to say at least three times before his eyes shut that she was mad at him. Knew she would pretend to resist his tongue only to give in. Knew she would lick him long enough to get an erection, then stop and start licking again and stop and wait for him to ask her not to stop—plead with her as if they were playing some game. He missed Olena, who was indeed skillful with her tongue, although she refused to swallow. Missed the sweet taste of honey between her thick thighs; the way she rode him; the nonchalant manner in which she handled him. Intrigued by her; loved the sound of her moans. Indeed, he was fascinated by her age and how youthful she both looked and acted. To him, there wasn't an age difference. Tanisha was his steady—the one who admired him for all he had, because to her he had the world. She was appreciative of the small things—for the chance to come over on weekends to wash her clothes, for the money he gave her to shop. Fifty dollars felt like five thousand. Matthew was to Tanisha what Jason was trying to be to Olena—a man willing to give as much as he could to please her.

"Can I check my myspace page?" she said as he turned on the computer after they finished soaking in the tub.

"Be my guest."

She picked up the wireless keyboard from his nightstand and logged on to her page and accepted a half dozen comments with Happy Valentine's Day graphics attached. If she was trying to make him jealous, she was wasting both his and her time.

TWENTY-EIGHT

Valentine's Day had come and long gone. The fresh flowers Matthew had sent to Olena had died and been replaced several times over. Now it was April. Three months in his city, and Olena still hadn't seen Matthew's David Weekly–designed home. Not because of his doing. Not completely. He had pulled away slightly, but as he reminded her, his work schedule was hectic. And even though it allowed her to spend more time with Jason, her thoughts were still on Matthew.

The invitation to go to Matthew's home stood and still remained. He could tell that it was as if she felt safer in her own territory—first, the hotel and soon her three-bedroom condominium at the Mansions that she would be moving in to.

Olena had Matthew's mind more than he cared to admit. While much of it had to do with the sex, not all of it was about that. He enjoyed the times they spent together both in and out of bed. To Matthew, Olena taste like cocoa butter, and when he replaced his tongue with his penis, he did glide in just as smooth. Some of his boys joked he would need to use extra lubricant, said a woman that old couldn't possibly stay wet, and wouldn't fit his penis like a glove, but more like a mitten. But he knew otherwise. He listened to their taunts with a smirk, because he knew the truth: Sex with her was some of the best he'd ever had.

He started having flashbacks of the two of them in bed. This occurred often—while he was at work—driving to or from—or even when the two of them were together eating and engulfed in innocent conversation. He loved when she called him her baby and stroked the side of his cheeks. He understood why older women were referred to as cougars, because she maintained an animalistic stare each time she would watch him undress. He wasn't sure if she realized that she would lick her lips while her irises pierced through every inch of him.

He had flashbacks of her lying on her back while his head was buried between her legs. He loved listening to her piercing moans of satisfaction as she swung her head wildly from side to side, her hair sweeping over her youthful face, hiding her large gray eyes. She told him that his tongue was magical, because it felt as if he was performing art. He entertained her in such a way as if to create an illusion of a supernatural feat, so it was no wonder she rubbed her hands over his head as if it were her crystal ball and she was in the process of scrying. But what would the future hold? He knew that she wanted nothing more than to please him and he her. And for him that pleasure came just as much before sex as during sex, as well as after sex when she fell asleep in his arms. Was it wrong for him to continue seeing her when he knew he couldn't commit? Knew a commitment was something she wanted just like most women, only the young women had more time and he didn't want to waste any more of Olena's.

It was a peaceful Thursday afternoon, and one of the rare times he had off from the dealership. But this week was an extra treat, because he also had the next day off, now that the dealership had started opening on Sundays. Matthew stood near the large picture window in the living room of Olena's hotel suite with his hands in his pockets. He took in the views of Phillips Arena and the CNN Center as light rain began to fall, remembering the tornado that had swept through downtown the year before and damaged the CNN Center and many other places throughout the city.

He wondered how to break it to her. After telling her he would never leave, how could he admit that he could also never give her what she was seeking?

"When will your condo be ready, baby?"

She walked up and hugged him from behind, resting her head on his back. "Let's not talk about when my condo will be ready. I'm ready. Are you ready?" Her full lips pressed against his neck while her tongue swirled his flesh. She nibbled his skin. "Mmm, I'm going to have to start calling you white chocolate."

He grinned as he thought about the popular stripper by the same name who danced at Stroker's, a strip club in Clarkston, where he along with a few friends had been on occasion.

"You're such a PYT," she said.

"Michael Jackson?"

"Pretty young thing."

"Pretty?" He turned to face her, studied her hands as her fingers unbuttoned his shirt.

With him, she loved being the aggressor and taking control. It was rare for her to be that way with a man closer to her own age. Perhaps it was the age difference—the fact that she felt she could be more in control with a young man since she was the more experienced of the two. But she also remembered what Dr. Phil had said on his show about Cougar Craze: He saw nothing wrong with an older woman dating a younger man, just like he saw nothing wrong with the opposite, as long as the person had the right mind-set going in, which was that it was just for fun and nothing serious. Otherwise someone was bound to get hurt and that person was usually the older one.

"Handsome young thing, then."

He swallowed hard after becoming aroused.

"Why do you make me feel so good, baby?" she purred.

By this time, she had loosened his belt. His pants had fallen to his ankles. He stepped out of his shoes and stood near the window in his boxers and a pair of socks while she undressed. He pulled off his socks and dropped his shorts. The curtains to every window lining the corner suite in the living room were open, and they both stood completely naked in full view.

"Maybe it's your fantasy to be with a younger man. Didn't you say I was your first?" She nodded as she rubbed her hands over his chest. "Maybe being with me makes you feel like a virgin, even though you don't act like one."

"What do I act like, baby? Tell me," she said as she took her hand and squeezed that part of him that made her wet. She took him by the hand to lead him into the bedroom.

"Are you afraid to give people a show?" He kneeled,

cupped his hands on her butt. Her soft flesh made his erection harden. He licked her clit, taste her wetness, the possibility that others might have been watching from their office windows aroused him even more. They were the stars of their very own porno that was free for all to view.

"Oh, baby," she sighed, her head dropping back while he caused her juices to steadily flow. "I can't help myself. You are the best thing that has ever happened to me. You can have your little girlfriends." Her hands began furiously massaging the top of his freshly cut hair. "Did you hear what I said? You can still date women your own age. I know what this is."

"What is it?"

"We're just having fun. It's sex. That's all it is, isn't it?"

"Don't sell yourself short," he said as he pulled at her arm so she would join him on the floor. "It's more than sex." They kissed for nearly five minutes. Passion made her forget how hard the floor felt. Instead, she focused on how hard he felt inside of her. "I love you," he said at the height of his orgasm.

"I'm in love with you," she said.

"Tell me about the women in your life," she said to him. It was late, close to midnight. They had moved to the bedroom, made love again, then fallen asleep for a few hours, and she had awoken with questions.

"I don't have any women in my life other than you."

"Matthew, you don't have to be a player with me. Tell me the truth."

It was something about the way she spoke to him, stern but still sweet, that made it nearly impossible for him to lie. Although he still did. He couldn't tell her that he had other sexual partners because he knew Olena and knew it would break her heart.

"I just have friends."

"Who are they?"

"My best friend, Angel."

"Your best friend is a female."

"Yes, baby. I've mentioned her before."

"I thought I was your best friend?"

"What? Angel is my best friend. I've know her all my life. We were born on the same day."

"Well, you said I was the best friend you've ever had."

"When did I say that?"

"Never mind."

"When did I say that, baby?"

She climbed out the bed and walked over to her purse resting on the dresser to retrieve the card that she kept inside her wallet from the flowers he had sent her the day before Valentine's Day. She handed him the card. "Those were your words, but I wondered how sincere they were."

"You're a good friend . . . one of my best."

Olena snatched the card from his hand. "Is she on your phone?" He reached for his phone on the nightstand and showed Olena a picture of Angel. "Is she white?"

"No, but she can pass. Not that she would ever think to."

"Have you slept with her?"

"No. We're friends and our parents are good friends. It's purely platonic."

"So you've never slept with her?"

"Well . . ."

"Well . . . ?"

"I have, but it's been a long time."

"Platonic."

"For the most part."

"For the most part."

"It's been so long since we've been together. When I was a freshman in college was the last time we had sex, so I don't even count that. Angel is my friend, but we don't have sex. I've always been straight up with you. I mean, I do have a lot of female friends."

"A lot?"

"Enough. But that's all they are."

"I don't believe you. You just lied to me about Angel, so who's to say you're not still lying."

"Well, maybe if you could handle the truth I wouldn't have to lie."

"I want the truth, so give it to me."

He turned to face her. Not sure how his words would come out. "If I give you the truth, you won't get mad, will you?"

"I don't know. I can't make any promises."

He shook his head. "Forget it."

"Tell me."

"No, I don't want you getting upset."

"I already know there's another woman in your life . . . and I want to know about her."

"You are so direct with your questions."

"That I am. I asked what I want to know, because if you don't ask, you'll never know."

"That's not always true."

"Answer my question."

"There's a young lady who I have deep feelings for, but she left me almost two years ago to be with another man— a man who beats her. I have a hard time with that. I mean, if you want to leave me because you feel I won't commit and that's what you are looking for, it's fine to move on, but move on to a man better than me. Take a step up. Don't leave me for the bottom of the barrel. Don't leave me for a man who is going to lay his hands on you. What sense does that make? Then you tell me that you got your tubes tied when you were twenty-five because you knew you never wanted to have children, but yet a month after you meet this fool, you're texting me to tell me you're pregnant. So you had unprotected sex with this fool that quick?"

Olena laughed. Young people had drama. She could remember being young and getting her heart broken. "She didn't have her tubes tied. That was obviously a lie."

"She didn't lie. She doesn't have to lie," he said, his voice escalating.

"Matthew, she probably told you her tubes were tied so you would feel comfortable enough to have unprotected sex so she could get pregnant with you and trap you. Did you ever think of that?"

"She doesn't have to trap me because if she wanted me she could have had me," he shouted.

"Well, whoop, there it is." Olena stood from the bed. "Get out."

"What do you mean, get out?"

"Get out! You yelled at me over a woman who claimed she had her tubes tied but still got pregnant by some man she had just met who she's still with to this day—a man who beats her. She'd rather be with a man who beats her than be with you, and you're mad at me. Get out. I'm too old and I've been through too much in my lifetime to have a twenty-four-year-old yell at me over another woman."

"I'm twenty-five. And I knew you couldn't handle it."

"You're right, I can't. Get out . . . *young* man."

"Olena, I'm sorry for yelling at you. I never said I was

perfect. But I do love you. You asked for the truth, so I gave it to you."

"I didn't expect to be yelled at."

"I'm sorry."

She stormed out of the bedroom over to the main door to the suite leading into the hallway and opened it. She stood in her robe with her hand strangling the doorknob. "Don't apologize. Don't ever apologize for being honest."

He took his time getting dressed, hurried only after she told him to, swung his overnight bag over his shoulder, and left the bedroom, walking toward her and the door. He stood eyeing her. "I don't want to leave."

"You don't have a choice."

He pried the knob from her hand and closed the door, tossed his bag on the floor, and took her in his arms. "You said I could have my little girlfriends, remember? Those were your words."

"I know what I said."

"Don't say things you don't mean."

"I mean it. You can."

He shook his head. "No, you don't. Don't say things you don't mean. I don't need my little girlfriends. I just need you, baby."

TWENTY-NINE

"Would you like to have lunch in the park and listen to jazz, beautiful?" asked Matthew. He had taken the liberty of ordering room service for the two of them so he could feed her breakfast in bed. He wanted to show her that he still cared. He knew he had been slacking off a little and blaming it on work, and now he could feel a little distance on her part also. He wanted her to know that even though the sex was incredible, there was more to him than his tongue and the flesh between his legs that she managed to keep hard.

"What park?" Olena had just pried her eyes open. Another long night of Matthew's oral stimulation had left her feeling hungover. The only thing she was in the mood for was remaining under her sweet-dreams bedding and relaxing in the governor's suite.

"Centennial—the park that's directly across the street.

I need to get you out a little more. This isn't New York. You're not working. You're on a sabbatical with just nine months left."

"Don't remind me. I can't believe it's April."

"And what have you done?"

"What have I done?"

"Have you been writing?"

"Not as much as I should, but when I settle into my new place, I'm going to write in the English gardens every afternoon."

"Well, beautiful, can we get out and enjoy ourselves today."

"I'm really exhausted."

"Please go with me to the park. It's only an hour of your time, and I'll leave you alone after that. I want us to start spending more time together outside of bed. Seems like we got away from that. We used to go out more, but now it is a lot more sex, and I don't want you to think I'm some typical young man in his twenties who just wants sex."

"I'm sure that you are." She sat up in bed and allowed him to feed her fresh melons and grapes. He poured her a glass of freshly squeezed orange juice and cut her Belgian waffle in sections.

"I'm going to go out and get a few things for our picnic."

"Oh, we're having a picnic. Someone's being romantic."

"Trying. I'll be back."

Matthew brought along two portable lounge chairs from his house and a picnic basket. He went out to buy some imported wine and a variety of cheese and crackers. He knew this wouldn't be something she would expect Matthew to do, which is exactly why he did it.

They walked across Andrew Young International Boulevard and headed for the Southern Company Amphitheater, where the Music @ Noon series was held.

"Who's performing?"

"I don't even know," he said as they continued walking toward the amphitheater.

The artist on stage was JPeele, an independent neither Olena nor Matthew had heard of. He started singing his single, "My Lady."

"Are you listening to the words?" Matthew repeated a couple of lines after JPeele sang them, " 'One of these days you're going to be my lady. Baby, I know you think I'm crazy.' " He took her hand and squeezed his love inside. "One of these days, baby."

She leaned into him. "I'm not right for you." She thought the acoustics had drowned out her confession because Matthew's head never stopped nodding. "Did you hear me?"

He nodded, but she wasn't sure if he was nodding in answer to her question or continuing to nod along with the music. "Did you hear what I said, Matthew?"

"Yes, I heard you."

"What did I say?"

"You're not right for me. So who are you right for?"

She shrugged. "Not sure if I'm right for anyone. I prayed to God to give me a sign, and He hasn't yet."

"Here is your sign staring back at you. You're right for me. I just have to take my time with you. That's why I'm glad I'm a patient man. I just have to prove to you that your age doesn't matter, because that's the only reason you think you're not right for me. I'm young and I still have a lot to learn and a lot to experience, but I know that I love you, and I know I will never leave you."

What does that mean? she wondered. He continued to say that he would never leave her, but one day he would have to—one day when he married, he would leave her, because the last thing she would do would be to have another affair. She wanted to ask him how he would pull off never leaving her, but decided against posing another question, preferred instead to leave it with what he said, because what he said sounded too good . . . too good to be true.

THIRTY

It was still April. Just toward the end of the month. And Olena was finally moving out of the all too familiar Embassy Suites to the thirty-second floor of the Mansions on Peachtree. And even though she had most of her furnishings, with the exception of her bedroom, which would be delivered to her house sometime that day, she still needed Matthew's help. She had accumulated so many things— mainly designer apparel, expensive shoes and handbags— that it took Matthew and her most of the morning and a few hours in the afternoon to box up everything.

In as little as three months, Olena was beginning to feel more alive than she ever had. And this had absolutely nothing to do with the two men in her life, although Matthew was a wonderful accessory.

One by one she was checkmarking her to-do list. And most important she was back to dreaming again. With three chapters of her book completed and the entire novel outlined, she felt like a real writer. She frequented the Margaret Mitchell House for literary events and even joined the Literary Center's Atlanta Book Club and read their monthly selections. And now she was moving, which was the icing on her well-prepared multilayered cake.

"Now here's the real trick—getting all of this into my convertible."

"Not to worry. I have that covered also. I borrowed an SUV from used cars—a big-ass Expedition. We'll be just fine."

"Oh, my baby thinks of everything." Olena kissed his forehead. "That's what a young mind can do."

He smiled. "Whatever."

"Baby, not whatever, because I need that young mind to keep me alert. I don't want to go into a nursing home. Please don't put me in one."

"The only way I'd put you in one is if I went with you."

She giggled, pretended that she was merely joking. But she wasn't. It was a reality that they could one day face if somehow they ended up together and if the statement he often made about never leaving her came true. She would grow old much before he did, possibly burden him and die before him. At forty-three, she was faced with premature thoughts of aging because his youth had accelerated the process. In short, at times he made her feel old simply from being young.

"What's next?" he asked as he headed for the door she was holding open with two boxes in his arms.

"How long do I have you?"

"All day and all night, for as long as you need me."

"Well, I was hoping that after we dropped these boxes

off, we could go shopping. I need bedding, kitchen supplies, and groceries. I really will have you all day if you don't mind."

"Like I'd mind . . . as long as I can have you all night," he said as his lips pressed against hers.

"Thanks for playing chauffeur," she said while he massaged her legs and feet as she lay on her stomach, relaxing in bed. "You were so patient with me, and a few times I could tell you were ready to go. I saw it in your face."

"Pottery Barn . . . so ready. And that's my store, but you took your shopping experience to a whole other level. You acted as if they were going out of business, like you couldn't come back another day—you had to get everything today. Pier One. I couldn't take you and Pier One at the same time. That's why I had to walk out of the store, wait in the car, and turn on Marvin Sapp to clear my mind." Matthew began singing the Marvin Sapp song "Never Would Have Made It," because it was so fitting as to how he felt during Olena's shopping excursion, but he altered the lyrics. " 'I would have lost my mind if I had to spend another hour shopping with you. Never could have made it. Now I'm stronger. Now I'm wiser. I'm better . . . much better.' "

"I just want everything to be perfect."

"But you're not going to get everything perfect in a day, baby."

"Your parents got you perfect in a day."

"I love you," he said. Those three words had always been easier for him to speak than to express.

"What do you love about me?"

"Everything."

"Some examples, please."

Olena felt a slight warming sensation on her back as sweet almond oil dripped out from the bottle Matthew held. His hands continued to sensually caress her soft skin. "I love waking up in the morning with you in my arms, your head resting on my chest. Feeling your heartbeat and knowing that I'm not alone. I love watching you sleep so peacefully—observing the beauty in your stillness. I love listening to your laughter. I love how easily we connect—no matter where we are or what we're doing. We could be at a restaurant enjoying a romantic dinner or taking a leisurely drive. I love the way even our silence brings us closer. I love that even when we're not together it feels like you're still with me. I love when your smell lingers in my sheets. I love the things you've taught me. How much knowing you has helped me grow. Consider a rose. Even if you pull away every petal, there's still the center. And I know, no matter what, you will always be there—my center. I love all the little things you do that come without me ever asking, that come from your heart. The dinner you will prepare for me even though you don't cook."

"But I never made you dinner."

"I know, and that's why I said the dinner that you *will* prepare for me even though you don't cook. I hope you didn't spend two hours in the Container Store to plan on not cooking."

"No, I didn't. I plan on cooking for you, baby."

"May I continue?" She nodded. "I love snuggling with you on the sofa and watching a movie late at night. Listening to your snores since you can't hang after midnight."

"I don't snore."

"*Shh,* don't interrupt me again. I was patient when I had to endure you shopping earlier. Now it's your turn to be patient. Even though I love when you interrupt me because I know you can't wait. I love your impatience, which is the only imperfection I've discovered so far—well, besides your possessiveness."

"I'm not possessive."

"Shit," he spit out. "You're not?"

"Not really."

"Really . . . yes . . . really. But this is about what I love about you, and not what I dislike. I love eating breakfast in bed with you, washing your back in the shower and you doing the same to mine. The massages—I love not only feeling your soft hands rubbing all over my body with the sensual oils you buy just for me. But times like these, when I'm smoothing my hands all over you. I love your simplicity, how nothing's ever a big deal. I love knowing the person you truly are—your spirit not your facade. When no one understands you, I do just as you do. I love your eyes. I love your smile. I even . . . even—and know this is a big one—I even love your age."

She pinched his nose as her laughter erupted yet again. "Even love my age, huh? Well, I even love yours too."

"Oh, I know you do. I know you want this young stuff."

"Whatever?"

"Am I lying?"

"No," she said as a big smile plastered her face. "Not at all. I want it and I'm not even going to lie."

The English gardens put her mind in a state of bliss. There was something about being among so much greenery and all of the vibrant colors that ignited not only an inner sense of calmness but also awakened her creativity. At last, she was able to exhale, even with her frequent thoughts

of Andrew. After all of these years, she still couldn't get
him out of her mind for some reason. Particularly since
she'd moved to Atlanta and had more time on her hands
to reflect on her past. If he could just see her now and see
how much she had grown, she was certain he would be
impressed. See how confident she was as opposed to the
Olena Day he had known. Even though she hated her mistakes, she loved herself and loved the way she looked. She
was secure enough with herself that she could acknowl-
edge her shortcomings without becoming depressed because she realized that no one was perfect and beauty truly
was in the eye of the beholder. Nearly two weeks after all
of her furniture had arrived, every box unpacked, and everything had been put in its proper place, Olena could finally explore the grounds. She had decided to put herself
on a schedule—a one o'clock writing appointment each
afternoon in the English gardens while the spring weather
was so beautiful. That evening, she planned to invite Matthew over to dine at Tom Colicchio's Craft, which, while
physically separated from the main tower, was directly on
Peachtree, steps away from the entrance to the building.
But now was not the time to concentrate on what would
occur much later. Now was the time to concentrate on her
character Clara.

Olena wasn't alone. Others would stroll through,
but one well-dressed and somewhat eccentric woman
had posted herself on one of the benches with a stack
of papers by her side and several in her hand. She was
reading and balling up pages, tossing them into a small
stainless steel garbage can that belonged to her and not
the Mansions.

Olena had noticed the woman in the English gardens
every afternoon. She always arrived before Olena and left

usually an hour before her. She was always reading stacks of papers, so Olena assumed she was an English professor, even thought about asking her how much she would charge to edit her manuscript.

"Trash . . . garbage . . . bullshit . . . rubbish . . . *waste* of my fuckin' time," said the woman. As each word was spoken, a page was discarded. She let out a loud sigh filled with her annoyance. "I don't need a therapist. I need a damn drink and some decent material to read." She rose to her feet, gathered up all of her belongings, including her garbage can, and huffed off.

"Strange," Olena said, before shaking all thoughts of the woman from her consciousness and preparing to enter her character Clara's world.

What became of Clara? No one knew. Not even her husband, or so he would claim—a husband who didn't love her and one who kept a mistress. But she had found love with Jeremiah. Made love to him the first day he arrived to cut their grounds. Took him in her husband's study to write a check and before handing it to him asked how much it would cost her to have him remove his shirt.

"Nothing," he had responded.

Had she run off with him? Were the whispers that spread throughout the exclusive subdivision true? Had she taken up with a commoner, left a renowned surgeon for a landscaper. Or was she dead, perhaps killed by her husband during a fit of rage after the discovery that she too had cheated? Had her body been cut into pieces, which would explain the right hand two boy scouts had discovered the day before in a wooded area not far from her home? Was it Clara's or some other poor soul's?

*   *   *

"It was the strangest thing," said Olena as they sat in the one-hundred-seat fine-dining restaurant. She watched as Matthew nearly devoured his steak while she picked at her organic farm chicken. "She seemed so bizarre."

"Maybe she's an English professor and her students can't get it right and she's frustrated."

Olena hadn't ordered a drink. Not after she thought about how much the crazed woman seemed possessed by the mere mention of one. One thing was for sure: The woman had money if she lived in the Mansions, if she wasn't one of the residents' guests.

"I don't like unstable-acting people."

"And I thought you were one not to judge."

"I'm working on not judging. But I do know that I prefer people who are self-confident, even slightly cocky, but definitely not crazy—the functioning insane scare me. Those are the ones you read about in the paper and see in news reports whose neighbors had no idea they were capable of such a thing."

"There's that fiction-writing mind at work."

"But it's true." She searched the booth, felt his pockets, knew something was missing. "Where's your phone?"

"In the car."

"You forgot it?"

He shook his head. "I left it. I agree. It was rude of me to text while I was with you, and besides, the one person that I would want to text I'm already with."

Her grin turned into a smile. "If you can leave your Moto Q in the car, then there's magic at the Mansions. I truly believe it."

THIRTY-ONE

"I don't want to argue with you. Why are we arguing, anyway?" she asked Jason as she shifted through the clothes hanging in her massive walk-in closet in search of an outfit.

"It's fucking with me that you aren't into me the way you should be."

It's fucking *with you?* she mouthed. She couldn't stand the way he used slang and profanity when he talked to her but spoke perfect English when he was on television. *Why the contrast?* she wondered, or maybe she was again being too picky.

"I'm not even one hundred percent up to par, and I think it's because of you."

"What do you mean because of me? What's wrong with you?"

"I'm sick . . . probably lovesick."

"Oh, shut up, Jason. I thought you were being serious. Nothing's wrong with you."

"Yes, it is. I made a doctor's appointment for next week. I haven't being feeling well."

"Your ego must be bruised."

"What ego? The one I had you destroyed. How is it that I can have a half-Brazilian chick playing Glenn Close's role from *Fatal Attraction* with me, and then I have you, who would probably hand-deliver to me another woman's pussy?"

"Afro-Brazilian," Olena toyed.

"You don't care about me. I have some of the most beautiful women in the world wanting me. Do you know who I am?"

"Yes, I know who you are, but am I supposed to worship you as if you're God? *Do you know who I am?* It sounds like you are saying that you don't understand why an average-looking woman such as myself isn't breaking her neck just to get beside you. No, I'm not Afro-Brazilian, and you probably won't catch me on any hip-hop videos, but for forty-three years old, I know I look damn good, and I'm in great shape. I mean, I could work on my abs, but hell, nobody's perfect. It's not about how the public perceives you, and it's also not about what you have, Jason. It's about who you truly are. And that's what I'm trying to figure out. Who are you? But not before I figure out who the hell I am." *Am I being unreasonable?* she sometimes wondered. Maybe a man like Jason needed to be challenged or maybe not. When they were together, his cell phone constantly vibrated with incoming calls that Olena could only imagine were from women, and what about all the times he excused himself to go to the bathroom, which for Olena was so obvious that he was returning phone calls. Better, she felt, to be the way she was toward him, which was indifferent, than to be the way they were toward him, which was desperate.

"I never said you were average. I must think you're beautiful for you to even make my list."

List? Olena mouthed, shaking her head and removing a pair of five-hundred-dollar jeans from the closet. "Maybe you really don't know who I am?" she muttered. "I don't need your damn money."

"What was that?"

"Nothing."

"What are you over there mumbling? I mean, do you realize for me to even continue calling you obviously means I'm attracted to you, and I can't get you out of my damn system?"

"How's Kitty?"

"She's fine."

"Raven?"

"Okay."

"What's the other one's name? There're so many."

"They're all doing well."

"See. That's what I don't want to be a part of—all those other women." She slid into her jeans and turned to examine her butt in the mirror to assess if hers could compete with all the young butts floating around the city. Now that she was dating Matthew—well, seeing him, since dating wasn't something he subscribed to, much like Valentine's Day—she paid attention to things that she never used to concern herself with, like fine lines and strands of gray hair. Her body would never again be that of a young woman half her age. At times, Olena contemplated plastic surgery. There was a black female doctor in Georgia, Dr. Nedra Dodds, who performed Brazilian butt lifts. Olena laughed at the name of the procedure, and the fact that black women had always been known for their large behinds, yet a black male surgeon who invented the procedure decided to call it the Brazilian butt lift. However, from a marketing standpoint, it did sound a lot better than the black butt lift or the African-American butt lift. Olena was tempted to get the fat sucked out of her stomach and placed in her behind, the same way the dancers did, so she could make her booty clap. But for them, their bodies were their business. For Olena, she would just be doing it to be vain to turn on a young man, whom she had already turned on, so she felt the surgery was unnecessary and she should avoid it. There was nothing wrong with looking good, but she didn't need instant results. Maybe she was old-fashioned or just plain scared, but she didn't want to go under the knife unless she absolutely had to.

"Who are you dating?" Jason asked. "I know you have to be seeing someone if you're not interested in me."

"Why do you know that?"

"Because I know women. So be honest. What can I say to you about seeing other men when you already know that I'm seeing other women?"

"I have a friend."

"Tell me about him."

"He's just a friend."

"Are you sleeping with him?"

"No. I'm celibate, remember?"

"I remember. I was just checking to see if you did. So tell me about him. He has to be one bad muthafucka if he's better than me."

"It's Idris Elba."

"Idris ain't got shit on me."

"Does any man have shit on you?"

"Denzel cuts it pretty damn close, but I know it's not him, because he's not leaving Pauletta."

"It's not Idris Elba, either. I wish it were. And it's of course not Denzel."

"So who is it?"

"Do you remember when you went with me to the dealership?"

"Yeah, I remember. Why?"

"Do you remember Matthew, the young man who helped me?"

"I can't remember what his name was, but I do remember that young-looking guy. Why?" He picked up on her silence. "I know it's not him. You want a car salesman over me?"

"He's not a car salesman. He's in finance."

"Same thing. That's who you want? How old is he? He looks like a kid."

"Huh?"

"How old is he?"

"Huh?"

"You heard me. He's much younger than me, isn't he?"

"Huh?"

"Say *huh* one more time, and I'm coming through the damn phone."

"He's twenty-five."

Jason began laughing uncontrollably. "And how old are you again?"

"Forty-three."

"Okay, Stella. You saw what happened after she got her groove back, didn't you? You older women are going to get enough of fooling with kids. He was just in high school."

"He wasn't just in high school. I will say that he was just in college."

"I've had my ten-year high school reunion. Has he?"

"You're young too."

"Baby, I'm a long way from twenty-five."

"Not that long."

"Yes, that long. And if you don't think you will be one of many, you're so sadly mistaken. I was his age once. The games twenty-five-year-old men play, you aren't ready for. It's a whole new vibe going on out there now. The young ones today are real free with theirs."

"What do you mean?"

"Let's just say they're overfriendly to others."

"Okay, and you're not his age now, yet you still have a slew of women, so you see, age really doesn't matter, does it? I'm sure he does have friends, as do I . . . as do you. But I just met the man not too long ago, so he has a right to."

"He's not a man. He's a boy . . . a child. And he will always have a bunch of women. The difference between him and me is that I'm willing to settle down when I find the right one, as I have in the past. I've been married before, remember? I have two kids I'm raising. I'm a grown-ass man while he still has a whole lot of play in him."

"He's just a friend."

"But you've gone out with him, haven't you?"

"I've gone out with him a few times, but mainly we just text every day," she lied.

"Text?" Jason said with continued laughter. "Baby, can't you see that he's a child. Are you reverting back? Why are you texting a boy, and you are forty-three years old? Do we text each other? No, we have adult conversation."

"Is it adult to hear about the women you sleep with?"

"You ask."

"Is it adult conversation to nag me about why I'm not in to you like you're some desperate woman?"

"Oh, so now I'm a bitch."

"And that cursing and talking to me in slang, like I'm one of your boys. It becomes rather exhausting at times. You're a nice man, and I enjoy our conversation, but I just want to have friends. We can continue this conversation another day, but right now I have to go. I have a date."

"Call me in six months when that shit's over, if it even lasts that long."

"So you don't want to talk to me anymore?"

"Why should I continue to talk to someone who's not in to me?"

"For the friendship."

"I have enough friends, remember?"

"Jason, don't be like that."

"Look, a friendship is fine, but I'm starting to feel like a phone buddy. Me? A phone buddy?"

"You love the challenge. You said so yourself."

"Yeah, but when you play a game you can't win, you will start to get frustrated, especially after you figure out maybe it's not you or your skills but rather it's the damn game. I already have more than enough games I can play, and I don't really need another one, especially one that doesn't work, so why should I try to make it work? I guess I'm young but just not young enough."

"Well, I'm sorry if you don't want to talk to me or see me anymore. I would still like to see you. I enjoy your company."

"Even though I nag you?"

"You don't nag me, Jason."

"That's what you just said."

"Okay, right now, you are nagging me. Can we move on?"

"That's what I'm about to do."

"Jason."

"What?"

"Okay, hopefully I will talk to you later."

"I'm a winner, not a loser. If you would rather deal with that little boy, go on with that. I wish you the very best of luck. And I mean that."

"I'm sure that you do. Can I work out with you tomorrow?"

"What time?"

"You like to go so early. Can we wait until eight?"

"That's fine."

She smiled as she ended the call. She knew Jason was all talk and couldn't write her off that easily, and she was glad, because even though she didn't love him, she couldn't do without his love, because she and Matthew worked better as long as she knew she had Jason. Jason made sense while Matthew made mind-blowing love.

The woman was quiet that afternoon. She had brought along her lapdog, a Yorkie named Queen B, whom she fed treats while she read her papers silently. Olena observed the woman, whose appearance seemed perfect. She wore a Kay Unger printed silk patio dress and a Loro Piana Johannesburg Panama Hat. She seemed engrossed with every page. Olena was excited that a student was finally going to pass the woman's class, but that was before she heard, "You fuckup. Two days I wasted reading this shit for you to end it this way. If you can't get it right the first time, don't waste my time." The woman stood and dropped the pile of pages into her garbage can, gathered her things, and scurried off.

Now it's Clara's turn, Olena thought as she began writing.

THIRTY-TWO

"So now I finally have your address. Maybe you really do live alone after all."

"I definitely do."

"I know you said you have a migraine, but do you feel like company if I promise not to make a lot of noise?" Olena asked Matthew as they talked over their cell phones. She was tired of having text sex; she wanted to lie beside him instead. He'd been busy with work, but nearly a week without seeing his baby face was sending Olena through more withdrawals. No, he wasn't perfect—even Matthew admitted to that—but he was young, so Olena could make concessions for some of his ways, like the distance he occasionally maintained.

"You wouldn't even know how to get here."

"I have nav. Now I can see if it works."

"You're driving a BMW. It works."

"I want to nurse you back to good health."

"I feel like shit, baby. No need for you to come all the way here. I'll be better tomorrow."

"I don't mind. Really, if you need me, I'll come."

"I know that you will baby, but I'll be okay. I'm getting ready to take my pill and crash."

"You can't just be popping by, Angel. I told you that I met someone that I really like," Matthew said to Angel just minutes after she entered his home, kicked off her flip-flops, and relaxed on the sectional in the great room.

He hadn't expected her. And while unplanned visits from Angel usually came as a pleasant surprise, he decided to let her know that they would now be a thing of the past.

She took a cigarette from the pack and a lighter from her purse. "I'm not going to smoke in here. I'll go outside on your deck."

Matthew snatched the cigarette from her hand and threw it in his garbage can. "Let me have the whole pack. You know I hate that you smoke."

"I know, but I need my cigarettes." She twirled her naturally wavy hair, which she had flat-ironed straight into a ball and clamped with a banana clip. "So now your house is off limits to me?"

"Baby, all I'm saying is next time call and let somebody know you're coming." He stood over her in his bare feet. He wore a wife beater and boxers.

"The last time I came to visit, I didn't call."

"Yes, you did."

"Yeah, when I was thirty minutes away from your house, just to make sure you were there and it wasn't a problem. I thought we were closer than that. You just met that chick."

"I met her back in January. And I don't want to mess it up before it really gets going. We're having a good time."

Angel shook her head. "You get more ass than a toilet seat. You should be worrying about Spellman dropping by instead of me."

"She doesn't even have a car."

"Never underestimate the power of a woman—one of her friends has a car, I'm sure. But, hey, if you think having me over here is going to be a problem, then I'll leave. Even though I just drove close to seven hours in mostly heavy rain, and I think there might be a tornado warning in effect, but I can certainly turn back around and try to make it home—all I can do is try. Now, if my parents should call looking for me in a few days because I never made it, tell them that I loved them."

"You're so dramatic. You know I wouldn't make you drive all the way back to South Carolina." He inched his way toward the kitchen. "I better drink a Coke and take my pill."

"And take a shower and let the water run over your head?"

"You know the routine."

"Yep. And that's because I'm your best friend and not just some chick you're fucking." She trailed behind Matthew as he trudged up the stairs holding a twenty-ounce plastic Coke bottle. He opened the French doors leading to his master bedroom, walked into his bathroom in silence, and turned on the water to his Jacuzzi bathtub.

Angel stood near the entrance to the bathroom to take in the surroundings, as if it might be the last time she would see them. She noticed a Walter Mosley novel lying on the bathroom counter. "I can't believe *you* bought a book, as if you have time to read."

"Olena bought that book for me after I told her that Walter Mosley was my favorite author. It's the little things."

"I thought you were taking a shower for your headache, baby?"

"I ran the Jacuzzi tub for you."

Angel undressed and stepped inside, sliding her body farther down in the tub so that her head was just above the water level. "So just because you met someone doesn't mean I can't get none while I'm here, right?"

"I have a migraine."

"Damn, I'm horny. Maybe you'll feel better in the morning. Wow. I know you drive her wild with your tongue." Suddenly, a somber expression appeared on Angel's face as she repositioned herself so that she was sitting straight up in the tub. She remained quiet for several minutes before Matthew broke the silence. "Is everything okay?"

"No, everything isn't okay. Seems like every guy I meet is fucked up in one way or another. Now even you're pulling away."

"I'm not pulling away. I'm still always going to be here for you. What happened, you and the cop fell out already? Just a week ago you were bragging that he was the first man to ever wash your hair and how romantic he was."

She sighed. "He was, but all that changed quickly. I almost didn't come visit you. Almost went to see that fifty-year-old to let him fuck my brains out."

Matthew shook his head. "And you give me a hard time about dating a woman who's forty-three when you're messing around with a fifty-year-old."

"Fifty-two actually, with plenty of stamina."

"He must be on the blue pill."

"I'm his damn blue pill. When he sees my naked ass, his shit stands to attention." Angel stood in the tub and reached for one of the towels that were thrown over the shower. She stepped out and walked into his closet, looking for a dress shirt to put on.

"Don't put on the tan pin-striped one. I'm wearing that one tomorrow."

"I'm just putting on one of your plain white ones. You have a million of them. How does your head feel?"

"I'm about to take this pill and crash, but I'm so hungry. I just don't feel like going downstairs and making anything."

"What do you have in your fridge? I'll make you something."

"I have some stir-fry."

Angel ran down the stairs and noticed a shadow at the front door and then the bell rang. "Are you expecting someone?" Angel shouted, as she peeked through the glass. Olena was on his porch holding a Whole Foods grocery bag.

"What did you say?" asked Matthew as he stood at the top of the stairwell.

Angel pulled the door open.

"Hello," Angel said.

"Who is that?" Matthew asked as he ran down the stairs. Olena gasped at the sight of Angel and Matthew, both practically naked and semiwet. "Olena, baby, what are you doing here?"

"Well, guess what," said Olena. "My nav works."

He noticed Olena's eyes glued on Angel. "This is Angel . . . my friend."

"Nice to meet you," Olena said.

"Thank you. And you also."

"I just wanted to bring you a few things since you said that you weren't feeling well. I'm sorry for bothering you and your *friend* Angel—your best friend that you haven't slept with since freshman year in college."

Angel gagged.

"You don't have to apologize, baby," said Matthew.

"I thought you had a migraine, and I know you would never go to Whole Foods, so I went for you." Olena forcefully pushed the bag into his bare chest. "The Naked Juice is really good. I hope that you like it."

"I'm sure that I will."

"I also bought you a chicken Caesar salad from their deli. It's made with organic chicken and organic Caesar salad dressing. Okay, well, I have to go."

"Baby, it's not at all the way it looks." Matthew reached for her hand. "Olena baby."

Olena snatched her hand away.

"No, it's not," Angel said. "We weren't doing anything. We just got out the tub." Olena's eyes exploded. "Okay, that didn't sound right. He just got out of the shower, and I got out of the tub."

"It doesn't matter. It's not my business," Olena said. "We're just friends."

"It is your business," Matthew said as he trailed after Olena as she walked out of his home. "I know I told you I had a migraine, and I said that I was going to be taking some medicine and that I would be knocked out. You decide to show your concern and come over, and you found me and Angel half naked."

"Jason was right."

"Jason was right? I thought Jason was just your friend," Matthew asked.

"He is. The same way she is—whatever way that is. I won't be coming back to your house again ever. And just lose my number, okay? Don't ever call me again."

"You're making a really big deal out of nothing. I didn't even know she was dropping by, just like I didn't know you were either. I'd never just drop in on you."

"I appreciate that, but if you did, you wouldn't find a half-naked man in my condo. Good-bye."

She smiled because she still couldn't cry and wasn't sure if tears were even appropriate. So what if he had a female visitor who he claimed was just his friend—best friend, at that. And she would be spending the night with him. Did Olena have a right to be angry—jealous maybe, but angry? After all, Matthew and she hadn't committed to each other, so what made Olena think she had the right to dictate that young man's life and whom he let spend the night at his house?

"It is what it is?" she said. "And that's all it's going to be."

"Can we talk?" Matthew asked. He'd called Olena after he was sure she had made it home. He'd given her a little time to hopefully calm down, but in actuality her wandering mind made matters worse.

"No."

"Please, baby, I want to talk."

"I asked you never to call me again."

"Yeah, right, like I was going to listen to you about that. I'm not letting you go."

"Just tell me this is she going to sleep in the same bed with you tonight?"

"No, she's gone."

"What do you mean she's gone?"

"She left."

"She drove all the way there just to leave."

"She was mad at her boyfriend, but evidently he followed her to Georgia and called her when he got into town. She loves drama. She's gone. Can I come over?"

"No. I just didn't like that whole scene and how it made me feel. Reality is starting to set in."

"I never said that I was perfect, but you're treating me like we're in a relationship."

"That's so true. I am. Thank you for reminding me that you're just my jump off."

"We're more than that."

"What are we, Matthew? Have you thought of a word to describe the kind of relationship you have with me and your other female friends? Because I'm starting to wonder whether or not you're making a whole lot of other women feel good also, and I refuse to be one of them. I'm forty-three years old, and I'm dealing with a young man who is afraid of commitment, but I'm not afraid. And I'm tired of feeling ashamed to admit that's what I'm looking for, so this is the end."

"I'm not afraid of commitment. I was in a relationship two years ago that lasted close to a year with a woman in her thirties, remember?"

"The one with the four kids?"

"Yes."

"But you told me that wasn't even a relationship and that you couldn't be with her after you asked yourself if you really wanted to have a ready-made family and your answer was no. So my question to you would be, why did you continue to string her along? Is that what you planned to do to me? Are you going to ask yourself if you could really be with a woman eighteen years your senior?"

"I never said I couldn't be with her because of her kids."

"Matthew, you never said that?"

"No, I never said that. She has beautiful daughters. She's beautiful. I'm just not ready for marriage. Not because she has kids. I've dated women with kids before."

"But, Matthew, that's not what you told me. And besides, she has four."

"I don't remember telling you that."

"You told me that, Matthew. I distinctly remember that."

"Well, if I did, I must have just said that, because if I were ready for marriage and I loved the woman, I wouldn't let the fact that she had kids stand in our way. I wasn't ready to take our relationship to the next level. She was ready for marriage, and I wasn't. That's what I should have said."

"Oh, so now it was a relationship. Before you told me it was just something that you did at the time, but nothing serious."

"Yes, it was a relationship. It was definitely a relationship, but time and my migraines became a factor, as they always do. I need peace in my relationship, and she wasn't giving me that. She's a very controlling woman . . . much like you."

"I'm not controlling."

"You are very controlling. You have to be in control at all times, which is why you have to plan everything so far in advance. You can never just let things flow."

"I may want to be in control sometimes, but with you

there's no such thing. And I think you love that woman with four kids just as much as you love Shayla and your best friend and all the other women in your life—some that I probably don't even know about."

"I do love her as a friend, and I respect her for being a single mother who went back to school and got a degree. She's raising her kids all by herself and taking care of business. More women should be like her."

"Well, I'm sorry that I don't have any kids to raise so you can respect me also."

"I'm not saying that, baby. Now who's acting young again?"

"I'm just telling you how I feel. She's so perfect, and I'm not."

"I didn't say she was so perfect. When did I ever say she was perfect? She has her faults."

"But she still wants you, doesn't she?"

"No, she doesn't still want me. She's moved on. She has a man in her life. And that's fine. I wish her nothing but happiness. But, baby, I love you. And I'm sorry that every time I turn around, I seem to fuck up, but I swear to you that the incident with Angel was innocent. I don't want you to throw away what we have. We never have to have sex again, but I don't want to lose your friendship, because you have changed my life."

"I love you too, Matthew. But I just don't think this is going to work."

"Stop being so negative."

"I'm not being negative. I'm being realistic."

"It is going to work. I don't care what you say. I know it can work."

"There you go acting like a stubborn little baby . . . like a mama's boy. You're a mama's boy, aren't you?"

"Yes, I am one, and I'm proud of it. There's nothing wrong with me loving my mother."

"Matthew, don't put words in my mouth. I never said anything was wrong with loving your mother, but I'm not going to be a mother substitute. Enjoy your life."

"See you tomorrow."

THIRTY-THREE

"**W**hy don't you like Jason, Auntie? Why would you rather have a man who had a naked woman hanging out at his house?"

"I know it sounds crazy, but that young twenty-five-year-old has got my mind. I can't explain it."

"He doesn't have your mind, Auntie. Let's be honest. We know what he has, and it's not your mind, unless your mind is between your legs. Maybe you need to let Jason bury his head down there. Do that tonight. Didn't you say you were spending the night with him?"

"Yes, I'm spending the night in a guest bedroom just so we can get up early and work out, since I stood him up this morning. I wasn't even in the mood to get out of bed. I'm depressed."

"Over Matthew? You haven't met Matthew's mother, but you've met Jason's. Jason takes you out—"

"Matthew takes me out."

"Yes, but you end up in the bed with him every time. Does Matthew take you out as much as Jason, or is it all sex?"

"Jason is a multimillionaire, so please don't compare him to Matthew. Matthew does well for himself, but I doubt if he has a whole lot of extra money lying around to use on taking me out, and besides, I don't require that. Jason likes to show off. His cars cost more than a lot of people's homes. What's spending a few hundred dollars for dinner and drinks to him?"

"Well, if Matthew's not taking you out, rest assured he is taking someone out. Let's really look at this, Auntie. Jason is on his way to pick you up so you can meet his kids. Men don't introduce women to their mother and children unless it's serious. Open your eyes and look at that fine man. Take the blinders off, because when I tell you there are so many women who would not just pay you, but kill you to be in your spot, I'm not exaggerating."

"I really don't care about all that he has or the fact that he was a professional football player. I don't want to love him just because of those things. I love Matthew for himself, and no, he's not perfect, but who is? Certainly not me? I can't explain love. Can you? All that I can say is, Matthew makes me feel alive."

"You used to tell me not to focus so much on men, but it seems like that's all you're focusing on these days. A man shouldn't make you feel more alive. Life should, in and of itself. Remember that? That's what you used to tell me. Don't you have any girlfriends you can hang out with?"

"No, I don't have any female friends, Alicia."

"Well, whatever happened to Renee?"

"I don't know, and if you ask me that one more time, I'm going to scream. Do you still keep in contact with everyone you went to high school with?"

"Quite a few people."

"Well, bravo to you. My friends must not like me very much. Look at Shelly. She moved to Arizona. Sent me an e-mail with fifty other names cc'ed, saying she was leaving her job to start a new beginning, and I haven't heard from her even though I called her several times. So her new beginning must have entailed leaving me behind."

"Why are you staring at me, beautiful?"

"You really are an attractive man." Olena watched as Jason's cheeks caved in as he smiled.

"Thank you, baby." He glanced at her while he stopped for a red light, then squeezed her hand, before raising it to his lips to kiss it. "You're looking at me like you want to say something."

"No."

"I'm just being respectful of you, beautiful. Respectful of what you're trying to do, and that's the only reason I haven't touched you. But, baby, all you have to do is say the word. Please believe that."

"I should have brought a gift."

"A gift for those spoiled brats? You are their gift. They're getting ready to meet their new momma."

"Ha . . . ha . . . ha. I thought you lived in Duluth," she asked after noticing the Alpharetta sign.

"I live in Alpharetta. I gave my mother my other house after I found one I liked better."

"So that was her Valentine's Day gift."

"Yes, a home that was appraised for two point five million dollars."

"Do your sons have everything and then some?"

"And some more. I'm sure they'll attack you with their Wii as soon as you walk through the door, and you'll be stuck playing with them for hours."

Olena studied Jason, not the Maybach he was driving. She thought of the conversation she'd had earlier with Alicia. "I wish I was there to slap some sense into you," Alicia had told her. "If you don't want him, tell him you have a niece his age who would love to be his woman, but knowing my luck he won't be into light-skinned women."

"And if he wasn't," Olena joked, "he would be one of the few black men who wasn't."

"How much money does an athlete make?" Olena said as they drove through the lavish grounds of the gated community Country Club of the South, and arrived at Jason's home on Leadenhall Street.

"It depends on the athlete, baby. I was one of the highest-paid football players in the league."

"I feel poor compared to you."

"You're not supposed to compare yourself to anyone, and I definitely don't want you making a comparison to me." He pulled into the five-car garage beside a Bentley. Her eyes raced at the luxury cars surrounding them.

"Who's watching your boys now?"

"My momma."

Olena smiled. "I get to see your mother again."

"Yep, and she loves you. Went home after our Valentine's Day dinner and told her girlfriends that I finally found a woman who wasn't a gold digger."

"And I'm really not one," Olena said as she stepped out of the car, "but I must say that I've never seen anything this beautiful in my life, and we're just in the garage."

"Then you're really in for a surprise." He opened the door and welcomed her into what she could only describe as paradise. His two terrors were more like little angels. They smiled upon introduction.

"What's with all this chucky cheesing?" Jason's mother said. "She has the same effect on y'all that she has on your daddy. Go on and tell her you want her to be your stepmom."

The smaller boy, the one not yet school age, tugged on Olena's hand. "Will you pick me up?"

"What did you say, little man?" she asked as she bent down.

"Don't fall for that trick," Jason's mother said. "Don't bend over. He's just trying to see your boobies." The older one, the six-year-old, fell on the floor in laughter. "Yeah, the little one is the Mack daddy. Thinks he's so slick. 'Will you pick me up?' Next it will be, 'Will you kiss me . . . not on the cheek but on the lips?' You gotta watch that one right there. You too big to be picked up, boy. Next year you're going into nursery school."

"Are you only three?" He nodded and stuck his thumb in his mouth, but Olena quickly removed it. "Aww, you're not too big." Olena picked him up, but struggled to hold him. "Well, maybe you are a little too big." She stumbled into the family room and toppled over near the sofa.

"That's why you need to start working out, beautiful. You can't even pick him up. I have a gym on the lower level, and we will be working out in the morning, just like we said. You need to build your arm and upper-body strength."

He gave a tour of his seven-bedroom, five-bathroom, three-level home. They ate the meal his mother prepared. And when it was time to put his boys to bed, he did so with Olena by his side. She read their favorite bedtime story, *Llama Llama Red Pajama*, to them along with Jason. Once the kids fell asleep, Jason decided it was time for Olena and him to write their own bedtime story. He stood outside of the guest bedroom and said, "Instead of sleeping in one of the guest bedrooms, how about being a guest in my bedroom?"

"No, baby. It's too soon."

He held her face and bent down to kiss her, but she drew back. "It's just a kiss. Damn it, it's just a kiss. I can't have a kiss?"

She shook her head. "Good night. We're getting up early in the morning to work out, so I need to get plenty of rest."

"Or we can stay up late and work out tonight."

"In the gym?"

"No, in my bedroom."

"Good night," she said again, this time from behind a door that was closing in his face.

"I have never had one of my own doors shut in my face. You're trying me. You really are trying me."

Before she turned off the lamp on the nightstand, she checked her phone for any text messages from Matthew. She knew he was busy this week—something about a new line crossing with his fraternity and a regional conference for his fraternity that he was going to attend in Jacksonville, Florida—but she had hoped he would at least send a sleep-tight text.

Sleep tight, baby. I miss U and can't wait until I'm in your arms again.

Matthew texted just seconds after she had turned off the light.

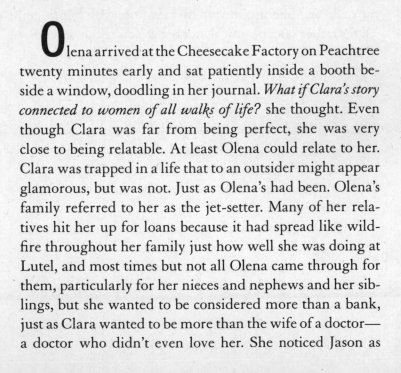

THIRTY-FOUR

Olena arrived at the Cheesecake Factory on Peachtree twenty minutes early and sat patiently inside a booth beside a window, doodling in her journal. *What if Clara's story connected to women of all walks of life?* she thought. Even though Clara was far from being perfect, she was very close to being relatable. At least Olena could relate to her. Clara was trapped in a life that to an outsider might appear glamorous, but was not. Just as Olena's had been. Olena's family referred to her as the jet-setter. Many of her relatives hit her up for loans because it had spread like wildfire throughout her family just how well she was doing at Lutel, and most times but not all Olena came through for them, particularly for her nieces and nephews and her siblings, but she wanted to be considered more than a bank, just as Clara wanted to be more than the wife of a doctor—a doctor who didn't even love her. She noticed Jason as he pulled up to valet his Rolls-Royce Phantom. The boys hopped out of the backseat. The younger one took Jason's hand while the older one played it cool in a pair of dark shades—a mini-Jason.

"You like this seat?" he asked as he stood over Olena with his two boys by his side. "Do you want to move, beautiful? I hate sitting at the back of a restaurant near the help. Where's the restroom?" Jason asked the waiter, who pointed toward the front of the restaurant. "I'll be right back, baby."

"Don't stay on the phone too long."

"Ha . . . ha . . . ha."

Jason's younger child asked Olena, "Do you want to move, baby?"

She smiled, focusing on him. "No, I don't want to move, baby." She smashed in his tiny nose with her finger. "Your father said, beautiful, not baby. You're the only baby here."

"I am not," he said with laughter.

"You are too."

"What's wrong, Junior?" she asked, recognizing the sadness in the six-year-old's eyes.

"You like him better than me because he's younger."

"That's not true. You too are both my little men."

"Watch out, sons. She may literally mean that," Jason said as he slid in the booth.

The younger boy was sitting beside Olena with his head on her shoulder.

"That was so wrong to say to them."

"You're forty-three years old," Jason said as he perused the menu.

His younger child's head rose from Olena's shoulder. "Dang, you're old. You're as old as Daddy."

"Daddy isn't anywhere near forty. I'm older than Daddy."

"Older than Daddy?" he asked in disbelief. Olena nodded. "Huh?" he gasped, covering his mouth.

"You're so cute," Olena said, smiling as she looked down at him.

"And so is that other little boy you got. He's the son you never had I guess."

"He's not the son I never had, and I don't want to talk about this in front of your boys."

"Why not? Maybe they can give you some advice, since he's closer to their age than mine."

"That was so low. He's twenty-five."

"I thought you were looking to progress, not regress. Why are you messing with an embryo?"

"An embryo?" She hated the way that sounded.

"That's what I said. What can a boy that young do for you?"

"He may be young—"

"Hold that thought. I have to go again."

"You just went."

"I have to go again."

"Now who's acting young? Just call her right here."

"I have to go."

"I'm ordering while you're gone."

"Get me the ahi tuna and the bang-bang chicken and shrimp."

"Two dinners?"

"I'm a big boy."

"You're not lying."

Jason returned to the table a few minutes later. "Well, when I was twenty-five, I had my own house and a damn good income, and guess what I was doing. Chasing as many skirts as I could, because once women saw what I had, they wanted it, and would do anything to try to get it."

"Yeah, but you were an athlete. That's a big difference."

"Maybe, but he's still living the life right now. And you're still dealing with a youngster. I know he has you running ragged. You can say what you want about me, but at least I've been honest." *Honest* to Jason meant admitting that he still had a hard time remaining faithful. When he met a woman who piqued his interest, everything seemed good in the beginning, but once he settled in with the person and knew her just as well, or maybe even better than he knew himself, then the boredom would set in. The problem for him with most women was that they told him too much. "I don't care about your past relationship and what man hurt you. It's none of my concern because I'm not him. The more you tell me about what you did in the past, the more I know what you will do in the present, because there is no better indication of future behavior than past behavior. That's why I'm still intrigued by you. Well, I was until recently."

Olena sat quietly, stroking Jason's younger son's head.

"Don't rub on my boy's head like that. I have to watch you now. You might be like Mary Kay Letourneau."

"Who?"

"Don't you remember the teacher who had a baby by her student and then went to jail and had another one somehow while she was in prison? And then she married the dude once she got out. I guess she's your role model, huh?"

"Maybe she is," Olena said, allowing him to win. She mostly picked over her food and listened to more of Jason's scolding.

"I'll be the first to admit that I'm not perfect, but at least

I'm honest. I told you that I've had a hard time remaining faithful in the past, but the only reason that I even told you those things is so you would know that it's different with you. Are you still celibate?"

"Of course I am," she said—a lie had never been spoken so easily. "Now let me ask you something: Why do you like me?"

"Why?"

"Yes, why? I know the type of women athletes go for. I don't look like those women. I'm not saying I don't look good by any means, but I don't believe I'm the type of woman you have dated in the past."

"I don't have a type. As I have told you before many times, I think you're beautiful. And what I love most of all is that you don't give a damn about who I am. You're not fazed by my status—the fact that I'm on national television every week during football season . . . the fact that I played pro ball and that I live on a ten-million-dollar estate. I love that."

"It's your home, not mine, and I want my own shit," she said, making Jason laugh because he often teased her about the fact that he had never heard her swear. "I'm sorry," she said, covering her mouth because she let the word slip out around the kids.

"Daddy says *shit* all the time," the younger boy said.

A young man armed with a digital camera anxiously approached their table. "Jason, do you mind taking a picture with me?"

"I sure do. Not to be rude, but I don't grant photo ops. I'll sign your napkin if you want but I'm not posing beside anyone I don't know. I'm trying to enjoy some lunch with my wife and kids, partner. Can I do that?"

"I'm sorry," he said, easing from the table.

"Your, *wife?*" Olena questioned.

"That's right, my wife."

"I'm not your *wife.*"

"Not yet. But you will be." Olena felt a sensual tingle shoot between her legs after Jason stared her down. "If I were to stand and pose for a picture with him, it'd be all over the Internet that he's my secret lover. You see how they did NeYo. I mean, it could be true, but you never know, and that's the same thing they would say about me—that you never know. So back to you. I would like us to start spending more quality time together—sometimes just you and me and other times you and me and the kids."

Olena took a deep sigh and said, "I'm not going to have that much free time because I've joined a writers' group." That was the second lie she had told. She hadn't even looked for a writers' group. "And I have this literary agent interested in my stuff." And there was the third lie.

"How long does a writers' workshop last? A couple hours? A few days? A week? I'm not asking for all of your time—just more of it."

"Okay, Jason. I'm sure that can be arranged, but I thought we had been spending a lot more time together recently."

"Really? You did? Maybe you have me confused with someone else. I am a young man, but I'm not the youngest one."

"No, Jason, I don't have you confused with anyone."

"I need more time," he said, tapping the face of his Breguet Swiss watch, while his two sons sat, mocking his gesture. "Tell me know if you can't bring it."

"Bring it on," his younger boy said.

"What are we going to do with you?" Olena asked.

"Marry my daddy."

"How much did he pay you to say that?"

"A hundred dollars."

"Did he?"

The boy nodded and pulled a hundred dollars from his pants pocket.

"Bribing your sons. You need to be ashamed of yourself."

"He's pulling your leg. That's his weekly allowance."

"A three-year-old gets a hundred dollars a week?"

"It's going into his bank account. So, baby, where do we go from here? I need more time. Are you willing to give it to me?"

"You have to be patient, Jason."

"What? I know you didn't pull out the P word on me. We meet in December. It's now May, and we haven't even kissed. Now, if that's not patience, what is?"

"But, in all fairness, you have friends for all of that, and what's wrong with having a friend like me who's purely platonic?"

"What is *platonic*?" Jason Jr. asked.

"She's not giving up any ass."

"Jason!" Olena said, gasping. "How can you talk to your sons like that?"

"How? These are boys I'm raising. And I've already talked to Junior about the facts of life. All I can say to you, Miss Day, is that I need more time, and I'm leaving it up to you to figure out how much you're going to give and when I'm getting it."

She checked her iPhone and saw a message from Matthew saying he was going out with the frat to celebrate someone's birthday. He told her at eight o'clock to sleep tight, and so she knew what that meant—she wouldn't be hearing from him for the remainder of the night.

"Well, how about you boys come and have a slumber party at my place tonight?"

"Do you have a Wii?" Jason Jr. asked.

"No, but I got me."

The boys' faces displayed disappointment.

"The mall is right down the street," Jason said. "I'll buy you another Wii to keep over your new mama's house, and we'll buy some pajamas too."

Olena shook her head. Like mother, like son, she was starting to see.

"I don't know, baby. I don't know what's wrong with me," Jason said as he rolled off of Olena. "I don't know what's going on."

"Maybe I don't do it for you."

"You do. Don't talk crazy. Maybe it's because the kids are in the other room. Maybe I'm out of my comfort zone. If we were back at my house . . . I don't know. In the back of my mind, I think you really don't want to do it. I know you're celibate."

She sat up, clutching the sheet against her bare chest. "It was a sign that we shouldn't be having sex. That's all."

He rolled on his back and stared at the ceiling. "In the morning . . . I always wake up hard in the morning."

Morning came, but neither Olena nor Jason did. And whether he'd woken up with an erection was anyone's guess, including hers, because by the time her eyes opened he was standing over her fully dressed, kissing her forehead.

"I have to take the boys to camp and then meet with my accountant."

"Are the boys up already?" Olena sat up in bed.

He nodded. "Don't get up. Go back to sleep, baby. I'm sorry about last night. I can't explain what happened, but it's not you. I'm very attracted to you."

"Are you sure? I know I'm not one of the exotic beauties that you're used to."

"Get up," he said, pulling her by the hand.

"You just told me to go to sleep," she whined.

"But I'm tired of hearing about all of those beauties. I want to show you something." He guided her to the mirror on her dresser. "Look at yourself. I want you to see what I see. Your skin is glowing, and you don't have any makeup on. Look how beautiful you are with no blush or lipstick, with nothing." He cupped his large hands over her breasts and squeezed. She felt something hard poking her lower back.

"Daddy, we're ready to go," Jason Jr. said as he stood behind Olena's bedroom door.

"I'm coming." he said to his son. Then he lowered his voice and said to Olena, "I wish I could have said that last night."

"Well, it was best because you know I'm not trying to be sexually active, anyway.

Olena was relaxing in her heated Jacuzzi bath, her head resting against the contoured pillow as all fifteen jets soothed most of her body. The phone was on the edge of the tub as she spoke to her niece through the speaker. "Oh, my God, Alicia, he couldn't get hard."

"Who?"

"Jason."

"You're lying."

"No, I am not. I wish I were, because I was surely going

to give him some. I was horny, and my baby was out last night doing who knows what to who knows who? So I was going to do what you said and give it to Jason to see if I could reverse this curse and leave Matthew alone. Concentrate on Jason. And he couldn't even get it up."

"Why didn't you let him eat you, Auntie? Did you try that?"

"Am I bad influence on you?"

"No. Why?"

"I have to remember you're my niece. To hear you suggest that I let a man eat me out seems weird, but okay."

Alicia laughed. "I'm thirty-one not thirteen. You could have sucked his dick. Maybe he needed foreplay. Did you all do any foreplay?"

"No."

"Well, Auntie, what do you expect? Maybe he needed to be put in the mood. I refuse to believe that Jason Nix is impotent."

"Men don't need foreplay. And I'm not saying he's impotent, because he was hard this morning."

"And did you get you some?"

"No."

"Why not?"

"Because his son was banging on the door."

"Oh, it was the Brady Bunch up in there. Well, no wonder. He's going to have to leave the kids at home next time."

"There won't be a next time. What happened was what should have happened. I would have just been using him, and that wouldn't have been right."

"Yes, it would have been right. I wanted you to give Jason some. I hope you're not going to give up."

"Yes, I think I am."

*   *   *

By midafternoon, Olena had retreated to the peaceful English gardens. The same woman was planted on her usual bench with her papers sprawled over her lap and a red pen flowing to make corrections. The woman's head shook and her nose occasionally twitched as she read through what Olena imagined was a student's English paper. At times, she let out grunts or tossed the papers in a large red vinyl and monogramméd-canvas Louis bag that Olena had eyed at the boutique but determined that for $2,940 it was too rich for even Olena's materialistic blood; she drew the line at $1,800 for purses and not a penny more.

"Come on, people. Please give me something good," the woman said as she snatched off her half-glasses. "Too much work for too little pay." She removed a pewter flask from her tote along with a matching shot cup and poured and sipped away most of the afternoon. For the most part, the woman operated in her own little world with the exception of one brief moment when she glanced toward Olena. Olena smiled until she realized either the woman was blind or she herself was invisible.

THIRTY-FIVE

It was going on two hours. Two hours at Whole Foods. Her shopping cart was nearly full as her mind wondered back to the story she was creating. It had finally leaped from her head onto the page. She was no longer interested in being the main character. She had decided that very few would care that she had lost her one true love in high school due to suicide or that the man she had hoped would replace him instead replaced her. She wasn't the only one who had cried in their lifetime. She wasn't the first, and she wouldn't be the last. Why not write a love story—one with a happy ending? Perhaps. She couldn't concentrate on the ending when she had barely gotten past the beginning. She was starting the fourth chapter, but something major was still missing.

At least when she experienced writer's block, it didn't last too long. There was something about living on Peachtree that inspired her. She loved the way everything was within walking distance and she enjoyed taking leisurely strolls. On occasion, she drove to the market because she knew she would be filling her trunk every time she went to Whole Foods, and to Lenox Square Mall and Phipps Plaza. She loved the shopping; in fact, she couldn't get enough of it. But most important, she loved stepping out into the English gardens and sitting on one of the park benches each day to write. It was there that she allowed the vibrant colors of a variety of flowers to inspire her next words, and allow her pen to let the most beautiful, unimaginable love flow. So what if life didn't always turn out that way? She was writing fiction. Writing the way she had hoped her life would turn out when she was young; writing about a character nearly half her age who found a knight her same age—writing the next *Love Jones*. Writing about two young lovers—a black woman and black man—because despite what many may have still believed, Olena knew the truth that black people knew how to love just as genuinely as anyone else, and she wanted her writing to portray that just as the movie *Love Jones* had. She hoped young women would realize after reading her story that money couldn't buy happiness and love could conquer all. She described Clara as an ordinary-looking woman whose inner beauty was extraordinary. Instead of saying she had long, wavy hair and light eyes, instead of making her so far removed from many black woman that any black woman reading would assume being beautiful meant living up to society's standard, which for so long didn't include black women and in many ways still didn't; when Olena believed there shouldn't be a standard; no one to ten scale. And maybe some would argue that was because Olena could never top it, but that was okay because Olena had the power to create characters who could top any scale. She wasn't God, but she could play God for the moment she was writing.

Olena had packed away her groceries and headed for the English garden. She sat in her usual spot and was accompanied by her usual guest—the English professor.

"Elliott, answer your damn phone. You're not too big to be dropped by your publisher. Six months behind on turning in your manuscript is unacceptable.... Elliott, thank God. I was getting ready to call the police. So you finally decide to answer your phone. What do you mean I didn't leave you any messages? I've been calling you for six months. You're not answering my calls. You're not answering the publisher's calls. . . . What more do they need to do for you, Elliott? You have to give it time. This is just your second book. Your first book did well. No, it didn't make the *New York Times* bestseller list, but so far it's sold fifty thousand copies. . . . You can't compare yourself to James Paterson. Do you know how many people would love to be in your shoes . . . ? What? The publishing company can't make Oprah select your book, Elliott. They advanced you two hundred fifty thousand dollars on a two-book deal. . . . Do you have the money, since you obviously don't have the second book." She ended the call, let out a long sigh of exasperation, and placed her BlackBerry Curve on top of a large stack of papers.

Now, Olena realized the woman was a literary agent, which for a writer was a cure to all of life's problems—the gatekeeper to the mysterious New York publishers. When Olena was conducting business in New York, she'd seen most of the large publishers' buildings, but it remained a mystery as to how someone like her could work her way inside. She'd mailed query letters to many of them in the past, only to receive the standard rejection letters, but that was so many years ago that it wasn't worth another thought. Nothing beat a failure but trying again, and she was going to keep trying.

Usually she forced herself not to stare in the woman's direction, but this time she did and realized that the woman looked familiar. "Excuse me, but did you go to Cass." The woman removed her expensive glasses and focused in on Olena's face. "Is your name Eugena Grayson and did you graduate in eighty-four?"

"Yes. Who are you?"

"My name is Olena . . . Day." The woman shook her head. "Candice Mason's cousin."

"Oh, my God, how is she doing? Of course I remember Candice, and I remember you now too. How have you been? All this time we've been sitting out here—six degrees of separation. Isn't that funny? Are you a writer?"

"I'm writing—let's put it that way."

"I'm now officially looking for new writers. I'll be in New York for a week so maybe next week you can drop me off a sample."

"Are you serious?"

"After that conversation . . . very. I just need to read the first three chapters, so work on perfecting those, because if you don't hook me in the first three, the rest doesn't matter."

"Okay. I'll have it for you by next week. It's was nice seeing you."

"And tell your cousin Candice that I said hello. Is she still fat?"

Olena was taken back by how direct Eugena was, but then she remembered Eugena was voted Class Snob. "No, she's slim now."

"Really . . . I'd pay to see that. Next week," Eugena said after gathering up her papers. "Make sure you get it right."

"That crazy woman that's always in the English Gardens is a classmate of mine, and get this—she's a literary agent."

"Really," Matthew said, sipping on wine and enjoying his salmon with asparagus and wild rice.

"She's going to read the first three chapters of my book and decide if she wants to represent me." Olena waited before she continued. Waited to see if he was listening, if he even cared. Waited for ten minutes but noticed his eyes were fixed on the television and the series *Lost*. "Can I ask you a question?"

"Sure, baby?"

"Do you care about anything that I say?"

"I care about everything that you say."

"Do you feel that I talk too much?"

"Well, you can go. Sometimes I do have to say, bring it back down, baby. Bring it back down . . . surface level."

"But I was telling you about an old high school classmate, who ironically is also a literary agent, and she's willing to read the first three chapters of my manuscript, and yet you asked not one question."

"I never ask questions?"

"No, you never ask me questions—only when you repeat what I say in a question form."

"So do you have the first three chapters ready?"

"See. You heard what I said, so you do listen."

"Yes, I listen to you all the time. I love the sound of your voice. I just don't always respond."

"But you don't ask any questions."

He shrugged. "Don't take it personal. I'm just like that—the same way with me not liking to talk on the phone. It's just who I am. I never said I was perfect, and lately it seems like I'm not good enough for you."

"What? Don't use that psychology on me."

"So she's your age?"

"Yes," Olena said with attitude.

"You say I don't ask you a lot of questions. Then, when I ask you one, you get upset by it. I didn't mean anything by the fact that she's your age. I just wanted clarification."

"It's the way emphasized *your age*. Forget it. I'm just being sensitive. Now, on to another problem. Do you know I went to Whole Foods today and spent over eight hundred dollars? That's ridiculous. I can't write that off."

"That is ridiculous, baby. But in your defense, for the past seven years you have been saving all of your income and your investments did pay off nicely."

"What I'm trying to say is, maybe I have a spending problem? I didn't have to go out and buy you this," she said as she slid the Movado watch case toward him.

"You bought me something? Why?"

She shrugged. "Because I remembered one time we were at the mall and you looked at it. You said it was nice, but said you were too cheap to spend twelve hundred dollars on a watch. But my mind said, 'Twelve hundred dollars—that's nothing.' What's wrong with me?"

"You're just so generous, baby, but I can't keep accepting gifts from you. I love them and appreciate all that you do, but it's unnecessary, really."

"I am very generous when I love someone, and I haven't loved anyone in a long time. It makes me feel good to give, so please don't take this feeling away from me."

He glanced into her hopeful eyes and saw her sincerity.

"Okay, but you do know that I don't need this watch, and if I really did need it, I would buy it myself, so let's take it back together."

"No, I want you to have it." She slid the case toward him. "Open it." He opened the case and tried the watch on. "You'll need to get a couple links taken off."

"Yeah, I can do that tomorrow. Thank you, baby. You're too good to me. I don't deserve you."

"Don't say that. It makes me think that you know something about yourself that I don't." Olena fell into a deep trance.

Matthew watched as her mind wandered, but he didn't disturb the process. "Tonight, baby, let's not make love."

Her eyes widened. "You're tired of me."

"Not at all. I just want to be with you. I want you to see that it's not all about the sex or the gifts that you love to buy me that I never ask for. Let's watch a DVD and lie in bed and just enjoy each other. I have come such a long way since we've met."

"Really? How so?"

"I used to have a very bad temper. I always had to be right. I never listened. That corny saying 'My way or the highway'—well, that really was me, but knowing you has calmed me down."

"You appreciate my unconditional love . . . that's what it is. That's what most of us strive to have: someone who will love us, regardless."

"I love you, regardless."

"Regardless of what?"

"Your age."

"I hate you for that."

He frowned. "Don't say that, baby. Don't ever say you hate me."

"You know I'm just playing."

"Still, don't ever say that, especially when I have a birth-day approaching."

"A birthday?" Matthew asked. "When is it?"

"On Sunday the fourteenth."

Later that evening, while she was in the bathroom pre-paring herself for another night lying next to her young knight, she examined her skin in the mirror, studying her pores to see if they had become more visible. She smoothed her finger over the fine lines underneath her eyes and de-vised a game plan—the hotel's spa was her best weapon for now and a wonderful prelude to a not-so-wonderful birthday. Forty-four was one year away from forty-five, which was closer to fifty. She was frightened of fifty. Not of the age, but for what she hadn't accomplished yet. For what she assumed she should have done years ago. What had happened to her house with the white picket fence and the love she was going to live inside of? What happened to her life?

As suggested on the spa's brochure, Olena had arrived thirty minutes prior to her spa appointment and spoke in a soft spa voice. Immediately, she was greeted by luxury from the crystal chandeliers to the concierge who offered her the choice between a glass of their signature wine or a grape seed antioxidant tea (of course, she selected the wine) to the classy decor that featured fifteen thousand square feet of wine extract and was named 29 Spa because it was inspired from Napa Valley and Highway 29 that ran alongside it.

There was a spa menu featuring a healthy organic en-trées, but what whet Olena's palate was the Southern fried

chicken salad—so much for her short stint as a vegetarian. Today, she deserved a break from black beans and soy
products. Today, she was planning to indulge.

After slipping into a cozy robe and sandals, she was
whisked off to one of the fourteen treatment rooms to experience over four hours of ecstasy. Her spa package included
the cream-of-the-crop facial, perfect pairing massage, and
a waterless exfoliating crush manicure and pedicure. She
was anxious to receive the perfect pairing massage, which
was highlighted as a Mondavi, the spa owner's, favorite.
The thought of two highly trained therapists utilizing a
warm grape-seed formula with natural essential oils spe-
cially blended for her individual needs and body type
elevated her mood. She relaxed on a heated water bed
outfitted with exquisite 29 linens, silk duvets and boudoir
pillows and allowed her mind to escape into Clara's world
while the warm oils were poured along meridan lines and
worked into her body by two sets of hands.

It was hard for her to concentrate on her character.
Usually, she could relate to Clara but not today. Not one
day before her birthday—one day before she would turn
forty-four. Not when Clara was just twenty-eight and settled for a man twice her age for the security of his money
and not for the comforts of true love. Yes, Clara could afford this type of treatment every week, even at the cost
of $535 for the package Olena had selected. And perhaps
Olena could too, but she wouldn't treat herself that often.
While Olena had to work hard to achieve everything she'd
earned in life. At Lutel, she had to smile on days she truly
didn't feel like it. Know the products and services her company provided better than she knew herself, which was the
precise reason she was suffering now. Even with the attention of two men and the affection she was enjoying from

one—there was still something missing that she couldn't pinpoint; something that didn't feel right, beyond the age difference. Perhaps, she had been focusing in on the wrong one. Was Matthew her surgeon and Jason her gardener? she wondered. He said that he loved her, and she said the same words back even more times. But was that love?

"Happy Birthday," Jason said. "I have your present, so when do I get to give it to you?"

"I don't know. I'm not feeling so well today." At least Jason had remembered her birthday, which was more than she could say for Matthew, who hadn't even sent her a happy birthday text.

"On your birthday you're not feeling well? You should be."

"I'm forty-four. Soon I'll be fifty. I'm not sure why I'm letting that bother me. Age never used to bother me. Maybe because the only people I meet nowadays are people who are so much younger than me."

"Do you want to go to church with me?"

"No."

"Do you know how many times you have said no to me when I've asked you to go to church?"

"Then stop asking."

"No. I'm a saint, and saints have to work on the sinners."

"You're a saint?" she said and laughed. "What church do you attend?"

"For the hundredth time, World Changers. Creflo Dollar's church. I know you've heard of it."

"Sounds familiar," she said, and then Olena's eyes bulged when she realized the reason it did was because it was also the church Matthew attended. No, she could never accept his invitation and risk the man she was in love with seeing her with the man who loved her.

"Of course, it wouldn't be like me not to personally deliver your gift and take you out to dinner."

"Can we dine somewhere not so froufrou?"

"Frou . . . frou, huh? Okay, tell me where you want to go?"

"I am really in the mood for some chicken and waffles."

"Well, I can take you to Mrs. Winners for that, and we can go through the drive-thru."

"I was thinking more along the lines of Gladys's and Ron's."

"I was going to suggest that, but I was just trying to make sure I didn't take you anywhere too froufrou."

She found it ironic that while they ate their meal at Gladys's and Ron's Chicken & Waffles that Jason presented such an expensive-looking item to her in a Kay Jewelers box. Not that there was anything wrong with Kay, but Olena knew quality. She had gone so far as to study the finer things enough to know when she was in the presence of superior quality.

"Show me the receipt for this." She couldn't stop smiling. "Don't try to outsmart me."

"What are you talking about?" he asked as he opened his wallet lying on the table and removed a Kay Jewelers receipt.

"You really did get this from Kay?" she said as she scratched her head while she eyed the receipt. "This didn't even cost six hundred dollars, and it's so beautiful."

"Will you please accept it?"

"Yes, since you didn't pay thousands for it. Not even one thousand. Five hundred dollars is like five dollars to you."

"More like five cents."

"Excuse me," she said as she cut her chicken with a knife and fork.

"Woman, you'd better pick that chicken wing up and eat it like you have some sense. I'm glad my momma isn't here, or you know you'd be in for it. I could hear her cussing you out now."

She realized something right then—realized that by trying to cut the chicken from her wing, she was more comfortable with Matthew than with Jason. Perhaps because they had shared intimate moments over and over again, or maybe to her Matthew was more down to earth than Jason, who came across almost greater than life. After all, during football season, he could be seen on FOX Sports and his new Fav five commercial that had just aired and was popular on YouTube.

When Olena was with Matthew, she didn't have to worry about fans approaching him for autographs, still, Jason didn't seem to let his fame and his fortune go to his head. True, he loved who he was, but as Olena soon learned, he also loved who she wasn't even more.

"Humor me some more," Olena said as she leaned on the table. "You could date just about anyone, so why me again?"

"Not this conversation again. You sure know how to beat a dead horse, don't you?"

"No, but seriously—and it's not like I feel that I'm not worthy, because I know I'm all that, but what is the biggest thing that you like about me. Stroke my ego for my birthday. I have one too, you know."

"I guess the fact that you're really nobody."

She frowned after replaying his statement through her mind. "I'm nobody?"

"Yeah, you're nobody, and you didn't think that I was anybody, either," he said after he wolfed down a few fried green tomatoes.

"Jason, I have to correct you because I'm definitely somebody."

"Baby, let's not get hung up on a word. I mean that you aren't famous. I don't want to date an actress or a model or a singer. I just want to be with a woman who has a stable head and who I know will always be there and love me for me and not for my money. Not just so she can say, 'Jason Nix is my baby daddy.' "

"Wasn't your wife a nobody? I'm just assuming she was by the way your mother talked about her, and your marriage didn't work."

"In my mom's mind she was a nobody as anyone who hurts her baby is. But my ex-wife is the singer Keena. She used to be somebody a few years back. I guess she's trying to make a comeback. She's ballin' out of control off my money. Has a house in LA and one in Florida."

"Keena, the singer from Detroit—that's your ex-wife?"

"Yeah."

"She did use to be all that, and she has a hit single they've been playing on the radio constantly."

"No, she doesn't have shit. She's singing vocals on Porter Washington's hit single, 'Rebound.' Yeah, everybody thinks it's hers, but it's not. It's on his new CD. Her CD hasn't even been released yet."

"He's from Detroit too. Did you know that?"

"Who? Porter Washington?"

"Yes."

"No, I didn't know where he's from. I just know that I like his music."

"And he's engaged to Winona Fairchild. I used to go to high school with her. I didn't really know her then, but we graduated in the same class and my cousin Candice knew her. Who didn't my cousin Candice know? Do you know that she's HIV-positive, and he's not. Can you believe that?"

"Who, your cousin?"

"No, my classmate."

"No, I didn't know that."

"Isn't that a trip?"

He shrugged. "That's real love, baby. That's all that is, and a lot of us won't ever truly get there."

"True," Olena said, knowing that only real love could allow for something like that, and here her shallow mind sometimes wondered if a man could love her even though she was five-nine and considered tall by a man's standard and perhaps because of that fact not as cute as the petite girls. She realized how often she allowed her mind to play tricks on her and how much time she wasted.

"Do you like your chicken and waffles?"

"I love my chicken and waffles," she said, then studied the phone as a text came in.

Jason snatched her iPhone from her hand and read the text.

Hey, baby, what R U doing? Sorry I haven't texted U today. The dealership is now open on Sundays, and it was hectic. Anyway, Enjoy the rest of Ur day.

"Can I reply?" Jason said.

"No," Olena said, snatching the phone from his grip.

"All I was going to say is today is, 'Olena's birthday, and you didn't even say happy birthday. She's out having a good time with a man who truly loves her. Have fun playing Nintendo later.'"

"He doesn't even play Nintendo."

"Aww, but I bet he does. He would never admit that to you."

She shrugged. "If he does . . . he does."

THIRTY-SIX

Olena sat on her patio with her laptop open. She had started to write but got stuck. She needed a change of scenery. Started debating with Alicia whether today would be the day she rode the train. "I have writer's block . . . and I usually write well on a plane, so short of flying somewhere, I want to see if it'll work while I ride MARTA. Outside of a cab, I haven't used public transportation since my freshman year in college. What would really be the point of this whole thing?"

"I don't know about riding MARTA, Auntie. It's all over the Internet about how that girl went off on an elderly lady on the MARTA."

Are you calling me an elderly lady?"

"No."

"So why did you bring that up?"

"Because it's MARTA, and you're thinking about riding it, and I saw on the Internet where some girl that they were calling Soulja Girl went off on an elderly lady. I can't believe you haven't seen that video. It's all over the Internet. I wouldn't ride the train if you don't have to, and you don't have to."

Olena googled *Soulja Girl Goes Off on MARTA, Atlanta,* and the first of several entries was the Youtube video. She watched the video and knew immediately, before she had watched the videotaped apology from her brother explaining that the girl was bipolar that she had to have had a mental illness. Was more appalled by many of the viewers who left cruel comments than by what the girl had done, because the girl couldn't help herself. It was obvious that she wasn't in her right mind and the fact that no one had considered that bothered Olena.

"I wish I could do something to help people. Help people who are hurting and those who don't understand them."

"Everyone can't be empathic like you, Auntie."

"I'm not all that empathic. I'm learning to be. But when it comes to matters of the mind . . . let's just say, I know what pain can do to a person." Olena thought back to her first love—back to Stanley. Didn't realize then at fifteen, what was obvious to her now, that he was manic depressive. Mental illness wasn't something discussed in the black community in the eighties, was barely discussed now. Just because a person behaved strangely didn't always mean they were on drugs and certainly didn't make them a hood rat as one of the Youtube viewers commented—sometimes it was a cry for help. If only she had heard Stanley's—she'd heard it, but if only she had known what to do back then she could have quite possibly saved a life.

"Don't ride the MARTA. Are you just trying to see if you can unblock your writer's block?" Alicia asked.

"I've read interviews where writers say they can write anywhere. Some writers say that they use digital recorders, and when they're driving, if an idea pops into their heads, they grab their recorders and dictate into them. Other writers say they can be sitting in a restaurant and overhear a conversation that sparks an idea, and they'll grab a napkin and start jotting down their thoughts or some dialogue. I don't think you always have to have the perfect setting to create a perfect setting, but I do believe sometimes you need to change your setting, so I'm going to ride the train and see if that helps, because I only have three days to get the first three chapters perfect."

A new e-mail had popped into her in-box from the Margaret Mitchell Museum as a reminder for the literary event. An author from Seattle—someone Olena had never heard of but whose novel had reached the *New York Times* bestseller list—would be speaking at the literary center and signing her latest novel, *Wrecked*. Maybe hearing from a successful author would be the inspiration she needed to polish off her first three chapters.

"Auntie, I'm tired of LA. Tired of struggling. I'm seriously considering moving to Atlanta and living with you."

"Living with who?"

"With you, Auntie."

"Not while I'm on my sabbatical you're not coming here living with me. I don't mean to be selfish, but this is my time."

"No, but when you're off of your sabbatical and you go back to work, you'll have an empty condo. I can come down there and work at one of the M•A•C stores and audition for movies that are being produced in Atlanta. I might even luck up and get in a Tyler Perry production."

"So my mortgage is twelve thousand a month. Can you pay half of that?"

"Twelve thousand dollars? Are you kiddin' me? I thought you said you borrowed against your four-oh-one-k and put nearly half down."

"I did. And my mortgage is still twelve thousand a month."

"Now, Auntie, that's a damn shame. No, I don't have six thousand dollars to pay each month. And I would hope you wouldn't make me."

Olena smiled. "I won't make you. Not before you get in one of Tyler Perry's movies, but after that and whenever you blow up, I want my money."

"After I blow up, I'll pay your condo off."

"Don't forget you said that, because I sure won't."

Olena rode the MARTA train to the Margaret Mitchell House. She sat in the front row and listened to the short, frail, unassuming author recite a chapter from her novel without so much as a glance at the page. She stood at the podium with the full attention of her audience. She stood in the place Olena hoped to one day.

"You made your first deadline. I'm impressed." Eugena attempted to take the manila envelope from Olena's grasp, but Olena wouldn't let go. "Olena, give it to me."

"If I didn't get it right, then what?"

"There is no *what*. If you didn't get it right, then I'm not interested, but, sweetie, that doesn't mean someone else won't be." She tugged at the folder. "So give it to me."

"But I believe in fate, and that's what I think this is. We went to high school together."

"Whatever you do, if you want even half a shot at me representing you, don't ever bring up our high school again.

If I'm going to represent you, it's not because you went to Cass. I barely spoke to you at Cass. And don't be offended, but I thought you were so lame back then. You dressed nice, but you were goofy to me. I loved your cousin. She was so bubbly."

"I had another adjective to use to describe her, and it too starts with a *B*."

Eugena tugged at the folder. "Get your hands off the material and let me have it." Eugena used forced and snatched the envelope away from Olena and then fell out in laughter. "Oh, maybe we're both desperate. I'm desperate to discover a new writer, and you just want an opportunity, don't you?"

"It's always been my dream to write full-time. Since my life didn't turn out exactly the way I wanted it to, I would love to be able to create characters and stories and to live vicariously through them."

"Royalty checks are what you're going to be living vicariously through. Not your fucking characters, because you'll be constantly creating new ones unless you do a series, and I am not into authors who write those, even though many have been successful with that gimmick."

Olena was nervous now, afraid to mention to her that her next book would be a series. "Are you hungry?" Eugena asked.

"Not really, but I can order an appetizer."

"I'm only in the mood for a wet lunch, anyway."

Olena sat in the passenger's seat of the Lexus LS hybrid as Eugena drove the pair to the Atlanta Fish Market on Pharr Road.

"I'm warning you—there's a big-ass copper fish in front

of this restaurant, and the first time I came here, the damn thing nearly scared me to death. I almost wet my pants."

"Really, just because of that?" Olena asked as Eugena pulled into the parking lot.

"Well, I was drunk at the time, so that may have added to it."

"You like to drink, don't you?" Olena asked as they exited the vehicle.

"I love to drink, probably as much as you love to write."

"I do love to write . . . just didn't have much time for it while I was working."

"Well, I can't say that about drinking." She stood at the door to the restaurant and held it open for Olena "When I'm working . . . when I'm not working. Some people prefer to drink eight glasses of water a day. I, on the other hand—"

"I hope you don't drink eight glasses of alcohol a day. I would like for you to live long enough to sell my manuscript."

Typical. You're only concerned with yourself, huh?" Eugena asked jokingly. They were ushered to a booth. They sat quietly while they perused the menu.

"So do you every run into anyone from high school?" asked Olena.

"I'm not looking for any of them."

"Really, from what I remember, you were quite popular."

"Popular enough to be voted class snob, so what does that tell you? What about you? Do you? The one thing I remember about you was you were so in love. Whatever happened to him?"

Olena spoon froze in midair while the gumbo dripped from the sides. "You forgot?"

"Forgot what?" Eugenia asked, and then allowed her mind to travel back. "What did I forget?"

"It was a big thing when it happened—he committed suicide."

"Oh, honey, I'm sorry. I really did forget, but now that you mention it, I do remember something like that. Did you ever marry?" Olena shook her head. "He was your one true love, wasn't he?"

"I thought . . . I'd hoped. But he managed to prove my love-conquers-all theory completely wrong." *Love could not and would not conquer all,* Olena thought. At least not for Olena. How could it when she had yet to experience real love? She couldn't think about Stanley this time; left him at his grave site today, didn't want to get too sad, because some times she realized that his suicide wasn't his fault completely. If he had known better he would have done better. If he would have known the hurt he was experiencing was only temporary and that being a teenager was also then maybe he wouldn't have blown his brains out. Maybe he would have waited for life to get better, because life did get better. . . even for Olena . . . even without Andrew.

"Well, I married a guy from high school, and we can't stand each other now, so I'm a witness that love doesn't conquer shit, because it rarely lasts."

"Who did you marry?"

"Marcus Johnson. He was a senior when we were freshmen, and he really wasn't that popular until he got to college and did real well playing basketball. He's a basketball coach at Indiana now. I couldn't live in Indiana, so we sold our house in New York after he was appointed head coach, and he went there and I came here."

"You don't miss your husband."

"Miss him? Miss him for what? After twenty years I was missing my freedom. So let's propose a toast to your manuscript. May it be everything I'm looking for and more." The two wineglasses clinked.

What if Andrew had married me? Olena wondered. *Would that had made me happy? Being Mrs. . . . .* She couldn't remember his last name and then questioned if she had ever known it, because back then she was so naive she would have allowed herself to be limited to first-name basis only. No, she wouldn't have been happy with Andrew. *Not if he didn't truly love me.* She thought about all the times she had heard a man say to her, "I love you." Only to discover they didn't mean that they were in love with her just that they loved her as they loved all of God's children as one man had said after she asked him for clarification. It seemed to Olena that two people in a relationship could never be on the same page at the exact same time. There was always one trying a lot harder, loving unconditionally . . . always one more sincere.

"What are you looking for?" Olena asked.

"A *New York Times* bestseller that's also an Oprah's Book Club selection."

"Well, I'm not sure if it's going to be all that, but it is a good read for anyone who still fantasizes about love."

"Is it a love story?"

"Yes. Why?"

"It's a damn romance novel."

"It's not a romance novel but it is a love story."

"I am only interested in sci-fi, thrillers, and mysteries. The shit like Walter Mosley and Dan Brown write. Not a fuckin' love story. I guess I should have told you that up front, but you didn't strike me as a romance writer, and besides, I was having a bad day, and I guess I forgot. I'm so sorry, sweetie."

Olena shrugged. "No big deal."

"I'll still read it. I might run into a colleague who likes that type of shit."

"Thanks."

"There's just not real money in that genre."

"I don't care about the money. Writing is my passion."

"Well, you may not care about money, but I do. I don't work for free or for books. Did you ever consider writing a mystery?"

"I have. Love is a mystery."

"That it is."

THIRTY-SEVEN

Olena checked Matthew's Myspace page almost daily, ever since she had discovered he had one. She was somewhat taken back that nearly all of his top friends, with the exception of one, were females, most in their early twenties—one was even eighteen—this coming from a man who swore he preferred older women. To his credit most of his top friends were relatives. *Hmmm.* Some were, Olena could tell after reading all of his bulletin posts. Those alone put together a story. She knew whom he was seeing and when. He was certainly dating the young lady who had sent him a Valentine's Day wish. And definitely the twenty-five-year-old who placed the comment "Enjoyed last night" under a picture of him standing on the Morehouse campus with his fraternity brothers, which was dated sometime in January shortly after Olena and he had started seeing each other, so she couldn't hold that against him.

Olena had to stop the madness, she would tell herself. She couldn't even concentrate on her novel because of thinking about him, messing around in cyberspace, and trying to figure Mr. Harper out. It was all part of her growing obsession with the young man. And when he didn't answer her phone calls or return a text in two hours, she let loose on her iPhone.

Finally, he replied.

Wow, U sent me 15 text messages in a row. I'm not going to get upset. I'm not going to say anything. But all of this just because I didn't text U right back because I went back to sleep. I can go back to sleep and I'm going back to sleep. please don't send me another text unless U have something nice to say for a change. Hope U enjoy Ur day.

Initially, she felt remorse for overreacting about his Myspace account. She even questioned what had made her spy the way she had. But then, she flipped the script. Thought about her old faithful—Jason. And so Olena decided she would do just that. Enjoy her day. Not just her day, but her week. *He isn't messing with some young girl,* she thought. She wouldn't merely pick up the phone and talk her girlfriend's ear off about how her boyfriend was doing her wrong. She was a grown woman who was dealing with Delta frequent-flier miles that had never been redeemed and so many Hilton Honors points it would take her entire lifetime to burn them, and she hadn't even considered her American Express Rewards. A weekend away wasn't something she needed to plan months in advance or budget for, because it wouldn't cost her one red cent, and even if it did, she had plenty of those too.

"Baby, I'm sorry about the other night," Jason said after calling Olena late that evening while she was perched in bed with her laptop, fleshing out some scenes in her book.

Olena stopped pecking on her keyboard to say, "Remember when you said we should do a trip?"

"Yes, beautiful."

"Well, I want to go somewhere. I feel like exploring."

"Come over here. I have something you can explore."

"Jason, I'm being serious."

"I am too."

"I want to get away for a few days."

"Where do you want to go, beautiful? Just name it. I'm game."

"How about Key West? I've never been there, but I've always wanted to go."

"I can arrange that with no problem. We can fly down to Miami and take my little boat into Key West."

"I'm not getting in a little boat."

"It's a nice little boat. You'll enjoy it."

Olena and Jason arrived at the marina. She was dressed in a new oufit, a floral dress that flowed, but hugged her figure. She felt like a princess, because Jason had a knack of knowing just what to say and how to act so she could feel as if she were sitting on a pedestal.

"You call this a little boat?" Olena asked as she climbed aboard the seventy-four-foot yacht. "This is the Love Boat."

"Mmm," Jason said as he held Olena by the waist and drew her nearer. "I like the way you said that. Does that mean we're going to make love on this boat?"

"No, wrong choice of words. I'm sorry. I'm simply pointing out how big it is."

"My boat isn't the only thing that's big."

"Oh, brother," she said as she walked into the main salon and sat on a sofa looking out at the bay.

"Why did you walk away from me?"

"I didn't want to go there."

"Go where? I can't help that I also have a big heart. I thought you could tell that from Valentine's Day."

"A big heart? Are you sure that's what you were talking about?"

"Get your mind out of the gutter, baby. Of couse that's what I meant."

She smiled from ear to ear. "I'm so excited. I have never been on a yacht before."

"Are you serious? Aww, I'm glad I'm your first. May I get a hug before we venture off into uncharted territory?"

"You're making me scared," she said as she stood and fell onto his large chest. "Thank you."

"For what?"

"Being my friend."

"Sometimes people have to get away, and I'm just glad I was able to accommodate. Now, my fair lady, if you would care to join me in the sky lounge, we can get this show on the road."

"Jason." She looked at him and sighed. Didn't want to do what she assumed Matthew had. Didn't want to tell every man who was her friend that she loved him, but in his case she really did love him, but she decided to keep that to herself. "Thank you."

"You've said that once, beautiful."

"When did I say that?"

"You were standing right there with those big, pretty

gray eyes like you were getting ready to say *I love you.* I'm standing here waiting to hear *I love you,* but instead what do I hear but thank you."

"I love this boat."

"Oh, you love the boat, but you don't love me."

"I love you too, Jason," she said as she followed him up to the sky lounge, relaxed on the built-in leather sectional couch, and watched him take his seat in the captain's chair.

"Thank you," he said as he turned to face her.

"What are you thanking me for?"

"For being here for me. I needed to get away just as much as you did. It's not always about the money. Money can buy a lot, but it can't buy everything. And you sure can't take it with you when God pulls your name."

"Tell me about it, and I don't even have near your money." Olena looked over at him and felt his somber mood. "Is everything okay, Jason?"

"It's going to be as soon as I'm in Key West with my baby."

THIRTY-EIGHT

Smiles flowed freely between Jason and Olena while they strolled along Duval Street, hand in hand. They had just grabbed a bite to eat at the Grand Café and were heading back to the Westin Resort and Marina when Jason stopped suddenly just as they passed Caroline Street. He clutched a chair with one hand and his side with the other.

"Jason, are you okay?"

"I'm fine, baby."

"No, you're not. Sit down, please." Olena helped him take a seat and stood with her hands on her hips and her eyes scouring their surroundings. "We need one of those little scooter cabs."

"Beautiful, a scooter only fits one person, and I'm too big to get on one."

"Well, baby, I'm not talking about a scooter. You know

what I mean—those electric car things that have been whizzing all around this place. That's what we need."

"I can make it back. I'm just a little tired, but I can make it back." Jason stood, took a deep breath, and sat back down. "Okay, get one of those things. I can't make it back."

"That's what I thought." She went inside the restaurant and asked for assistance with calling for transportation. She stood by the bar while she eyed Jason, whose hand covered his mouth while he appeared to be deep in thought.

Olena had managed to track down an electric Gem taxi, which took them back to Jason's yacht. He was able to make it on board and into the master stateroom.

"Maybe I can get us back. Is it hard?" she asked as she patted a cold compress over his forehead.

"Yes, beautiful, it's very hard."

"I'm talking about steering a boat, nasty man."

"That's what I was talking about too, beautiful. This is the second time that your mind went into the gutter. I think that's because you want me."

"I don't want you," she said playfully.

"I want you," he sat up in the bed and leaned toward her. He peeked under his sheet. "And by the way, it is hard."

"Baby, see, you're nasty."

"Okay, can I have some?"

"You don't even feel well."

"Tell me I can have some and watch how quickly my condition improves."

"No, baby. I want you to rest. I'm not ready to have sex."

"That's right. You're celibate. How could I forget? Or is it that you're giving it to somebody else?"

"No, it's not that. Are you going to tell me what's wrong?"

"I'm on the Love Boat and I'm lovesick."

"You're impossible. I'm going to the sky lounge, and I'm going to figure out how to maneuver this thing."

"No, baby, don't get near the controls. I don't want to die before I have my surgery."

"Surgery?" Olena stood at the door to the stateroom. "Why are you having surgery, Jason?"

He waved his hand. "It's no big deal. I'm going in for a prostatectomy next month, but before then I'm getting a second opinion and a third."

"Is it that serious? What is a prostatectomy?"

"I have cancer, beautiful, and they need to remove my prostate. But I'm not going to just accept that. I want to see all my options. Get a second opinion even a third if necessary."

Her body went limp. She wanted to show her strong side, but at that moment, she felt so weak. "Prostate cancer?"

"Yeah, baby," he said and laughed.

"It's not funny. I know it was a stupid question, but I also thought that was a cancer older men were at risk for."

He sat up in the bed and shrugged. "Evidently not, because when I had a biopsy, it confirmed the cancer. I'm at stage two. The doctor said it can start in younger men around my age, but usually there aren't any symptoms. For me there were."

"How many stages are there?"

"Four."

"So that's good if you're just at two."

"I'd rather not be at any. But I do feel some encourage-ment that it hasn't spread to the lymph nodes or any other parts of my body." He shook his head as his mind traveled. "I've always been in great shape. I exercise and eat right. I mean, I did suffer a football injury, but aside from that, I don't understand why this is happening."

The more Olena thought about Jason's surgery, the more anxious she became. She found herself hyperventi-lating, which she had never done before.

"Are you okay?"

"Yes," she said, trying to catch her breath. "I'm okay, I guess. I don't understand why you didn't tell me sooner. I'm in a state of shock, and I want to be able to say things to you that will make you feel good, but I just have so many ques-tions." She walked over to his bed and sat on the edge of it.

"I didn't want to think about it, and I still don't. I'm thirty-one years old, and I have cancer. I could die. I have two young sons, and I have you. I don't want to die. I have to live so I can take care of all of you."

Olena didn't want to cry. She wanted to stay strong for Jason. And besides, she didn't think she remembered how to, but then the tears came streaming down her face quickly. She covered her eyes and balled her palms. "You won't die. I can't lose another person I love. You won't, so don't you even think about that."

"You love me?" he asked, his eyes perked up with the slightest bit of hope that maybe things would get better between them.

"Yes, Jason, I do love you. And I know that I haven't always been around and that you've complained about me from time to time, but I want to help you get through this. I want to help you recover from this."

"But there's a chance—"

"There's a lot of chances in this life that we take, and most of them turn out well, just as this will."

"I may never be able to have an erection again."

"Sex isn't everything."

"To who? Maybe not to a celibate woman, but it means the world to me. Do you think I don't want to make love to you? Right now I can't. Honestly. I haven't had an erection in months."

"So is your illness why you would always excuse yourself and go to the bathroom?" she asked as she wiped away the tears.

"Yes."

"Baby, I had no idea."

"I know. You thought I was going to call some woman. I never thought about another woman while I was with you. I bet you weren't the same way."

"Yes, I was. I never thought about another woman while I was with you."

"Ha . . . ha . . . ha. But you thought about another man . . . a very young one."

"This isn't about him. This is about getting you back on the road to recovery."

"Well, right now I need to get us back to Miami, because I don't think you can."

"I can if you tell me how. It can't be that hard. It didn't look hard."

"Did you see it?" he said, making as if he was turning back his bedsheets.

"The yacht, silly."

"I'm scared," he said.

"I know you are, baby. But I promise you it's going to be all right. God brought me into your life for a reason. I'm going to be here for you."

"Can I buy you a nurse's uniform? That could be sexy."

"You can, if it it'll make you feel better."

"Not having cancer at all will make me feel better." She noticed the glassy look in his eyes and realized he was getting ready to cry. The one and only time she had seen a man cry was her father after he had learned his mother had passed away. Olena had been just seven years old at the time, but she would never forget that nor the way her mother had consoled him. Now it was her turn to tell Jason, "It's okay. Let it out." She held on to him firmly, didn't want to let him go. Felt his tears land on her cheeks and dance on her shoulders. " 'Thus says the Lord, I have heard your prayer. I have seen your tears; surely I will heal you.' "

Jason looked at her in amazement. "That came from the Book of Kings. I didn't know you even read the Bible."

"I don't."

"So how did you know that verse?"

"God must have placed it on my heart to give to you."

"Are you serious? You had never heard that verse before."

"Not that I can recall . . . no."

"Okay, I'm definitely keeping you around. I was keeping you around anyway, but after that, I am definitely going to. You must be my angel. Where's your cross, baby?"

"I still have it."

"I've never once seen you wear it."

"I'll wear it. I guess I need to learn how to steer this boat. Is it difficult?"

"It's not that difficult to steer it in open water. You just have to keep your eyes on the water current and the wind, but don't you worry, I'll get us back. I just need a little nap."

As Jason rested, Olena thought about life and how fragile it could sometimes be. She meant the promise she had made to Jason to watch after him. She would dedicate herself to helping him recover and belong to him entirely. *But what about Matthew?* she wondered.

THIRTY-NINE

It was Monday morning, bright and early. Six a.m. Olena and Jason had boarded the plane and were seated in the first row of first class.

"May I lay my head on your shoulder if I promise not to slobber?" Olena asked.

"Not if you promise not to slobber."

"So I have to slobber?"

"That's right. For good old times' sake," Jason said, forcing a smile that Olena knew he didn't feel like wearing. Not today. It was early and the day would be a long one, because they were flying to Houston to meet with specialists at the University of Texas Anderson Cancer Center. They were making the trip to Houston because that particular cancer center was ranked number one nationwide for cancer care. Jason had always heard the phrase "What good is money if you don't have the good health to enjoy it," but he wanted to flip that script, because his money would give him the ability to search for the best care, the best surgeons, and the best alternatives. Today, he would endure another series of tests, and Olena and he would need to stay in Houston for the entire week, and Olena would encourage that when they weren't in the hospital, they should make the best of their time. She called it their vacation, but he didn't like the reference. And they'd argue at times.

"Stop sounding like a broken record. I don't need no damn encouragement today."

"Okay," she would say. Allowing him to vent, to take his anger out on her, and not even five minutes later, he would apologize and admit to her again that he was scared.

Jason had gradually told her more about his condition and how he had discovered that he had cancer. He explained that he had become concerned the first time he discovered blood in his urine. But he waited to see if the next time he used the bathroom he saw any, and he didn't. But before long he began to urinate a lot more frequently, nearly every twenty minutes or so, and it was painful whenever he did. Then he started having a constant throbbing in his lower back. At times the throbbing crippled him, as was the case in Key West. So he had consulted his doctor, who performed a digital rectal exam. Jason's urologist had inserted his gloved finger into Jason's rectum to feel the prostate gland to see if it was enlarged. It was then that a lump had been discovered. The prostate biopsy confirmed Jason's condition. He was given an enema and an antibiotic. A biopsy needle removed ten tiny core samples of tissue from the prostate gland, and in three days he learned he was about to play the biggest game there was—life or death.

When they finally arrived at the cancer center, after a slight delay on Will Clayton Boulevard, the staff was friendly, and the wait was short. Olena went with Jason everywhere, held his hand at all times, and allowed herself to be referred to by him as his wife before any I dos were exchanged. She understood life better as a result of what Jason was experiencing. Understood how the book *Don't Sweat the Small Stuff* could be so popular after so many years. It was all small stuff. Not Jason's cancer, but so many things Olena had worried about in her past.

After all of the tests were performed, Olena and Jason checked into the tycoon suite at Hotel ZaZA, which was located in the heart of Houston's museum district, and dined privately in an elegant cabana in Urban Oasis. Olena had set aside her Hilton Honors and researched a hotel that she hoped would distract Jason from the situation each evening when they returned to the hotel. He paid for all of the expenses of the trip, but he agreed to let her handle all of the details outside of the hospital.

"Wow, the menu looks great," Olena said as she perused it. "Don't you think so?"

"Huh," Jason said, looking down at the menu, but not paying attention to any of the entrées.

"What are you going to have, baby?"

"I'm not hungry."

"You're not hungry. Since when? Now you love crab cakes, so let's order some hot and crunchy crab cakes and salt-and-pepper rock shrimp, just for starters."

"I don't want any shellfish. I need to eat healthy, remember?"

"Okay," she said, not even fazed by his anger. She couldn't let his attitude bother her; she had to put herself inside of his Berluti shoes and endure all that he dished out to her.

"Well, then how about the grilled wild salmon?"

"How about you just order what you want, and I won't order anything, because I don't know what I can and can't eat? How about that? And how about you stop acting like we're on some *Fantasy Island* retreat when my fucking life is at stake? How about that?"

She stood, and threw the menu down; she had finally had enough. She had endured his cursing, his ranting and raving, and his fits. "How about you feel sorry for yourself by yourself? If you want company, find someone else who will sit up and cry and feed into your belief that you're going to die instead of live. I know you're going to live, so I'm not going to join your pity party. I don't know about you, but this is a beautiful hotel and a lovely restaurant, and I'm going to order some food back in our suite and enjoy it by myself."

He grabbed her hand as she attempted to walk away. "Sit down. I found something on the menu that I would like to order."

"Really?" she said as she went back to her seat.

"Yes, I'm going to have the organic spinach salad and grilled wild salmon."

"I think I'll have the same," she told their waiter.

"I know I've been an asshole."

"You have. And I can't say that I blame you. I've developed some thick skin because of you, and I'm willing to take your abuse. All that I ask is that you let me enjoy my meal. You can cuss me out before dinner and even after, but please don't cuss me out during dinner."

"How about I don't cuss you out at all? How can I expect God to forgive me if I cuss out the angel He sent?"

She smiled. "Okay."

"Thank you again for being here for me. I don't know what I would do without you. Whatever happened to your friend?"

"What friend?"

"I'm not going to call him a kid. And I'm going to actually apologize for putting you down about him and giving you such a hard time. It was just my ego speaking. I don't even know him, so I didn't have any right to judge him or you. Are you still seeing him?"

"No, I'm not seeing him." She had no other choice but to lie, because this wasn't about her love for Matthew. This was about her concern for a good friend, and in his mind, he had to believe she was one hundred percent all about him.

"You are such a good friend to me. I don't know what I would do without you. My mom has to watch the boys because I don't want them seeing me this way, and I wouldn't have anyone by my side right now."

"You have other friends that I'm sure would be there for you."

"Nobody besides my mother and my sons would. Most people are only around when it's all good."

"I'm around you now, and it's still all good. I truly believe that. We're going to make it through this. I promise. Oh, I almost forgot." She pulled out her diamond cross pendant. "I meant to ask you at the airport to put this on me, but I forgot. Do you mind?" She turned her back toward him.

"Not at all," he said as he placed the pendant around her neck and kissed her shoulder. "Just in case I haven't told you this in a while, I love you. And by the way, this did come from Tiffany's."

"Baby, and I bet it cost a mint."

"Yeah, it cost a peppermint. But guess what. If you gave it back now, at this stage, it may affect me."

She gasped. "Yeah, you're going to be just fine with your manipulative self, but I love you." She turned her face toward his and kissed him on the lips.

FORTY

It was Olena's intention to see Matthew one last time. To wean herself off him so she could concentrate on getting Jason healthy again. Making sure Jason recovered meant more to her than anything—even more to her than her book. This, she believed, was her mission or higher calling. It made her want to get closer to God, brought to her a better understanding of the importance of cherishing each day and letting go of any regrets. She couldn't say that all of her problems were over. She still had issues, particularly when it came to Matthew. The love she felt for him was different from the love she had for Jason. She was in love with Matthew, and she wasn't sure if that was how it should be. For the first time in a long time, she got down on her knees and prayed to God to give her a sign as to where her heart belonged. She was still waiting for Him to show her. But with two weeks left, even if Matthew wasn't the man for her, she wanted to gradually ease herself away from him. She couldn't stop seeing him cold turkey. Every time they argued he found a way to make up with her, even with a simple text to apologize, which made her forget that anything had ever happened, and this time was no different.

They drove down I-20, took the Thornton Road exit, and turned left at the light. She noticed landmarks like Country Inn & Suites, several fast food chains, and a Team Dodge store, but once he turned down the windy road on Factory Shoals, her mind went blank.

"This is creepy," Olena said as she turned toward him, flashing a nervous smile. "I didn't come this way that one time I tried to visit you."

"It's a short cut to my subdivision." He squeezed her thigh, letting her feel his desire in the forcefulness of his touch. "I missed you. Why did you ignore my text messages and my calls for so long? Where have you been for nearly two weeks?"

She shrugged. "I wasn't in the best mood, I guess. But I am happy to see you again."

"I don't let everyone into my home, so you must be special."

"But look how long it took me to get here."

"That was by your choice, not mine."

"Let's not go back there. We know what happened when I tried to surprise you."

"Which is exactly why I say that I don't like surprises."

"Well, I promise that there'll be no more of those."

Their passion wouldn't allow them to make it any farther than the middle of the staircase, where they sat. His legs sprawled open and an erection awaited her arrival. She sat in his lap with her back facing him, and grinded her lower half. He kissed her nape and cupped her full breasts as she bounced on him. She felt bad that she was enjoying sex while Jason was lying in bed worrying about his life. She felt worse than bad. She felt selfish.

"What's wrong with me?" she said aloud. Her movements began to slow as her thighs stiffened. Then she took a moment and peered through the railings into his bare living room, trying to figure out how to say stop without offending him. She didn't want him to think she wasn't enjoying the sex, but her mind was preoccupied with her other friend. "I'm not trying for the Guinness world record, baby," she said with one last bounce. "It's okay for you to come." And he did. Just not inside of her.

He said, "It's obvious that you're not used to a young man."

She remained still in his lap as he held her in his arms, running his tongue down her spine as he leaned his chest to her back.

"Is that your family?" she asked as she stood to examine the framed pictures hanging on the wall opposite the staircase. Her heart began racing, beating uncontrollably. "Is this your family?" she repeated. She pointed at the man standing beside Matthew. "Is this your father?"

"Yeah, that's my dad." Matthew stood beside her. "And that's my mom and my little sister."

"Matthew, you said they were in their fifties."

"How do you know they're not?"

"They don't look like they're in their fifties."

"You don't look like you're in your forties."

"Matthew, how old are your parents?"

"Forty-seven and -eight."

"So you lied?" Olena said. She studied his father and realized that twenty-five years had made him more handsome. It was Andrew. Matthew's father was Andrew. The man she had known so intimately her freshman year in college. Then she looked over at Matthew and immediately saw the resemblance. Aside for the complexion, he was definitely his father's son.

She went up each step, taking in one photo after the next until she had seen all five. "You can never tell your mother you're seeing me. You can never mention me to your parents. You told me they were in their fifties. They're my age."

"No, they're not. They're three and four years older than you."

"We were in college at the same time, which means we're the same age."

Matthew shook his head. "I'm sure they were out of college when you got in."

"No, Matthew. I'm sure we were in college at the same time. That's only a four-year age difference."

"It doesn't matter, baby."

She felt light-headed, almost as if she were about to faint, as if this was another one of God's tricks. First, Jason and now this, as if He was refusing to let her have any happiness. She couldn't believe the turn of events. How feeling so wonderful could crash so suddenly. If only she had never gone to Key West, maybe she could have prolonged the inevitable, knowing that the friend she had neglected was in trouble. If only she hadn't looked up and noticed the smiling faces and stood to investigate, curious to see if his parents appeared friendly, but instead found them to be familiar.

"Don't tell your parents about me. Don't tell them anything about me. Not my name, my age, or my occupation. Let's just keep what we share between us a secret."

"So now you're ashamed of me."

"Never ashamed, but I just want my life to be as simple as it possibly can. I don't want anybody telling us that we shouldn't be together just because they might not understand."

FORTY-ONE

"If men can do it, why shouldn't women be able to?" Matthew asked. He was lying on his bed beside Olena, who was staring at the red digits from the clock, which reflected off the ceiling, thinking about how upset Olena seemed when she learned she was closer to his parents' age then she originally thought. She started to leave right then, go back to the mansions and ring on Eugena's door. Drown her sorrows away in the lounge-bar area with a few blue motherfuckers, but instead she allowed Matthew to continue his tour of his home that stopped in the bedroom. First, they showered together and then they were back in each other's arms, but this time in bed.

"Why shouldn't women be able to do what?"

"Fall in love with a younger man."

"They do, baby, all the time."

"Yes, they do, but it should be just as acceptable for a woman as it is a man, but you know it isn't."

"It's just different when the man is older. An older man can still have kids, but by a certain age a woman can't. You know that."

"So."

"So? So, baby, one day you are going to want to settle down, and you're going to want children. I can't give you that. I mean I can, but there's a time limit."

"Who knows when or if that one day will come? I'm more interested in being happy, and you make me happy. Besides, I'm not one hundred percent sold on the idea of kids any way. Just stay looking sexy for me, baby. Don't ever let yourself go. Because you know once you do, I'll have to leave you for Pam Grier."

"Pam Grier, huh? You probably would."

"If it will make you feel better, I won't mention you to my parents, at least for the time being."

She drew a deep sigh of relief. Maybe this was just fun and nothing more, but she knew it went deeper. Too deep for her to stop, even after discovering that Matthew was the child Andrew had conceived with another woman, a woman who later became his wife, around the same time that Olena and Andrew had conceived twins. Only Matthew was given life.

She glanced down at Matthew as he rested so peacefully. Pressed her hand against his chest and realized for the first time that her children would have been his age, and for the second time in twenty-five years, she shed tears.

His eyes opened as he felt her tears rain down on him. "What's wrong, baby?"

"I love you, Matthew, and I just wanted it to be right because so little has been."

"But why are you crying? Did I do or say something to hurt you again?"

"No, Matthew. It isn't you."

He sat up in the bed. "You're worried about the age difference. That's why I lied to begin with. I knew you would have a hard time accepting that my parents were only a few years older than you. This relationship is between you and me—not you, me, and my parents. Don't worry, baby. Everything will work out fine." He kissed her forehead. Simplified a complicated matter that wasn't going to change no matter how long she hid from Andrew. She had lived long enough to know that whatever was done in the dark would always come to light.

"Listen to this." He grabbed his iPod from its radio docking station and selected the track, "You Don't Know What Love Is" and allowed the all too familiar sounds of John Coltrane to play through his speakers. She was lying in Matthew's bed, but it was beginning to remind her of Andrew's, and so, when reality quickly brought Olena back down, she sighed.

"What's wrong, baby?"

Now would have been the time to tell him the truth: that he was his father's son as he already knew of course and that she had been his father's mistress, a huge detail that had taken her several months to discover—two facts that could never be erased no matter how hard they tried. And she had made attempts to wipe both from her consciousness. Pretend she had never seen the family portrait hanging on the wall. Pretend she never pried into his family history, never commented that they looked younger than their midfifties and listen to him confess that his parents were actually forty-seven and -eight, because in that case, a lie was much better than the truth. And then there was her guilt, or maybe it was more shame that now if she and Matthew made love again, she might think of his father instead of him. See his face in his son's—the good side of him—the side that once loved her. Not the side that left. Now she was afraid that Matthew would leave if he knew the truth. She didn't want to cling to him. But instead of telling him who she was, she straddled his erection and took what she wanted. Let him feel her from the inside and discover what his father already had years earlier— that she enjoyed making love.

"I'm starting to feel like you're using me for sex. Am I your boy toy?" His hands clutched her buttocks. She leaned her chest toward him and gained pleasure as she observed him taking her left breast in his mouth. She gazed at him, stroking his head as he sucked on her nipple. His eyes clenched shut.

She picked his hands up from his side and placed them back on her buttocks. She held his face as she continued to ride him. Told him how good he felt inside of her. How much she loved making love to a younger man; called him her baby—made him come inside of her.

"I need a fresh washcloth," Olena shouted from the bathroom. "I never reuse them."

It was the next morning—time for Matthew to get ready for work and Olena to do some more writing . . . this time at the library in Buckhead, for a change of scenery.

Matthew knocked on the door before entering; he always remained polite. She stood at the sink with an electric toothbrush stuck in her mouth while he lingered behind her, nibbling on her neck and squeezing her behind.

She bent over to rinse her mouth out. Used the towel

to wipe the water away and spit out a long strand of dark hair.

"What is this?" she said, yanking another strand of hair from her mouth. She examined the last thing to make contact with her face—the towel—filled with hair. "Why are long strands of hair in this towel, Matthew?"

"What? I don't know."

"It's not your hair, and it's not my hair, so whose hair is it?"

"I don't know what you're talking about." He shuffled out of the bathroom. Plopped down on the edge of the bed and ran through the channels with his remote.

She followed behind him, stood with the towel in one hand, and used her other to snatch the remote from his hand.

"You had the nerve to give me a towel some other woman used—a dirty towel. I guess those sheets weren't clean, either. I can't believe you. I thought you told me you weren't sleeping with anyone."

"I'm not."

"Stop lying, Matthew. I'm too old for all these damn games. Whose hair is that?"

"I don't know," he yelled, the rage building. He hated being questioned and, worse, hated being caught.

"You do know." Olena wasn't afraid to stay on course with the questions until every last one was answered to her satisfaction.

"One of my friends'."

"Your *friends'*?" she shook her head. "I'm so sick of hearing about your friends. Which friend?"

"You don't know her."

"Angel?"

"No."

"Who?"

"Spellman?"

"Who?"

"She goes to Spellman."

"I thought you told me you weren't into young chicks, but of course you would tell me that, since I'm not a young chick. I'm an old one. You're such a liar. I asked you who you were sleeping with before we started having sex. I asked you again the other day also, after I found Angel in your house and you said me, myself and I. So I guess Me is one of your friends, so is Myself, and so is I, huh?" He snickered. "I'm glad you can find humor in hurting me. So you're sleeping with her. I'll just call her I?"

"Yes, I'm sleeping with I."

Olena froze in position. The truth smacked her harder than the revelation that he was Andrew's son, which she could pretend wasn't true. But this she couldn't.

Her eyes scoured the room quickly. Suddenly, instead of feeling like their love den, it immediately become a crime scene. She checked the opening in the middle of the nightstand, saw a half-empty bottle of warming lubricating gel, which had never been used on her. She picked it up and threw it at him. "So this is what you use to get her ready?"

"Olena, what's wrong with you?"

"Is that what you use, you whore?" Olena snapped. Everything came crashing down. In a little more than a week, Jason was going in for surgery, and she was just as nervous as he was. Now she was starting to see she had wasted too much time on loving the wrong younger man.

Matthew sat very still, focused on the television instead of the anger steadily raging inside of him.

She snatched open the drawer to the nightstand, saw a

box of condoms with a few unused ones inside and several empty Lifestyles wrappers lying on top of his papers and more receipts. "And I know this is what you use on her because you don't bother to use those with me either. Why is that?"

"You never asked me to."

"Oh, so what are you saying? I'm not concerned with safe sex the way she is? So I guess you eat her pussy the same way you eat mine. You eat her pussy and then come to me and kiss me and eat mine too, don't you?"

He shook his head. "I don't do that with her. She doesn't like it."

Olena spit out laughter. "What woman, especially a young woman, doesn't want a man to eat her? So you mean to tell me you don't have oral sex with her at all?"

"Not in that way."

"In what way, then? She sucks on you?" He nodded. Olena held her heart. She was losing her breath and in the middle of a full-fledged panic attack. "So you mean I'm between your legs sucking on a dick that was just sucked on? I hate your ass so bad."

"You hate me?"

"That's right. You are nothing more than a fuckin' whore. And there is no telling how many other men she's fucking, and you put me in the middle of all that bullshit. Correction: My dumb ass put myself in the middle of it, because only a forty-three-year-old fool—excuse me: I'm forty-four now—so only a forty-four-year-old fool would fuck a twenty-five-year-old freak. You didn't even have the decency to admit when I asked you who you were sleeping with that there was someone else—didn't have the decency to allow me to decide if I wanted to be one of many."

"You're not one of many."

"Let me tell you something: More than one is too many."
She looked at the open nightstand drawer. Noticed credit
card receipts and investigated further. "Oh, so you don't
have time to fucking date? Well, what do you call going
to the show?" she said, throwing several movie tickets in
his face, "There you go, Mr. I Don't Have Time To Go To
A Show."

"Do you know how old those are? Half those movies
came out before I even met you."

"And I bet if I kept digging, I'd find more that came
out after we met. You never took me to the show. What?
You're ashamed to go out with me in public. Like my
niece said, if he's not spending money on you, he's spending it on somebody. I guess she knows what she's talking
about."

"Are you on drugs? We go out all the time."

"We go out to eat on occasion. And who pays for it?"

"Sometimes I do. Sometimes you do."

"Most times I do."

"I didn't ask you to pay."

"You didn't ask me not to, either. You just say *Thank
you, baby.* Let's see where you take her to eat after the
show."

"Why are you doing this to yourself? You are blowing
this way out of proportion."

"You gave me a used towel to wash with. I'm not blowing shit out of proportion."

Olena went to the matching nightstand, which was
across the room and closer to the bathroom. She opened
the drawer and pulled out another handful of credit card
receipts and movie tickets. "So much for your migraines.
Now I see what you were really doing all of those times
that you sent me text messages saying you were getting

ready to go to bed because you didn't feel well. Well, look here," she said, retrieving a gift bag.

Matthew stood, because she was overstepping her boundaries, and it was time for him to stop her.

"This wouldn't happen to be a Valentine's Day card given to a man who doesn't believe in valentines, would it? Let's see what it says:

Valentine, The Lovin' Is Good. It just doesn't get any better than this—our "grateful we've got it," sweet, everyday bliss.

We've got the real thing, and I have to confess—when it comes to good lovin', baby, yours is the best. Happy Valentine's Day.

She took the card and slapped him in the face with it.

"Olena, stop." He snatched the gift bag from her hand and held both of her arms firmly. "Stop acting like one of those possessive young girls."

"Why? You must like it?"

"No, I don't like this at all."

"You could have been honest." She freed her arms from his grip.

"You're right. I could have been."

"So why weren't you?"

"You didn't want to hear that. I know you, and I know you wouldn't have been able to handle it, and . . . I was thinking about myself."

"Your cake and ice cream with the cherries on top."

"Yeah, you're right."

She gritted her teeth. She had never been the violent type, but she wanted to clench her hands into fists and beat him all over. He wasn't Matthew. He was Andrew in the new millennium. "Déjà fuckin' vu," a song came into her consciousness: Lauryn Hill's, "Nothing Even Matters."

"It doesn't matter," she said.

"What?"

"Nothing even matters at all."

"I don't matter?" he asked as he watched her storm out the room. He walked to the staircase as she toppled down it. "I don't fuckin' matter?"

"Nothing!" she shouted.

"How are you going to get out?" he asked as he stood at the door leading from the garage to his laundry room.

"Either you're going to open the garage door, or I'm going to crash through it." She shrugged. "Either way . . . doesn't matter to me. Do you know why? Because nothing even matters to me."

"I'd like to see that." He leaned on the doorframe with his folded arms. She climbed into the car, sat behind the wheel, started the engine, pressed her foot on the gas, and proceeded to back out.

She stuck her head out the car window. "I have so much shit on my mind. You have no idea," she said as she revved the gas. "But if you want to test me, come on."

"This woman has lost her mind." He pressed the garage door opener when her bumper touched the door. "What the fuck is wrong with you? Do you want to ruin your car and my garage door?"

Her car tumbled out while the door was still in the process of rising. She backed out of the driveway, let her top down, and selected, "Nothing Even Matters," from her iPod playlist. She snapped her fingers as she looked over at him. "Geico, baby, so nothing even matters."

She sped down Bankwell Close Street with the music blasting.

She knew it. Wasn't surprised at all that he had someone else—someone younger. Just like his best friend was probably another one of his sex partners. She'd fallen for his lies long enough. She was half Olena's age—still in college—someone who believed those silly little cards could change a man's heart. Cards women displayed proudly while men tossed them in a drawer, hidden away.

"Silly little college girl!" Olena exclaimed. "You have no idea." Or was Olena the one who still had no idea. She'd bought Andrew cards like those when she was in college. Only she had always selected the ones that were blank on the inside so she could express her own feelings instead of relying on someone else's words that could merely come close to her emotions, but couldn't possibly describe how much she loved him. But in the end not a card in the world could save their relationship.

"I'll be damned if I go through another heartbreak. Like father, like son."

The ringing phone cut into Lauryn Hill's song. It was Matthew. Olena thought about answering, reached toward the radio controls to pick it up, but instead, turned up her music.

" 'Nothing even matters to me . . . nothing . . . but you,' " she sang. " 'But you.' " She repeated, " 'Nothing but you.' " She checked for tears, but there wasn't any evidence of them. " 'Maybe nothing really does matter . . . not even him.' "

FORTY-TWO

"Olena, what are you doing?"

"Sleeping. Who is this?"

Olena slid off the silk eye pillow and sat up in bed.

"It's Eugena. I take back everything I ever said about love stories. Yours will be the first one that I'll represent, because like you said, love is a mystery, and this one certainly is and so much more. I can't begin to tell you how much I love what you have written. I have to know where Clara disappeared to. Did she leave on her own, or was she forced to go, or, worse, is she dead? I need more chapters ASAP. Is the book finished?"

"No. You only asked for three chapters."

"Well, what the hell are you waiting for? How many more chapters do you have?"

"Six in rough-draft format."

"Well, give those to me."

"I have to edit and type them first. And right now is not a good time for me."

"Damn, Olena. You should have already had them typed."

"You told me you weren't interested in a love story, so I sort of put everything on the back burner, and then some more important things came up."

"You stopped writing just because of something I said. What the hell do I know? I'm two drinks away from being an alcoholic, and just because I never experienced real love, I was too afraid to read about it, but your story is quite nice and it provides more depth than I thought love stories would."

"So what made you read it in the first place?"

"Well, as fate would have it, I grabbed your envelope instead of the one I meant to take to my hairdresser, and while I was under the dryer, I decided to read the first page just out of curiosity. When I finished I passed it on to the woman sitting beside me, and she had the same reaction. You said so much in thirty pages, it was unbelievable. I have to represent you. It would be an honor."

"Are you serious, or are you drunk?"

"Both. But I'm sober enough to know what I'm saying."

"Well, I don't know what to say other than thank you."

"No. Thank you. Now get to work. I'll see you next week."

"Next week. I'm not sure if I can do all of that in a week."

"Opportunity sometimes knocks only once, darling. If you want it bad enough, you will. And next time you can come to my condo, because we have business to discuss."

*   *   *

Olena was sitting in Eugena's living room. She wasn't sure how to tell her that she hadn't been writing and had no more material to give her. In a few days, Jason was going into the hospital for surgery. He had moved into her condominium because he wanted to recover somewhere away from his home, so when he returned to his home he wouldn't have to think about his illness. His sons were staying with his mother.

"So you know what that means, don't you?" he asked Olena. "We're selling this place."

"And where will I live?"

"With me, where you belong."

Jason hadn't moved in yet, but he had stayed over in her condo for a couple days, and she was noticing her mood change. She wasn't sure what to say to him. If she talked about the cancer, he became angry, and if she didn't, he took it as if she didn't care. He cursed at her for going on the American Cancer Society Web site, but then asked what she had learned.

"Will I ever have an erection again?"

"Of course."

He inched toward the computer. "What does it say about that?"

"Don't worry about it now. But the odds are more in your favor than not."

"Stop trying to make me feel better and state some facts."

"I don't care about a damn erection. I care about you."

"But I want to make love to you. I want to show you that I'm a man."

"When I look at you, I see a man. Sticking your penis

inside of me won't make you any more or any less of one. Don't worry. I will be here to help you recover, and everything will be fine."

"Olena, snap out of it," Eugena said. "I asked about the chapters. Do you have them ready?"

She shook her head.

"Listen, Olena, I only represent clients I honestly believe in. I already know which publishing houses will be interested in picking you up. Now will this book go into a bidding war? I'm not promising all of that. Is it going to be on the big screen? Who knows? But will I get a two-book deal for you and a decent advance? Yes, those two things I can commit to."

Olena sighed. "I'm willing to give it a shot if you are."

"What's wrong with you today? You don't seem your same bubbly self."

"Eugena, I have to get this off my chest, but can I run to Starbucks first?"

"What? No, Olena. You don't need to drink Starbucks just to tell me what's wrong. Are you addicted to that shit?"

"No, but I'm craving a grande café mocha."

"I can make you a cup of coffee and stir some chocolate syrup in it, and it will taste just as good."

Eugena walked into her kitchen to prepare the coffee. Olena followed behind her.

"Starbucks is right down the street, and it will only take a minute. Right now I need what I need."

"I can make you some cappuccino, and it will only take a minute. So please tell me what your problem is."

"I'm in love with a younger man."

"I know that's not what you needed coffee to tell me. Big deal. That's happening more and more these days. I can't even pick up the newspaper without reading an article or log on to the Internet without seeing a headline about cougars."

"But my story isn't the typical one. Just when I got past the eighteen-year age difference—"

"Wow, now that's quite a gap. I know he makes you very happy," Eugena said with a wink. "I can't even imagine."

"This isn't all about the sex, but yes, he did make me *very* happy—in and out of bed."

"So what's the problem?"

"I don't think you're ready for this. I need my coffee." Olena took a few sips and nodded. "Not bad." They returned to the living room.

"I'm waiting."

"I was in love with a man named Andrew during my freshman year in college. He got married right after he graduated from college and his fiancée was pregnant at the time."

"What does he have to do with the man you met?"

"The young man I met is *eighteen* years my junior."

"Yes, what does your college boyfriend have to do with him?"

"What does Andrew have to do with the young man I meet who is eighteen years my junior?"

"Is this a quiz? If so, I'm waiting for the answer."

"Matthew is Andrew's son."

"Who is Matthew?"

"He's the young man that I'm in love with."

Eugena's mouth fell open. "Are you telling me that you fell in love with the son of one of your ex-boyfriends from college?"

"Yes . . . and I'm also in love with another younger man who is thirteen years my junior, but I didn't realize I was in love with him until I found out he had cancer and he could die."

"And all you needed was a cup of coffee." Eugena walked to the kitchen and took a bottle of wine from her cabinet, "No, wait. This isn't strong enough either." She removed a bottle of Austin Nichols Wild Turkey bourbon and poured two glasses. She returned to the living room and took the cup of coffee from Olena's hand, replacing it with the whiskey.

Olena took one sip. "Damn." She shook her head. "Who needs Starbucks?"

"I reserve that for moments like this. There's nothing you can do with the young man besides chalk it up as having had good sex with the father and his son. As for the other one with cancer, what kind of cancer is it?"

"Prostate?"

"At thirty-one?" Eugenia's face signaled concern. "That seems so unusual for someone his age."

"That's what I thought, but the more research I do online, the more I find that the prognosis for recovery is good. There is a high probability, though, that he could be impotent—if not permanently at least for a while."

Eugena downed her first drink and returned to the kitchen to retrieve the bottle. She sat across from Olena and refilled both of their glasses. "The younger one you have to give up. Scratch him off. Nothing can be done there."

"I can't give him up. I can't leave him alone. I know it's crazy, but I can't."

"But what about when you finally meet his parents, if it were to ever get that serious."

"It already is that serious, but I told him that I don't want his parents to know about us."

"So he knows you dated his father?"

"Of course he doesn't know. Are you kidding me? No, he would not go for that. Even if I wasn't who I am, I still wouldn't want to meet his parents, because we're in the same age group, and that's embarrassing."

"But he's grown up."

"My nephew is grown up, and I would smack the shit out of him if he brought some—"

"Ah, ah, ah." Eugena raised a finger and stopped Olena in midsentence. "Don't talk about our age group. You mean you would discourage your nephew from dating an older woman even though you yourself are dating a younger man."

"I don't know, Eugena. I feel so lost, and at forty-four I really shouldn't feel this way."

"Let's look at the bright side. This could make one hell of a book."

"Spoken like a true literary agent."

"I don't mean to come across as insensitive, but I have far too many clients with personal problems, and I'm not about to sign up another one. Is this issue that you have with your younger men going to prevent you from finishing this book?"

"It shouldn't."

"Shouldn't? Not exactly the response I was looking for. From the time you sign the publishing contract, you're going to have about six months to finish the book."

"Get me the contract first."

"I'm not worried about that. If I say it's good, it's good. I'm just making sure that you're okay."

"I'm fine. Couldn't be better."

"Now you're lying. Don't ever lie—at least not to me. I know we don't really know each other, and we're really complete opposites. But I love the book you're writing, and I'm somewhat surprised, considering the genre, so I'm actually more excited than I would be if it were in the standard genres I represent. It's sexy and mysterious, and it makes me want to consider love again. And you achieved all of that in thirty pages, so I can't even imagine what more you have in store. So now I'll ask you again: Are you okay?"

Olena smiled. "Yes, I am."

"So when can you get me the rest?"

"Can we shoot for a month? Just let my friend get through his surgery, and give me a few weeks to concentrate solely on him. After that, I should be able to free up a little time for myself."

She made certain not to mention her friend's name to anyone when discussing his illness, not even to Alicia, because he didn't want anyone to know what he was going through. Not even the network to whom he had written requesting a six-month personal leave of absence.

"You can have two. I know that what your friend is going through is very trying. I lost my father to prostate cancer."

"He died? Why did you have to tell me that? I'm sorry for your loss."

"It's been ten years, but I know what kind of battle your friend will be facing, and it's your job to keep him fighting."

FORTY-THREE

It was August now and time had flown, which wasn't a good thing. Only four months of her sabbatical remained unless she decided to place herself on permanent leave—unpaid. The discovery of Jason's illness had deflated Olena. Why couldn't Jason be one of her characters so she could fix him as easily as cutting away the illness in Word and pasting in the cure all in the same paragraph? Why couldn't she play God this time for real? Instead of playing God, she prayed for Him to watch over her dear friend. Her lack of energy mirrored Jason's on some days. She was trying to get her spirits back up, trying to continue writing and focus on life, but it was hard. Some of the things and even some of the people who used to make her smile were starting to disappoint—mainly Matthew.

Olena had done it again: accepted another one of Matthew's apologies—an admission that he was young and in all fairness had been honest from the very beginning that he wasn't looking for a commitment and that she had always known that he had other female friends. Yes, he had lied about having sex with anyone else, but only because he was too afraid if he came clean with her, she would wipe the slate clean of him. Now she had somehow allowed him to convince her to go to one of his frat brothers' housewarmings. Being away from Jason for a few hours wasn't difficult, because he was at his mom's, spending time with his boys before his operation.

"It's a step in the right direction, because it proves I'm not ashamed of you," Matthew had said about his party invitation.

Olena's back straightened as Matthew drove through the manned gatehouse at Sugarloaf Country Club. Her eyes danced between mansions until finally settling on the one at Carmichael Place.

"Who lives here, honey? What's your frat brother's name? He must really be doing well. Is he your age?" Olena asked as Matthew pulled his seven series BMW into the circular drive and parked behind a long line of expensive cars.

"No. It's Andrew Harper—my dad."

"Your who? I thought you said your frat brother was having a housewarming."

"Well, my dad is also my frat brother."

"Oh, no. Take me home right now."

"It's time for you to meet my parents. I want you to see that I'm serious about us and that I don't want to keep you hidden. I'm not ashamed of you, because there's nothing to be ashamed of. It's my life, and my parents understand that I'm an adult and capable of making my own decisions."

"I'm not ready to meet your parents, Matthew. I can't . . . trust me."

"You'll never be ready. And it would be so rude if you didn't come to their housewarming."

"No, it wouldn't. Don't use your psychology on me." Olena eyed the large brick home with stucco trim and at least a dozen cars in the circular drive.

"I see my uncle Rick is here with his family and my cousins from Monroe. They didn't think they were going to make it. Perfect. You can meet mostly all of my relatives, even my grandparents on my father's side. Don't be nervous, baby." He leaned over and kissed her. "My parents are very cool."

"They're not that cool. Not when they find out who I am."

"Who you are?"

"My age, I mean."

He nodded. "They already know you're thirty-two. I mean thirty-three," he said with a wink.

"Matthew, did you tell them I was thirty-three?"

"No. I told them you were twenty-three. You can't be older than me, or my mother would kill you."

"Take me back home."

He laughed. "Your age never came up. Come on, baby. You look beautiful . . . and *young*, because I know that's the one word that you want to hear. It will be fine, I promise."

"It won't be fine, Matthew."

"What's wrong? They won't even think to ask your age. Trust me."

"*Trust me.* I can't walk through those doors."

"Yes, you can. It's really no big deal. Come on." He snatched the keys from the ignition. Left the car with

Olena inside and stood in front of it, gesturing for her to join him.

She heaved one long and deep sigh, then remembered the last time she had seen Andrew in the yard of Howard University. Recalled the aloof manner in which he breezed past her without exchanging any words. Not even a glance in her direction, as if she were a stranger who had not even shared a minute alone with him. She had changed, and so had he. Maybe he wouldn't recognize her. It was possible. Anything was. Besides, in some ways she wanted to stare into the eyes of the man she had once loved—the man who left her. She wanted to study the woman who was better than her, and who had what Olena could never capture— Andrew's heart.

"Nothing even matters," Olena said and exhaled. She climbed out of the car and stood under the arched entrance of the covered front porch with Matthew, holding hands as they waited for someone to come to the door.

"You don't have a key," she whispered.

"Not yet, baby. They just moved in."

She heard someone at the door, so she prepared her signature smile, and as the door opened, she prayed that it wouldn't be his father on the other side.

"It's about time you made it," Matthew's sister, Rhonda, said. "This must be your friend."

"My girlfriend."

"Your who?" Rhonda said excitedly. "I am so honored to finally meet the woman he doesn't mind labeling. Please come join us and allow me to introduce you to our entire family as Matthew's girlfriend."

Olena whispered into Matthew's ear. "I'm too old to be someone's girlfriend."

"She doesn't know that."

"What don't I know, Matthew?" Rhonda asked as she turned back and eyed the pair suspiciously.

"Nothing."

"Mom," Rhonda said as she took Olena by the hand and led her into the kitchen. "I want you to meet Matthew's girlfriend."

"Matthew's what?" his mother said, nearly choking on the wine she was sipping.

"I'm sorry. He so rudely forget to tell me your name."

"Lena," Olena said.

"Lena," Rhonda said.

"Olena," Matthew corrected his sister.

"She said Lena."

"She didn't say Lena. Her name is Olena. It's pronounced O-Lay-Na."

"She said Lena, but okay, Mom, please meet O-lay-na, Matthew's girlfriend. Where's Dad?"

"He's in the back grilling with your uncle. It's very nice to meet you, Olena. I wish that I could say I've heard so much about you, but I haven't heard one word for some reason." Matthew's mother stared him down. "My son has always been very private."

"Mom, you can talk to Olena later. I want to finish the introductions." Rhonda tugged Olena's arm.

Olena felt her head begin to spin as she saw Andrew through the large picture window standing beside the grill wearing a chef's hat and a big smile. "May I use your restroom?"

"You must be nervous. It seems like you would've been more nervous to meet my mom than my dad." Olena could feel herself perspiring. "The bathroom is at the end of the hall. I'll be right here, waiting for Matthew's girlfriend to return."

Olena felt as if it were the green mile she was walking. She wanted to open the bathroom door and lock herself inside. No, this wasn't happening. No, she wasn't in
Andrew's home, surrounded by his family and being introduced as his son's girlfriend. She laughed as she stared
in the mirror—with a sound of wickedness and a feeling
of confusion. Her focus shifted toward the small bathroom
window as she wondered if she could squeeze through and
escape to freedom.

She heard a knock on the door.

"Are you okay, baby?" Matthew asked. "My sister ran
out and told my father she was getting ready to introduce
him to my girlfriend. Sorry she's making such a big deal
about this. But in a way I'm glad, because maybe you'll
believe me when I say that I love you and that you are very
special."

"I'm okay," Olena said, unlocking the door and finally
removing herself. "I'm very nervous."

"Why? The worst part is over. You met my mother
and passed her test. She said you seemed sweet and that
you were beautiful. So you know if Mom thinks that, Dad
will only have good things to say. And don't worry. I'll introduce you to him. I know my sister can sometimes act
rather juvenile, but only around family and friends. She's
actually a very intelligent woman who loves teaching, but
she hates living in Kansas."

Olena walked through small patches of Matthew's relatives and friends and stopped alongside Matthew for the
introductions, but she couldn't gather up enough energy
to even flash her signature smile. All she could do was
focus on Matthew's father, who was coming into view. She
walked through the French doors leading to the spacious
covered porch and deck, but lingered on the porch near the

fireplace as Matthew approached his father without her. Andrew glanced back at Olena, using his hand to block the sun from his view. Then he signaled to Olena to come join them.

She trod through the beautifully landscaped backyard and stood in front of the man who had broken her heart and prayed he wouldn't recognize her.

"Dad, this is Olena. Olena, this is my father, Mr. Harper."

Matthew's father eyes fell off of Olena and back toward the barbecue.

"Nice to finally meet you. My son has told me a lot about you, and I just wanted to finally put the name to a face."

Olena was shocked. "You've told your dad about me, but not your mom?"

"Well, you know," Andrew said as he turned over a slab of ribs that were grilling, "there are certain things a son can tell his dad that he can't tell his mom, like the age difference. And nowadays it's really no big deal. Son, I need some more barbecue sauce and a few more slabs, but make sure you get the ones that your mom marinated overnight."

He waited for Matthew to enter the home, and then waited for his brother to relax with his beer on the deck, leaving him alone with Olena.

"It's a small . . . small world. Don't you think?"

"I've heard it described that way many times," Olena said.

He grinned. "You knew who he was, didn't you? You knew that was my son, didn't you? What did you do, hire a private investigator to hunt me down? How long have you been stalking us?"

"Are you serious? You think that I knew Matthew was your son? I found out after I fell in love with him."

"Fell in love with him? Until my son said your name, I had forgotten it. So I asked him to bring you here so I could tell you nicely to leave my son alone. He will not settle for his father's leftovers."

She tried to catch her breath; she held her chest when she felt like she was going to lose something more than her mind. The anger raged inside of her. He had been too cool while he delivered his blows, as if she were nothing and had always been nothing.

"You never loved me, did you?"

"That's right. So now what? You want to try to make my son love you since I never did? Who's going to tell him, you or me?"

Matthew returned with a jar of homemade barbecue sauce. "Mom said you have the last of the ribs."

"Matthew, I can't stay for dinner. I have to go," Olena said.

"Why? What's wrong?"

"I'm just not feeling well."

Matthew looked down at Olena and noticed how glassy her eyes were becoming. He knew she was seconds away from ruining her makeup.

"Just like that you're not feeling well?"

"I'm very dizzy. Please take me home, or I'll call a cab."

"No need to call a cab. My son will take you home."

Matthew took her by the hand, then led her to the driveway and back to his car without reentering his parents' home.

"I'm listening," Matthew said while he drove south on Interstate 85. "I've given you time, but now I need to know.

Are you really not feeling well or did my father say something to upset you?"

"You told him how old I am?"

"I'm very close to my dad, and I can talk to him about everything. My mom still thinks of me as her baby."

"And do you honestly think that your dad didn't tell your mom?"

"Trust me, if he had told my mom, you wouldn't have made it out of the kitchen."

Olena shook her head as she turned to face the window, riding the rest of the way in silence as she pretended to take interest in the billboards. She understood how ridiculous loving a younger man was, particularly one that young. He hadn't even reached thirty. He was at the age where hanging out and sleeping with as many women as he could was still of interest. She was much too old for him. Even if he wasn't Andrew's son, it still wasn't something that would work, or so she tried to convince her mind as they traveled along the interstate. She was trying to figure out how to tell him the truth—tell him something he wasn't prepared to hear and she wasn't certain he could handle. She couldn't. She wouldn't. She would just disappear like the character from the movie *The Vanishings* and eventually he would move on, perhaps even sooner than Olena imagined.

She had two days to pull herself together, to keep a strong face for Jason and make sure she proved to him that the saying *Love can conquer all* was much more than a cliché.

Matthew turned into the driveway to the Mansions, waving off the valet.

"Can I come upstairs so we can talk and I can find out what's really bothering you?"

"No, Matthew, you can't."

"But you left my parents' house so abruptly, and I don't get it. I knew you were nervous, but you seemed to be holding up. What changed so suddenly?"

"The truth."

"What truth?"

"That I am in love with a younger man, but that younger man isn't you."

"It isn't me?"

She shook her head. "No, it isn't."

"Who is it?"

"That doesn't really matter, now, does it?"

"So you discovered that while you were at my parents' home, because that's when your entire demeanor changed?"

"No, actually, I realized it on the ride back from your parents' home." She had three choices: she could say nothing at all, but knowing Matthew, she believed he wouldn't let it rest; she could tell him that she was in love with Jason, which she had discovered after learning that he could die; and last but certainly not least, she could tell him about her relationship with his father.

"Do you really want the truth, Matthew?"

"Yes."

"Okay, then I'm going to give it to you." She closed her eyes and blurted it, "I went to college with your father. I was a freshman when he was a senior, and for my entire freshman year, I was with him."

"What do you mean when you say that you were with him?"

"Your father and I were lovers at one time. I think we loved each other. I know that I loved him."

"Lovers? That's impossible. My father and mother were high school sweethearts."

"I realize that. But your mother didn't go to Howard."

"She went there for medical school."

"Right, but she wasn't there during my freshman year. I didn't know your dad had a girlfriend. We never discussed any of that." Matthew sat silently with his face tight. She saw the disgust. "I'm sorry, Matthew. I didn't know who your father was until the other day when I saw those photos."

"So why didn't you tell me then and save me the embarrassment of taking you to meet my folks?" He shook his head as the reality of their situation became clear. "So you fucked my father is basically what you're saying?"

Her eyes closed as she braced herself to take the wrath of his displaced anger. He stepped from the car and walked around to her car door to hold it open for her.

"Well, I can't say you're not a gentleman," Olena said as she stepped from the car. "I don't want you to hate me."

"I don't hate you. I could never hate you. But I don't see how I can love a woman who used to be in love with my father."

She walked not with her head down, but not high, either. And to think, she had left out the part that she had gotten pregnant with twins by Andrew. That would have been too much for even a sane person to handle.

Olena waited for the elevator. The best way for her to put the past behind her was to pretend Matthew didn't exist, to think about all the things that were occurring right then and in the near future and to plan ahead. Jason was her first priority and then the book. Matthew flashed back into her consciousness for longer than she could bear. She loved him, and why was that so wrong? She shook the nonsense from her head. She knew nothing could be done with it—not one thing at all besides moving on.

Olena and Jason would fly back to Houston the first thing in the morning, and she would stay with him in his private hospital room for four days after surgery. From there, they would spend another week at Hotel ZaZa and then fly back home.

Olena checked the messages on her cell phone, which she had had turned off for most of the day. There were two new messages, and one new message that had dropped in while she was listening to the other two.

"Olena, this is Eugena, dear. I don't want to come across as insensitive. Truly, I don't. But when do you think you can put an outline together and have the first one hundred pages for me? I think I have a publisher interested in your manuscript, but I'm trying to get you the best advance, so I am going to parlay this thing into an auction. Drop me a line. Let me know where your mind is and how your friend is doing. I do have him in my prayers."

"Beautiful, this is Jason. Not that I have to remind you about tomorrow, but instead of meeting me at the airport, can you come over to my mom's? She wants to see you and give you something before we fly out."

The new message that had just been delivered was from Matthew.

"Olena, I was driving home, and I realized I can't live without you. I called my father and told him the same thing, and there's no need for me to repeat what he or my mother said, because this is my life, which is exactly what I told him. So, baby, what I want to know is, where do we go from here? We've come this far, so why not keep it going? It's not my place to judge you based on your past. Everything happens for a reason, and you are right for me. I know that in my heart."

Her body collapsed on the bed. She was only one person with so much ahead of her—too much at that moment to even think about. So instead she decided to close her eyes, press the imaginary PAUSE button in her head, and wake up in the morning to continue it all.

In Love with a Younger Man

cheryl robinson

A CONVERSATION
WITH CHERYL ROBINSON

Q. Tell us about In Love with a Younger Man. *What inspired you to write a novel about a mature woman in her forties falling in love with a twenty-five-year-old man?*

A. I met a younger man, and while he looked extremely young, I never once thought he was any younger than thirty. We met in a professional business setting, and I was really smitten by the way he carried himself. I smiled the entire time we interacted. When I told him I was a writer and had a Web site and a Myspace page, he sent me a friend invite. I looked on his Myspace page and saw an age that I assumed he simply put down the same way I had put I was ninety-nine on my page. The next day I questioned him. I believe I asked him how long he had been working on his job, and he said three years, and then I asked what he did before that and he said, "I was in college." That's when I realized the age on Myspace was not just a number—it was his true age. I felt compelled to tell him my age, but he didn't seem to want to know. I would hint to him almost daily for about a week and finally he said, "If you want to tell me how old you are, go ahead." I told him and then he moved on to another subject and never mentioned it again. As our relationship blossomed, and I was considering my next novel, I thought to myself, *I'm in Love with a Younger Man.*

Q. So, if the book was inspired by an actual person, is it a true story?
A. No, not at all. While there are some similarities between Olena and myself, such as the high school and college I attended, her story is not my own. I can, however, relate to a woman who feels as if she has lost a lot of years and decides to reassess her life. And I wish I could go on a one-year paid sabbatical to reconnect with myself—what a wonderful benefit. Can you imagine?

Q. Was there any other inspiration for In Love with a Younger Man *aside from the fact that you had met and fallen in love with one?*

A. Yes. There was an article in the collectors' edition of *Essence* with Nia Long, Gabrielle Union, and Sanaa Lathan on the cover. Their article discussed the lack of quality roles for black women in Hollywood. As a writer, I took that as a challenge for me to create a story that a producer would be interested in. This is the first book I have written with that goal in mind. Every one of my books, readers have asked me who I could see playing this part or that one, but with *In Love with a Younger Man*, in the back of my mind, I was saying to myself this book is for those ladies or actresses just like them. I plan to do what I can to promote the book and get it into the right hands so that one day we can see *In Love with a Younger Man* on the big screen.

Q. Instead of saying, What's love got to do with it? *what does age have to do with your book? Olena seemed very preoccupied with the fact she had reached midlife. Was there a point you were trying to drive home?*

A. I am around a lot of people who are much younger than me. Most are in their twenties and early thirties. A person my age is considered old to them, although I don't consider myself to be old. It is my personal belief that the way society has handled the issue of aging, particularly where women are concerned, is unfortunate. While most young people will agree that they don't want to die, young, they do seem afraid of getting older. When someone in their forties and fifties dies, the sentiment is, *Oh, they were so young.* Then we need to ask ourselves if they were too young to die, why does society as a whole seem to view them as too old to live or at least live in the same vein as a younger person?

Q. You left In Love with a Younger Man *with several unanswered questions. What will happen to Jason? Will the surgery be successful? Will Jason and Olena end up together? Then there was the possibility of a book deal for Olena. Also, there was Matthew's voice mail message to Olena, with his love-can-conquer-all speech. Why end the book this way?*

A. If you think I ended the book abruptly, just wait until you see how the continuation opens. When I was writing, I realized as I reached page four hundred that something was happening here that I had never experienced. I couldn't stop writing. I knew that I would either have a very long novel and still not be able to say all I needed to say, or I would need to stop at some point and continue later. I decided that Olena's story would continue very soon.

Q. *Aside from the continuation to* In Love with a Younger Man *are you working on any other novels?*

A. Yes, of course. I have started sketching the conclusion to *If It Ain't One Thing/It's Like That*, which is the love story between Porter Washington and Winona Fairchild.

Q. *Any advice to women who are involved with a younger man or considering becoming involved with one?*

A. Not really, because everyone's experience is different. They say age is nothing but a number. Whether that is true or not may be on a case-by-case basis. I would say you shouldn't feel bad about who you love. If you were a man, most people wouldn't even blink, so older women who date younger men are faced with the double standard. I am not in a relationship with a younger man. I have a younger male friend I love. There was one point where I found myself falling in love with him, but then a couple things happened, and my own reality set in for the two of us. As I began to picture us becoming involved in something that was more than friendship, it seemed somewhat unrealistic. Not only is distance a factor, but he is at one point in his life and I am someplace else. He is still exploring all of his options, while I know exactly the type of man I both want and need. And while I can't say if he'll be eighteen years younger than me, I wouldn't be surprised if he was younger. All I ever meet are younger men.

QUESTIONS
FOR DISCUSSION

1. Olena Day is introduced to readers as a college student with hope in her heart. In your opinion what was Olena desiring as she ventured off to Washington, D.C., in 1984? Would you consider her to be an outcast? If so, why?

2. What did Olena's college experience tell you about her character? If you attended college, particularly if you stayed on campus, what was your own experience? Were you vulnerable as a freshman? If so, how? If you didn't attend college, do you feel you missed out on that experience?

3. What was your opinion of Olena and Andrew's relationship and how they connected in the novel years later?

4. Beginning with chapter six , readers are reintroduced to Olena twenty-five years later. It is at this point that she says she has twenty-five years' worth of regret. How did you feel about that statement and how

she had handled her life? Do you think she wallowed in her pain or pretended to have it all together (put on a good front)?

5. In what ways did Olena evolve from when we are first introduced to her in 1984 to years later, and in what ways was she the same? What was your opinion of the mature Olena?

6. Olena was successful in her sales career; she earned a very high six-figure income with great benefits. Do you feel she should have been happy with her income and not worried about her failed love life?

7. How do you feel about a woman who is seeking love? Is it something you feel women should just be open to, and if and when it happens, let it happen, or should they search for love? How do you feel society views single women, particularly those who are older and who have never been married and have no children?

8. What would you say was Olena's true desire?

9. Did love happen for Olena? If so, with whom, and when did you feel the connection began?

10. Let's discuss the two love interests in Olena's life: Jason Nix and Matthew Harper. What were your opinions of both men? If you were Olena, who would you have chosen to love, and why?

11. Have you ever dated someone much younger than you? If so, what was the end result? Was age a factor in the relationship? What is your opinion of a woman who dates a much younger man? Do you feel society still frowns on that union? And why is that so different from older men who often marry much younger women ?

12. In your opinion what was the central theme of the novel *In Love with a Younger Man*?

13. Consider your age. If you are over the age of forty, how do you feel about being considered *old*. If you are younger than forty, how comfortable are you with getting older? What is your opinion of women who are *older*?

14. What is your opinion of an older woman who has sacrificed her life for her career and a family for mutual funds? Do you know any women like this? Are you one?

15. The story ends with Olena's life just beginning to blossom in terms of her love for two men, her decision to care for one of them, and the possibility of selling her first novel to a publishing company. As the story continues, which characters would you like to see more of?

Georgia sat in her boss's office, her worst-case scenario finally realized as the day ended the same way it had started—not good. Not good at all.

The day before, on Christmas, her father-in-law had continued insulting Marvin about his recent car purchase and his lack of a stable job—the usual. Georgia received the shock of her life after Marvin handed her a large box with a red bow tied around it. Inside was a long wool dress coat with a five-hundred-and-seventy-nine-dollar Saks Fifth Avenue price tag dangling from the sleeve.

"You didn't need to buy me anything."

"That's your Christmas and your birthday present rolled into one," Marvin said.

"He left the tag on to let you know how much the coat cost. Not that he paid that much for it," Marvin's father said. "Did you buy it off one of those boosters at your barbershop?"

"No, Pops, *I* bought it."

"Stop being so negative, Charles," Marvin's mother said.

"Marvin, we can't afford this," Georgia said as she hugged the coat.

"It's cashmere. Did you see the regular price? Twelve hundred dollars. I really wanted to buy you a mink, but that's coming one day."

"I don't need a mink. I don't even like fur coats. And you paid way too much for this wool one. Saks, Marvin? You know we can't afford anything in there."

"Well, that's where your coat came from, so I guess we can." What Marvin hadn't told Georgia was that he had taken the last twenty dollars he had to his name to the Motor City one night after his routine and won close to a thousand dollars off the poker slot machine. It was his first time gambling, and he actually won. He was happy with himself that he knew when to stop.

The next morning, Georgia woke up with her husband on top of her. Her eyes strained to open just as he made the sound—the one letting her know when it was all over. And in this case, it was over at the same time her alarm sounded at six.

She didn't feel well—whether her illness was mental or physical, she really couldn't say. But one thing was certain: She didn't want to go to work, especially the day after Christmas, even with a new wool coat.

Her head hung off the side of the full-sized bed and she stared at her flower-print head scarf on the floor. Half of her black sponge rollers had fallen out of her hair, and she now knew that the generic sleeping pills from the dollar store worked because she had slept through most of Marvin's lovemaking.

He thrust his dick inside of her one last time, a move that caused Georgia to fall off the bed entirely and land on the cold, hard wood. By the time she had gathered her hair essentials from the floor and made her way into the bathroom to hurry for work, Marvin was fast asleep and snoring.

It was freezing outside.

The snow had just started to fall as Georgia backed her Shadow out of the driveway, gas needle teetering between a quarter of a tank and empty, when it dawned on her that she could drive the new car. She pulled the Shadow back into the driveway and took the Maxima to work instead, but a new car and a new coat still didn't equate to a new life.

She looked down at her fingers, the red polish chipped on all but two of her nails. She twirled her loose-fitting, tarnished wedding band and wondered if all of the struggling had truly been worth it. But Georgia was just doing what she'd always done—be a good woman by supporting her man emotionally, financially, and sexually. She had to keep the faith that Marvin's dreams would come true. But still, the question remained . . . what had being good ever gotten her?

At work, she mainly kept to herself. She worked through her lunch, eating a snack or two at her desk to avoid the office gossip that occurred in the lunchroom. The further away she was from controversy of any kind, the more secure she felt with her job, because the last thing she needed was the one thing she feared most—unemployment.

For the past several weeks, at least two or three people

had been escorted to their desks to gather their belongings and then ushered out of the building by security. For this reason, Georgia started taking most of her personal effects home so that if her D-day were to ever come, she wouldn't have to face any unnecessary embarrassment. She could just leave.

The rumor circulated that this last wave of firings was due to time card issues—claiming overtime not worked. Georgia, though, knowing most of those accused, found it hard to believe. JoAnna, especially, was a die-hard corporate type who lived, slept, and breathed the core values. It all just proved to Georgia that no matter how well liked you were, no job was secure.

Five o'clock came quickly, but a last-minute call kept Georgia a few minutes over. When she hung up the phone, she noticed that her team leader, Ernie Dixon, stood by her desk.

"May I see you in Mr. Marshall's office?" he asked.

Georgia nodded quickly, signed off of her computer, and followed Ernie to Mr. Marshall's office in silence.

The office was down a long hallway at the very end of a row of managers' offices. The door was closed, but when Ernie opened it, Georgia saw three people waiting in the room: Mr. Marshall, the company's human resources manager, Mrs. Fallen, a group leader, and a male security officer.

Georgia knew before anyone said a word that her worst case scenario was finally realized—she was getting fired.

But for what? she wondered.

Mr. Marshall began speaking after Georgia took a seat.

"We had cause to tap into your computer because our corporate security team identified your ID address as visiting several unauthorized Web sites, particularly thelastlaugh.com. We have proof that you submitted an application online through our Web server for your husband, Marvin Brown. We also traced several calls you made from your work phone to Burbank, California. You also utilized our overnight packaging service to send mail directly to a Los Angeles studio and billed it to our company. For this reason, Georgia, we must terminate you on the grounds of disorderly conduct."

"Okay," Georgia said. What more could she say? It was all true, and she knew it was against company policy. Since they didn't have a computer at home, she had taken a chance, and that chance had cost Georgia her job.

They had papers for her to sign, but Georgia, feeling like she might faint at any moment, had only enough strength to turn in her badge before hurrying out of the building for some much-needed fresh air.

She heard them mention withholding her last check until she signed the termination papers, but her goal at that moment was to not pass out.

She made it out of the building and into the parking lot, her head spinning and her stomach queasy. Once inside her car, she sped away, her wheels skidding on the newly formed ice as she made her way onto Big Beaver Road.

At the first light, she leaned over and removed her prepaid cell phone from her purse, but with just one minute of talk time remaining, she couldn't even place a call. Now she was outraged about the car and the so-called free cell phone the dealership offered as an incentive—the phone was free but not the monthly service. She was an hour away from home. An entire hour she had to wait before telling Marvin that she had lost their primary means of survival because she had tried to help further his career. So either his dreams needed to come true, or he needed to find a job and let Georgia sleep in for a change. She was officially tired of having all of the burden fall on her shoulders.

Once she made it home, she didn't have a chance to drill into him, because Marvin greeted her at the door with a glass of champagne and cause to celebrate. Aside from the fact that it was Georgia's birthday, after two months and three mailings to the producers of *The Last Laugh*, including a videotape of Marvin's performance, he had been selected as one of a hundred to audition live on-air during their season premiere.

"We're on our way, baby," Marvin promised. "Wasn't this the best birthday present I could give you?"

Now it was Georgia's turn, but her news was far from joyous.

"Today is my birthday and I was fired, Marvin. Called into the human resources office the day after Christmas and terminated. I can't explain how humiliating that was or how scared I am right now. I don't want to live like this. I don't want our kids to live like this. I was looking forward to the new year, but now what do we have to look forward to . . . a year of unemployment and more bills?"

"You're not going to have a year of unemployment," he said, trying to encourage her.

"You're right, because you only get six months. All I know is there's a whole world out there much bigger than this, and that's the one I want to live in. We've struggled enough."

"And that's the one we will live in," he promised. "When I hit LA, I'm coming back to Detroit as the winner of *The Last Laugh*. And we're going to get our own place. It's going to be that mansion in Grosse Pointe Farms with luxury cars in the garage, the best schools for our kids, anything and everything that money can buy."

"Happiness?"

"Of course, happiness," Marvin said, embracing Georgia. "You stuck by my side, and I'm not going to let you or the boys down. We're always going to be together and we're always going to be happy. We're never going to be poor again. That much I promise."